# HARD
# GIRLS

# HARD GIRLS

*A Jane and Lila Pool Thriller*

J. ROBERT LENNON

MULHOLLAND BOOKS

LITTLE, BROWN AND COMPANY

NEW YORK  BOSTON  LONDON

Copyright © 2024 by J. Robert Lennon

Mulholland Books / Little, Brown and Company
Hachette Book Group
1290 Avenue of the Americas, New York, NY 10104
mulhollandbooks.com

First Edition: February 2024

Mulholland Books is an imprint of Little, Brown and Company, a division of Hachette Book Group, Inc. The Mulholland Books name and logo are trademarks of Hachette Book Group, Inc.

The publisher is not responsible for websites (or their content) that are not owned by the publisher.

The Hachette Speakers Bureau provides a wide range of authors for speaking events. To find out more, go to hachettespeakersbureau.com or email hachettespeakers@hbgusa.com.

Little, Brown and Company books may be purchased in bulk for business, educational, or promotional use. For information, please contact your local bookseller or the Hachette Book Group Special Markets Department at special.markets@hbgusa.com.

ISBN 9780316550581
LCCN 2023934817

Printing 1, 2023

LSC-C

Printed in the United States of America

# CONTENTS

# Contents

# HARD
# GIRLS

# 1

# Nestor, NY: *Now*

Nineteen years after she ran away from home, thirteen years after she married a stonemason, twelve years after her daughter was born, and eleven years after she got out of prison and pretended to put the past behind her, Jane Pool sat at her desk in the history department office surrounded by travel receipts, supply requisitions, and reimbursement forms, spring rain pounding the window behind her, and stared in shock at an email.

It wouldn't have looked unusual to anyone peering over her shoulder. It would have looked like spam. That's where she'd found it, the spam folder. But it wasn't spam. It was from *her*. Jane knew this despite the anonymous, clearly temporary email address (ovbxvz7tdrbqtc1lxqs@vbr.la) and the innocuous subject line, *Prescription drugs via UK rail, lowest prices, no wait for approval!* She wouldn't have opened it if not for *UK rail*. That's what meant it was from her.

The contents of the email consisted of one line of text and one image. The text read, "No appointment needed, no waiting, call today!" The image had been hidden from her by the email client, leaving only a small broken-image icon beneath the text.

She moved the cursor over to the icon. The words LOAD IMAGE

appeared beside it. Her finger hovered over the mouse button; if she clicked, she could see what had been hidden.

Instead, she took her hand off the mouse and hit the delete key. The email disappeared.

Jane involuntarily gasped. Sweat had broken out on her face and under her arms. She stood up, and her chair rolled backward and crashed into the bank of filing cabinets. Across the room, Lydia and Carmen looked up from their computers.

"Are you going to the commissary?" Carmen wanted to know. "Can you get me a scone?"

"I wasn't— No, actually, yes. Yes, I can get you a scone."

"Currant, please, cranberry as a last resort. *Not* the one with the figs."

"Got it."

"All I have is a twenty, can I pay you after lunch?"

"Anytime."

Jane drew a deep breath, smoothed her sweater, and slipped her bag over her shoulder. She walked to the door, opened it, and entered the hallway.

Students hurried past her on either side, about to be late for class. Their shoes squeaked on the linoleum, wet with tracked-in rain. This building, Seddon Hall, was 150 years old; it was drafty in the winter and roasting hot in the summer, and on rainy days it felt as clammy as a big canvas tent. History occupied the second floor, with philosophy upstairs and the dean underneath. And below that, in the basement, the commissary.

She took the stairs. Students sat on them, gazing at their phones. Jane was thirty-five, hardly old enough to start bemoaning the habits of youth, but she could not understand the students' obliviousness to the space they took up. They sat on the floor outside professors' offices with their legs extending across the hall and looked shocked when you asked them to move. They blocked doorways with their enormous backpacks and spread their possessions over as many chairs and tables as physically possible. And then there were these two, the stair sitters. It was like they wanted to be kicked.

"Excuse me," she said to the two girls in her way. She couldn't go around them, as the custodian was mopping the stairs; he clearly was annoyed with them as well but perhaps had hoped they'd move of their own accord.

They didn't look up. "Kids," Jane said, more loudly now. "You're blocking the stairs."

One of them craned her neck to look up. She blew a lock of hair out of her eyes and said, "You can go around."

"Get the fuck up," Jane said. "Now."

She hadn't heard this tone of voice come out of her own mouth for years, not since Chance insisted that they enter therapy to talk about her anger and its effect on their marriage. It was the voice that had frightened their daughter, the one Jane deployed when her bare foot was jabbed by a wayward toy, or when she was pestered too long for a snack. For much of her adult life this voice had been a vital tool in her defensive arsenal, a warning and a threat.

But here, as at home, it was too much. The girls were up and scurrying away in an instant, the "go around" girl muttering "Jesus" under her breath. Even the custodian seemed shocked. She apologized as she passed, head hung. She'd left the office to calm down! Instead, every muscle in her body had tensed up and her pulse throbbed at her temples.

The crush of students in the commissary made it worse; she felt exposed, cornered. She tended to avoid the building's public spaces when classes were letting out; only when the campus drew in its breath every hour did she feel comfortable away from her desk. In line, she mastered herself, closing her eyes, slowing her heartbeat. She bought Carmen's scone and a coffee for herself, and, as an afterthought, an oatmeal raisin cookie. "Separate bag, please."

At the second-floor landing, she walked not south toward the history office but north, to 263, the final door in the cul-de-sac that also contained 261, the supply closet, and 259, the IT storage room. Like all the doors on this floor, 263 was of stained hardwood, and dominated by a large frosted-glass window through which you could discern the hunched silhouettes of professors puttering among their books.

You couldn't discern any professors in 263, though. The window was covered from the inside with an old, yellowed map of the Soviet Union. The map was the last thing she saw every time she visited 263. She frequently visited 263 because it contained her father, Professor Harry Pool.

She awkwardly transferred the snack bags to her coffee hand so that she could knock. A frail voice issued from inside: "Office hours are tomorrow!"

"It's me."

Sounds of thumping and shuffling came closer, and then Jane heard the rattle of a turning lock. The door fell open. "Hi, Dear."

"Hi, Dad. I got your cookie."

He extended a trembling hand and accepted the bag. "Thank you. I'm truly moved. Thank you."

Harry Pool was seventy-three, hunched and frail. His face was blotched, his nose crooked, the result of a fall on the front steps of Seddon Hall three years before. Surrounded by books, as he was here, in his small, cluttered office, he should have looked like the platonic ideal of an elderly professor. Instead he resembled a defeated wizard or guru, a magician whose tricks have been rendered obsolete. He gestured toward the only other chair in the room, an industrial-looking armchair upholstered in cracked vinyl. Jane picked up the pile of books from it and moved them to the floor.

"Ah. Oh. Those. Yes," her father said.

"How are you today, Dad?"

"I've run out of shirts, I'm afraid."

"All right," she said. "Are they in the bag? I'll take them for you." The dry cleaner was accustomed to rush jobs from Jane; her father tended to spill things on himself at work. The jackets were probably in even greater need of cleaning than the shirts, but brown tweed—in the feeble light from windows blocked by stacks of books—hid stains. They could always wait.

"Yes, yes. A student startled me." He removed the cookie from its bag and began its slow and loving decimation. The empty bag fluttered to the floor.

"Dad. I have to tell you something. She emailed me."

He gaped. Jane could see the partially chewed cookie.

She said, "Close your mouth, Dad."

He nodded, swallowed. "Not—"

"No, not her. Lila."

"Oh. What did she say?"

"Nothing. I mean, I don't know. I didn't open it." Jane sipped her coffee. "Do you think I should?"

"Yes," he said, but he was shaking his head no. "I don't know. I would like to know that she's all right."

"When was the last time you heard from her?"

After a moment's thought, he said, "It's been a long time, Jane. More than a decade. Not since . . . before everything happened." He looked up. "Has she contacted you? Before this?"

"Never. Not since I came back."

"Mmm."

They sat in silence, he eating, she drinking. After a while she rose, took the garment bag off the coat rack in the corner. She raised her coffee-and-scone hand in farewell.

"Please let me know," he said. "If you do respond."

"I will. If you really want."

He took another bite from the cookie and nodded. He was staring at a spot on the wall now; he'd forgotten Jane and was thinking, no doubt, about her sister. She wordlessly greeted the former Soviet Union and slipped out the door.

She got through the day. The afternoon's distraction was a pile of travel receipts from Dr. Lutherson, who treated most research travel as vacation time for herself and her wife, and never bothered to untangle which expenses were hers alone and which were incurred by Fiona. This always necessitated a long phone call or office visit, during which the professor would pretend not to have noticed the extra expenses, and Jane would pretend not to have noticed that she knew it all along. This time it was Italy. How many risottos dove la foresta incontra il mare scampi e funghi does it take to generate an endowed-chair-worthy monograph? Professor Lutherson seemed determined to find out.

When the clock read five minutes to four, Jane clicked open the email archive and selected the *UK Rail* message. She undeleted it. This time, she clicked the broken icon and loaded the image. It was a cropped jpeg of a page from a book, with a phone number added below the last line.

> and flung her aside very roughly indeed; if they
> had been playing, such roughness would have
> made Bobbie weep with tears of rage and pain.
> Now, though, he flung her on to the edge of the
> hold, so that her knee and her elbow were grazed

*1-877-883-4821*

As the words sank in, she experienced a rising sense of anxiety and anger. Lila could have chosen anything from the book, but she chose this: siblings fighting on a boat. Did she even want Jane to call? Or did she just want to drive her further away?

Jane closed her eyes, drew breath, calmed herself. She printed the email, then rushed to the shared laser printer to snatch it up before anyone else got there.

Lydia was standing beside the machine, shrugging on her raincoat. "See ya tomorrow?" she said. Lydia was the calm, fiftyish single woman who figured out when and where all the classes should take place. Jane liked her workspace aesthetic, which was to cover everything with a shifting collection of different-colored sticky notes. Her desk was like a boulder overgrown with lichen and spattered with gull droppings. The paper emerged facedown into the tray, and Lydia watched Jane snatch it up and fold it discreetly in half.

"Bright and early!" Jane said.

Lydia glanced once more at the folded page and winked. "See ya."

Back at her computer, Jane peeked at the printout, then permanently deleted the email. She said goodbye to Carmen, who always stayed a little late to wait for her boyfriend in another building, and walked to her car.

At home she found her mother-in-law playing Monopoly with Chloe. The triumphant look on Susan's face was not, Jane surmised, a reaction to the game, but to her successfully appearing to have engaged Chloe in something "wholesome" and analog, rather than the video games or movies the child would presumably have been enjoying under Jane's supervision.

"Sadly, dear, we'll have to continue this another time," Susan said with a sigh. "Your mother is here."

"Come on, I'm about to win!" Chloe said. But Susan's martyrdom could not be postponed. She got up and shouldered her purse.

Jane thanked Susan for picking Chloe up from the private school Susan paid for, half an hour's drive from home. "Tomorrow?" Susan said.

"Tomorrow's drama club after school. I can pick her up myself."

"Very well," Susan said, with a skeptical lilt. She was a resentful, calculating person who could display blithe condescension or strategic meekness, depending on the situation. She was the kind who entered a party with great fanfare but left without saying goodbye. Jane guessed she'd learned to be flexible while dealing with her now-diminished asshole of a husband. Or maybe she was just born that way and was the reason he was now diminished. It was no secret that she believed Chance could have done better. She was probably right. The two women glared at each other.

"So long, then?" Jane said.

"I suppose. Goodbye, Chloe! See you on Sunday!" A questioning glance at Jane, as if she might forget, or find some way to sabotage, the weekly extended family meal that, for Jane, was an excruciating waste of time, and which Susan imposed for this exact reason.

"Bye, Grandma," the girl said, putting her colorful money back in the game box.

Susan clopped down the front walk, climbed into her Prius, and drove away, sitting straight-backed like an equestrienne.

"Mom," Chloe said. "Take over, so I can win."

Jane said, "I just got home. I need some time to myself."

"You don't have to talk to me. You just have to lose."

With her wispy blond hair and long face, Chloe resembled her mother-in-law far more than she resembled Jane's mother—although, old photos notwithstanding, it was difficult for Jane to conjure up her mother's face. Often away and never truly present, Anabel Pool had left for good twenty years before. Jane's canonical memory was of her trying not to betray emotion—usually irritation. Her signature quality was the effortful absence of feeling. Occasionally, in the couple of years after her disappearance, Jane would see something in her sister that reminded her of their mother—the way she got up out of a chair, or slipped quietly through a door in the dark—but now she hadn't seen her sister in more than a decade, either, and her memory of both women was beginning to fade.

Jane sat down and let the girl beat her. She could see Chloe getting angrier as her Pyrrhic victory grew nearer, its pointlessness more clear. At some point Jane rolled the dice and accidentally moved her piece the wrong way around the board, and Chloe sighed. "All right, Mom, I give up."

"Great," Jane said, getting up. "I need to go on an errand."

"I'll come."

"I need to do this alone, Chloe."

"What, are you buying drugs?"

"Chloe!"

"Grandma thinks you do."

"She said that?"

Chloe crossed her arms. "She said you get wild eyes, like you're back on something."

"Jesus."

"Did you used to be an addict?"

"No," Jane half lied. "The wild eyes are because of her."

"Ha!"

The two faced off, staring, the girl's head angled slightly, like a fawn that has heard a distant, suspicious noise. Now she resembled Chance, whose displeasure was rarely expressed in words. His tight vocabulary of gestures could convey, with masterful efficiency, precisely which of Jane's flaws was bothering him.

It's not their fault, she told herself. She did have many flaws.

"It'll be boring," Jane said. "Bring a book."

Chloe hopped down from her chair and strode past Jane to the hallway, where she tugged her jacket down from its peg with a practiced snap of the wrist. "Where are we going?"

"The mall."

"Where in the mall?"

"The parking lot."

"That does sound boring. Why?"

"I have to make a phone call."

"Use your phone!" she said, slipping the jacket on. She struggled, briefly, with the zipper. Jane watched her face as she considered asking for help, then rejected that possibility, then drew a sharp breath, then worked the tab into its slot and pulled it up to her chin.

"I need to use a pay phone. Maybe we can go inside for ice cream after. Isn't there a yogurt place?"

"A pay phone? You *are* buying drugs!"

"I am not."

"I don't believe you."

It wasn't clear if Chloe was kidding or, if she was, how much. Now she reminded Jane of Lila—the unaffected bluntness that could be hostility or could be an ironic joke. They'd taken her to a child psychologist years ago — or rather, Chance and Susan had, at Susan's insistence — to find out if the girl was on the autism spectrum, but it turned out she was just sarcastic.

"Whatever," Jane said. "I need a minute. Meet me in the car."

Jane went upstairs to the bedroom, opened the closet doors, and knelt on the floor. From a cardboard box behind the shoes, she produced a tattered paperback book: *The Railway Children,* a British children's novel by E. Nesbit. It was about three children living in London in the early 1900s whose father, an employee of the British Foreign Office, is falsely accused of espionage and is arrested.

She remembered the scene Lila had excerpted: In it, the children are trying to save a baby from a barge that has caught fire. The bossy brother, Peter, tosses Bobbie, the eldest sister, to the side, trying to save the day. Sitting on the bed, book in her lap, it took Jane only a few moments to find the passage. She took a pencil from the bedside table drawer and worked out their code, jotting the results on the printout she'd made at work. Chapter 8, page 148, lines 22 through 26.

08 148 22 26

She put the book away, folded the paper around the pencil, and tucked them into the pocket of her dress.

They rode in silence. Their quiet neighborhood lay halfway between Jane's job in Nestor and Chloe's school in Rochester; the ride to the mall took them through the golf course, past several farms and the power station, past the nature preserve. The rain had been done for an hour, and sun appeared between speeding clouds.

The mall had been in decline for a decade; most people went to the mega-mall in Syracuse. The Old Navy had closed, then the American Eagle, then Best Buy. Only Target and the movie theater kept the place open. As she pulled into the parking lot and beheld its vast emptiness, Jane hoped the only nearby pay phone kiosk she could remember was still there.

It was. She found it outside the theater, amid the ragged-shrubs-in-white-gravel landscaping, beside the standpipe and wheelchair entrance. Part of her had wanted to just use her own phone, but she knew her sister would criticize her for it, or ignore the call altogether. She ought to have wanted to defy Lila's preposterous, theatrical cloak-and-dagger nonsense, but her better angels held her back. Besides, she was curious.

She parked in the nearest space, about thirty feet from the phone. She said, "Five minutes."

"Mhm." Hair covered Chloe's face; she licked her finger and turned the page of her book. Jane took a long look at her, then stepped out of the car.

The phone still worked. She dialed the provided number. While she waited, she spied a Target employee about fifty yards away, leaning against a red wall, smoking. A click gave way to a robotic voice that prompted her to enter the code.

08 148 22 26

"Thank you. Please wait." The call cut off and the dial tone returned.

The hell? She replaced the receiver. Stickers on the phone's casing advertised a strip club—correction, a *gentlemen's* club—and take-out wings. A local band, a dog groomer. Had it been worth even the modest effort to stick the stickers here? Jane turned around, gazed again at the clouds. The Target employee threw her cigarette on the ground and returned to work. Her exhaustion and defeat were visible even from here—the feelings were infectious. Should she try again, or get in the car and leave?

No—the pay phone was ringing.

"Thanks for finding a pay phone," said the voice on the other end. *Her* voice. Her twin's. Lila's. "I know you didn't want to."

"What do you want, Lila."

"You have to come," her sister said. "I think I've found her."

# 2

# Nestor, NY: *Then*

There was no goodbye, not even a moment of realization that their mother's absence was permanent. She just wasn't around, as had often been the case, and then, instead of coming back, stayed gone. Their father never told them she'd left for good; maybe he didn't know, either. Their mother was, as a rude parent of a friend once said to her years before, a rolling stone. Her parents' marriage was a sham. There was never any point in wishing, waiting, or wondering.

The first time she disappeared, they were six and had stayed after school helping their teacher hang the harvest decorations in their first-grade classroom. This was supposed to be a privilege, because of their superior artistic skills. Jane was a little in love with their teacher, Miss Conover, who was cheerful and talkative and young. She always let them stay in the classroom during recess, silently reading while she painted her fingernails. Once she painted the twins', too, and they wore the deep purple polish all day, until Miss Conover frantically rubbed it off in the last moments before the bus arrived. On this day, though, the three of them kept busy cutting red and orange leaves out of construction paper and compiling a list of words that evoked autumn: cool, dry, wind, branches, pumpkin.

After a while Jane noticed that Miss Conover kept glancing at her watch, and then at the clock above the chalkboard, then back at the girls. She peered out the windows overlooking the school parking lot, and out into the hall.

"Girls," she said. "Will you behave yourself while I go talk to Mrs. Vainberg?" They heard her heels clicking away, down to the main office, and then returning a few minutes later.

"Is there a place where you think we can reach your mother?" she asked them.

Lila looked up, alarmed, at Jane. She set her scissors down. Jane turned to Miss Conover.

"At our house?"

"No one is answering there, or at your father's office. She was supposed to have picked you up quite a while ago."

"I'm sorry, miss," Lila said.

"It's not your fault, Lila. Perhaps she forgot that you were staying after today?"

Jane could remember their mother reminding them, that morning, that she would pick them up. "I don't think so."

"Do you think," Miss Conover said, "one of your grandparents could pick you up?"

"We don't have grandparents," Jane said.

"Yes, we do," Lila said. "They're in *Europe*." That's what their mother had told them when they asked why they'd never met her mama and daddy. With a wave of the hand, as though she couldn't care less. Their father's parents, they'd been told, were dead.

"How about a neighbor? Does somebody live next door who could come for you?"

"We live in the woods," Jane explained.

"Well," Miss Conover said, "let's wait a little longer, and I'll give you a ride. Maybe there's something wrong with the phone."

Miss Conover's car was extremely clean and had a sweet-smelling pine tree dangling from a knob on the radio. As they arrived at their house, she mumbled, "This is hardly in the woods," and Jane realized, with a start, that she was right—their house was low, long, and sheltered by trees, but in a neighborhood of houses otherwise set closer together. You could even see the other houses from their yard. But Jane didn't know who lived in them. She and Lila stayed in the yard and played with each other.

No one was home, but the front door was unlocked. The girls followed Miss Conover inside. Lila made peanut butter sandwiches, and Miss Conover politely turned down her offer of one. They sat in the kitchen until it was nearly dark. Then their father walked in, carrying his stained leather satchel bulging with books and papers.

"Oh!"

"Mr. Pool? I'm Fern Conover, the girls' teacher."

Fern! It had never occurred to Jane that she had a first name.

The adults talked, apologizing to each other. It was all a misunderstanding, they agreed. Their father rubbed his hands together as though it was cold inside, and hung his head. Miss Conover thanked the twins for their help and left, pulling the door gently closed behind her.

When she was gone, their father went into his office to make phone calls. The girls stayed in the kitchen, gazing at each other in alarm. They could hear his voice but not the things he was saying. After a while he came out, looking very tired. "Your mother's away," he said. "What do you—that is—it's Friday. Are you hungry?"

"Can we have fish sticks?" Lila asked.

"Yes! But—I don't—"

"They're in the freezer," Jane said. "You put them on a pan."

"A *tray*. In the stove," Lila said.

"The *oven*," Jane clarified.

"The oven."

The girls bathed and dressed themselves, told their father which books to read them, put themselves to bed. Their father seemed distracted and upset. In the morning, he wouldn't come out of his room, so they ate toast and cereal and read and played with their dollhouse. Eventually it got warm out, so they went into the yard. Their clothes got dirty and their father didn't seem to notice.

Their mother came back before dinner. She seemed tired and her eyes were red. She kissed them on their heads and went into her bedroom and closed the door. For a little while their father tried to talk to her through it, and eventually he went in and they argued. Then their father came out and ordered a pizza, and the three of them ate it. This time it was better.

He oversaw their bath and picked the books to read. He remembered to make them brush their teeth. In the morning, everything was back to normal. No explanation was offered for their mother's absence and they didn't ask.

Normal, in their house, was a studious quiet — the sound of people indulging in their own preoccupations. The girls were expected to make their own fun. Their father, at his best, seemed gently amused by their existence, but they generally encountered him as he furtively retreated to his home office to work on the book he was perpetually a few months away from finishing. Their mother was more attentive, at least until a few years into her "times away," which is what their father came to call these unexplained absences. Before, she had discharged the basic chores of motherhood with a wry, eye-rolling efficiency, always telling the girls how much they were inconveniencing her before dispelling their guilt with a smile and a wink.

Their mother winked a lot. She dutifully attended school functions — bake sales, choral concerts, the science fair — and winked at the fathers. The other mothers did not wink, and did not seem to like her. The fathers did. Jane had never seen other people see her mother until these events; she saw how people reacted. Their gaze lingered on her, their expressions changed. Her mother dressed differently from the others, whose attire was college-town casual — jeans, sneakers, university sweatshirts, and plaid flannels. Jane wouldn't have known at the time what to call the clothes her mother wore, but from the few photos that remained, she could see that she was trying to look like Jean Seberg in a movie from the sixties — sleeveless dresses, floral cigarette pants, a man's shirt tied at the waist. Headscarves and sun hats in the summer, long wool coats and fur-lined hats in the winter. Eventually, after she stopped attending such things, after she discovered her love of horticulture and spent what little time she was at home among her plants, she wore long khaki skirts or shorts, chambray shirts, vented leather clogs.

But for now, when they were small, she would respond to their attention, at first with resistance, even offense, before she capitulated, rewarding their persistence with stories of her childhood adventures in Russia or Spain, raised by servants whose care was easily escaped, wandering narrow cobblestoned streets, befriending stray cats and friendly shopkeepers, stealing lipstick out of tourists' handbags and pastries off their tables. Only later would Jane learn these stories were invented, or at least greatly exaggerated; their mother had spent her childhood in the US and traveled to Europe infrequently, if at all.

The girls liked to be read to, but what they really liked was when their mother grew bored by whatever whimsical children's story she was reciting and instead regaled them with these apocryphal tales. With the book abandoned, she could encircle Jane and Lila in her arms, tip her head back, beanbag ashtray balanced on the back of the sofa, and expel cigarette smoke into the air as she lied to her heart's content. A standoff with a vicious guard dog, over which she triumphed with a poisoned sack of meat scraps. A necklace found in the gutter that turned out to belong to a dissipated heiress, who, in exchange for the lost item, taught her how to smoke. ("But you, girls, must never smoke. You *shall* not.") A brooding Russian couple who kidnapped her, whom she escaped by leaping from their moving car into a river. A teenaged boy with a motorcycle who tried to rape her when she was ten, "but I crushed his jewels, girls, like my mother taught me, and I would have stolen them if I could."

Years later, when the girls were ten themselves, Lila wondered aloud what this story meant.

"You don't know what a rapist is?" Jane said. "It's a man who tries to do it with you when you don't want to."

"I *know*," Lila said. "I mean the *jewels*. How can you crush, like, diamonds? Or, like, if you can crush them, why can't you steal them?"

They were sitting in front of the television. It was too late for them to be up, but their mother was halfway through another unexplained absence, and their father was locked in his office. Jane was half watching a James Bond movie, and Lila had a math textbook open on her lap — not the fifth-grade one she was assigned but a seventh-grade one that she'd stolen from school. She wanted a head start, she'd said.

"Oh my *god*. Are you kidding me?"

"What!"

"It's *balls*," Jane said. "That boys have under their penis. That's the jewels. She hit him in the balls, that's how she escaped."

Lila gaped. "Really?"

"Yes! It makes them barf. Remember Kevin Guong?"

Kevin Guong was their classmate who slipped climbing over a fence and went home early in a vomit-stained shirt, cupping his crotch. The other boys would never let him live it down.

"Oh."

"*Oh,*" Jane said.

Her sister punched her, hard, in the arm.

"Hey!"

"Don't make fun of me. Just because I'm not so obsessed with boys I know what their stuff is called."

"Shut actually up right now."

"Watch your movie, ball fiend."

They stared at each other. "*Ball fiend?*" Jane shouted, and they managed to hold back for a second or two before collapsing into laughter.

"But," Lila asked ten minutes later, "do you think that's true? Do you think she really did that?"

"Why would she lie?"

Lila closed the book, idly stroked its cover. "I don't know," she said.

# 3

# Nestor, NY: *Now*

———

I assume," Jane said, "you mean Mom."

"Of course I mean Mom."

"What do you mean," Jane said, "you *think* you've found her."

"A reliable source."

"And you're calling me about this why?"

"So that we can go together."

"Your idea is . . . I'm supposed to drop everything and come find our mother with you."

"That's the idea."

"Hi, by the way," Jane said. "Nice hearing from you. I'm so glad we're getting to catch up."

"There's no need to be sarcastic."

"Lila! It's been a dozen fucking years!"

The two were silent for a time. But it was pointless to try waiting Lila out. Jane listened closely for any evidence of her sister's environment — a workplace, a partner, a child? But there was only silence.

Jane said, "Okay, look. She didn't want us, she didn't want Dad, so she left. Isn't that more than enough information? She doesn't want to be found, why should I want to find her?"

"Jane," her sister said, and Jane knew the tone: patient, unflappable, absolutely confident that her position would win the day. It usually did; Lila was guided by impulses, but she tended to have the data to back them up. A mathematician's sixth sense. "I know you want to put everything behind you. I know you *did* put everything behind you. I've been . . . keeping track. But all of our speculation . . . it wasn't bullshit. Something was going on with Mom."

"*Your* speculation. We knew what was going on. She was fucking around on Dad."

"You know that's not the whole story."

"You *don't* know," Jane said. "She left him utterly bereft. You haven't been taking care of him for the past decade. The man's a wreck. You haven't been getting his fucking shirts cleaned." Oh shit — she'd forgotten to drop the shirts off. She glanced at her watch: 5:42. The cleaner closed at six.

"I'm not saying she was a saint. But she didn't just . . . run away from us. There was something she was running to. Don't you want to know what it was?"

"So you've been sleuthing it out this whole time?"

"Mmm, let's say . . . some information came to me. It piqued my interest. I asked around. Then I heard something from a guy who heard it from a guy."

"What kind of life are you leading?" Jane asked her. "Where you talk to guys who know guys? About *Mom*? And you need a secret code to call your sister?"

"Come find out."

"So what did you hear? From the guy, who heard it from the guy."

Lila hesitated. "He wouldn't talk about it over the phone. He's . . . he's pretty paranoid, for good reasons. All he'd say was that a woman he thinks is Mom is in the country. In the Northwest, he says. And she'll be there for two weeks, max, his contact tells him. So, we go talk to him and find out the details. If it turns out to be bullshit, we can just turn around and come back. But if it sounds like good intel, we go after her."

"Where is this guy?"

A little laugh. "Montana."

"Oh my god, Lila."

"Consider it a vacation. Or . . . a family emergency."

"So you're telling me you think she lives abroad," Jane said, hating herself for the note of curiosity in her voice.

"Some of my intel said otherwise, initially, but I think so. Yeah."

"With what, international playboys?"

"Jane," she said, "it was more than just the men. Mom and Dad . . . weren't an ordinary couple."

She sounded like she did when she was twelve, full of wild paranoid theories and furious enthusiasm. It was infectious, but Jesus Christ. They were adults.

"Once we know," Lila went on, "you can go back to your nice, quiet life."

Amazing. The woman could not keep the contempt out of her voice. "I'm not sure what makes you think my life is quiet or nice." It was as if she didn't remember, or didn't care, what had happened, how they'd parted, what Jane had been through. "Aren't you going to thank me?" she said. "Now that we're talking again after all these years?"

"For what?"

"You've got to be kidding me."

Jane could hear the scrape of a chair against wood, a distant car horn. All right, so she's someplace that has cars. Finally, Lila said, "I didn't ask you to do what you did. You should be thanking *me*."

"I didn't ask you to do what *you* did, either."

"I *saved* you."

"And then you kept going. You never stopped. You nearly saved me to death."

The silence that ensued was familiar: it was the sound of Lila clamping down hard on her anger, flattening it, absorbing it. In a monotone, she said, "It was about you *once*. Just once. It hasn't been about you since."

"Okay."

"Okay."

Some tension seemed to have broken between them. Jane peered across the parking lot, through the open window of the car. Chloe wasn't paying attention to her at all. Or she was pretending not to be paying attention.

"You got married," Lila said.

"I sure did. Chance, from high school."

"I remember him. And you have a daughter."

"Yeah. She's right here. Waiting for me in the car."

"You're at a mall?"

"Of course you know that. Do you know my daughter's name?"

"Yeah," Lila said.

"Uh-huh. Do you know who named her?"

No response.

"My mother-in-law," Jane said. "Her sons are Chance, Charles Junior, and Christopher. And *their* children all have to start with *Ch,* too."

"No," Lila said.

"Chelsea, Chuck, which is Charles the Third, Charlotte..."

"The cousins?"

"You already know all this."

"Yes." Lila snorted, then burst into laughter. Jane joined her. Soon she was doubled over, weeping. The laughter felt like an attack of something; it felt like it might snap her in half. She hadn't laughed like this in a long time. Or cried. She didn't think she'd laughed or cried like this since she was married.

"Mom!" Chloe shouted, leaning over to look out the driver's-side window. "Are you okay?"

"Yes, yes," she said, waving her off. To Lila, she said, "Oh god. Dad ran out of shirts because he keeps spilling things on himself at work, and I'm supposed to get them cleaned, and I'm too late. The fucking cleaner is going to close."

"Jane."

"Lila."

"Jane, come see me. Give me two weeks. Ten days, even. See this through with me. Dad isn't helpless. He made his bed. Let him clean his own damn shirts. It isn't going to kill him."

"Oh god," Jane said, "it might."

"Something will. Any of us could die tomorrow. Come find her with me."

It was true that Jane had regrets. She missed her sister. Not the one she left behind, but the one she grew up with, the one who made the world seem so complicated and interesting. And, somehow, understandable. "It's not Dad, though," she said. "I have to be here for Chloe."

Lila seemed to take a second to digest this. She said, "Sure, but."

"But what?"

"Let me put it to you this way. Are you a great mother?"

"What?"

"Are you? Do you think you're an excellent mother?"

"I don't know what to say."

"You're not answering the question, which is interesting to me," Lila said. "It sounds like you're afraid you're not a very good mother, and maybe you're wondering why not. Am I right?"

"You have no fucking idea what you're talking about." Also, Jane didn't say, you are right.

"I wouldn't know —"

"No, you wouldn't!"

"—but it seems to me you aren't at peace with your role as mother, and why do you think that might be?"

"None of this is your business," Jane said, gazing at her daughter's head, bent over in the car. Inhibitions loosened by the laughter, she began to tremble. She was crying again.

"Part of it, I'm sure, is that our mom *was* a terrible mother. That's a verifiable fact. Part of it is that she didn't seem to care about how bad she was. You're different, Jane. You care. That's why you're crying right now."

"You absolute shit," Jane said, gasping.

"You think maybe you're like her. That something in you is broken, is dead, and you can't love your husband right, and you can't love your daughter right. And I know this about you because I know it about myself. So what you're going to do is find her and confront her. You're going to prove to yourself that you aren't like her after all. You'll look her in the eye and make her explain herself, and you'll finally know."

"Why did I call this number?" Jane said quietly. "Why am I doing this to myself?"

"Do you have a pencil? I'm going to give you an address. Do not type it into any computer or phone, ever, do you understand?"

"Are you kidding me?"

"I'm not. You are my sister, and I am not kidding. You don't have to come, Jane."

"No shit."

"You don't have to, but I think you need to. Don't do it for me, do it for yourself. Are you ready? I'm going to give you the address."

Heart racing, Jane wrote it down: 21 2nd Street, Timber Fell, Missouri.

"Timber Fell, Missouri?"

"If you have to fly, fly into an airport at least 150 miles away. Do not rent a car, or drive a car that can be connected to you."

"Lila."

"Don't bring your phone. Buy a phone at a truck stop on the way."

"Lila, for shit's sake. How am I supposed to get there without a car? Or a phone? Hitchhike?"

"You'll think of something. I'm serious. None of my clients knows where I am. Not anymore, anyway. It's peaceful here. I like it. Locals think I grew up a few counties over and that I make websites. I've even made a few for them, as cover."

"Clients."

"Yeah, well, we'll talk when you get here."

"I didn't say I was coming," Jane said.

"I know. I won't hate you if you don't."

"Is all this secrecy really necessary?"

"It is."

"Why can't I just meet you in Montana? At this guy's place?"

Another silence, not so tense this time. Jane knew she was going to go. Lila knew it, too.

"I want to go on a road trip with you. Like old times. We can catch up on the way."

"Those times weren't exactly fun."

"Weren't they, though?"

Jane didn't reply. Instead she placed the receiver, gently, back onto the hook. The mall parking lot was so quiet. Beyond the pebbled verge, the line of neatly spaced pines, cars flashed on the highway, clouds massed. She wasn't sure if this was the rain that had passed or new rain that was on the way.

Her sister was right. She wanted to know. And now was the time, wasn't it? Chloe was, at long last, old enough to be without her for a week or two. And soon she'd start asking unavoidable questions about Jane's past, about her childhood. It had already begun, in fact—little passive-aggressive nudges about Jane's secrecy, her moods—and her deflections were becoming less and less effective, and it was becoming harder and harder to abide by the deal she had made with Chance and Susan. Soon, Chloe would know everything. She would know that her aunt Lila existed. She would know what happened, and why.

When it came time to tell her, Jane had to be armed with the truth. She would go find it, and when she came back, the life she had made for herself would finally make sense—enough sense, anyway, to make her daughter understand why she wasn't a normal mother, why their family wasn't a normal family.

A week or two, that was all it would take, and she could do right by Chloe.

In the car, without looking up from her book, Chloe said, "What was that all about?"

"An old friend," Jane said, wiping at her eyes.

"An old . . . boyfriend?"

"No."

They circled around to the main entrance, parked, and went inside, but the yogurt place was gone. Instead they went to the nature preserve. The parking lot was nearly empty thanks to the rain. No leaves on the trees yet, but their branches shuddered and groaned in the wind. The path took them around a small lake, really a glorified pond, with its tiny, lonesome island in the center.

"Has anybody ever lived on the island?" Chloe said as they walked.

"Maybe?"

"Buy it! We could build a cabin there!"

"You think this is a skill I possess?"

"It would be easy. You just stack the logs on top of each other."

Jane laughed, but what did she know? Maybe you did just stack logs on top of one another. Susan had given Chloe a huge Lincoln Logs set for her fifth birthday. It seemed a miscalculated gift for a little girl who, in spite of Jane's admittedly weak best efforts, had been obsessed with Disney princesses, but the set would become Chloe's favorite toy for the better part of that year. She made elaborate, physics-defying castles of logs. Building-code-defying, anyway.

Chloe deserved to build a cabin on the little nameless island. She deserved to have a mother who could build it with her.

She had a father who could, though.

The temperature had dropped five degrees and now the rain started again. They ran back to the car, squelching through the mud. Chance called just as they were climbing inside.

"Where are you?"

She told him. "We'll be home in ten minutes."

"Did you forget? Doug and Nancy and Astrid for dinner. They're here now."

"Oh Jesus."

"I ordered from Imperial Garden. Please pick it up."

He hung up. Chloe said, "Why did you say 'oh Jesus'?" and Jane told her. Chloe began to hyperventilate. "Astrid is there *now*? She can't go in my room!"

"Why not?"

"She messes things up!"

"The price of friendship."

"Mom, I am getting too old to be forced to play with your friends' kids."

Jane started the car and pointed it toward the restaurant. "Sometimes the people we have to be with aren't our favorites. You need to pretend."

At home, she greeted Chase's co-worker and his wife, who sat awkwardly on the sofa, staring at her with tight smiles. Chloe ran to her room to assess the damage. Jane handed over the food, which Chance began to set out on the table. She carried her father's garment bag into the laundry room and shoved the shirts into the washing machine. DRY CLEAN ONLY, read the labels. It was hard to imagine her father noticing the difference.

She endured an evening of unpleasant conversation with their boring guests while periodic minor arguments erupted upstairs. When it was over, Chloe took a bath while Jane scrubbed dishes in the sink. Chance sat at the table behind her. She heard a bottle of beer opening, and his sigh.

"Come on, Jane. You could've tried."

"I thought I was."

He didn't answer.

"I have to talk to you about something," she said. Outside the kitchen window, across the alley, a neighbor was dragging a heavy trash can through the gravel. It was nearly dark. She could see her own reflection, her expressionless face, Chance's defeated slump at the table. "I need to go away for a little while."

"All right." It was almost, not quite, a question. To indicate that he expected elaboration but that it didn't really matter, because she was already in the wrong.

"Don't get angry."

"What."

"It's . . . Lila. She thinks she knows where our mother is and wants to go look for her."

Chance exhaled loudly, theatrically. "Where, exactly."

"I don't know, exactly. Out west?"

In the window, she watched him drain the beer, place it gently on the table, push it away. His head fell into his hands. "Uh-huh. You can't, though."

She stiffened. This was the thing they'd gone into therapy for, his patronizing, sexist fear that her distant past would rise and overwhelm her, leave her drugged and drunk in some alley, send her back to prison. The therapy hadn't worked, because Chance hadn't wanted to believe she could be trusted. He'd walked out, literally, mid-session. "Which part can't I, Chance," she said. "And why not." She was almost finished with the dishes. Pretty soon she'd have to sit down and face him.

"You can't get pulled back into all that," he said. "This is your life now."

"I'm not getting *pulled back*. I'll be taking a trip. Getting to be alone, for the first time in — what — ten years? You get to go to Daytona with your brother every winter. You get to go fishing with your buddies."

"You don't have any buddies," he said.

She turned away, rinsed off the beer glasses, held herself back from throwing them across the room.

"For how long?" he said, slightly contrite.

"A week? Maybe two."

"Maybe two," he repeated.

"This is my life, Chance," she said. "But that's my life, too. I need to settle things. I want to know."

She placed the last dish on the rack, dried her hands, sat at the table. Upstairs, Chloe was splashing, singing a song from *Moana,* the way she used to when she was little. Jane realized she would stop if she knew they could hear her, and she was gripped by a wave of sadness.

"This is so like you," Chance said, still talking to the table's surface. "You can't just *plan* a trip. For, I don't know, summertime. Like a normal person. You have to go *now*."

"Chance."

"Because your sister called you and she needs you to go *now*. Your sister you sacrificed so much for, and then she didn't talk to you for . . . how long?"

"It wasn't like that," Jane said. But, of course, a day ago she would have made the same argument, for the same reasons.

He rubbed his face, then looked up at her, at last. "So, when?" he said.

"I have to check flights. Go to work, try and take off. Tomorrow night?"

"Right." Throwing his hands in the air. "Of course."

"Your mother can help out with Chloe. I'm sure she'll relish the opportunity to —"

"Hey, man, don't," he said, getting up. "Just don't." He walked out, leaving the empty bottle behind, in its little nest of paper, bits of the label he'd torn off. She heard his feet on the stairs, heard him pause. Draw breath. Come back.

He gripped the doorjamb. His eyes were red, with exhaustion and with the fire of indignation. "You know it's never going to end, right? You're never going to decide you're not as shitty as they are."

"That is not fair."

"It's a fuc — a freaking complex, or whatever it's called. You're always either too traumatized by them to be any good, or too boring compared to them to be cool. Whatever makes you feel like shit about yourself. Which is the goal."

"I hardly think that —"

"What kind of attitude is that for Chloe, huh? I'm here trying to teach her to be confident, make stuff, succeed at stuff." He waved his hands, gesturing toward their large and tidy house, whose down payments had come not from his labor but from his parents. "Both of those dumb bitches could be dead and you'd still be using them to prove what a self-sacrificing loser you are. What kind of message is that sending her?"

"She can hear you."

Chloe had stopped singing, stopped splashing. "No, she fucking can't."

"She can. You're sending her the message right now, not me. You're shouting it for everyone to hear."

He gripped the jamb harder. She heard his knuckles crack, and she flinched.

"I'm running out of time," she said. "To be a positive influence. She's almost cooked, Chance, she's like a whole, full person. And I still don't know how to explain myself to her. The time is going to come to tell her the truth, and I won't know."

"Don't you get it?" she said, more quietly now. "I don't know what to tell her."

He opened his mouth as if to speak, but never did. Instead he went out to the garage. A moment later she heard a crash — tools being swept onto a cement floor.

The splashing started again, too loudly.

In the morning, Jane got up early and ironed her father's shirts. She got Chloe off to school, managed to avoid saying goodbye to Chance. At the office, she explained the situation to the department manager. Family emergency. A week or two. She had the personal days banked. Spring break was next week, the professors wouldn't be making so many demands. Carmen and Lydia could handle the work.

Of course, of course. Take all the time you need.

Her father's office door was shut. A few students waited outside, looking at their phones. "He's not in there," one of them said.

She let herself in with her key and closed the door behind her. Her father was there, of course, gazing up at her like a frightened animal. "You have some visitors," she said, hanging the clothing back on the rack.

"I know. I didn't — I wasn't — Yes."

She lowered herself into the chair, uncharacteristically still empty of debris from the day before. "Dad, I need to talk to you about something. I have to go away for a little while."

"Oh no," he said.

"She said she found Mom."

To his expression of fear was now appended a terrible sadness. His eyes seemed to recede a little further into his skull; he sank deeper into his chair.

"No," he said.

"She heard something from somebody. She wouldn't tell me what it was, just told me to come."

"I assumed your mother was dead," her father said in a near whisper.

"Yes, I know. But you never say why you'd think that." She leaned forward, bracing herself against the desk. "Dad, is there anything you want to tell me before I go? Anything that would be useful for me to know? I understand that this topic is upsetting to you. But please help me out if you can."

He sat in stunned silence for a long, uncomfortable minute. Above him, the clock clacked and hummed. His breaths came loudly, shallowly, and his bony fingers gripped the chair's arms. He moistened his lips as if to speak, but nothing came out.

Then, finally: "I just . . . I can't imagine she's still alive."

"Because you think she would have contacted you? Or because she was in some kind of danger?"

He didn't reply.

"Lila thinks there was something going on with you and Mom. Something besides the . . . other men. Do you want to talk about that?"

His hand flew up, stroked his necktie. "No," he said.

They sat in silence for a while. Jane stood up.

"It's spring break next week," she said. "I shouldn't be much longer than that. You'll be fine while I'm gone. Call Carmen if you need anything." She picked up her bag from the floor. "Maybe this would be a good time to do something fun with Chloe."

He blinked at her, as if he wasn't sure who that was.

"Or not," she went on. "Do you need anything else? Dad?"

"Tell them —" he said, very quietly.

"Dad?"

"The students," he said, staring at the window. "Tell them to leave."

At her desk, she searched for the town Lila had given her — not the address, as requested — then studied photographs of half a dozen prospective regional airports. She was looking for a particular kind of place: small but not too small, flights departing in the morning, before the rental car counters opened. After half an hour she booked herself a one-way ticket to Highfill, Arkansas, a good two hundred miles from her destination.

She left work half an hour early and withdrew $500 at an ATM. At home, she packed light, tee shirts, bras and underwear, a pair of jeans. A baseball cap, sunglasses. A paperback to fall asleep reading. Her bag would fit in the overhead or even under the seat in front of her, in a pinch.

She zipped it up, set it by the door, and drove to the school to pick up Chloe.

Drama club had been Susan's idea. She had fond memories of Chance's summer camps, the dreamcatchers he brought home, sculptures made of twigs, rubbings of leaves. She wanted Chloe to do "activities" and offered to pay for the after-school, though money wasn't the issue. The issue was that Chloe didn't want to do it, at least not at first. On the one hand, Jane couldn't help but think that every effort of Susan's to keep Chloe active was really an effort to keep her away from home, away from her mother. On the other, Jane appreciated the extra time these activities gave her to think, to breathe.

The choice of drama club, specifically, seemed passive-aggressive, given Jane's past. But she hadn't taken the bait. It was a normal thing for a child to try.

She nodded, smiled politely at the other parents who stood by their cars in the bus lane. Jane knew she ought to be friendlier but she couldn't retain the faces and names, did not feel akin to these wealthy people. When Chloe emerged, aloof from the other children, she scanned the row for Jane, then wordlessly, carefully made her way to the car.

"I'm no good at this," she said as Jane pulled away from the curb. "Some of these kids have already done summer stock. Do you know what that is?"

"Yes."

"I didn't. They laughed at me. I don't know how to be somebody else! I'm not sure why people want to."

"Well . . . it can be fun. You don't have to be a natural at it. Some people pick it up slowly."

Chloe scowled. "You were good at it as a kid, right?"

"Not really."

Her eyes narrowed, as though she sensed a lie. But she let it go, and they rode in silence for the half-hour drive home.

The neighborhood where they lived was friendly, leafy, well-groomed. There was objectively nothing to dislike about it, yet Jane felt a growing excitement about her impending escape from it. When they pulled up in front of the house, Jane drew breath. "Chloe," she said.

"Oh god."

"No, no, it's not bad. I just . . . have to go away for a little while."

Chloe frowned and narrowed her eyes. "That *is* bad, Mom."

"Somebody in my family needs me. I'll be back soon."

"Grandpa?"

"No, somebody else."

"There's somebody besides Grandpa?"

"People I haven't seen in a while. People you never met."

Chloe looked out the window at the house, theatrically sighed. Maybe she was learning something from drama club, after all. "Can we go inside now?"

"Of course. But . . . are we good?"

"We're fine," Chloe said, unbuckling her seat belt. Then she stopped, looked up, scowling. "I just don't like that you lie and keep secrets. I heard you and Dad arguing." She leveled a serious gaze at Jane, one that was clearly "acting." But she also meant it. "I'm old enough to know everything."

"Not quite."

"You'll be saying that when I'm forty!" the girl said, climbing out, and she slammed the door behind her.

Jane followed her into the house. Chance was there. So was Susan, an expression of smug triumph animating her face.

"So you're really doing it," Chance said, performing for his mother.

"Come on, Chance. You'd go, too, if your brother needed you."

Susan rolled her eyes.

"We'll talk about this when you get back," Chance said. "But it's going to be a different kind of conversation than the one we had last night."

"I don't know what that's supposed to mean."

He shook his head. "I guess you'll find out," he said, turning his back and following his mother to the kitchen. "I'm off to make our daughter dinner."

Jane found Chloe sitting on the floor of her room, playing a handheld video game. On the screen, a small person with a round head cast a fishing line into the sea.

"Can I say goodbye?"

"That's it? Just, all of a sudden, you're going?"

Jane sat down beside her. "People's parents go on trips all the time."

"Not you."

"I'll call you every day. Can I have a hug?"

Chloe shrugged. Jane got on her knees and wrapped her arms around her daughter. "I love you, Chloe."

"Love you, too," Chloe muttered. Her hair hung down, concealing her face, and she didn't lift her head to be kissed. Her game character caught an enormous fish and reacted with surprise and delight.

Jane stood up. She took one more look at Chloe. Then she turned, descended the stairs, picked up her bag, and walked out.

# 4

# Nestor, NY: *Then*

Jane's earliest memory of her mother:

Jane and Lila, playing in their crib. They can't be more than a year old. The room is illuminated only by late afternoon sun, filtered through an orange curtain. Jane wants something; she is hungry, she's wet. She hasn't cried yet, but soon she will. Voices in the hall, Mama and Daddy. Music plays from a radio somewhere, far away. The doorknob turns, and Mama enters. The hallway is bright, she's just a silhouette. Jane uses the crib's bars to pull herself up, then, standing unsteadily, raises her arms into the air. "Mama, Mama," she says. She wants to be lifted out.

Instead, her mother bends over, reaches down into the depths of the crib. She's near enough to the window now for the yolky light to illuminate her, while Daddy stands back, in the shadows. Mama's smiling face is full of love. For Lila, not for Jane. She scoops contented Lila up, and Daddy moves into the light, his young face animated by delight. Mama and Daddy exclaim over the favored twin, the one who needed them less. Rewarded for her indifference, as Jane, left behind, cries and cries.

None of this could be true, could it? The handful of photos Jane had of their childhood bedroom showed two cribs, placed against opposite walls. Would they really have been left alone together in one of them?

And her father's young face: this is something Jane never saw, except in photos; he was already middle-aged when they were born. In this memory, there was only one window, nearly the width of the wall. In pictures there were two, both small. No orange curtains, either; rather, cheap vinyl blinds, hanging crookedly, casting slats of unfiltered daylight across the rug.

And why would their mother have favored Lila? Even if this event had really occurred, if she came in and picked up Lila first, surely she bent over a moment later for Jane? What she recalled as an eternity of sorrow might only have taken seconds.

She couldn't remember being held by her mother, being nursed, smiled at or laughed at or praised. But could other people? How clear are anyone's memories of their earliest years? Jane sometimes wondered whether the twentieth-century notion of an idyllic childhood might have been the illusory product of photography — the fact that everyone took pictures, but only of the best times. You want to know if you were happy? There's the proof, in the photo albums, on your parents' refrigerator, in the box of Polaroids on the closet shelf. Everyone smiling, laughing, celebrating. Good times and special occasions, gradually taking the place of the real memories of boredom, worry, and displeasure.

Jane possessed none of her childhood photos. As far as she knew, few existed. School pictures, mostly, and a few outliers: her father had owned an old film camera, acquired in his youth, that he still had today. What he photographed, when he traveled for research, was buildings and battlefields, churches, barns. A few shots of the girls might sneak in at the beginning or end of a roll, posed in the yard, playing on the floor, but their mother didn't like it. Didn't like the idea of some stranger at a photo lab coaxing the images out of the emulsion, fishing the prints from the chemical bath. Staring at her children, at their faces. Memorizing the moments of their lives. She was paranoid, yes, but she also disdained sentimentality, the idea of happiness as an ambition. They didn't need photos to prove they were happy.

They were happy, sometimes. Weren't they?

Jane's clearest memories of her father began later, when she and Lila were older, and their mother's absences had grown longer. She remembered him struggling to buy them clothes for school, make them meals.

Help them with their homework. He was literally a college professor, and couldn't seem to make sense of what their teachers wanted.

"Why are all these adjectives in here?" he asked them. He was proofreading their work. They must have been nine or ten. "You don't need all these adjectives."

"That's what we're supposed to *do*," Lila tried to explain. "We're doing adjectives."

"There has to be three in every sentence," Jane said. "It's in the instructions."

He took up his pencil and started crossing them out. "No, no, none of this is necessary."

"Stop!" Lila snatched up her notebook. "Now I have to do it over!"

"I can't condone writing like this!"

"Daddy," Jane said, "it's the *assignment*!"

"Then don't follow the assignment!"

But he was also the source of her small store of truly happy memories. When their mother was at home, and content, and available, he could be warm and funny, passing through the room on the way from his office to the bathroom and back; he called them his little bits, affected a Tin Pan Alley accent, sang, "Shave and a haircut, two bits!" and tousled their hair. Sometimes they would ask him to tell them something funny, and they would laugh and laugh at his extremely unfunny responses, which usually described disasters that had almost but not quite happened during the Cold War.

"In 1983, a Soviet missile warning system reported that the United States had launched a nuclear attack. The military officer in charge, a man named Stanislav Petrov, was supposed to retaliate, but he defied his training, believing the report to be in error. He was right! If it weren't for one man, disobeying his orders, we would all be dead, and the world would be a wasteland!"

"In 1958, the United States developed a plan, known as Project A119, to detonate a nuclear bomb on the moon, to frighten and intimidate the Soviets. Cooler heads prevailed, but imagine if they'd gone through with it — nuclear fallout would have rained down on our heads!"

"Back in the early seventies, there was a code that American military technicians had to enter in order to launch a Minuteman nuclear missile. Can you guess what it was? Eight zeroes! They didn't change it until 1977!"

Their father made a show of being appalled by their laughter, clutching his chest, recoiling in mock horror. "How can you think this is funny? Imagine! Just imagine!" But at night, in bed, the covers pulled up over her head, Jane would worry herself to tears contemplating the ruined world these stories implied. The moon story was the worst. It was so vivid. She imagined herself, strangely enough, alone, sitting on a hill. (It was the hill from her father's computer desktop, grassy underneath blue skies.) Night had fallen. The moon was full. She gazed at it, feeling safe and content, knowing that, as long as she lived, she could look into the sky and find it there, same as ever.

And then, suddenly, a flash. A slowly expanding cloud of dust, mushrooming into space from the moon's surface. A horrible crack, the moon rupturing, breaking in two, and the two halves falling to pieces. The pieces falling toward earth with terrible slowness.

Suddenly, Jane's pleasure in being alone was gone. The ones she loved were far away — some other country. Everyone would be killed, everyone on earth, and she had to wait here, completely alone, anticipating the inevitable. There in bed, she worried herself to tears, which she tried to suppress so that Lila wouldn't hear.

Eventually, she realized that it was their mother's audience that really mattered to their father. When she wasn't around and they demanded his stories, he typically found some way to deflect them: he was too busy, it was time for bed, he wasn't in the mood. Only when they were all together did he find the energy to entertain them; only when their mother laughed did he resemble the young man from her false memory.

Where did he tell them their mother had gone? Later, once an explanation presented itself — once they understood what love affairs were, and that their mother had them — all her absences could be made to make sense. But then? "Your mother is away." The implication was that she was visiting the family that she seemed to despise or, more plausibly, working — though they never knew their mother to have a job, at least not one that could be easily explained. She seemed to share some of their father's expertise in history; when they were getting along, he would come to her with ideas, draft pages, and she would criticize them, slashing at the paper with a red pen. But she didn't teach; there was no office she went to, not even a place in the house that was hers alone. When she was gone, she left no trace; it was as though she'd never lived there at all.

# 5

# Nestor, NY: *Now and Then*

Harry listened with gratitude as his daughter told the waiting students that Professor Pool was not feeling well and would have to cancel office hours this week. Then he sat and pondered for an hour. Then he fell asleep. Then he went downstairs and bought a cup of coffee and a sandwich. Though he intensely disliked talking to his students in the office, he enjoyed being among them in the commissary; he felt comforted, shielded by their anonymous mass, their frivolous chitchat. It amazed him how much personal detail they were willing to betray in casual conversations to whomever happened to be standing around: the names of their friends and enemies, their social and sexual habits, their conflicts with family and plans for employment.

The commissary was extra crowded today; students seemed elated that spring break had arrived and were buying provisions for their drives and flights out of town. In the sandwich order line, he overheard two young men discussing their powerful fathers' plans for them, and their ambivalence about assuming roles in the family businesses. One, a Korean boy, would seem destined to inherit a microprocessor-manufacturing empire. The other, a white American, was the scion of a conservative media mogul. Harry took his little spiral notebook out of his breast pocket and jotted down:

*Labor investigation in chip fab*
*Design assistant fired, corporate espionage?*
*Gun lobby pay to place editorial*
*Female intern threaten harassment lawsuit*

There was no particular utility to this work; it was the force of habit that compelled Harry. He had a box at home containing dozens of these notebooks, all of them useless. A forty-year history of doubt, bravado, and naivety among the children of the wealthy and powerful. No one had asked him to do this in many years, but he kept the notebooks just in case. Or perhaps just to remind himself that history is always in the making. Every second, the present transforms itself into the past.

Oh, what pretentious drivel. He reached the front of the line and ordered the seitan pita with hummus. He'd stopped eating meat many years ago, when he visited a slaughterhouse in the commission of research. Meat now seemed pointless and barbaric. The last time he became truly angry was a couple of years ago, when a student, visiting his office for a conference, killed, unprompted, with the nearest book (Michael Beschloss's *Mayday*), a bee that had alighted on the desk. Harry welcomed the bees, they lived in the sash, they did not harm him and had their own jobs to do. He pounded the desk and shouted at the student, who appeared truly alarmed. Later his friend Julius, the dean of arts and sciences, came and had a talk with him. This was the first time Julius hinted that, if Harry wanted to retire, a very handsome package could be prepared for him. The suggestion had nothing to do with Harry in particular, of course, only that, due to post-pandemic budgetary considerations and reorganizations, opportunities were available that previously were not, and might not be, down the line.

No, thank you, was Harry's reply, and it is rude of you to bring it up. Julius hadn't approached him this year, but Julius was about to retire himself, and must have figured Harry would soon be someone else's problem. At seventy-three, he knew that he was, in fact, various people's problem. He couldn't seem to retain information any longer. His classes, which had once featured bold presentations of carefully researched material, followed by dynamic and inspiring question-and-answer sessions, now consisted of him desperately gripping the podium with his head hung while reciting lectures from twenty-year-old typescripts. Or maybe they were always this way, and student expectations had changed? The most appalling thing he'd witnessed in the last decade was a video of himself, posted to YouTube for the purpose of mockery, mumbling his way through a lecture on America's failed dealings with Fidel Castro. He had been searching for video of Castro himself!

Harry accepted his sandwich and returned to his office to eat it, hurrying up the back stairs so as to minimize his exposure to possible attack—violent or verbal, he feared the two equally. Safely ensconced inside, he ate in silence broken only by the branches that the wind flung against his window.

This is where he met his wife, in 1983, he sitting here, behind this very desk, she poking her head around the edge of the doorway. Her name was Anabel. She was the TA who had been assigned to his Cold War survey course. Was he Professor Pool? Was this the right office? Harry was desperately attracted to her immediately; she had an arboreal air, furtive yet self-assured, like an extremely sexy deer.

He was very surprised. He had thought she was, as they said, out of his league. Perhaps it was her unusual upbringing that made her seem so elegant and exotic to him: the child of diplomats, one Spanish, one Russian, she had traveled the world and spoke five languages with what sounded to Harry like fluency. (It was an enduring shame of his that he had no knack for languages and had barely made it through his high school and college German classes.)

He loved her passionately, without reservation. But he never understood her. She was fierce, mercurial. Often she was distant; sometimes he thought she pitied him for loving her. The less he understood her, the more he adored her; he loved her best when she was away—when, alone, he pondered her, puzzled over her. He never met her father, who had divorced her mother when she was still a girl and returned to what was then the Soviet Union; he met her mother once, in New York, at the Russian Tea Room. The two argued in Spanish for most of the meal.

It was clear to Harry that Anabel had her own money and did not need his. But she would never share her finances with him, would never volunteer to cover household expenses when they ran low. They fought often, but he didn't understand why. Something he said or did would set her off and she would rage at him, push and punch him, then retreat in shame to her solarium, a little greenhouse addition a previous owner of the house had built, which she had filled with exotic plants that she was forever tweezing, pruning, pollinating, and germinating. To his surprise, she didn't pursue what would have been a stunning academic career; her work on postwar France and patriarchal Gaullist politics was superb. She would later blame the twins for this, but Harry was no fool. He knew by then that she had abandoned those ambitions, despite her frequent open-ended research trips. She did not have to become pregnant—it had been something she said she wanted. Yet the pregnancy infuriated her. She railed against him, told him he was trying to control her through the baby. He said he would support an abortion if that was what she wanted, and she said he was a pig.

But even at the time, her logic was too twisted to be wounded by. Clearly, for whatever reason, she had wanted motherhood to rescue her from the life she had made, and belatedly realized it wasn't going to work. Her anger was really for herself, for the corner she'd backed herself into. On the ride home from the obstetrician's office, where they learned that they would be having twins, she wept bitterly and pounded the dashboard with her fists.

And yet, for years, they had what seemed to Harry like a normal marriage. Whatever Anabel had been trying to convince herself of, the girls seemed, at least at first, to have persuaded her. She was a kind and compassionate mother to the infant twins, and thank goodness, because Harry himself proved an inept and distracted father, a role he had continued to inhabit to this day, to his great shame. Until the girls began preschool, it seemed as though their unconventional and sometimes mysterious union would last, that their family would thrive.

Harry had assumed that, given her newfound school-day freedom, Anabel would resume her academic career. Instead, she kept putting off her return, first by a semester, then by a year. She smoked more, grew restless. Started taking day trips, then overnight ones. To the city, she said, to research a book. This gave way to trips abroad: more research, she claimed, and to visit family. Harry was hopeless with Anabel away; the girls didn't like the food he made, he couldn't remember to pick them up at school or to make sure their clothes were clean. His own work suffered. He should have known, given her refusal to talk about her research with him, that her trips weren't really what she claimed. Oh, he understood that there must be other lovers; Anabel effortlessly commanded the attention of men younger and handsomer than he was, and her beauty and confidence seemed to grow with age. That part made sense to him. That, he could bear.

It was the other thing that haunted him, the thing for which he had only himself to blame.

Sandwich eaten, Harry slept once more. He was awakened hours later by a robin at his window, pecking at its own reflection. Bird, stop. You'll hurt yourself. He didn't want to leave campus. He didn't want to leave his office! It was spring break now, the time of the school year he liked the least, when the halls seemed emptiest. He turned on his desk lamp and read in the yellow pool of light. Another hour, he thought. But he lost himself and by the time he became hungry again, darkness had fallen. The robin, no longer confused by its reflection, had returned to the nest. If only it knew! It had brought the enemy home.

Eventually Harry began to long for the comforts of his own house. His grocery order likely waited on the porch. Peanut butter and raspberry preserves on sliced deli rye, a combination the girls had found vile. When Anabel lived at home, Harry enjoyed his eccentricities. He could imagine his absentmindedness and frailty in the domestic sphere as endearing. Not so when she was gone. He had failed. He lied to everyone; he didn't want them to know he'd been abandoned.

Outside, the air was moist and cool. Clouds raced across the moon. He stood at the bus stop behind Seddon Hall, waiting. On the other side of the road, another man waited to travel in the other direction. Not a student, nor a professor. White, broad shouldered. Middle-aged. The man wore a collegiate windbreaker and smoked a cigarette. He stared at Harry, smoking. Unable to contain himself, Harry raised a hand in greeting. The man did not respond; he stared and smoked.

Harry prided himself on his rationality. He was a man of research, of deduction. His job was to make sense of the chaos of human endeavor. By his own standards, then, it made no sense that he should harbor this fear: that someday, they would send somebody for him. He understood that this should never happen; that if it was going to happen, it would have happened a long time ago; that, the more time passed, the less likely it became, and it was never very likely to begin with. Harry was old; he was nobody now.

And yet, that man. He wore a baseball cap without a logo on it — just plain black, pulled down low. Cigarette smoke curled up around the brim. Who wore a cap without a logo? It should say something. Buffalo Bills. MAGA. The university's own mascot: that fierce, rotund, and strangely sexual bear.

The bus would be here soon. In fact, here came one — on the man's side of the street. It pulled up to the stop. It was empty, save for one dozing student. It pulled away. The man remained. He was here to kill. Or perhaps he was waiting for a different bus. Harry peered left, leaning into the dark as though it would help him see better. No homeward bus was visible in the distance, coming down the hill and over the bridge.

Harry turned and fled with as much dignity as he could muster. The tails of his overcoat flapped in the wind. He hurried around Seddon, dashing from one pool of lamplight to the next, then speedwalking across the arts quad. He shouldn't look over his shoulder. He did. The man wasn't there. But they were experts at concealment, weren't they. Head down, already winded, he darted between Manfred and Pace, their windows dark, save for a basement lab where someone peered into a microscope. He longed to be that person, young, absorbed in a miniature world.

On the winding street between campus and the Creekside neighborhood where he lived, someone fell in line behind him, footsteps clacking on the pavement. What kind of shoes was the man wearing? Surely they were not hard-soled. The footsteps drew closer. What had he been taught? Turn, confront your attacker. Harry pivoted, jerking around on his toes, and found a young woman behind him, black dress and heels, white earbuds in her ears. She appeared startled, stopped, removed an earbud. "Are you all right?"

"Yes, yes."

"You almost fell."

"No," Harry said, "no, just forgot something. I think. I think I have to go back."

She resumed her listening, clacked into the darkness and out of sight.

At home, he dragged the grocery box inside, closed and locked the door behind him. Then he went and checked the back door and all the windows, turned on every light. The house still smelled a little like his cat that had died three years before, his companion after the girls left. He thought some litter must have fallen into the heating grate in the bathroom, and now it tainted the air every time the furnace kicked on.

He went into the basement, turned all the lights on there, too, peered behind the moldering boxes where he kept Anabel's clothes. Checked the lock on the basement door, too. This was the weak spot. The wood was old. To add a deadbolt would require replacing the door. To replace the door would require a handyman. To call a handyman would be to invite a stranger into his home. He went back upstairs, locked the door to the basement, checked all the other locks again.

Nine days alone, and Jane away. If she learned the truth, would she ever come back?

# 6

# Nestor, NY: *Now and Then*

————

She wore sunglasses on the shuttle to the airport, through the security line (removing them briefly for the TSA agent), at the gate, down the jetway, into her seat. First to St. Louis, then a connection to Highfill. A high school boyfriend once called her a monster because she said she didn't miss him when he was away. Jane didn't miss anyone when they were away, missed them even less when she was the one away. Maybe that did make her a monster.

It was dinnertime at home. They ordered pizza on Friday nights, but not when Susan was over — Susan expected a home-cooked meal, which Jane always prepared resentfully. With distance, though, Jane couldn't recall Susan ever insisting that she cook. And it wasn't as though Susan ever complimented the food. Maybe Jane was the one who insisted. Who needed to prove herself. Susan had probably come straight over, as soon as she learned Jane was leaving. Maybe they'd ordered pizza, maybe they were eating it now. She could have texted Chloe — *what are you eating?* — but she didn't have a phone. She'd done as Lila asked and left it at home, in the bedside table drawer, powered down. Cutting herself off entirely from her own child.

Verdict: monster.

Her own mother never seemed to miss her. Jane and Lila were

expected to raise each other, always when she was away, and most of the time when she was home. The person to ask for help first, she told them, is your sister. Only demand something of Mama when Sister couldn't. They took the policy as a challenge, and it often resulted in messes and minor disasters. Burnt toast and hands, crudely hacked-off locks of hair, bleach instead of peroxide dumped on a wound. Any of it was better than the dread sensation of asking Mama for help and watching her face stiffen.

It was easiest in summertime, when life had always been unstructured. The house stood on a double lot their parents had let go to seed; a rotting garden shed held old tools, scrap wood, cans of dried-up paint, weed and insect killer. They had managed to restore a mechanical push mower with a file and some 3-in-One Oil, and used it to carve paths through the wild. They built forts, made miniature towns in little clearings. Their attempt to erect a hideout in the apple tree had been foiled by a fall and a dislocated shoulder (Lila's), but they did manage to create a wooden platform, a rope ladder, and a pulley out of a wagon wheel, which they used to haul their possessions up and down. Today the place seemed sad and small, but then it was immense, thrilling, entirely theirs.

Jane had a fanciful notion of her mother's solarium suddenly appearing one day, a whole miniature world just off the kitchen that had been dreamed into existence during the night. But of course it was always there, disused, filled with moldering boxes of what Jane now assumed was the detritus of their parents' academic lives. Ivy grew in the yard beside it, covering the glass entirely, making it feel, from inside, like a clammy closet with a slanted outside wall. Sometimes one of the girls would conceal herself there during hide-and-seek; it was a good spot, because both of them were afraid of the spiders and mice. If you were brave that day and your sister wasn't, you could go undiscovered for ages.

Unburdened of the boxes and thick vines, with the baseboard heat switched on, the tile floor swept and mopped, the solarium felt like a forgotten room from a dream. Their mother must have done most of the work while they were at school; Jane could remember dropping her backpack onto the tile and gazing in wonder at the light and space. Shelves once cluttered with books and papers now bore plastic seed-starter trays, terra-cotta pots. Bags of soil and fertilizer slumped on the floor. Grow lights blazed overhead, dispelling the gloomy day outside, and a series of narrow pipes emitted a gentle mist, which mingled with their mother's cigarette smoke.

A few weeks before, Mama had brought back seeds from her last trip, and Jane, awake from a nightmare, had wandered into the kitchen to find the kitchen table covered in newspapers. Cracked china cups, tuna fish tins, and jelly jars were filled with dirt, and her mother was poking her finger into each one, creating little depressions. "What are you doing?" Jane asked her from the doorway, and to her surprise, her mother gestured for her to come sit with her.

"When I was away," she said, "visiting family, I collected some seeds."

"Are they vegetables?"

"No. Flowers and other things. That grow where it's warm."

It was late winter, and snow still melted in patches among the trees outside. "It's cold," Jane said. "Will they die?"

Her mother picked up her cigarette from the saucer she was using as an ashtray and, smoking, began to pick up seeds from a little plastic sack and drop them into the holes she'd made. "No. They'll grow inside, not out. By the window." A bag of potting soil stood on one of the kitchen chairs, and now she sprinkled some into each of the holes, covering the seeds. "Here," she said, handing Jane a glass of water. "Water them. Pour gently, a little bit in each."

Jane did as she was asked. "Who did you see, Mama?"

"What?"

"On your trip. Did you see your parents?"

"No."

"Who, then?"

She took the glass from Jane's hand and resumed the watering herself. "Why are you awake?"

"I had a bad dream."

"Well, it's over now. Go back to bed."

In the weeks to come, seedlings appeared all over the house, on windowsills and on side tables. Their mother would alight, beelike, on each of them in a lazy circuit, watering, pinching, rotating. The rehabilitation of the solarium was the culmination of this process, and once the project was finished, the seedlings all disappeared into it, and their mother with them.

If the solarium removed their mother even further from the domestic sphere—this is when Mrs. Vesey, the woman who still cleaned the house weekly for their father, first appeared—it at least rendered her more docile. She left the door open when she was inside, almost as if inviting them to visit; if Lila or Jane slipped through and sat on one of the folding chairs that used to be stored here when it was a closet, she would acknowledge them with a nod and let them watch her work. Sometimes, if her mood was right—contentedly muttering a tune in some foreign language was the tell—she would answer questions before ushering them out.

"Mama, what are you growing?"

"Heliconia. Also called lobsterclaw. This one will go in a big pot in the corner. It will be tall and the flowers will be long and red and orange."

"Mama, what is your daddy like?"

"My daddy was too rich and important for me ever to know him."

"Is he dead?"

"No."

"Do you miss him?"

"I miss him like the wind misses the trees."

"I don't understand."

"Think for a moment before you ask such a thing."

Over time, the shelves filled up. Baskets hung from hooks; grow lights appeared to replace the sun the baskets blocked. There was an old VHS videotape Lila loved, that Jane sometimes watched with her, late at night, when their parents forgot to put them to bed. It was a compilation of episodes of *The Muppet Show,* from before they were born. The text on the box was in another language—Russian, Jane supposed now, perhaps a gift from their mother's family—and one of the skits featured Kermit the Frog in a hospital bed, prescribed some strange concoction by a doctor. The characters sang a song as the room slowly, horribly filled up with vegetation and wild jungle creatures, and the characters transformed into what Jane suspected she'd now recognize as aboriginal caricatures. Of the two of them, Lila was the more risk averse, the more buttoned down, and Jane the agent of chaos. But Lila loved this sketch, and Jane found it terrifying.

That's what the solarium came to remind Jane of, as her mother withdrew further into her private world, seemed more foreign to her, more mysterious. But she couldn't stop entering that world, which was suddenly more fascinating than anything that had ever been visited on their house.

"Mama, what are you growing?"

"Salvia microphylla, a type of sage. Some refer to it as 'hot lips' but I do not. Its blossoms are red and white, and if it were summer, and this plant were growing outdoors, it would attract hummingbirds."

"Mama, what is your mother like?"

"My mother is a cheat and a liar, just like yours, dear daughter."

"You're not a liar, Mama."

"Ha!" She pointed, in mock anger, with the lit end of her cigarette. "You admit I'm a cheat!"

"You're not, Mama, you're nice."

Her mother did not soften at the compliment. Her lips went pale and tight and her eye twitched.

"If there is one thing I am not, Jane, it is 'nice.'"

"I'm sorry, Mama."

"You've worn out your welcome. Go pester your father."

# 7

# St. Louis, MO: *Now*
# and Nestor, NY: *Then*

———

She woke from dreamless sleep on the tarmac in St. Louis and wandered, slightly dazed, down the concourse to the food court in the main hub. Her connection was in terminal E, at the other end of the airport. She bought a croissant and a cup of black coffee and took her time, watching.

It had been a while since she'd allowed herself this kind of attention to strangers. She was out of practice: for the moment, they looked like an undifferentiated mass, the same mass they considered her to be part of. Each person was enveloped in an invisible shroud, a barrier, impersonal and impermeable.

She began to imagine, for every given passerby, what she could say or do to break that barrier. To the once-handsome business traveler whose eyes flickered between his phone and every passing woman under forty: Whoa, Breitling, my dad had one of those. Is that vintage? To the disheveled goth kid in the Killing Joke tee shirt: When I was your age, I saw them in Poland, on the reunion tour. To the elderly woman being conveyed by hospitality attendants to her gate in a motorized cart, after a glance at the ticket she clutched in her ring-encrusted hand: Mrs. Halloway? Do you remember me? Nearly everyone could be breached, something could always be extracted, even if it was just information.

At her gate, she studied her fellow passengers. Mostly college students: Arkansas State's spring break must have been ending this week. A few business travelers, dressed in cheap shirts and shoes. Some rural-looking men, rough-edged, well-heeled: farm equipment conventioneers, maybe, agribusiness owners. A genuinely rich-looking guy in business casual, khakis, button-down shirt, Patagonia vest, loafers without socks: probably a lawyer, land use, oil and gas, something like that. He had a weathered look, rough skin and hair, like he still spent his vacations pretending to be a country boy. A lesbian couple in their sixties, one of them doing a sudoku, the other one reading *The New Yorker*. A man, early twenties, in ripped jeans and flannel shirt, cello case propped between his legs.

Jane could lie to these people, gain their confidence. She knew how. She could feel distant parts of herself yawning, stretching, dusting themselves off. She had an impulse to pull out her phone, text Chloe good morning, check the news, and was glad she couldn't; she hadn't forced herself to focus on the moment like this in years. She was rested and alone and all her senses were alive. She felt like the precocious child she once was.

Their mother had given them *The Railway Children,* the 1960s paperback edition she'd had as a child. Its blue cover bore a sentimental-looking sketch of a locomotive and a little girl in a hat, and they ignored it for months, until Lila finally read it and pressed it upon Jane with a breathless excitement that was wildly out of character. "It's about *spies*." They'd watched a couple of James Bond movies, but ultimately Jane found them frightening — there was one where a man almost got cut in half with a saw, and it was hard to care about the guns, gambling, and sex. *The Railway Children* started their obsession, but also *The Adventures of Mary-Kate and Ashley, Harriet the Spy*. A school book fair produced a book about the Revolutionary War; from it they learned about dead drops, used by the Americans' Culper Spy Ring to pass on information about the British. A doctor named James Jay invented an invisible ink that George Washington would call "sympathetic stain," and the rebels used it to hide military messages in otherwise ordinary letters. There was also a loyalist spy, a woman named Ann Bates, who infiltrated Washington's army by pretending to be a peddler. Once she was caught and managed to lie her way out of captivity. Bates wore or carried a symbol — a "token," the book called it — identifying her as a spy to other British loyalists. The book didn't say what the token was, but Lila and Jane decided it was a stalk of wheat, stuck through a buttonhole. They and their friends went around the school "wearing the wheat" — probably some grass gone to seed from the verge of the playground — to identify themselves as part of a spy group. At first they didn't want Ann Bates to be their hero. She was, after all, one of the bad guys. But then they learned about double agents and began to think of themselves as loyal only to one another, a cabal. They defined themselves by their hostility to authority. They would play the big powers against each other, and keep their secrets until death.

They created their own dead drops (a loose brick behind the dumpsters, the underside of a drawer in the science room) and tried to write secret messages in lemon juice. Jane couldn't remember what the messages were about — probably manufactured dramas involving the teachers and the kids they didn't like. That ended when one of the spies started a fire trying to read a message on an electric baseboard heater and ended up in detention.

It might have ended there, but one day another girl brought a new device to school — a pen that could record your voice and play it back at different speeds, and played sound effects. It was called Talkgirl. Lila became fascinated and managed to convince her to trade overnight — the pen for her favorite Polly Pocket, the Toy Land one that looked like a magical book, with a large plastic key, and inside, an airplane ride, a rocking chair, a swing, plus Polly, Tiny Tina, and Ted the Bear.

"What if she breaks it?" Jane said. "What if she loses the dolls?"

Lila shrugged, already trying to pry the pen apart to see what was inside. "I'm over it," she said.

The next day, the girl would return the toy unharmed, but that afternoon Lila and Jane played with the pen, spying on their parents, whispering their observations into the tiny microphone, dead-dropping it to each other in a rotted-out tree in the yard.

"Subject is cultivating a new seedling. It is suspected to be a deadly poison."

"Subject has deposited papers in the locked file cabinet. The key is concealed in the bottom desk drawer."

"Subject's lighter may be a listening device."

"Subject has placed a notebook into his safe. Last number of the combination is twelve."

The following week, with their mother away, they managed to convince their father that they each needed a recording pen for a school project. "What kind of project?" he asked them, as they drove to the mall.

"Science," Jane said, knowing the word would cause his brain to shut off. It snapped back to life, though, once they found a couple of the pens at RadioShack, after first striking out at Target and Circuit City. They were the boy version, Talkboy, with slightly different sound effects and more muted colors.

"These cost twenty dollars!" he exclaimed.

"I know," Jane said with a theatrical sigh. "I feel bad for kids who can't afford it."

"I can't afford it! I'm still paying off the roof!"

"Dad," Lila said. "Come on. It's our education."

In the end, he bought them one that they had to share. It was fine. At school, the spy girls used the pens for a week and a half, muttering messages and trading in the hall. It wasn't until they actually owned one of the pens that the twins began to chafe at the toy's limitations: the silly sound effects, the brief recording time. Their mother came home, as she usually did, without fanfare, appearing one early morning when it was still dark. Jane, creeping into the kitchen to refill her water glass, found her sitting alone at the table in the dim light from the oven hood. In her hand was the spy pen.

Startled, Jane let out a small scream and dropped her empty glass. It bounced harmlessly on the linoleum.

"This toy belongs to you," their mother said.

"Yes."

"It is used to make recordings."

"Um . . . yes?" She bent over and picked up the glass.

"The prerecorded sounds. What are those used for?"

"Not much, I guess? They're just dumb."

"Hm," their mother said, setting down the pen. She turned her eyes to the unbroken drinking glass. "That's your good luck for the day," she said. "Better look out."

"Huh?"

"You only get one piece of luck. It's important to know when you've run out. Don't be reckless today."

"Okay. Are you home now?"

She looked around in mock bewilderment. "I seem to be."

"I mean, for a while?"

"Ah." She nodded once. "Sure."

There was nothing more to say. Jane filled her glass and went back to bed.

The following week at school, a clownish attention-grabber named Emma tried to trick their teacher with the fake sound of a ringing phone from her Talkgirl, and all the pens were confiscated until the end of the term. But by January, Jane and Lila's friends had moved on to something new. It had always been a point of contention in the group that the twins had never owned electronic diaries, plastic clamshells with a notebook inside, that would open up only in response to the owner's voice. Jane had asked for one for Christmas the year before and been given a conventional diary instead, bound in red leather, with an easily picked lock. She and Lila had declared the password diaries stupid—it was easy to imitate a friend's voice, and the plastic wings would spring open, and nobody had used theirs for long. But this year those girls were given the Secret Sender, a foldable device with a tiny keyboard and a screen, that would let them send typed messages to each other across the room. It cost $120. Jane and Lila didn't even bother asking for one. Before long their friends were using the devices to declare Jane and Lila stuck-up and poor. At one point, in a snowy berm at the edge of the playground during recess, Jane managed to snatch one away from Emma and found an ugly little digital approximation of a face—hers or Lila's, she supposed—alongside the text *duh im a dumb bitch.*

"We're not *poor,*" Jane said, smacking it against Emma's chest and letting it drop. The girl caught it, gasping.

"You're not even twins!" she said, unexpectedly.

"What?"

"You don't look alike!"

"We're *fraternal,* dumbass," Jane said, and Emma repeated it back to her in a singsong voice. "And we don't look like your stupid picture."

The spy girls, it seemed, were splintering.

It was fine with Lila and Jane. They formed a spy ring of two, dedicated to mocking and belittling their former friends. They traded messages using a code they devised that required you to have their mother's childhood edition of *The Railway Children*. The girls had two — Lila had seen another copy at a used bookstore and stolen it for this very purpose. You constructed sentences out of words picked from the text, identified by page number, line, and position: page 89, line 7, third word in. Unless you knew what the key was, the messages were just random lists of numbers. This game occupied them for weeks and made their ostracization feel like a badge of honor.

Later in the spring, a teacher told Jane she had a flair for the dramatic and encouraged her to try out as a child extra in the summer musical at the local community theater. They were putting on *Annie*. Jane had never seen a musical and persuaded their father to rent the movie of *Annie* for her. After that, she used her allowance to buy the original Broadway cast recording on a CD and listened to it constantly.

"Why are you into this?" Lila wanted to know, after Jane pressed it upon her one night in early spring. Their bedroom window was cracked open and moist cool air gushed in, carrying the scent of melting snow. She handed back the headphones, frowning. "It's dumb."

"It's not! I'm going to be in it. I'm going to be Annie."

"I don't get it. You want to be on a stage with everyone looking at you?" Lila had pretended to be sick for the winter concert last year and was rewarded by getting to stay home alone for the first time in her life. She later told Jane she'd smoked one of their mother's cigarettes.

"I don't care about *that*," Jane said, though she did. "It's fun. You have to do it with me."

"No."

"Come on. Tryouts are in May, there's lots of time to practice."

But Lila was still thinking about recording. Their teacher had returned the spy pens in December, and now Lila idly played with theirs while Jane sang "It's the Hard-Knock Life," speeding up and slowing down her voice, making them both laugh.

"These only record, like, ten seconds," Lila said. "They should go for hours. Or send the sound to another pen, like it's a cell phone. What if you could put it in somebody's purse or something, and hear everything they say, no matter where they went?"

"Who do you want to listen to, Emma?"

Lila gaped at her. "No. Mom."

"Why?"

"Are you serious? She's not visiting her family. She says she hates them. Sometimes she's gone for weeks, sometimes it's just a couple of days. Like, if it's her family, how come we never see them?"

"We're in school."

"Kids take off from school all the time. Robin Leffler went to Disney World and her parents wrote a note saying she had mono."

"So, where do you think she's going, then?"

Lila stared at a blank spot on the wall. "I don't know," she said, in a way that suggested she had an idea but didn't want to say. "But I'm going to find out."

Jane's seatmate on the plane to Highfill wanted to talk. A woman who hadn't flown on a plane since she emigrated from Pakistan decades ago, she was on her way to visit her son at college. Nervous, she adjusted her headscarf and dress, licked her lips. She'd applied a little too much perfume. She gripped Jane's hand during takeoff, then fell asleep suddenly, as though she'd short-circuited. Jane tried and failed to sleep herself, imagined Chloe in school, wondered what kind of crushes, conflicts, and other dramas she endured that she never talked about. I should ask more often, Jane told herself. I should ask her later today, when I call. After I find a phone.

On the tarmac, her seatmate now seemed embarrassed by their earlier interaction and refused to look her in the eye. That was fine. Jane didn't want to look anyone in the eye — it was time to get to work. She put on her sunglasses and waited until the plane emptied out before getting up and calmly disembarking.

It was 7:34 a.m. and surprisingly crowded in this small airport. Chloe would be getting ready for school. No — it was the weekend. She'd be reading in bed, pretending not to have woken up already. Jane reached for her bag to call, then remembered. *Stop it.* She found a restroom and when she emerged picked up an abandoned copy of the *Democrat-Gazette* and pretended to wait for a flight out. Instead, she watched.

# 8

# Highfill, AR and Timber Fell, MO: *Now*

―――――

She was looking for a particular kind of person — ideally a business-woman who carried a big handbag, moneyed but a little harried, fidgety. There was one candidate here, a woman in her twenties with a grad student look, dirty eyeglasses, hair pulled back, leather tote. She was reading a hardcover book. But she appeared alert and vigilant, and she kept an arm over the bag.

Jane had arrived on the far end of concourse A; there were eleven gates here, and another ten on the west side of the airport, on concourse B. She decided to make her way to the central corridor, get a coffee and a pastry, and survey the scene.

Most of the gates were empty at this hour. She'd looked it up; fifty flights left here every day, most of them clustered in late morning and early afternoon. But the woman she wanted was most likely to be here now. If she was traveling alone on a Saturday morning, she was likely single. And if she was married, her husband or wife was probably asleep. Either way, she would probably drive her own car and leave it in the long-term lot.

Jane walked, watched, ate her scone, sipped her coffee. She found two more women, one in late middle age, angry-looking, expensive shoes, big unstructured floral canvas bag, appearing to be headed off on vacation; the other younger, talking on the phone and reading what looked like legal documents, Kate Spade work tote. She finished the scone, threw out the coffee, and was about to settle on the lawyer when the perfect mark suddenly appeared, hurried past her, and ran into the women's restroom.

The woman was in her midthirties, blowsy, and ill at ease in her clothes, an off-the-rack gray pantsuit that made her twitch and fidget. She was blinking furiously, poking and tugging at the corner of her eye, and talking on the phone. A big navy-blue suede bag hung from her shoulder, gaping open. As she passed, Jane heard her say, "— be there by one, Greg, the flight was delayed half an hour. I will be there."

Jane pocketed her sunglasses and entered the restroom. The mark was standing at the row of mirrors, rummaging in the bag. Her phone lay facedown next to one of the sinks; its case bore the image of a dog — labradoodle? — that she vaguely resembled. There was one other woman in the room, visible only as a pair of Keds underneath the door of a toilet stall.

It quickly became clear that the woman's contact lens had gotten lost in her eye. She was leaning over, squinting at the mirror, rolling her eyes around in an effort to snap it back into place.

"Contact?" Jane asked, putting her duffel on the floor and drawing a small compact from her pocket.

"Always at the worst moment, the thing gets lost!"

"Oh geez," Jane said, "your phone's in a puddle." Without hesitation, she picked up the woman's phone, wiped it on her sleeve, and dropped it into the open tote. She stole a glance at the bag's contents; the woman's keys were clearly visible at the bottom of a zippered side pocket, which was also gaping open. A bottle of contact lens solution was among the items haphazardly scattered throughout the main compartment.

The woman seemed slightly taken aback by Jane's having touched her phone but appeared reassured by her smile. "You know the trick?" Jane said.

"Trick?"

"It feels like it's way back there but it's really always just stuck to the underside of your eyelid. You have to get it wet, then you can just close your eyes, look up, and kind of wiggle it around. Like you're watching a tennis match."

"Yeah, I guess I usually do something like that."

Jane patted her chin and cheek with powder. "I've got some solution if you need it."

"No, no, I've got it."

From her bag the woman produced the bottle Jane had seen, and she tipped her head back and squirted some into her eye. She gazed into the mirror and then, after a glance at Jane, closed her eyes and started moving them around. Swiftly, with her free hand, Jane reached into the woman's bag, closed her hand around the keys, and transferred them to the pocket of her cardigan. Behind them, a toilet flushed, and a small woman in her forties emerged. She moved toward the sink row.

The mark opened her eyes, blinking.

"Did you get it?"

"Oh my god. Yes."

Jane snapped her compact shut. "There you go!"

"Thank fucking god," the mark said. The wiry woman, washing her hands now, scowled at the curse.

Something about the sound of her own voice reminded the mark of her earlier suspicions. She peered into her own bag, then pulled out her phone with obvious relief. She threw the contact lens solution back in.

"Cute dog," Jane said, pocketing her compact. She shouldered her bag.

"That's Big Ed."

"Big Ed!"

"I feel like a heel kenneling him. But what are you going to do."

"He'll make some friends, maybe."

"Ha! Hope they like slobbering."

"Well," Jane said, "see you around. Safe travels."

"You, too."

Jane couldn't tell if what she was feeling was paranoia or exhilaration. She was sweating freely under both arms and felt calm only after she'd passed the security checkpoint. There was no going back now; if she'd missed her guess, she'd have to find some other way to Lila.

The air was warm and moist here, despite the bright sun. Thin pink clouds were dashes over the flat distant horizon. Pickup trucks and SUVs dominated the long-term parking lot. The mark's key ring was awkward and busy, its house and work keys color-coded with plastic sheaths. A keychain ornament bore another picture of Big Ed, another one the name VENESSA. And there was a long metal whistle, presumably to ward off attackers. The key fob was from a Scion.

She could just double-lock it now and the horn would lead the way. But she wanted to forestall the moment she learned she was wrong. The lot was moderately sized, about twenty double rows of cars stretching about a hundred yards into the distance. She positioned herself in roughly the middle and made her way from row to row, in between the cars, alert for the familiar boxy outline. The car could be a sedan, but Jane doubted it. The woman had a big fluffy dog and considered herself quirky. No doubt she had the cube, didn't want to let it go despite its age. She thought she found it once, but it was a Honda Element.

And then, in the third row from the end, there it was. A bright red dusty shoebox. She approached, walked around it. Dent in the driver's-side door where the mark once opened too fast at a gas station. MSU Bears window sticker. MY OTHER CAR IS A UFO. HILLARY 2016. Inside, a mess. Dunkin' Donuts iced-coffee cups, a pair of running shoes, some junk mail. Dirty tennis balls. Chewed-up frisbee. Back seat covered in gray dog hair. Jane squeezed the fob, the car unlocked, and she climbed inside.

There was no parking receipt that she could find, so she took off her sunglasses, messed up her hair, and made herself cry.

It took ten seconds. Her technique was to recall her moment of greatest joy. It would be hard to explain to somebody like Chance, so she'd never bothered to try, but this moment had occurred when she was in prison. It was late winter, a time when, due to the vagaries of the HVAC, her cell was always either too hot or too cold, and she was always either throwing off her blankets or, shivering, pulling them back on. Being pregnant made it worse; she'd just spent her first trimester nauseated and ill at ease. Then, one night, it would have been in March, a heat wave moved through the state. It started in the evening; as they were led back to their cells after counseling, they peered up through the high window of the block to watch the clouds traversing the moonlit sky. During the night, the heat stayed off, and she slept better than she had in years. The whole prison was buzzing with excitement the next day; in the cafeteria, and in the laundry where she worked, you could feel it. Then, at three, they were let out into the yard. The sun shone. The snowmelt had left paths across the concrete. The air was cool and dank; you could smell the mud, the dankness of the pulp mill on the other side of the valley. She slipped her hand under her uniform top and felt the swell of her belly. A collective sigh from the inmates seemed to lift Jane up; she was glad, for the first time in months, to be alive.

That's what she thought of now, in the mark's car, as she backed out of the spot, navigated to the end of the row, and turned toward the toll kiosk. She relaxed the muscles in her chest and face and shoulders. She smiled at herself in the rearview, showing her teeth; she blinked. Out loud, she said, brightly, "Ten." Then she imagined herself being pulled down into darkness, the force of gravity increasing, the air thickening, pressing more and more heavily on her. As she counted down, she let her cheeks sag, her shoulders slump. It was more about the physical sensations of joy and misery than about the emotions themselves; she didn't have to think of sad things. Her body responded naturally. Her face in the mirror aged five years. And as she pulled up to the kiosk, the tears began to flow.

"I'm sorry, I'm sorry," she said to the old man sitting there. "I just got here, do you remember me? I just passed through. I'm sorry. I don't have my ticket, I don't know what happened to it. I had to cancel my trip. I'm sorry! The kennel called."

"Ma'am—"

"They don't know what happened, he just died, Big Ed, he had a heart attack or something, I don't know. I should have never put him in the kennel!"

"Okay, if you could just—"

"I'm sorry, could you let me out, I don't know what to do, I have to go pick up his b-b-b-body . . ." She sobbed, covering her face with her hands.

"All right, ma'am. All right. There you go. Next time, keep the ticket somewhere safe. There you go."

The gate rose. "Thankyouthankyouthankyou," she said as she passed under it.

When was the last time she'd stolen a car? They'd used to do it all the time, easy as bumming a ride. She had to admit, it felt good. By the time she reached the highway, she was laughing.

She pulled over at the first truck stop she found and paid cash for a map, a folding knife, a $20 burner phone and some minutes, and an egg-and-sausage

English muffin sandwich, neatly wrapped in foil-lined paper in a heated cabinet on the counter. In the car, she used the knife to open the blister pack and plugged the phone into the cigarette lighter. The little color screen lit up. She called to activate it and added the minutes. Then she ate the sandwich with the window open while plotting out a route on the map with a ballpoint pen she found in the glove compartment.

She drove through Rogers and Garfield, then crossed into Missouri at Gateway. State Highway 37 was farms and pastures, silos rising out of flat towns, lumber and auto parts, tire stores, abandoned houses. She turned on the radio, listened briefly to some religious music, then some local sports talk. Turned it off again. She stopped in Bolivar to pee and fill the tank.

Three hours after leaving the airport, she pulled into Timber Fell. She was impressed; there were two traffic lights. The town had a main street, called Main Street; it was intersected by three numbered cross streets, and a few other named ones that quickly petered off into gravel and then dirt. It was fairly bustling for a remote village; there was a fly shop and a wilderness outfitter and several burger joints. A bank, a church, an auto mechanic. A real estate office in whose window were taped faded ink-jet printouts of log cabins. Jane assumed its relative health was the result of tourism to the nearby reservoir.

She parked on Main, shouldered her duffel, and walked around the corner to the address she'd been given. The building was on the second block down. In fact, it *was* the second block down: a long, three-story warehouse with windows on the top two floors, sided in white clapboards. Number 21 was a featureless steel security door with a dead-bolt lock, right at the corner of Second and Lake Streets. The far end of the building was windowed on the first floor as well, and a glass corner door was marked 23. It also bore, in elegantly painted gold script, the word ANTIQUES.

Jane pushed open 23 and walked in. The place was neat and organized: tasteful arrangements of furniture, display cases full of glassware and old cameras, ornately framed landscape and portrait paintings. Fan lights hanging from a pressed-tin ceiling. Classical music issued from a radio. Facing the door, behind a long glass-topped counter, stood a stern-looking woman with a prominent chin and nose and piercing gray eyes.

She wore a blazer over a white shirt buttoned to the neck and greeted Jane with a nod and a look of recognition.

"You're Jane," she said, in the smooth, husky voice of a noir femme fatale. Not a style Jane was expecting to encounter in rural Missouri.

"I guess you know my sister."

The woman gestured around the space. "This is all hers."

"She didn't mention the antique store."

The woman laughed. "I'm sure there's a lot she didn't mention. I'm Loretta." They exchanged a firm handshake. "I'll tell her you're here."

"Thank you."

Loretta pressed a button on an intercom unit that sat on the counter beside what Jane assumed was a functioning rotary telephone. She said, "She's here." A moment later, the phone rang. Loretta listened.

"Come on up."

Loretta beckoned her around the counter, then led her down a dim hallway lined with ledgers and folders. They waited at another brushed-steel door, which emitted a buzz and a click. The door fell open and Loretta ushered her in before heading back.

"Thank you."

"Of course."

Jane climbed a flight of stairs into a long, brilliantly illuminated, high-ceilinged space. The air was cool and recirculated by the same kind of ceiling fans she'd seen downstairs. Before her stood a work table surrounded by aluminum military-issue office chairs and covered with papers, maps, and electronics; behind that, a U-shaped counter lined the far end of the room. It was clearly used as a standing desk and bore several computer monitors, a soldering station, an enormous printer, and other machines and devices — a laminator, a metal punch. She turned. Behind the stairs, a walled-off space that Jane presumed was the bathroom; a bed, an end table bearing a lamp and a stack of books, and several wheeled steel-pipe garment racks filled with clothes. A blue and orange duffel bag advertising RC Cola and the 1986 Mets gaped open on the bed, and leaning over it, holding a stack of folded tee shirts, was Lila.

She hadn't aged so much as sharpened. Her long nose had been broken and healed since Jane saw her last. Her sandy hair was pulled back in a tight ponytail. She wore minimal makeup, no lipstick, eyebrow pencil, a little concealer; it made her look like a kickboxer in a movie. She was wearing close-fitting slacks, tennis shoes, and a crew-neck sweater. Lila put down the shirts, turned, put her hands on her hips, and laughed.

"What?"

"You look good."

"Thanks." She didn't feel like she looked good. She felt weak.

"Although, I'd lose the cardigan. We might have to climb over a fence or something."

Jane had dressed for the plane: stretch jeans, Blundstone boots, the cardigan, and a tee shirt from a fun run in 2017. "Wait, really?" she said.

Lila shrugged. "Maybe! So do I hug you?"

"You're seriously asking me that."

They stared at each other for a few moments. Then Lila walked toward her, gripped her shoulders. Her eyes welled with tears. "Fucking hell." She gathered Jane into her arms with surprising gentleness. Jane let her head fall onto Lila's shoulder, breathed in the scent of her.

"Goddammit," Jane said.

"You see? I knew you'd come."

"Goddammit."

Lila took her hand, led her to the work table. Offered her a chair. They sat.

The two women stared at each other. Age and experience had changed them differently. There had, at times, been a savage calm to Lila that Jane had found unfathomable, even disturbing. This seemed to be her signature quality now. She exuded a sense of control: over her body, her face. Her hair was beginning to gray. It looked good. They were both thirty-five, but not the same thirty-five. Jane was the one who had married, who'd been to prison, who'd given birth. But she felt like she was still a child. Like she was visiting an older sister instead of a twin.

"How did you get here?" Lila asked.

Jane fished the mark's keys out of her sweater pocket and dropped them on the table.

Lila laughed. "Oh no! Poor Venessa."

"If I smell like dog," Jane said, "Venessa's car is why."

"Where is it?"

"Second and Main."

"I've got a guy. First leg of the trip, we'll go to him."

"Why am I not surprised you have a guy."

She laughed again. This was a new sound to Jane. Levity wasn't part of Lila's repertoire. Or was it, and Jane misremembered?

"You're different."

"Yes," Lila said, nodding. "You're different."

"Tell me about Loretta. How'd you convince her to move here?"

"I found her here."

"Were you . . . a couple? Are you?"

Lila shook her head. "It's complicated. Or it used to be. Now, no. She's my employee. There is no one I trust more than Loretta." She paused. "There's no one I trust *besides* Loretta."

"Including me, you mean?"

Her sister stared hard at her. "You're in a different category entirely," she said. Which did not answer the question.

Lila had her bring the car around back, where she was met by a row of four galvanized-steel garage doors. One of them was rising. She pulled into a large space that contained a Volvo station wagon, three motorcycles, a rolling tool rack, and shelves of solvents and lubricants. Lila met her at the driver's door.

"Do you fix cars?"

"Not really. I like to restore bikes, though."

"Right."

"Loretta," Lila said, as the woman came out to the garage through a door to the antiques shop. "Could you call Tyler in Lakehurst and see if he can take a wreck tomorrow?"

"Sure."

Lila turned to Jane. "I assume you don't want to leave tonight? You've probably had a long day."

"I could eat."

"Let's eat. Not out. I don't want anyone here to know about you."

"Prairie Empire?" Loretta asked.

"Sure."

"Done."

The three women ate the Chinese takeout together at the work table. Jane asked about Loretta's past. "I grew up here," she said. "My folks died when I was seventeen. They were farmers. Dad went broke and killed them both. I'm sure he would have killed me, too, if I hadn't run off with a girl. That didn't work out. I sold the land and joined the army. Made it to staff sergeant and did three tours in Afghanistan. I transitioned over there."

"Wow."

"They treated me right. But, I dunno. Once I figured out why I was so angry, I didn't want to die. So I came back here. I bought the shop. You'd be surprised, people who knew me back then have been okay. About my being trans, I mean. Some of them say congratulations or whatever, some just pretend nothing changed."

"Nobody harasses you?"

"Mostly outsiders. Locals know I'm armed and dangerous."

Lila said, "So, I bought the building and was going to kick her out."

Loretta shrugged. "I proved useful."

"She's handy," Lila said. "And the shop's good cover."

"It's a nice shop," Jane said.

"Thanks."

The sisters shared the bed for the night. Lila gathered her in, held her tightly, seemed to think better of it, and released her. "I'm glad you came."

"I don't know if I'm ready to say the same."

Lila rolled over onto her back, away from Jane. The separation gave her a sick feeling, and she was flooded with guilt.

"Oh god. I didn't call Chloe today," Jane said. "I promised."

"Do you want to get up?"

"No," Jane said, after thinking for a few minutes. "I'll call in the morning." But Lila was already asleep.

Jane was awakened in the night by a torrential rain that beat the roof and windows. Beside her, illuminated by streetlight, Lila's chest rose and fell. She got up, used the toilet, returned to the bed, and lay stiffly on her back. She lay awake, dwelling in the guilt at having broken her promise. She imagined Chloe, alone in her room, waiting for the call that never came. When she was little, Jane was perpetually bewildered by her need for companionship, her desire to share her every thought. What on earth kind of child required this kind of constant attention and validation?

A normal one, it turned out. It took raising Chloe to realize that it was strange to never feel lonely, to feel most calm and safe in solitude. Not for the first time, she wished she'd had another child, someone for Chloe to love, teach, and eventually depend upon. Or—also not for the first time—she wondered if this was just something she told herself, because she couldn't accept the possibility that it might have been better never to have had Chloe at all.

For a time, Chloe had salved her loneliness with an imaginary friend. It was when she was six or seven, had been in school long enough to find it alienating, to feel that nothing could change, that Jane heard her talking in her room, as though to a doll. But when she knocked and went in, Chloe was sitting cross-legged on her bed, empty-handed. This happened several times—Jane heard the phrases "going to be *punished*" and "don't tell Mama"—before Jane asked who Chloe was talking to. But all Chloe would say was that the question was very rude.

Chloe asked to be assigned the task of setting the table for dinner—something she'd been reluctant to do before—but bewildered them by setting an extra place and scowling at Jane when she failed to provide the invisible guest with food. Her laundry doubled in volume, and it eventually became clear that she was throwing clean clothes into the hamper along with her dirty ones. One night Jane heard a shout from her bedroom and went in to find her waking from a nightmare on the floor, where she had arranged one of her bed pillows and a blanket.

"Chloe, why aren't you in your bed?" Jane asked, comforting her, and half-asleep Chloe answered, "I gave the bed to Violet."

A few days later, Jane asked how Violet was doing. Chloe's response was a curt "You *know*." After a few similar exchanges, she finally asked Chloe—now many weeks into sleeping on the floor—if something was wrong with Violet, and, with a determined expression, Chloe said, "You always ignore her."

"But we can't see her."

"Yes, you *can*."

"I'm sorry."

"Apologize to *her*."

Jane did as she was asked. "How did you meet her?"

This seemed to inflame Chloe further. "I *met* her when she was *born*."

"And when was that?"

"You should know! She's your daughter!"

Ah. So, Violet was an imaginary sister. Jane went along with it, tried to acknowledge the invisible girl when she could, waited for Chloe to grow tired of the charade. Chance couldn't make himself engage; the few times he tried, he sputtered and blushed like a child. But his ineptitude didn't anger Chloe. His attention wasn't important to her; Jane's was.

One night Jane was idly supervising Chloe's bath — she was capable enough to wash herself but Jane feared leaving her alone — and was startled by a piercing scream. Not a shout, but a genuine scream of pure terror. Jane dropped the book she was reading and jumped up from her perch on the closed toilet seat. "Chloe! What is it!"

"She's drowning! She's drowning!"

Both of them flailed in the water, trying to save the girl who didn't exist, as Chloe shrieked her name. Eventually the panic subsided, and through tears Chloe declared her sister alive and well. She let Jane hold her for a moment before climbing out of the tub, drying off, and going to sleep, chest hitching.

Jane couldn't remember how it ended. At some point there was an argument that Chloe must have overheard: Susan insisting the child needed to see a therapist, Chance disagreeing, Jane secretly thinking this was a good idea, but reluctant to admit to taking Susan's side. Soon Chloe started second grade, got into chapter books — Junie B. Jones or the Wayside School, something like that. She returned to her own bed and stopped setting an extra place at the table. But Jane never stopped feeling guilty about the whole ordeal, was convinced that she'd handled it badly. And she didn't forget the real fear she felt that night, thrashing in the bathwater, powerless to save the drowning Violet. It returned to her in nightmares.

When she thought of her own strange childhood, Jane rarely took the time to consider herself lucky. She'd had Lila — the only thing in life she could take for granted, at least until they grew up. Chloe had friends, but never close ones. She held herself apart from her peers. Jane was her best friend. She too often forgot that.

Today, Chloe's best friend had let her down.

It was half past 4 a.m. She closed her eyes and tried to find the thread of sleep.

# 9

# Nestor, NY: *Then*

---

In the end, Jane and Lila both tried out for *Annie*. Lake Overlook Community Theater was housed in a rustic multipurpose center in a small state park on the eastern shore of Onteo Lake, about a half hour's drive north from where they lived. The open call happened on a summery Saturday morning, just a few weeks before the end of the school year. The girls were full of excitement and optimism about their impending vacation. Their mother, in a rare good mood, agreed to drive them, and they rolled the windows down and sang along to the cast recording.

The community center was a sprawling log structure with three square buildings that extended from a central covered outdoor pavilion: a cafeteria; a recreation room with board games, log chairs and sofas, and a gigantic fireplace; and the theater, a cozy two-hundred-seat space with a movie screen and projector, a sturdy stage, and a small orchestra pit. This casting call was just for kids; the rest of the show was already cast, including, to the girls' initial disappointment, Annie herself, who would be played by a semiprofessional child actor from Rochester. The available roles were for Annie's orphan friends Molly, Kate, Tessie, Pepper, Duffy, and July.

Signups were taking place under the pavilion, where a handful of adults sat at a picnic table, behind a clipboard. There were about twenty girls horsing around as their parents chatted and sipped coffee out of take-out cups. Ms. Langford, the school music teacher, recognized the girls immediately and waved them over to the table. She was the pianist in the pit band, she explained.

"This is Mr. Framingham," she said, gesturing to the man sitting beside her. "He's the director. And a playwright himself!"

Mr. Framingham was a wiry man in his late twenties with a fleshy face: a baby's cheeks, full lips, large piercing eyes. He wore his hair short in the back, long in the front, like he was in a boy band, and an oversized moth-eaten cardigan over a pink tee shirt. "Hello, girls," he said, giving them a cursory glance that nonetheless made Jane feel exposed and embarrassed. "George," he said, turning to the girls' mother and extending a hand. To Jane's surprise, she took it.

"Anabel," she said.

It was so strange, hearing their mother say her own name. She smiled at Mr. Framingham and Mr. Framingham smiled back.

"Girls, just put your names on this clipboard," Ms. Langford said, pushing it toward them. "You'll be signing up for"—she glanced at the page—"10:10 and 10:20. You've got a little while to wait, but there are nature trails along the creek. Maybe your mother would like to take you for a walk. Or you could meet the other kids."

"We'll walk," Lila said.

They expected their mother to take them on the trails, but she told them to go without her. Ms. Langford, overhearing this, suggested that she might want to go along; the trails ran up along a mountain gorge, and there were high bridges. "They can take care of themselves," their mother replied, with a dismissive wave, and headed for the coffee urn. Ms. Langford appeared dismayed and leveled a serious look at them. "Girls," she said. "Don't leave the trail, and don't go too far."

The trails were crowded with parents and kids, carefully stepping among the wet rocks and roots and stopping to gaze into the creek, with its waterfalls and pools. Jane clambered down into the gorge at the first available opportunity to dip her hands into the water, still cold with spring runoff, while Lila looked down, disapproving, from her perch on the trail. They took a side trail and found an overlook that offered a yawning view of the lake in the distance; the wall that separated them from the drop-off was made of stones that bore the impressions of tiny whorled fossil shells.

When they got back, they found their mother and Mr. Framingham smoking in the shade of the tree line outside the community center. He was tall, as tall as their father, and his jeans were tight. Colorful socks peeked out from under scuffed loafers. As they approached, their mother laughed at something he said, touched his shoulder.

"Mom!" Jane called out. "We saw fossils!"

"Ah." Tapping ash. "Hello, girls."

"There were fossils and we could see the whole lake."

"Dinosaur bones?" their mother said.

Mr. Framingham laughed. She winked at him.

"No," Jane said. "Snails, I guess?"

"Ammonoids," Lila said dryly, her arms crossed. She was scowling at their mother.

"Ah, impressive," Mr. Framingham said. His voice was sweet and low, and Jane would have bet he was a good singer. "Did you learn that in school?" He brought the cigarette to his lips.

"No. In a book."

"Well," he said, expelling smoke. "A self-starter."

Back in the pavilion, they sat nervously at a table by the rec building entrance, trying to ignore the other kids' auditions. Mr. Framingham was in the theater, listening. Their mother was pacing in the parking lot.

"They sound good," Lila said.

"Yeah," Jane agreed. "Really good."

"I don't like him."

"Who? Mr. Framingham?"

"He acts like he's a cool guy."

Jane said, "He kind of is one." They could hear his voice behind the closed theater doors, a rich baritone, singing "Santa Claus we ne-ver-see." A girl's tremulous voice echoed the words. "No, Rachel, like this. Santa Claus we ne-ver-see! Santa Claus, what's that, who's he!"

"Hm. Maybe. But it's like he knows it and wants you to notice."

"Maybe."

The sisters' auditions went fine, but it was clear by that point that they were in the bottom half of the pack. Jane couldn't believe how talented the other kids were. As they were getting ready to leave, gathering their things under the pavilion, Mr. Framingham burst out through the theater doors and stopped them. "Girls," he said, "Anabel. Listen — I don't think you're going to make the cut for this show, but you've got real presence onstage. You might be very good little actors."

"Is that so," their mother said.

"We do a drama day camp after the summer musical," he said. "Three weeks, beginning the last week of July." He picked up a flyer from a pile on the signup table and held it out. "There are still openings. Sign up, it'd be a blast to work with you."

Their mother accepted the flyer, gazed levelly at him. "Say thanks, girls," she said.

As school began, they forgot about theater camp, assumed they wouldn't be allowed to go. Their mother disappeared for the weekend and wasn't home when they returned from the last day of school, and left the next weekend, too. Family, she said. Then a research trip. "Your father's semester is over," she told them, before leaving the second time. "Please make him his dinners."

That night, in their room, having provided their father with spaghetti and canned sauce, Lila said, "What kind of research? She doesn't have a job."

"I don't think these family members are real," Jane said.

"I want to know where she goes." She sat up in bed. "Do you still have that tape recorder?"

She was referring to a battery-operated RadioShack machine, about the size of a volume of the encyclopedia, that their father had used to take notes and cast off years before. The girls had used it to make a fake radio show about Beauty and the Beast.

"Maybe?"

"What if I put it in her car? Like, under the seat. Maybe it could tell us something."

They dug around under Jane's bed until they found the recorder. The batteries were dead, but they found working ones in a flashlight in the hall closet and swapped them. "Okay," Lila said. "Next time she goes."

The next time turned out to be the following week, but, unexpectedly, she was to be gone for a long time — two or three weeks, potentially. "It's a family emergency," she said, throwing clothes into a duffel bag. Jane and Lila exchanged a look, and Lila stole away. Jane intended to delay her mother somehow, but she needn't have worried; her parents were now arguing. Lila reappeared at her side and slipped something into her hand.

"Let me know when she's about to walk out," she whispered. Jane found herself holding a walkie-talkie, one of a pink plastic pair they'd been given instead of the expensive texting devices last Christmas. The speaker was decorated with little flower stickers, and another sticker bore the Morse code alphabet.

"Got it."

When the argument ended and their mother shouldered her bag, Jane pressed the talk button and muttered, "She's leaving." Two minutes later, Lila strolled in the front door as their mother strode out.

"Well," she said, when the car rolled out of sight and their father slammed his office door behind him, "I guess we'll know whenever. The tape's forty-five minutes on a side, so, hopefully something will happen before it stops."

"Will it make a sound when it does?"

Lila shrugged. "Beats me. Maybe if she's driving she won't hear it."

They didn't exactly forget about the tape recorder, but it came to seem silly and childlike, and they moved on to other things — reading, mostly, and wandering around the neighborhood. The nature trail at Lake Overlook had gotten them interested in hiking, and they found that they could sneak over the train trestle across the street from their house, then creep through a culvert to the dirt paths wending around the big city park along the creek. Fishermen and homeless guys greeted them, and sometimes they frightened a deer.

Then, a week into their mother's absence, their father called them into the kitchen. He was clutching a pile of mail, and in it was a large envelope addressed to them. He'd already opened it. "What's this all about?" he said, handing it to them.

Lila accepted the papers, then looked up, bewildered, at Jane. "It's theater camp. We're signed up for it."

"What!"

"I didn't know anything about this," their father said, sounding pained. The packet included instructions for what to pack each day, what supplies they would need, and directions to the community center. A schedule promised activities like "Trust Exercise," "Improv Workshop," and "Voice Training."

"I hope your mother plans to bring you to this," their father said, throwing his hands in the air. "I have a lot of work to do this summer and I don't have time."

"Oh, she does," Lila said, her face a mixture of excitement and concern. "I'm sure."

# 10

# Timber Fell, MO: *Now*

———

When Jane woke the second time, her sister was frying eggs. She hadn't even noticed the stove the night before; it was over by the work table, just another piece of equipment for sustaining Lila's existence between sessions of work. She sat up, rubbed her face. Noticed two plates on the table behind Lila, two slices of buttered toast.

They ate together in silence. Jane remembered all the other times they'd made breakfast for each other and ate it alone. Lila cleared away the empty plates, washed them in the sink. Said, "Let's get on the road at nine."

"Okay." Jane glanced at her watch. "I'm going to call her."

"Do you want some privacy?"

The correct answer was yes, but Jane said, "Doesn't matter." Lila nodded once, went to the bank of monitors, started working on something.

Chance didn't answer the first time she called. Probably the unfamiliar number. She left a voicemail, then called again. The third time, he picked up. "Jane, what the hell."

"Hi. Sorry, using a different phone."

"She waited up for you last night."

That hurt. Which was the point in saying it. "I was catching up with Lila. Can I talk to Chloe, please?"

"She's not here," Chance said. "Mom has her."

"Okay. I'll call your mother, then. What are you doing with your day off?"

Chance sighed. "I'll be honest with you, Jane. I hate to do this on the phone. But I'm researching lawyers."

Jane felt a sharp snap in her chest, like a twig breaking underfoot in the woods, and then relief, radiating out through her entire body. Hot on its heels, shame. She said, "Oh."

"We both know you've been checked out for a long time."

"Come on. That's an exaggeration."

"You don't like being married to me and you don't like how much Chloe is like me."

This stunned her into silence. She hadn't believed Chance could be this perceptive.

She could hear a rustling, like the turning of a page, and she realized he had a notebook he was reading out of. He said, "I've been writing it all down for years. You're cold. You refuse intimacy. You ignore Chloe, forget the promises you made to her."

"You've been . . . planning this? For years? You have a notebook filled with my flaws?"

"The therapist said we were supposed to keep journals, remember?"

"You can't just hit me with this out of nowhere."

He laughed. "It's not out of nowhere. Our marriage was failing! So we went to therapy together. Until you walked out."

"Chance, *you* were the one who walked out."

He snorted. "It was *you*, Jane, how can you not remember this? I know I'm right because I'm still in it. I kept going without you."

This genuinely shocked her. "What?"

"Yeah. You didn't notice. You didn't ask why I was late every Thursday night."

"I noticed you were late sometimes!"

"See? Yeah. Not sometimes. Every Thursday."

Lila had stopped working and was staring at her from the other side of the room. Every muscle in Jane's body was tensed, like she was in the middle of a car crash. Her jaw ached. She said, "Chance, please. We need to talk about this. I'm coming home. I want to see Chloe."

"Don't bother. Mom has her for now. I'll let you see her when you get back."

"*Let* me?"

"I'm going for full custody."

"Come on."

Until this moment, he hadn't seemed to be uncomfortable with this conversation; she could hear in his voice the satisfaction of a long-harbored plan finally being executed. But now he paused, let out a sigh. "I don't want to say it, Jane."

"Chance, you *have* to."

"You're a criminal," he said. "I know you served your time. I didn't think I could see it in you, at first. But the longer we've been together, the less I trust you. You don't have normal emotions. I don't know what you're capable of."

"You absolute bastard," she said, her voice cold.

"See? Right there."

"You have no idea what you're saying. I am not a danger to our child."

"Yeah, well. You can argue that in court."

"I fucking hate you, Chance. I hate you, and I hate your mother."

"Right," Chance said. "Jotting that down. March 28 . . . *I fucking hate you . . .*"

That, at last, silenced her. They stayed on the line, breathing. Chance said, "I'm going to hang up now. I'm sorry, Jane, I really am. Our marriage was a failure and I have to move on and do what's right for Chloe. You can try calling Susan if you want. Maybe she'll put Chloe on, but I can't make her."

"No, you can't, can you."

But he'd already hung up.

She called Susan several times. It went straight to voicemail. She left a message the last time: "Susan, it's Jane. Please call me back and let me talk to Chloe. You can't let her think I'm not calling. I need her to know that I love and miss her. Put yourself in my shoes. As a mother, please." She regretted it immediately.

She lay back on the bed, willing herself to cry. Instead she trembled with rage. Lila came to the bedside, sat down, put her hand on Jane's. Jane swatted it away.

"He's just like his mother. He's a fucking monster."

"I never understood what you saw in him," Lila said. "He was just a jock with no sense of humor."

"Fuck you!"

She held up her hands. "Just trying to help."

"It's not helpful." She groaned. "Susan took Chloe. She's off eating ice cream with that witch, being told her mother abandoned her."

"You don't know that."

"You don't know Susan."

The two were silent for a while. Jane managed to calm her body enough to stop shaking, but the tension remained. She willed herself to cry, failed. Squeezed her eyes shut hard enough to hear the muscles vibrating inside her skull.

Next thing she knew, Lila was shaking her awake.

"What time is it?"

"Eleven? Why don't you take a shower." She glanced at her watch, an enormous disc with a complicated face. "We're getting a late start."

Jane wanted to argue—of *course* I'm not going on this idiotic mission *now*, Lila—but what else was there for her to do? Go home, share a house with her sworn enemy, worry about Chloe? Lila seemed to know this, sat patiently as she worked through it in her head. There was no point. And Lila could help her make a plan. Lila solved problems.

Jane got up, took a shower, and got dressed, swapping a flannel shirt for the cardigan. She repacked her duffel and shouldered it; the two women exited by the back stairs into the garage. They threw their bags into the back seat of the Volvo, a 960 model that looked like it was from the late nineties. In the back, a couple of military-style storage and transport crates were strapped in place. There was also a gasoline canister, a five-gallon jug of drinking water, two bedrolls, and what looked like a camping tent.

"Are you kidding me with this car?" Jane asked her.

"Just wait. It's customized—there's a 380-horsepower Ford Racing V8 engine in it. It's supposed to have been made for Paul Newman."

"Really?"

"Well. I doubt it," Lila said. "The guy did make one of these for him. But then he made a bunch more. I got it in payment for a job." She walked over to the antiques shop door and knocked.

"What kind of job gets you paid in an old customized Volvo?"

Lila said, "An easy one." To Loretta, who had just appeared in the doorway, she said, "Could you call Tyler and tell him we're on the way?"

The woman nodded. "Will do." To Jane, she said, "It was nice meeting you."

"Likewise."

Lila pushed a button on the wall and the garage door rose. "Follow me," she said. She climbed into the Volvo. It roared to life, then settled down to a deep, smooth thrum, like jet aircraft idling on a runway. Jane got into the stolen Scion.

They pulled out of the garage. Jane peered over her shoulder and saw the door descending behind them. She followed Lila onto Second Street. It was a brilliant spring day. Jane rolled the windows down and propped her elbow on the doorframe, pantomiming an easy confidence she did not feel, and a moment later saw her sister, up ahead, doing the same.

Lila turned left off Main and onto a winding road that passed a cemetery and a lumberyard. Then she led Jane down a series of lettered country highways — B, K, EE — along the reservoir's edge. Woods, horses, a trailer park. Now and then they crossed a bridge and saw a fisherman in a creek. They passed few other cars. After half an hour they arrived at a rusted metal gate that appeared disused. But a pylon bearing a numeric keypad rose from the ground beside it. Lila pressed a couple of buttons and Jane heard her exchange words with someone.

Jane's truck-stop burner rang. It was Lila. "Stay behind me and don't get out of the car," she said.

Jane didn't remember giving her the number to this phone. "Is everything all right?"

"Think so. Not sure. Keep the line open."

"Uh . . . okay?" Jane said. The gate swung smoothly open and she followed her sister through.

# 11

# Nestor, NY: *Then*

Their mother's car had barely passed underneath the Lake Overlook Park arch before Jane noticed George Framingham, standing at the threshold of the pavilion, bending over to greet a pair of kids who'd just scrambled out of a minivan. Jane, riding shotgun, looked up at her mother, trying to clock her reaction. Her eyes were concealed by her sunglasses, but a small, confident smile had crept onto her face. When she turned back to Lila to convey this intel, Lila refused to meet her gaze, instead staring out the window, scowling.

The tape recorder experiment had been a bust. Lila had been worried that their mother would just listen to the radio, drowning out any evidence, but the recording was clear. The problem was that it didn't reveal any useful information. About twenty minutes into the recording, the engine turned off, and they could hear a car door open and close, and then the trunk. After that, the rest of the tape was silence.

"I bet she just went to the airport," Lila said.

"I guess?"

They were sitting on Lila's bed, replaying the part where the car stopped, hoping to hear some kind of clue. When Jane asked Lila what kind of clue, she said, "You know, like, on a detective show, when the suspect is supposed to be in the city or something, but on a phone call there's seagulls in the background." But there was nothing like that—just the door and the trunk, then nothing.

The only unusual thing about the recording was the sound of their mother's voice, unintelligibly audible during the last few minutes before her arrival. It sounded like she was on the phone, but their parents didn't have cell phones, as far as they knew. "Or maybe just talking to herself?" Jane said. "She does that sometimes." They couldn't make out the words and had determined that she was speaking in a foreign language. But they didn't know which, or how to figure out what she was saying.

Though they didn't say it out loud, it was clear to both of them what they were looking for: evidence that their mother was seeing Mr. Framingham. Now, at the beginning of camp, they were on high alert for any nuance that suggested romantic interest. This idea had seemed shocking at first—it was Lila's—but the more they talked about it, the more plausible it seemed. And once the possibility had entered Jane's head, she couldn't stop thinking about it. What if their mother had love affairs? What if that's what all her trips were, just romantic getaways? What if there were no family emergencies? What if there was no family? She and Lila had only been told they existed—they'd never met a single one of these relatives. They'd overheard phone conversations, but those were never in English.

Now her mother's smile seemed to Jane a confirmation of her suspicions. She was instantly angry and excited.

Their mother parked and they all climbed out of the car. By now Mr. Framingham had withdrawn into the shade of the pavilion, where he stood behind the same picnic table where they'd signed up for tryouts back in May. He was flanked by two older girls, high schoolers by the look of them, who would serve as teacher's assistants. Their name tags read AMBER and CRISSY.

"Hi, girls!" Crissy said. "Find your name tags here, and take a schedule. Do you have your swimsuits for later? Sunscreen?"

"In their bags," their mother answered, staring at Mr. Framingham. She had removed her sunglasses and hung them from the buttons of her blouse. They pulled down her neckline a little and Jane could see the lacy edge of her bra. Mr. Framingham was riffling through some papers and didn't look up.

"Great," said Crissy. "Girls, go on over there, by the trees. Amber will introduce you to the other kids. We'll get to know each other there and then break into groups."

"Should I leave and come back later?" their mother said casually. "Or do I need to stay?"

Mr. Framingham looked up and said, coolly, "We can take it from here, Mrs. Pool."

"Nice to see you again, Mr. Framingham." She was gazing at him intently. Amber looked up at her, then at Mr. Framingham, and back again.

His smile was polite. "Likewise." After an awkward pause, their mother turned and walked to the car.

A crowd of girls was scattered in the grass, in the shade of the tree line. On the way there, Lila said, "Did he even remember her?"

"Are you kidding?" Jane said. "That was, like, majorly intense."

"Yeah, but . . . I don't know."

"Trust me. There's something going on."

There were about twenty kids in total, most of them girls, ranging in age from around eight to thirteen. As an icebreaker, Mr. Framingham had them all stand in a circle, facing him in the center, as the two teenagers loitered outside. "I want everyone to look around the circle, and silently, without letting them know you're doing it, choose one of the other campers. This person will be your twin."

For a moment, Jane thought he was mocking them and felt herself reddening. But of course it was just an exercise. It would be happening whether they were here or not. She glanced around the circle and chose a boy, a little younger than she was, with red hair and glasses. She kept looking around afterward, to disguise her decision.

"All right. Now, I want you all to close your eyes. And, with your eyes closed, strike a pose. Any pose at all, doesn't matter how uncomfortable."

Giggles as, presumably, everyone contorted themselves into awkward shapes. Jane thought of a western Lila had been watching, and fell into a crouch, brandishing a pair of finger guns.

"All right," Mr. Framingham said, "now open your eyes."

Laughter all around. The kids were wilting flowers, ballet dancers, fierce monsters. One boy lay on the ground, pretending to be dead.

"Now. Look at the person you chose to imitate. Slowly, carefully move your body so that you have the same pose they do."

Jane's red-haired boy had adopted the stance of a baseball batter. She began to move to match him, but he was already in motion, slowly adapting to someone else's pose. All around the circle, the bodies slowly changed, as though some mysterious force were in control. When the boy stopped, he had the appearance of a beggar: slightly stooped, palms up, mouth open, begging for food or spare change. Once she'd imitated the boy, she glanced around the circle. To her astonishment, they were all beggars now, every one of them.

Several kids gasped. One girl screamed, and they laughed.

"Hold your positions," Mr. Framingham said. "Look carefully at yourselves. What you've just done is to draw out the collective desire of this group. You want something, but you feel powerless to achieve it. You hope someone here can give it to you." He brought his fists together, pounded his chest with them. "What we will learn this week is that what you want is *within* you. The only person who can give it to you . . . is yourself." He let his hands fall. "All right. You can relax now."

A collective exhalation. "How did he *do* that?" someone whispered.

"That was interesting," Jane said to Lila.

"I don't like it."

"I dunno, I thought it was cool?"

As the day wore on, they did an exercise where they addressed remarks to various rocks. Before lunch, they did exaggerated descriptions of food, making everyone laugh and their mouths water. Later they broke into groups and did a "table read" of a one-act play; each group would put on their play at the end of the summer. They went swimming, and then their parents came to pick them up.

The girls sat together in the back this time. Their mother was in a foul mood and dismissed their excited tales from the day by tuning the radio to a random station and drowning them out. When they got home and retreated to their room, Lila said, "What's her problem?"

"I guess her *boyfriend* didn't pay enough attention to her."

Lila scowled. "Shh! Don't let her hear you say that."

"Why not?"

"I don't want her to know we know."

"Whatever," Jane said, flopping down on the bed. The watering hole at the camp was fed by a waterfall and had been ice-cold; she was physically exhausted and mentally energized.

"Seriously," Lila said. "Be careful. Something weird is going on with her."

# 12

# Lakehurst, MO: *Now*

O kay, be on the alert. Something weird is going on here," Lila said. They'd just driven the two cars another mile along a gravel road that wended its way through woods and had arrived at a high chain-link fence threaded with privacy slats. Beyond an open gate lay a structure like a warehouse or airplane hangar. People moved around inside it, in the gloom, and neat piles of debris filled the paved yard that surrounded it. As they approached, the hangar doors slid closed. A few men stood around the open yard, each with a hand resting on a holstered pistol. Lila had slowed to a stop; Jane did the same.

"What is it?" she said.

"The guys out here. Just . . . let me do the talking. Stay in the car, okay? Leave it running, just in case."

"You're the boss."

The call cut off and the Volvo's door opened. Lila stepped out slowly, her hands in the air. One of the men spoke into a walkie-talkie and moved toward Jane; the other two converged on Lila. She could see Lila speaking to the men, but for now, at least, they ignored her.

The man nearest Jane had put away his walkie-talkie and now approached the Scion, gun drawn. He was broad shouldered, narrow hipped, like a swimmer, and his face looked battered and squashed, like he was pressing it against glass. Jane couldn't remember the last time she saw somebody's sidearm out of its holster. She thought of Chloe. With his free hand, the man motioned for Jane to roll her window down.

"Hands on the wheel."

Jane dropped the phone into the drink holder and complied.

The man opened her door, leaned in, and patted her down: her waist, up under her arms. His wrist brushed the side of her breast. Her entire body tensed and broke out in a sweat and she wanted to kill him. He ran his hands over both of her ankles, then felt around under the dash. Then he turned the engine off and pocketed the keys.

"Get out, please. Keep your hands raised."

"What's going on?"

He ignored her. She climbed slowly out of the car and he gestured for her to move away. He shut the door behind her and, gun still pointed at her, told her to widen her stance. Then he patted down her thighs. Over his head, she could see Lila being given the same treatment. He took a step back and used his free hand to speak into the walkie-talkie. "Second driver's out and clean," he said.

A crackle, and a voice saying, "Bring them in."

The three men led them toward the warehouse, and the doors opened again to admit them. It took a moment for Jane's eyes to adjust. A busy shop, with multiple vehicles up on lifts, over work bays populated by wheeled tool carts and men in greasy jumpsuits. The cars were in various stages of disassembly, their parts lying on the cement or on work tables. In the back, an open loading bay door offered a view of the back lot, where white panel trucks were parked. By the door, a forklift, concrete ramp, piles of wooden crates full of stolen car parts or, Jane was beginning to suspect, other things. Everyone on the floor stopped to watch them enter. Somebody wolf whistled.

A steel door inset with a wired window separated the work area from what must have been an office partition. The door opened and a man in his forties emerged: small, compact, he wore a Dickies work shirt tucked into unbelted black pants. His head was shorn to de-emphasize his male pattern baldness and he affected a stubble of beard.

"Who's that," the man said, pointing at Jane with a pencil.

"An associate."

The man, Tyler, cocked his head, looked Jane up and down. "Are you her sister?" he said.

Jane glanced over at Lila, who shrugged. She decided not to answer. It didn't matter. He said to Lila, "What exactly is going on here."

"I was going to ask you the same thing. We brought you a car."

"You brought me two."

After a beat, Lila said, "Come on, man." The swimmer still had his gun out, pointed at Lila now.

"Do you know how many acres I have out here?" Tyler asked. "Fourteen hundred fifty-six. That's more than two square miles. Most of it's just woods, thick underbrush, no paths. Anything that gets dumped out there would probably never be found. The bobcats and mountain lions would make sure of it."

"Yes," Lila said, "that's very threatening, Tyler, we get it."

Behind them, engine noises. The two cars were being driven in through the main doors. As soon as they were parked, workers began emptying them.

"Tyler, leave my car alone. I'm here to drop off the Scion."

"Are you sure?"

"Of course I'm sure. What is this? We're unarmed. Tell this guy to put the gun away."

He stared at her for several seconds, then nodded at the swimmer, who holstered the gun.

"This morning," Tyler said, "about an hour before you were originally supposed to be here, the motion detectors out back started going off. I send my guys out there, somebody's been snooping around. Somebody was on my boat. Shoe prints in the dirt on the road up to the facility. Dirty shoe prints on the dock." He pointed his chin at the swimmer. "Then Rick sees a car in the pull-off by the entrance and when he rolls up to check, they peel off down the highway."

"What does this have to do with us?" Lila said.

"You tell me."

"Why would I even know you had a boat launch?"

"You tell me."

He slid his pencil behind his ear, crossed his arms, and stared. Lila stared back.

"I don't know what you want me to say. I'm trying to unload a car. I've been your customer for five years. I'm as concerned about security as you are."

"I doubt that."

Though her expression didn't change, Lila was clearly infuriated by this remark. The tell was the slightest adjustment in the angle of her head, the rolling of her shoulders.

"What do you want from me? I don't have a boat and I wasn't parked on the road. I've got my own business concerns and I don't give a shit about yours, except for whether or not I can sell you a car."

"Why were you late?"

"We slept in."

"Why were you late?"

"Tyler. For fuck's sake. Are your clients usually particularly punctual? I called ahead. I don't know about your mystery lake monster or whatever."

The two stared at each other. After a moment, Tyler dismissed the three men with a nod. They turned and stalked off. To Lila, he said, "Where's your cross-dresser?"

"She's working. She's not a cross-dresser, she's a woman."

"You don't bring a stranger to my place without my approval."

"Message received. Jesus. Now can we go?"

Tyler turned to Jane and stared at her until she looked away. To Lila, he said, "I've had you followed before. I know where you live. Above that antique store. I want to leave you alone just like I want to be left alone, understand?"

"Yeah, I thought we both already understood that."

"So did I."

"Whoever's sneaking around, it has nothing to do with me. I have my own business to mind."

"So mind it."

Behind them, everything had been taken out of the Volvo, the seats removed, the carpets pulled up. Now the jumpsuit men were putting it all back. Tyler reached into his pocket and pulled out some bills. He handed them to Lila.

"I can't be too careful."

Lila let out breath. Jane could tell that she didn't want to accept the olive branch. "No worries," she said.

They waited in the yard for the Volvo, scuffing their feet on the gravel.

"So I guess that doesn't usually happen?" Jane asked.

"No," Lila said. Her mouth was tight and her eyes gazed unfocused into the woods.

"You meant it, right? It was a coincidence?"

"Has to be." Then, a minute later: "It's odd, though."

Jane heard the Volvo's engine turn over. "Okay." The car emerged from the warehouse and stopped halfway to where they stood. A jumpsuit man got out and headed back inside.

They walked to the car. Lila rummaged in the back, felt around under the seats, peered into the glovebox. Finally, they climbed in. Lila drove down the access road and waited at the gate until it rose. Then they were past it and free.

"So," Jane said, as her sister turned left onto the county highway. "Montana?"

"Montana," Lila said.

# 13

# Nestor, NY: *Then*

―――――――

For the next couple of days, their mother dropped them off at theater camp in the morning without getting out of the car and waited for them in the afternoon in the far corner of the parking lot, wearing her sunglasses and gardening clothes. She didn't ask what they did and endured their stories in stony silence.

Jane felt a growing excitement about the play they would put on at the end of the three weeks. It was a mini-mystery about a man found dead in a locked room, and she was playing one of two detectives assigned to the case. The other one, played by the red-haired boy she'd mimicked — his name was Frederick but he asked to be called Fritz — had a lot of wild theories. Her detective was the coolly logical one. She confessed to Amber, the teen assistant assigned to their group, that she wished she'd been given Fritz's role, which seemed to her much more fun, and Amber said, "That's where the acting comes in. That's why I gave you the part — I know you can make it interesting."

"Really?"

"Really. And actually, don't tell the other campers, but George says you have potential as an actor. Like, for real."

Jane felt a mixture of pride and disgust at Mr. Framingham's having noticed her; the pride quickly won out.

Both of the older girls called Mr. Framingham George. Sometimes, when one of them approached him with a question, or with some papers to deal with, he would briefly rest his hand on her shoulder. Sometimes the girl would let her fingers brush his arm. The girls seemed to have some special relationship with each other as well; on a bathroom break she found Amber and Crissy standing close, their pinkies linked, passing a cigarette back and forth. One time Amber whispered a joke that made Crissy laugh; she gently moved the other girl's hair out of the way and lingered with her lips touching her ear. Jane got a chill watching it. Amber caught her watching and gave her a wink that reminded her, with a jolt, of their mother.

"What's going on with Mr. Framingham and the girls?" she asked Lila.

"They're a cult," Lila said.

"They live in a cave together."

"And wear diapers."

"Diapers and nothing else."

"No, aprons. And sombreros."

"Only on Friday nights."

"Friday night is sombrero night!"

The last thing they did that week, during afternoon circle, was an exercise involving hands. "I'm noticing a lot of stiff, self-conscious bodies," Mr. Framingham told them. "You don't just act with your voice, you know. Acting is in the body! When you're on stage, people are looking at you, not just listening. Inhabiting a character means inhabiting their body as well." One of the teen girls produced a small bronze urn and paused with it in front of each camper. "Without looking, choose one slip of paper," Mr. Framingham said. "Each of you will act out the emotion printed there. But you can *only* use your *hands*."

Lila's slip of paper said "frightened." Jane's said "tenderness."

"Yours is easy," Jane said.

Lila's hands were already shaking. "Help, the sombrero gang is coming for me!"

"Like, what am I supposed to even do?" Jane imagined she was helping an old person get up from a chair. She pretended to hold their hand in hers, and stroked it with her other hand. "Can you even tell what this is supposed to be?"

"Sure, it's bowling."

"With *tenderness*."

"Just ask the pins nicely to fall down."

Jane pantomimed laying each pin carefully on the ground. "Spare!"

They were interrupted by Mr. Framingham, who had been making his way around the circle, giving advice. "Jane," he said. "You should be taking the exercise more seriously."

"Sorry."

To her surprise, he took her two hands in his. "Tenderness," he said. He raised her hands to his face and pressed them to his cheeks. She felt his beard stubble and the slight greasiness of a moisturizing cream. She smelled his coffee breath. His eyes were green and his gaze bored into her. "Imagine I'm someone beloved in your life," he said. "I'm very sick. You're trying to remind me that you're here, that I'm loved. What do you say?"

"Uh . . . there, there? You'll be better soon."

"Is that what you'd say to . . . your brother?"

"I don't have a brother?"

He released her hands, clearly disappointed. "We're actors here, Jane. You don't need to have a brother in real life."

When he'd moved along, she and Lila gaped. Jane wiped her hands on her shorts.

"I don't even have to act anymore," Lila whispered, exaggeratedly shaking her hands, twisting her face in mock terror.

That afternoon, when their mother came to pick them up, Mr. Framingham met her in the parking lot. They seemed to be on better terms now and joked around in French, which Jane could recognize but not understand. She caught sight of Crissy and Amber rolling their eyes at each other over this. Their mother was full of questions on the ride home.

The following week, more of each day was dedicated to rehearsing the plays in groups. Jane was now excited about her logical, calculating detective; she decided the character had mild autism and affected a flat, dry tone that proved a comical foil to Fritz's crazed fantasist. "I like the direction you're taking, kids," Amber told them. Every morning their mother lingered for a little while, sipping coffee with Mr. Framingham, and every afternoon they had a cigarette together in the parking lot and chatted. They were now speaking exclusively in French, and the two assistants huddled in a little cluster, muttering to each other and stealing glances, as though this development were in some way concerning. "I want to ask Dad to drive us," Jane said, in bed one night. "The whole thing just feels gross."

"I already did, yesterday. He said he's too busy. He was transcribing his notes off of his tape recorder. Like, one Dad talking, and the other Dad going, like, 'Uh-huh! Interesting!'"

"Double-Dad Danger."

"Double-Dad Madness." Then Lila sat up straight. "Wait. I just realized something."

"What?"

Wordlessly, Lila slipped out of bed and crept into the hall. Jane heard the squeak of her father's office door. When Lila returned, she was clutching their father's little tape recorder in one hand and a pristine tape in the other. "Look at this," she said, climbing onto Jane's bed. She pointed at the controls on the side of the machine. "I was in there when he was talking to it last night. He didn't turn it on and off, he just talked to it whenever he got an idea."

"So?"

"Look!" There was a button marked AUTO. "I think it turns on and off with your voice. So the tape doesn't run out." She unwrapped the fresh tape and swapped it with their father's notes. With the AUTO button depressed, she hit RECORD. Nothing happened. But when she said, "Testing, testing, please turn on," the little wheels in the tape began to turn. They turned off again.

"It works," Jane said. The wheels started up, then stopped.

"You know what this means?" Lila said. Start, stop.

"Yes, I do." Start, stop.

"The next time she goes away . . ." Start, stop.

". . . we hide this in the car." Start, stop.

They would have their chance that weekend. But first, on Friday morning, during improv hour in the little theater, Mr. Framingham asked the group what their parents thought about their theatrical ambitions. Most of the kids eagerly related their parents' excitement and dedication; they talked about previous theater camps they'd attended, summer stock productions they'd auditioned for. Many of their parents had been theater kids themselves.

"Lila? Jane? What about your parents?"

They had opted out of the conversation for a reason. Mr. Framingham glared at them now, with intense interest and what seemed to Jane like hostility. She said, "They think it's okay, I guess."

"Why don't you ask our mom," Lila said.

An uncomfortable silence settled in. Some of the kids looked in bewilderment at Lila, then at Mr. Framingham.

"All right, let's get to work," he said now, clapping his hands. "Today's improv will be about, you guessed it, parents. Lila, Jane, take the stage."

"To do what?" Lila said, crossing her arms.

"Find out when you get there."

All eyes were on them. Warily, they climbed onto the stage and stood in the center spotlight.

"Jane, you play your mother. Lila, you're your father. I want you to give us a scene of them . . . getting up in the morning."

For a minute, Jane thought Lila would refuse. She was scowling at Mr. Framingham, who gazed coolly back. Then Jane saw something shift; Lila turned to her and said, in a nasal, wheedling voice that sounded nothing like their father's, "Anabel . . . would you make coffee? I can't do my important research without coffee."

A titter of laughter from the group. Jane lit an imaginary cigarette. "Harry, I'm too busy smoking. You'll have to do it yourself."

"But I'm too absent-minded to work the machine!"

"You should be glad I'm here," Jane said. "I could be locked away with my exotic plants I am obsessed with, and you wouldn't be able to eat at all."

"I don't need you! I can make toast."

Jane remembered the recording they'd made, the one where their mother was talking to herself in a foreign language. She began to mumble something unintelligible.

"Anabel," Lila whined, "what are you saying! I don't understand you!"

"I am practicing my Swedish for my trip to Sweden tomorrow, to visit my cousin I never mentioned to you before."

The kids screamed with laughter as the bit continued. Mr. Framingham leaned back in his seat, feet up on the row in front, beaming.

That afternoon, when their mother picked them up, she and Mr. Framingham exchanged what seemed to Jane knowing glances.

The next morning, while they were making him his breakfast, their father asked, "Girls, did you see what I did with my Dictaphone?"

# 14

# Nestor, NY: *Now and Then*

———

Harry drank. Of course he did! He always did so when solitude was a probability rather than a certainty, but he did so with even greater gusto now that his loneliness was guaranteed. He liked his drinks cold, kept the gin and vodka in the freezer. He felt most satisfied when, while holding a pint glass filled to the brim with ice cubes, spritzed with half a lime, and topped off with as much liquor as the glass could contain, he heard the rumble and clunk of the ice cube maker discharging the next drink's ice into the tray.

By Sunday night he had achieved a rare flow state, whereby day and night became indistinguishable and sleep arrived whenever convenient. It was only in this state — accessible mostly during breaks, summers, and sabbaticals — that he permitted himself to indulge most fully in the treasured memories that haunted and beguiled him. Today he was enjoying them in his home office, where he had opened the floor safe beneath the folding buffet table that served as his desk and removed from it the papers, letters, and notebooks that documented the days he usually strove to forget.

The Factor had first come to him in 1970 when he was only twenty-one, and a precocious PhD candidate in history at Nestor College. The man never introduced himself by name, and Harry never addressed him;

he was only ever the Factor to Harry, though Harry would eventually learn his real name, and that he had a legitimate, if marginal, professional role at the institution. But that's not how he approached Harry. He was tall, nearly as tall as Harry himself (Harry was six foot four, which lent him, he was beginning to realize at that age, an authority that he did not deserve and needed to learn to exploit), with a long, boyish face, thin blond hair, long, bony arms. He wore a trim gray suit with narrow lapels and high-cuffed pants, out of style for the time, yet somehow fitting on his strange, elongated, scarecrow's body.

It was silly to think of him as the Factor—an archaic term he read once in a Scottish novel—as he wasn't much older than Harry himself, but that's what he thought as the man ambled toward him across the quad that bright September afternoon: Here comes the Factor, with an offer I can't refuse. It's amazing, in retrospect, how close this was to the truth. The Factor's head was tilted, his smile was crooked, the gentle breeze whipped his hair and suit coat like it was a hurricane. He said, "Mr. Harry Pool."

"Yes?" Harry was sitting alone on a cast-iron bench in front of the library, perusing his interlibrary loans and carefully marking paragraphs for further reading with a modest penciled dot in the margins.

"I've been told," the stranger said, angling his head forward as though to drop the words discreetly into his lap, "that you're an up-and-comer."

"Oh! Well," Harry said. "You could say that about everyone here."

"Yes, yes. May I sit down?"

"Of course."

The Factor flipped his coattails up fussily, like an elderly banker, and planted a sharp elbow on Harry's book pile. "You have the undergraduates' trust, I'm told. They admire you."

"I hope that's so."

"You attract, I believe, young strivers from all over this institution: the historians, of course; the political scientists, the government majors, the psychologists and sociologists."

"My class is a requirement for the school of arts and sciences."

He waved a pale hand dismissively. "Yes, yes. I'm told, as well, that you're a patriot. When your number failed to come up for Vietnam, you enlisted."

"I tried to."

"You had polio as a child. Fully recovered, or so you thought."

"My left leg is weak and a little out of whack."

"You thought you could help some other way. Offered yourself up. You were turned down."

Harry shrugged. "I don't think I caught your name."

"Harry, I'm coming to you with an opportunity. To help your institution, your field of study, and your country."

"Ah."

"I'd love to tell you more, but I must count on your discretion. Would you meet me for a drink in"—he glanced at his watch, then up at the sun, as though confirming its accuracy—"four hours? At, if you please, the Turf Exchange in Binghamton."

"Binghamton?"

"Tell no one," the Factor said, standing and smoothing his jacket. He fished in an outside pocket of his jacket and pulled out, as though from a hidden pack, a single cigarette. "Do you have a light, Mr. Pool?"

"I'm afraid I don't."

The Factor grunted and drew from the other pocket an engraved gold Zippo, which he flicked open and raised to his face. "See you this evening."

"Why — Why did you ask me for a light?"

The Factor's only response was a wry, knowing smile. He turned wildly, as though blown by the wind, and crossed the quad without looking back. He disappeared around the corner of Manfred Hall.

Harry wished that he'd thought to keep the safe up on a table instead of on the floor. He'd put it down there when he was thirty-six and it didn't occur to him that he'd ever regret the decision. Now it hurt his back to bend down, it hurt his knees to crouch, and it hurt his ass to sit on the hardwood, which he had done an hour and a half ago without much hope getting back up again. He still recalled with embarrassment that time in 2007 when he sat cross-legged in front of the bookcases in his office and had to summon Professor Aitkins down the hall to help him up. Since then, when he needed to get on the floor, he took pains to sit with his legs extended and his back to a solid vertical surface. But tonight he had mistaken his wheeled office chair for that vertical surface, and it had simply rolled away, and now he lay among his papers on his back.

Luckily, he had just refilled his glass, which he kept in a little divot on the rug even when he was sitting at the desk, to prevent it from falling over onto whatever he was working on. So it was conveniently within reach, even if it was something of a challenge to prop himself up on his elbows to sip from it. It was hot down here, at the mouth of the cave his desk made, because he'd cranked the electric baseboard heat beneath it. So he had shed his bathrobe and sprawled upon its terry-cloth island in his underpants.

It was dark. He wasn't sure what time it was. Papers lay all over the floor. Still inside the safe were nestled his gun — a stubby Colt revolver he had bought in the 1970s at the Factor's recommendation and which he hadn't fired since the training he signed up for at the gun shop and quit after one session because he was the only person there not dressed in jeans — and a pile of letters, tied with a bit of thick green yarn, presumably left over from a Christmas-present-wrapping session now lost to memory.

Harry held in his hands the tiny spiral reporter's notebook where he had recorded the instructions the Factor gave him. He closed his eyes and remembered that night.

The Turf Exchange, he learned by asking around (and already, he would later realize, this was a violation of protocol), was a hotel on Main Street in Binghamton. Driving there (and how Harry hated to drive, even then), he imagined a towering Art Deco edifice that harbored a long, dark, elegant bar where a jazz trio lugubriously labored on a dimly lit stage. Instead, Main Street didn't look particularly main, and the Turf Exchange didn't look like a hotel. It was a long, two-story clapboard structure with an uninviting and nondescript facade. Inside, it really was as long as Harry imagined, and not entirely without charm; there was indeed a small stage in the back, which was empty. The low ceiling was of pressed tin, and the floor, white tile; the Factor occupied a booth near the stage. Harry went to the bar and ordered a club soda with lime from an indifferent old man. He wasn't much of a drinker then.

"This used to be a speakeasy," the Factor said to him as he slid into the booth. "There are secret rooms below."

"Fascinating," Harry said, fearing he sounded sarcastic, though he was in earnest.

No other patrons occupied the place. No music played from no jukebox. If anonymity was the Factor's aim, he'd achieved it. It was hard to imagine noticing the existence of this place if you weren't invited directly to it.

"You're an historian," the Factor said, leaning on the *n* in "an."

"Of postwar European history, yes."

"Fascinating," the Factor said. Was he mocking Harry? Or were they simply two tall men liable to say "fascinating" in a bar in Binghamton? "Do you enjoy your work, Harry?"

"Yes, I do."

"The students. Do you get on well with them? Long, rambling conversations in your office, perhaps? Standing by the door outside the lecture hall, expounding upon some finer point as those young, curious faces gaze at you in wonder? A dinner party for those most treasured acolytes?"

"Well, not that," Harry said.

"No dinner parties?"

"I'm a private person. Also, I live in an apartment smaller than this bar."

"You should have a house, Harry. You're a professor!"

"Ah, not yet. I haven't completed my dissertation. And then I'll have to find a permanent job."

The Factor leaned over the table, grinning, his eyes unfocused. Harry noticed that his drink, a whiskey judging by the smell of his breath, had been a double and was now nearly gone, and was probably not his first. "If you could, Harry, would you stay at Nestor College? Would you own a house? Perhaps someplace leafy and quiet, with a book-lined room you'd call the library?"

"Ah . . . well . . ."

"A beautiful wife and two beautiful children, a boy and a girl? Would you like to pull the children in a little red wagon to the playground, where they would frolic in the sun?"

"Sure," Harry said, sipping his club soda through a straw. The straw suddenly seemed foolish. He removed it, then took a more generous gulp directly from the glass.

"Harry, do you know for whom I work?"

In fact, it had been pretty obvious to him from the start. CIA recruitment had been on the wane through his undergraduate days as sentiment against the war had gathered strength, and the Agency's interventions overseas were increasingly blamed for this and other American misadventures. (Someday books would be written about this, perhaps by him.) But he knew that campus recruitment had continued, if less overtly, and he assumed the moment the Factor spoke to him on the quad that he was Agency. The question, though, was what use the organization could make of an absent-minded doctoral student with a limp.

"I think I do," Harry said, trying to keep his cool.

"Then you know what I'm hoping to persuade you to do."

"Actually," Harry said, "no, I don't."

The Factor's grin could be described as Mephistophelian, his eyes as watery. He stood up, grabbed Harry's glass. "What are you drinking, Harry?"

"Club soda."

"Hmph."

The Factor loped to the bar and returned with two new drinks, another double for himself and another club soda for Harry. Except it wasn't.

"Vodka tonic, Harry. We enjoy a real drink now and then, in my line of work."

"Uh . . . thank you."

"Now. As I'm sure you're aware, domestic agitation has interfered with the war effort, especially on college campuses. I believe there has been some protest activity at Nestor?"

Harry nodded, sipping the drink. It didn't taste particularly boozy. He took a second swig. "They seized the provost's office last year. Said he invented napalm at Harvard."

"Yes, well," the Factor said, draining half his drink in one big slurp, "that wasn't him. But guilt by association is more than enough for these crackpots to justify their preposterous actions. The fact is, Harry, there are more and more of these agitators, and they're better and better funded, thanks to the flow of foreign money into the university's coffers, thanks to the scientists and the exchange students."

"I see."

"Harry, I don't want to take you out of your comfortable life here in Nestor. I don't want to put you in danger overseas. I want you to be a permanent fixture here, living a good life. I want you to have the house you want, the tenured position. I can help you get those things."

"How?" Harry said, already feeling the effects of his drink. When he looked down at it, he was surprised to see that it was nearly gone.

"By inviting you to be the best teacher you can be, Harry. By giving you the incentive to open your heart and your mind to your students, to invite them into your life, to become their mentor, yes, but also their friend."

He snaked a hand out to seize Harry's glass, which he appeared determined to fill up again. "I want you," the Factor said with a wink, "to spy on them."

Harry was awakened by the sound of a door falling shut. He opened his eyes and saw, smeared by sleep, a single bare light bulb screwed into an ornate, cobwebbed cast-iron fixture. He believed for a moment he was upstairs in the Turf Exchange Hotel; that's where he found himself the morning after his bender with the Factor, alone in a musty bed, his suit stained with vomit. Then he remembered his sentimental journey the night before and recognized the ceiling of his own home office. He was lying on his back on the floor. He seemed to have wet himself.

Another noise: heavy footsteps. Someone was in the house.

Harry tried to sit up and failed. He tried again and succeeded, this time, in propping himself up with his hands. Somewhere in the house, something was being dragged, another door opened and closed. Whoever had come for him, they were making no effort at stealth. That meant they didn't care if he heard them coming. That meant they intended to kill him.

He paused a moment to catch his breath and still his stomach. He saw his robe spread out around him, his soaking underpants. He saw his papers, his box of notebooks. (Is that why they were here? Is that what they wanted?) He saw his gun.

How was it, again, that he was supposed to get up from the floor? He ran through the steps in his head, then commanded his body to obey: Turn over. Check. Prop yourself up on hands and knees. Check. Now, hands up. Check. Bend one leg, foot flat on the floor. Check. And now, finally, grip the table's edge and stand.

Slowly, shakily, he did it. He stood, snatching up the Colt in the process. Was it loaded? He had no idea. How to check? He couldn't remember. Behind the closed office door, the intruder continued to move around the house. Harry gripped the Colt tightly and took three unsteady steps across the room. His head pounded and his stomach churned. Not now, body, I need you to do as I say. His left hand closed around the knob and he drew the door open slowly. No one was there, in the hall, but the noises were coming from the other end. The bathroom.

The bathroom? Well, maybe they thought he hid things there. He remembered seeing in a movie somebody taping a bag of drugs to the inside of a toilet tank. Regardless, he had them cornered now. He crept down the hall, hand against the wall for support, until he stood just outside the threshold of the bathroom. He heard the medicine cabinet open and close. He heard the scrape of heavy feet, a grunt. They'd sent a big man, a bruiser. But he would be no match for the Colt. Time to make your move, Harry!

"Freeze!" he shouted, lurching into the doorway and leveling the gun at the intruder. Mrs. Vesey, the cleaning woman — oh yes, he forgot, it's Monday morning — gasped, screamed, and jerked backward. She lost her footing; tangled in the shower curtain, she tumbled into the tub, pulling the curtain rod, its mounting hardware, and a rain of drywall down with her. Soon all that was visible of her were her two skinny legs with the white Keds at the ends, dangling over the tub's edge.

The sudden movement was too much for Harry's guts, which promptly unknotted and prepared to unburden themselves of the previous night's meal. Thinking quickly, he leapt across the room and vomited in the general direction of the toilet, which was shut. Much of the resulting torrent splashed onto Mrs. Vesey, who was luckily protected by the shower curtain. Well, not her legs.

"Oh dear," Harry said, panting. He gently set the revolver down on the toilet tank. "I'm very sorry, Mrs. Vesey."

"I quit!" the shower curtain cried.

# 15

# Nestor, NY: *Then*

All that weekend, the one before the last week of theater camp, their mother absented herself from their presence. She went on a couple of unexplained errands and made several phone calls in French.

"Dad doesn't speak it," Lila said on Sunday, dangling from the ancient gnarled apple tree in the yard. When they were younger, they used to climb all the way up into its branches. Jane sat on the ground, trying to pull blades of grass up from the roots without breaking them. "That's why she uses it."

Lila had gone to the library and got a French textbook, in an unsuccessful attempt to cram the entire language into her head in a weekend. "Do you understand anything at all?" Jane asked her.

"I think she said 'nuit,' which is night, and 'parc,' which is I guess park? Maybe they're meeting in the park at night?"

"She never says she's going out, she just does it."

"We have to assume she's meeting him tonight," Lila said, dropping onto the ground beside Jane. "I'm going to put the recorder in her car right now. It should be quiet enough in there so that it doesn't start up until she goes out."

Their mother didn't want to make dinner, so Jane made egg sandwiches and brought one to her father in his office, among his papers and books. He was drinking whiskey and looked exhausted and sick. "This is so nice of you. You even cut it on the diagonal."

"Are you all right, Dad?"

"I have a little allergy," he said, rubbing his face. "Nothing to be concerned about."

Lila had been determined to stay awake long enough to learn whether their mother had been out, then sneak out of bed and retrieve the tape, but when Jane woke up Monday her sister lay tangled in her sheets, crumpled paperback book beside her, much as Jane had left her the night before. They were late getting off to camp; their mother had failed to wake them, Jane had to prepare their lunches, and everyone was in a bad mood.

The girls sat in back together on the way, as they usually did when their mother was in a state. She wore her sunglasses despite the overcast day and played the classical station loud, to preclude conversation.

This suited Jane and Lila just fine. After a few significant glances, Lila unlatched her seat belt, slid to the floor, and snaked her hand underneath the driver's seat. A moment later it emerged holding the Dictaphone. Jane leaned over eagerly and together they squinted at it.

Lila nodded in excitement. The tape had recorded all the way to the end.

It would be several hours before the girls could steal away to listen, and, strangely, their mother hung around the camp for the duration of the morning. During improv circle, they could see her silhouette under the pavilion. At one point Jane noticed her staring into the swimming hole, smoking and watching children splash and play. And before lunch, their mother seemed to be having an intense conversation with Mr. Framingham and Crissy. Their mother was pointing at Crissy while directing what looked like a stream of invective at Mr. Framingham.

"This is weird," Jane said, as they carried their sack lunches into the woods. They'd found a disused stone bench on a high outcropping, surrounded by chain-link fence, and adopted it as a private hideout.

They turned off the path and onto the narrow dirt trail that led up to the bench. Lila said, "Is it, though?"

"What do you mean?"

"Just . . . it seems obvious what's going on."

"Why are they arguing with Crissy?"

Lila shot her a look. A moment later they arrived at the bench. "Let's just listen."

They took out their sandwiches. Lila rewound the tape, pressed play, and turned up the volume. She set the recorder down on the stone between them.

The first couple of minutes consisted of neighborhood noises: a loud truck going by, some kids shouting. A fire siren. Then, the sound of a car door opening and closing, and the engine starting up. The recording seemed to fade in and out as their mother shifted in her seat. She talked to herself again, in a foreign language, not French.

Next, they heard the jingle of keys, and the engine turning off. And then doors opening and closing.

Suddenly, their mother's voice was louder and clearer, and another had joined her. Mr. Framingham's.

"It's French, right?" Jane said. "Can you tell what they're saying?"

"No," Lila replied, staring out blankly into the trees. Jane had the impression, probably incorrect, that she was lying. "They're in the back seat," Lila went on.

"How do you know?"

"You can hear them. Their heads are right behind the driver's seat. The recorder is, like, right there." She took a bite of her sandwich, chewed thoughtfully. "They're lying down."

They laughed. Mr. Framingham moaned, and now their mother did, too, followed by a gasp.

Jane said, "I don't think I want to hear this."

"I do," Lila said.

The moaning intensified. Their mother's was ragged, animal-like. It didn't sound like her at all. They heard the jingle of a belt buckle, the creak of the seat springs. Then their mother's voice, in English, saying, "Fuck me."

"Stop it!" Jane said. She swallowed the bite of peanut butter and jelly she'd been working on and put the rest of the sandwich down. "Just stop."

"Cover your ears if you don't want to hear it," Lila said, continuing to eat. She was scowling with concentration, as though trying to commit the tape to memory.

"Lila, seriously!"

Lila turned to her. "I *am* serious."

They stared at each other as the squeaking back seat, and their mother's grunts, settled into a rhythm. Jane couldn't stand it anymore. She left her uneaten food and walked away.

She wasn't to find relief down at the camp, however. Back at the pavilion, everyone sat at the picnic tables, ignoring their food, as the argument in the parking lot continued. Crissy was yelling at their mother now, while Amber looked on, arms crossed, from the edge of the pavilion. "I will expose you for what you are!" her mother shouted, shaking her finger in Mr. Framingham's face.

Jane wanted to jump into the swimming hole, sink to the bottom, and never come back up. She must have made a noise, because about half the campers suddenly turned their heads to her, then hung them in shame.

Before she could decide what to do, their mother broke off from the group and stalked toward the pavilion. "Where are my daughters!" she shouted. The campers busied themselves with their lunches. Amber shied away as she approached, and their mother spun on her heel and said, "Don't go thinking you are so innocent! I will expose you like the rest!"

"Please leave," Amber said, just loud enough to be heard.

"Oh I will most certainly be leaving! And you will be refunding my fee!" She stopped in the center of the pavilion, swiveling her head. "Jane! Get in the car!"

"No," Jane said.

"Do you want to live here now? Is this your new home? Do you want that pervert for your new father?"

"Mother, stop."

"Where is your sister!"

"I don't know."

"Lila!" she shouted, muscling past Jane and striding off toward the trailhead. "Lila!"

Jane stood, stunned, with everyone's eyes on her. She turned, exited the pavilion, and went to the car. She climbed inside, shut the door, hung her head, and cried.

Some time later she heard a knock on the window. She looked up, expecting to see Lila, and was appalled to see Fritz staring down at her.

"Fritz, go away."

"Roll the window down."

"No!"

"Aren't you hot?"

He was right—it was stifling. She opened the window a crack. "Please leave."

"Are you quitting camp? Are you quitting the play?"

"I guess?"

"You can't quit the play. You're really good! We're going to be the best one."

"Amber will take over for me."

He frowned. "She's not the same."

"Fritz," she said, wiping her face with her sleeve. "I really want to be alone."

"It's not your fault your mom's crazy," he said.

"Fritz! Go! Away!"

Fritz backed away from the car. Incredibly, Jane immediately fell asleep. She was awakened by the sound of a car door. Lila had climbed in beside her. "You look terrible," she said, rolling her own window all the way down. "It's hot in here."

"I don't care. Did you tell her about the tape?"

Lila appeared surprised. "No. A spy never betrays their craft. Remember?"

"I guess."

She reached out and stroked Jane's back. Jane let her. Lila said, "I guess that's it for theater camp. She made them refund her money in cash. Mr. Framingham didn't even have enough, he had to borrow some from Amber and Crissy."

A minute later they heard their mother's frantic footsteps and the door flew open. The engine started and the car screeched and jerked across the lot. "Not one word of this to your father," she warned.

Jane could not think of anything she was less likely to do than share any of the day's revelations with him.

# 16

# Sioux Falls, SD: *Now*

———

"So tell me about your guy in Montana," Jane said as they picked up speed along the county two-lane.

"He's called Gramps. I know him because of the bikes. He's got more old parts than anyone in America."

"So . . . why him?"

"He has other connections, too."

They were coming into the village of Tightwad. It really was called that. They passed a Dollar General, a church, a bank.

"You enlisted a random guy in your search for Mom? A guy with 'connections'?"

Lila shot her a look. "It isn't like that. We just got to talking."

"So, are you going to share this information with me?"

"He hasn't given me any."

They drove through Coal, Clinton, Creighton, Garden City, mostly in silence. This was something Jane had missed, Lila's comfort with quiet companionship. It made most people anxious. After Kansas City they filled the tank. They stopped at a diner near Sioux City, where they were served fried chicken, green beans, and mashed potatoes covered in white gravy. The food was shockingly good. "It's actually excellent," Lila said, reading her mind. Then: "What was the first thing you ate when you got out of prison?"

Jane studied her sister's face, trying to figure out whether she was trying to wind her up. She'd fantasized for years about this conversation, or some version of it. It had been more than a decade. Would Lila apologize? Break down in tears? Would she fall into stony silence, unable to face the truth?

But she never imagined this. What did she *eat*?

"Pretty sure it was a Twix," she said. "In Chance's truck." It had melted and resolidified, probably more than once, and was white with crystallized sugar. He'd bought it at a convenience store on the way to the prison to collect her. It irritated her that he hadn't thought more carefully about this, hadn't packed her a proper meal for the nearly four-hour drive back to Nestor, but she was grateful that he'd bought the right car seat for Chloe and installed it correctly, grateful for his touch, his kiss, the smell of him. She shoved the candy into her mouth, licked the chocolate off her fingers, while Chloe fussed in the car seat between them and the gates of Boynton Ridge Correctional Facility closed behind her for the last time. "Then I think we went to Dad's and I had a slightly wrinkly apple." That apple she ate at the kitchen table in Nestor as the sun set outside; she drank from the glass of red wine Dad had poured her, and he held the baby, allowing her small hands to explore his unfamiliar face. He cried as Chloe babbled and stuck her fingers into his laughing mouth.

Lila laughed. "Wow. The taste of freedom."

She wanted to tell her sister these things. She wanted to talk about the joys and disappointments of being released, of becoming a mother in the real world. The way it felt to go to the supermarket for the first time, with Chloe's seat latched onto the cart, to watch her eyes roam over the boxes and cans and jars, to see her turning toward the voices of other children, the music coming over the PA, the announcements of sale items and cars in the parking lot with their lights left on. And she wanted to tell her sister that the sudden lack of routine, the structurelessness of freedom, terrified her, it reminded her of her darkest moments, made her want to drink and take drugs to fend off the horrors of possibility, like she had before her time inside. And to tell her that only Chloe kept her on the straight and narrow—maybe the force of the child's need, the responsibility she represented, but maybe nothing more complicated than the reliable cycle of feeding and playing and diapers and naps. The healing power of monotony.

And yet . . . she never lost the feeling that she was a danger to Chloe, and that Chloe was a danger to her. She remembered the nursing strike, when the child had been home for three weeks, that kept her awake nights, that banished her from the marriage bed so that Chance could sleep, then wake refreshed for his superfluous work that didn't pay the bills. (Susan, of course, did that.) She remembered the trips to the pediatrician's office, sessions with the lactation consultant, Susan idly musing that the damage she'd done to her body had poisoned her milk. And she remembered Chloe's deep satisfaction when Jane at last caved in and let her have a bottle of formula.

Today, she would die for Chloe. But was that because of the depth of her love, or her relative indifference to her own life? All the risks she'd taken, the disrespect she'd shown, and let others show, to her own body and mind . . . fights she shouldn't have picked, situations she shouldn't have gotten herself into . . . whoever was collecting the tickets on this ride had somehow missed how many times Jane's had been punched. To have never had a child, to have ceased to exist soon enough to prevent it, would have healed a rift she was still tearing in the fabric of existence. Which was just a fancy way of saying the world might be better off without her.

She wanted to tell Lila all of this. Instead, she kept her mouth shut. A few minutes later, Lila had switched on the radio and was quietly singing along.

They stopped for the night at a motel in Sioux Falls—the kind they preferred, where you can park your car directly outside the rooms. The clerk, a young woman in an orange polo shirt and baseball cap that matched the glowing sign they'd seen from the highway, was standing in the empty parking lot, pacing and smoking with a crooked grin on her face.

"I'll be with you ladies in a sec," she said, staring past them to the service road. She bounced on her toes.

"Waiting for something?" Jane asked.

"I just dumped my boyfriend. Over the phone," she said, triumphantly. "He threatened to throw out all my stuff. So I sent my friends over there to get it. Looks like he was bluffing! He begged them to talk me out of dumping him."

"And they're bringing your stuff here?" Lila said.

She nodded. "I'll be checking in for the night myself, lol."

As they spoke, the friends were already pulling into the parking lot, in a station wagon and a jeep, both filled to the roof with the clerk's possessions. They were leaning out the windows and cheering. They parked in front of the office, leapt out, and embraced in a jubilant cluster, like they'd just won a championship game.

"Whew!" the clerk said when they'd had enough. "Let me get you checked in." They followed her into the office, a surprisingly homey space decorated with framed family photos.

"Your family owns this place?" Lila said.

"Yeah, well, my mom, technically. It's her, me, and my brother now. Driver's license, credit card?"

"We'll pay cash."

"Still need your license."

They stared at the clerk. The clerk stared back. Jane leaned over the counter and said, "My sister's husband's a cop. He thinks we're having a girls' night out. But she's not going back."

Lila hung her head so that her hair fell over her face.

"Ah. Got it," the clerk said.

"Once he figures it out, he's going to track her down. So, we'd just as soon not have a half dozen state police cars come screaming in here to drag her away."

The clerk said, "Mmm. Okay."

"Maybe put us in a room in back. Facing away from the highway," Jane said.

"Sure." She reached behind her and chose a key from a peg rack, then dangled it at the end of her finger. Lila lay down two twenties on the counter, then, after a moment, added two more. The clerk nodded, swept up the bills, and handed her the key. "Good luck, ladies," she said. "I never saw you."

"Good luck to you, too," Lila said. "And congratulations."

They lay in the dark on their narrow beds. The walls had reduced the noise of the highway to a gentle wash, the party at the other end of the motel to a distant murmur. Jane opened her phone, called Susan again. She didn't answer. She tried to think of someone else she could call — a neighbor or friend who could have their kid ferry the phone over to Chloe? But it was hopeless. She didn't know the neighbors, or have friends. She had deliberately held herself apart, and now she was isolated and helpless. Could Chance really get sole custody? It was rare for a judge to cut out the mother, and the abandonment charge was preposterous. But most mothers weren't ex-cons. In her peripheral vision, she could see Lila wordlessly watching her think, and finally Jane said, "What."

"You know I have ways of solving this problem for you."

Jane ignored this. She tried to call their father. He didn't answer, either.

"They're being unfair to you," Lila went on. "I have the means to . . . make them stop."

"There's no need."

"I mean," Lila said. "There might be."

"I'm afraid you'll . . ."

"What?"

Jane set the phone down on the bedside table. "Overreact," she said.

Lila didn't respond.

"Chance is a good father," Jane said. "And I haven't been good to him. If he wants to divorce me, fine. But as for Chloe . . . I am hoping he will see reason."

Fifteen minutes passed. The traffic was dying down. The clerk's friends said good night; car doors slammed shut, engines started. Jane said, "Are you awake?"

"I am."

"Let me ask you something. What . . . do you *do,* exactly?"

"I am a security consultant and investigative services contractor, with specialties in missing persons, network technologies, and data recovery."

"Come on," Jane said. "That sounds like a business card. You don't have a business card."

"I actually do have a business card." She leaned over the edge of the bed, reached into her duffel, and pulled out a rubber-band-wrapped bundle. She drew a card from the pile and handed it to Jane across the gap between their beds. In the streetlight Jane read what was printed there.

PERKS LOCKSMITH SERVICES
"ALL OUR CUSTOMERS GET THE PERKS"
NORTH MAIN ST., RIVERSIDE
LOOK FOR THE BIG GOLD KEY

The phone number that followed was the one Jane had called a few days before.

"Clever. Bet there's a lot of Riversides."

"Just about every state. And even more North Mains. I actually am trained as a locksmith, by the way."

"Trained," Jane said, "as in actual school? You went to school?"

"Night school. After you . . . left. I figured I should go straight, learn a trade. But that got me into electronic locks, which got me into encryption, which got me into corporate espionage. And then other kinds of things."

"Perks."

"Yeah. Perks."

Jane said, "Just describe one job. One recent job you did."

Lila seemed to think about it for a moment. She said, "A woman hired me to find her adult daughter, who she said had been lured away from home by a cultist, and persuade her to come back with me. I was given photos, a description, a cell phone number, the names of some people who knew the daughter who might have information. I investigated for a couple of days, found the daughter pretty quick. She wasn't in a cult, it was more of a commune—like, an organic farm and animal sanctuary, and she'd gotten married to this guy, who was just this kindly hippie who made vegan leather bags and sold them on the internet. Then the daughter wanted to pay me to help her fake her own death and get her name changed."

"Whoa."

"I had to talk her out of the fake-death thing, but I did show her how to do the name change. Anyway, I went back to the client, told her that I found the daughter and she was fine, and there was no cult and she wasn't coming back, and the woman wouldn't pay me and threatened to sue to get my retainer back."

"I assume that wouldn't have been successful?"

"Litigation threats often get results, especially when the litigant is rich and angry and is happy to pay a lawyer more than the job is worth. But no. She had no case. Also, she did end up paying my fee. I don't think she ever realized it, but she paid it. Plus a tip."

"Oh. I see."

"Yeah. Most people know what I'm worth, though, and don't complain."

"How do they find out about you?"

"Word of mouth, mostly," Lila said. "Sometimes I see a situation unfold and realize I can make myself useful. In the beginning I placed discreet ads in a few carefully chosen places, but that, uh, I don't think that actually brought in any clients." She added, with a sigh, "I'm . . . known."

"Sounds like you don't like that?"

"No. I don't need a lot of money to live, and I don't want to call attention to myself. I turn down a lot of work these days. Some clients, I don't like the feel of them. I don't like being manipulated."

The sisters lay silent for a little while longer. Lila had gotten herself worked up, and Jane listened as she forced her breathing to slow. Jane wasn't tired, but she closed her eyes, trying to go through the motions of sleep. She opened them to dawn light and heard distant shouting.

Lila was standing in her underwear and a tee shirt with her hand on the knob of the cracked-open door.

"What's —?"

"Shh."

A man shouting, a fist pounding a door. "Go away!" came a voice — the motel clerk's — muffled by the walls.

Lila sprinted out the door. Jane could hear her bare feet slapping the pavement. She scrambled out of bed, pulled on her jeans, and followed. When they'd arrived last night, the rear lot of the motel was empty of anything but Lila's Volvo and a dumpster, beyond which lay a cornfield. Now, though, there was something else. The motel consisted of two long, two-story sections, forming an L shape, with a breezeway between. A black SUV was parked behind the last room on the other side of the L. As Jane jogged toward the breezeway, a light switched on in the room behind the SUV, and the curtains parted. A face appeared, a man's. He seemed to notice Jane, then quickly vanished. She was given only a brief glance into the room, and it was twenty yards away, but Jane believed she saw another person in the room behind the man.

She followed the voices into the front lot. A pickup truck was parked crookedly across several spaces, and a young guy, muscular arms, around six feet, stood in front of the room nearest the front office. In his raised hand he held a fragment of cinder block, of the sort lying outside many of the rooms, doubtless used to prop the doors open when a guest wanted a smoke. It appeared he was threatening to throw it through a window.

"Hey!" Lila said, slowing to a trot, and while the guy gaped at her panties, she lunged forward and sucker-punched him in the trachea. The cinder block fell as his hands flew to his throat, and Lila took this opportunity to knee him in the groin. He doubled over. She hooked her right foot around his right ankle and pushed him sharply backward; he twisted and fell, and she threw herself down on him and broke his nose with a fist. Jane heard the wet snap from twenty feet away. He gargled in pain.

Someone somewhere was screaming, it wasn't clear who. Then the room door opened and the clerk rushed out, hands extended. "Stop! Stop!" She hopped up and down in terror, flapping her hands in the air before her. "What are you doing! Let him up!"

The guy gasped and coughed, spitting blood. Lila looked up at the clerk, back down at him. She let go of his shirt, stood, and took a step back. As the guy rolled over, clutching his balls and gasping for breath, Lila said, "I could have killed you with the first punch. And if I'd caught you hurting her, I would have."

"Jesus fuck!" the clerk said. Her face was damp with sweat and tears and her blond hair stuck to her cheek. "Dylan!" she said, addressing the guy. She knelt on the ground beside him, laid a hand on his shoulder, gingerly, as though it might burn. "Are you all right?"

Dylan's body convulsed and he vomited onto the pavement.

Lila glared at the clerk. "That's how you treat somebody who wanted to throw a cinder block at you?" she demanded.

"He wasn't going to *do* it!"

"None of them are ever going to do it. And then they do."

The clerk gaped. She leveled a shaking finger at Lila. "You're not hiding from your husband," she said.

"I'm not hiding from anybody," Lila said. "And I'm certainly not cowering in a motel room from *Dylan*."

Here she was, the Lila Jane remembered, the one she'd run away with, and the one she'd run away from. The Lila brought to life that night almost twenty years ago. If she weren't Lila's twin, she might not find this kind of confrontation so viscerally repellent, but she was, and Jane did. To watch it emerge was to feel a part of herself stir from sleep: not the violence, of which she was, or at least had once been, capable, and to which she had, on occasion, been forced to resort. Rather the hunger to unleash it. To exact retribution. To induce surprise, then humiliation, then terror in anyone who might cross her — that's the part of herself she feared. Jane had never killed anyone. She'd been on the run, been assaulted, defended herself, escaped with her life. She'd desired the death of many men, and could easily have seen that desire fulfilled, many times. She didn't sympathize with the people who hurt her, at least not while they were hurting her. But to allow herself the satisfaction of revenge would be to ruin something in her, the part of her that was already deformed and broken enough, the part that let her exist with other people in the world.

She wanted other people. She wanted to return to her daughter, to the ordinary, unhappy life that had saved her a decade ago. She didn't want to watch Lila murder this man.

But that life was unraveling. The only direction was forward.

Jane lay a hand on Lila's shoulder. If she was surprised to learn Jane was there, her body didn't betray it. "Maybe we should get on the road," Jane said quietly.

"Learn to defend yourself," Lila told the clerk. "Don't kneel on the ground blubbering over some piece of trash."

"Get the fuck out of here before I call the cops!"

Jane said, "Come on."

"Hey, Dylan," Lila shouted. "I know your name, and pretty soon I'll know where you live, your phone number, your mother's maiden name, and your place of work. I'm going to keep tabs on you, and if you ever hurt this woman or anyone else, I will kill you. Do you understand?"

"Fuck *off*!" the clerk screamed.

Lila picked up the broken bit of cinder block. "You drive a 2012 Silverado 1500, South Dakota plates 1BX 344," she said. Then she flung the block at the truck. The clerk flinched as it bounced off, leaving behind a gouge. "With a dented passenger-side door. See you around, Dylan."

Back in the motel room, they threw their last few possessions back into their bags. Lila surprised Jane by waking up Loretta with a phone call and reciting the details of Dylan's truck. Maybe her body was flooded with adrenaline, as Jane's was. Lila ended her call and tossed the room key onto her unmade bed. They walked out. Climbed into the Volvo. Lila started the engine and steered the car around the end of the motel and out of the lot, as slowly and deliberately as an elderly tourist leaving a national park. The end room's window was dark and the black SUV was gone.

"I thought we didn't want to call attention to ourselves," Jane said as they accelerated up the on-ramp.

"You didn't have to show up and give them another good look," was the growled reply.

"Come on, Lila. I wasn't the memorable part of that scene."

Lila moved back into the right lane and set the cruise control. The road banked west. The purple sky was lightening, the earth was flat, and the clouds were wisps against the horizon.

"Did you see the SUV?" Lila asked.

"Yeah, I was going to mention it. When I came out, the light switched on in their room. There's two of them. At least one's a man."

"They were already gone when we left."

"Okay . . . what does that mean, though?"

"I'm not sure."

Lila was peering into the rearview. They'd passed a big rig and a minivan, and, aside from their headlights, the highway behind them was empty.

An exit was up ahead. Without signaling, Lila took it. A county highway ran underneath the freeway, and she turned left onto it and, a minute later, into the shared parking lot of a cluster of buildings: a gas station, a thrift store, and a restaurant that appeared closed for good. She pulled in behind the restaurant, shielding them from the highway.

They stepped out of the car. Lila threw open the hatchback and hauled out a black plastic case the size of a messenger bag. She opened it, revealing a collection of devices recessed in protective foam, and pulled out two of them: a black rectangle, equipped with a screen, that resembled an old smartphone, and a foot-long plastic paddle. She connected the two with a wire, then walked around the car, waving the paddle close to the ground and observing the readout on the screen.

"What are you doing?"

"Looking for a tracking device." Lila grunted, climbed into the back seat. Held the paddle over the passenger-side footwell. "Goddammit." She set the scanner down on the seat, stepped out, and crouched on the ground. She stuck her arm under the car and groped around. A moment later she produced another black ABS plastic object.

"Is that . . . a bug?"

"A GPS tracker. I'm an idiot. I should have been scanning for these all along. I didn't imagine we could be followed."

Jane was baffled. "Why are we being followed?" But then she got a sinking feeling. A bad idea was beginning to worm its way into her head.

"No idea," Lila said. She was peering over the roof of the car. A pickup truck had just pulled in, and its owner headed for the convenience store. "Hold on," she said. She leaned back into the Volvo and grabbed a balled-up receipt from the inside pocket on the door. Then she trotted over toward the gas station.

A trash can was positioned between the pumps. Lila arrived at it, tossed the receipt, and deliberately missed. She crouched on the ground, retrieved the receipt, and threw it in properly. Then she walked slowly back to the Volvo. It took a moment for Jane to realize what she'd done.

Lila said, "If they're any good, it shouldn't take them long to realize they're now tracking a 1996 Ford F-250. We'll see them again."

Lila put away the scanner. They got back into the car and onto the highway. "I think I know who they are," Jane said.

"Who?"

"Chance hired them. Chance and Susan. They want to prove I'm having an affair or something."

Lila considered. "I dunno. Maybe? But . . . I don't think the guys they would hire would have a rig like that." She fell into a scowling silence for a while, then said, "What was he wearing?"

"Who?"

"The guy you saw through the window."

"White shirt? Button-down. Something you'd wear a jacket over. In fact, now that I think of it, the person behind him was wearing a suit coat. I think it was another guy."

Lila said "hm" and nodded. A while later she asked, "What's she like?" In response to Jane's blank stare, she added, "Chloe."

"Oh!" Her desire of half an hour before, to unburden herself to Lila, had evaporated. But before she could stop herself, she said, "She's like Chance."

"Just Chance?"

"Sometimes I see them sitting at the kitchen table together," Jane said. "Chance has his colored pencils out, working on his landscape renderings, and Chloe is there beside him writing something in her notebook, and they have their heads down, and they're just . . . identical. I've seen them reach for the same pencil, then look up at each other and smile, like they're in a TV commercial or something. It's like there's no agitation, no struggle to be in the moment. They're just there, existing together." In spite of herself, she went on: "Whereas I always feel I'm at war with her. I'm always trying to get her to do something or be a certain way, and it makes me feel like shit."

Lila said, "It sounds to me like you're the one doing the heavy lifting, and he just gets to enjoy her. And enjoy thinking he's the better parent."

"He is the better parent." Nobody said anything for a minute. And then: "But you're not totally wrong. It pisses me off when I come home and need to get her to hang her things up, and do her homework, and make her something she's actually willing to eat, and he walks in and all that shit is already finished and he's like the prize she gets to have for enduring me for three hours."

"Well," Lila said, "now she'll get to find out what it's like to be with him all the time."

"Is that supposed to reassure me?"

At a truck stop, Lila pumped gas and they bought egg sandwiches on flavorless croissants. The black SUV did not appear. Men were wearing cowboy hats, not as a costume. Jane perused a rack of tee shirts that bore messages like I'D RATHER DIE ON MY FEET THAN LIVE ON MY KNEES, ALL GUNS MATTER, and I'LL KEEP MY GUNS YOU KEEP YOUR CHANGE.

"Here's one that just says, 'Fuck gun control,'" Lila said.

"Direct and to the point."

"Gun control? Personally, I don't like it."

"That's just my view, I'm against gun control."

"I wanted you to know."

"Look, I don't have time to discuss this, please just read my shirt."

Back on the road, Jane kept nodding off. "Sorry," she said.

"It's fine. I'm pretty alert," Lila said. She held up her giant cup of truck-stop coffee. "If I need you to take a shift, I'll wake you up."

"Thanks."

But now that Jane had permission to sleep, she couldn't. She closed her eyes and tried to slow her breathing. The confrontation with Dylan kept running through her head, and her conversation with Chance, and every moment of conflict she'd experienced in the past two decades. Her body stiffened, her neck ached. She thought about her mother. She thought about George Framingham.

# 17

# Nestor, NY: *Then*

Lila and Jane were dimly aware that other parents weren't like theirs, that most kids could expect attention, believed that their parents' lives revolved around their needs. But there was no way to be sure: They weren't invited to other kids' houses and didn't want their friends to visit theirs. They had each other, their games and secrets, their books, their yard. They weren't pariahs at school, but they weren't popular, either. They didn't get in trouble, because getting good grades was easy for them; and they weren't demanding, like many of their peers. The spy ring affair had taught them that social groups were strange, that other kids were petty and dishonest, and that they should keep their feelings to themselves.

Things changed after the theater camp disaster, both at school and at home. Only a couple of kids at the camp went to their school, much younger ones at that, but when seventh grade started, everyone seemed to know what had happened over the summer. Kids began to perceive them as weird, took note of their old, unfashionable clothes, got wind of their strange home lives, and began to mock them. All at once kids seemed to know what sex was, and girls called them sluts. Their mother's affair with Mr. Framingham had rubbed off on the twins; a rumor went around that they'd done it with a pedo in the state park and liked it.

Lila would react to these insults with detached curiosity, like some kind of wild animal, a powerful and inscrutable creature who was puzzled by the folly of humankind. Jane took them more personally. After a couple of months of torment, she screamed at a girl in the hallway, said, "A pedo wouldn't touch you, you ugly bitch," and ended up having to apologize to the girl in the principal's office with their parents present—in Jane's case, her father, who was utterly baffled by the entire ritual and seemed to have forgotten about it the next day.

Before theater camp, their mother's neglect could be seen as benign, and her occasional intervals of active parenting as a treat. Now, the girls learned to avoid her, resent her. If she was paying attention, she was most likely angry. Much later, Jane would understand that she felt tainted by her sexual desire and her daughters' witness to it; her rejection by George Framingham was an unforgivable humiliation. But now, it just felt like they were being blamed for the entire debacle and that their relationship with their mother was forever ruined.

The following year, they began to awaken longing in certain boys— stoners, punks, edgy outsiders. Their attraction manifested, at first, as teasing and harassment. The girls taught themselves to fight from a book they got out of the library and vowed to each other that they would each win one fight inside of a week. They beat the boys who mocked them, and they beat the boys who liked them.

Later Jane would wonder if they'd won so easily because the boys didn't actually want to fight. One boy, during their fourteenth year, definitely did not want to fight Jane, he wanted to have sex with Jane, so after Jane fought him, bloodying his nose, she had sex with him. She told Lila that night, in the shed, which they'd repurposed as a kind of hangout. They'd found old wooden chairs in the basement, and an end table with a drawer that they kept cigarettes and weed in. They were smoking the cigarettes now.

Lila said, "Why?"

"What do you mean, *why?*"

"Why did you have sex with him?"

"I wanted to," Jane said.

"Did it feel good?" Lila wasn't taking notes, but she might as well have been; she was leaning forward in the light of the citronella candle, eyes narrowed. She looked like a TV reporter asking a corporate CEO why he'd just laid off a thousand workers.

"It started to. Near the end. Next time I'll tell the boy what to do." She stared at Lila, smoking. "You should do it."

"Why?"

"Just get it over with, then it won't be a thing anymore."

"It's not a . . . thing."

"Don't you want to?" Jane asked. "Don't you think about it?"

"No."

"Come on, yes you do."

Lila appeared to consider. "Some people look okay to me," she said. "But I don't want to touch them."

"You should have sex with Will. I'm sure he'd want to. The twins thing, boys think it's hot."

"But — he's your boyfriend now."

Jane said, "He is *not* my boyfriend. I beat him up, remember? I only did it with him because I was cleaning the blood off his face after I hit him, and his face was literally right there."

They didn't discuss sex or romance anymore after this; looking back, Jane saw this as the moment her intimacy with her sister began to wane. Lila became more private, more furtive — more like their mother. The boys stopped harassing her, probably because her beatings weren't followed by sex. She seemed to judge Jane for the escalating chaos in her life, which featured more drinking, more boys, more drugs. Maybe Lila wasn't judging her; maybe she wasn't even paying attention. But Jane didn't feel as close to her as she once had. She resented it, the way she resented their mother's neglect. She began to experience a feeling that would extend through the next two years, which she would eventually recognize as loneliness.

The summer before high school, their mother went away for what would prove her longest trip yet. Their father was depressed. The girls made his meals, laundered his clothes. The research he was supposed to have been doing seemed to consist of little more than moving various piles of paper to new locations in his home office. Lila had long ago learned to pick the lock on the door and discovered that he was actually writing mostly unsent letters to their mother. He'd also been in contact with a woman named Ruth Bortnik, whom the girls recognized as their aunt, a woman they'd never met. They'd supposed many of her mysterious trips were to visit this sister, but the letters to their father suggested that she and their mother hadn't been in contact in years.

"So where's she been going?" Lila wanted to know.

"Off with men, duh." They were in the shed, the one place where they still felt close.

"For a month and a half?"

Jane shrugged. "Maybe she's gone for good. Maybe she's got a second family."

"I don't think Mom would leave us so that she could have more children."

"I was *kidding.*"

"Did you notice," Lila asked, "that she takes plant stuff with her? Seeds, her gardening notebook?"

"So, what. You think she's going on . . . secret gardening trips?"

"No, but . . ." Lila grabbed a book off the stack by her bed, a hardcover journal she'd stolen from a college girl who'd left her bag unattended outside a coffee shop they'd been walking past. The girl had only filled the first few pages, with lists of her own positive attributes, some kind of self-esteem project. Lila had left the pages in and had added parody items to the lists in a surprisingly accurate imitation of the girl's loopy hand: "Secret third boob," "French fry odor," "Can usually spell own name." Lila opened the journal, fanned the pages, said, "I've been making lists of the stuff she brings back, based on her notes. Look. 'D. oerstedii,' 'D. wendlandii,' 'D. grayumii' . . . these are weird plants from all over the place. Not here, I mean. I looked them up. One's a medicinal plant from, like, Colombia. Another one's from Costa Rica. I called the plant store, they don't sell anything like that."

"Okay?"

"So, her family's from, what, Russia and Spain? Did you ever hear of a cousin or something in Costa Rica?"

"No, but . . ."

"I just think it's weird. She disappears for *weeks,* is supposed to be visiting family, but she never mentions them, or anything else she did when she's away. Other people's moms aren't like this, they never shut up about every meaningless thing they do."

"So, what? You think she's a criminal or something?"

"Maybe?" Lila said. "Maybe the plants are contraband? Like, they're not allowed to cross international borders, and she's collecting them to make money."

Jane raised her arms, looked theatrically around. "So where's this money going, then? This place is a dump."

"I don't know," Lila said.

"I still think it's just vacations with her playboys. She's lying on beaches somewhere a million miles away, in a bikini, getting massaged by some beefy Latin lover."

"Maybe."

"Why do you even care? She doesn't pay any attention to us. What's the point of paying attention to her?"

Lila glumly closed the notebook, laid a pale hand on the cover. "I guess I'm a freak for caring."

"Well, somebody in this family should be that kind of freak, I guess. Congratulations."

She meant it as an insult, but Lila just said, "Thanks."

Their mother returned soon after school started. No greeting, no explanation; she was simply back in her solarium, chain-smoking, starting new seedlings. "Wow, hi," Jane said to her upon finding her there on a sultry afternoon.

Her mother turned, looked her up and down. "They permit you to wear that to school?"

Jane was wearing flip-flops and a sheer vintage nightgown she'd repurposed as a dress. Her bra and underwear were visible through it, and the neckline was torn. "Actually, no. That's why I'm home at lunchtime. They told me to change."

"Good," her mother said.

Jane changed, then didn't go back to school, instead wandering into the woods behind the city park to get high. She considered moving out, getting an apartment. But then she'd need a job, *and* her parents' permission. It was hard to imagine enduring four years of high school like this—something had to change.

That change came in the form of a xeroxed poster that started appearing on the school's bulletin boards the second week of September. FALL

DRAMA TRYOUTS, they read. Jane ignored them until Lila handed her one, out in the shed one night.

*"Bombshells?"*

"I looked it up," Lila said. "It's about women fighting against the Man. It seems kind of stupid. But I bet you'd get the lead."

"Why would I want that."

"Something to do," Lila said. "Also, you're depressed."

"Oh, and you're not?"

"No."

"Well good for you."

"I'll do it with you," Lila said. "There's a ton of parts. We can become 'theater kids.'"

"Woo-hoo."

"Mom will hate it."

That gave Jane pause. "Maybe it would chase her away for good."

"I mean, maybe," Lila said. This had become a habit of hers — reacting earnestly to what was obviously a joke. But maybe it wasn't a joke, maybe it was what Jane really wanted.

Lila was right that their mother would hate it, but not for the reasons she'd assumed. The girls stayed after school the following Monday, gathering in the auditorium for tryouts. The curtain was open, the house lights off, the stage lights on; kids turned to watch as the twins entered, then looked away. A couple of boys Jane knew nodded knowingly. She and Lila went and sat next to one of them.

"There's a new guy for theater director," he said. "He actually writes plays. He's legit."

A few more students filed in, but Jane was no longer paying attention. She thought she remembered something — *he's a playwright himself.* "Do you think —" she started to say to Lila, but then the auditorium was hushed by the sound of hard-soled shoes treading the boards. They looked up, and there he was: the new theater director, George Framingham.

# 18

# Bridger Range, MT: *Now*

---

The Volvo cut through the northeast corner of Wyoming and entered Montana. It was cold here, and rain battered the car; the digital thermometer behind the steering column read thirty-five degrees Fahrenheit. Darkness was falling. The sisters had traded places and Lila had gone to sleep; now she woke up and said, "We should stop for the night. We'll get to Gramps tomorrow."

In the village of Broadus they found a rustic log motel. Lila, alert for their pursuers, circumnavigated the place on foot, but there was no sign of them, not yet. They walked down the street to a small bar and casino. The casino portion consisted of arcade-style games of chance, most of which were occupied by elderly people in plaid shirts. There was a digital streaming jukebox you could control with a phone app, but the loud contemporary country music others had chosen suited them fine. They ate hamburgers and drank beer and ignored the stares of some men playing pool nearby.

At some point Jane felt an unfamiliar vibration in her bag and remembered the phone. She pulled it out and saw Susan's number on the display. "Jesus. It's her."

"Go outside."

Jane accepted the call as she hurried out the door. "Chloe!" There were a few cracked pieces of plastic porch furniture here, shielded from the rain by an awning. Jane fell into one, hugging herself against the cold.

"It's Susan."

"Ah."

"Chloe's asleep."

"Asleep! It's . . ." She glanced at her watch. "It's just past nine where you are."

"Ah. So, you have gone to another time zone."

"Yes. Is she really asleep already?"

"We had a long day. A good, long day."

It wasn't clear what she was expecting of Jane. The rain fell. A truck pulled into the bar's parking lot and Jane shielded her eyes from the bright headlights.

Jane said, "I've been trying to call, Susan. Why haven't you answered?"

"I suppose my phone was off."

"Susan. Come on."

"I'm not calling to put you in touch with Chloe, who I think is benefiting from this time alone with me. But Chance persuaded me to update you. So, I wanted to let you know that we've been swimming at the state park, we went to the mall for some new clothes, and we've visited the zoo."

"Well, thank you," Jane said, as the truck doors slammed shut and a couple of strong-looking middle-aged women hurried underneath the awning with their lit cigarettes. They smoked and looked out at the rain. "But it's important that I speak with her right away."

"That's very surprising," Susan said, "given that you've abandoned her like this."

Rage flooded her body. "Susan," she said, jaw tense. "I am on a brief trip, attending to family problems."

"According to Chance, you promised not to return to your old life. You broke that promise."

"I have not returned to my old life. I am with my sister." She hesitated, then said, "As you would know, if your people have reported back to you."

"I beg your pardon?" Susan said.

"You know exactly what I mean, Susan. Call them off. I will be back next week."

"Oh, you have a return date? What is it, please, so that I can tell your husband and daughter."

"Next week, Susan. I don't know what day yet."

"And next week, you won't know what week, and next month you won't know what month."

"Please get Chloe and put her on."

"I don't know what kind of chaos you're accustomed to, Jane," Susan said, "but in this house, we don't wake children out of a sound sleep on a whim."

"It's not a whim. I'm her mother, and I've been calling for two days."

"I'll have to pay better attention to my phone. But it's difficult, when there's a child to attend to."

She gripped the phone harder. The plastic creaked. "You utter sadistic bitch. How dare you."

It was hard to hear in the rain, but Jane believed she heard a grunt, perhaps of offense, more likely of satisfaction, before the call cut off. She threw the phone on the ground and screamed, then lowered her head into her hands.

Beside her, a voice: "Hey."

Jane looked up. One of the women was offering her a cigarette. Jane took it, drew in the smoke, exhaled. Handed it back. "Thank you."

"Phone's getting wet."

"Yeah," Jane said. She got up, feeling old, and picked up the phone from the ground. The plastic display was cracked but it was working. She put it back into her bag.

Inside, Lila had accepted a challenge from the pool-playing men and was in the process of running the table while they looked on in embarrassment. Jane sat down and stared at the remains of her burger and fries. A part of her knew that she should fly home immediately, that Chloe ought to take priority over this trip, over Lila, over their mother. But what purpose would it serve? The die had been cast. Susan had always despised her, and sometimes she thought Chance always had, too. He had loved her, but maybe what he loved the best was the sense that he had rehabilitated her, done her a favor by accepting her.

Going home now wouldn't prevent divorce. It wouldn't prove anything to Susan, whose nonsensical charge of abandonment was intended exclusively to infuriate and humiliate her, or to Chance, who had clearly been plotting to get rid of her for months, if not years. It would probably prevent Chloe from getting some new toys. And if she wanted a future in which she didn't have to look over her shoulder, in which she could feel she was a net benefit to her own child, she would need to reckon with the past.

The two men groaned as Lila sank the eight, but they followed her back to the table. They weren't bad-looking—a little beefier than Jane liked, but fit, one of them taller, the other broader in the shoulders. The shorter one feigned surprise at the sight of her—they had obviously noticed the sisters walking in—and said, "There's two of you?"

"I'm different," Jane said. "Not so good at pool."

"I wonder what you are good at," the guy said, winking.

She shot Lila a pleading look, and Lila nodded her understanding. "Sorry, boys," she said, slapping the tall guy on the shoulder. "Going to have to take a rain check. Thanks for the fun."

"Anytime," Tall said, and the two moved off, ceding the pool table to a couple of older women.

"Did you talk to her?" Lila asked, taking her seat.

"No. Just Susan."

"And?"

"Chloe was too tired to come to the phone, thanks to their thrilling day together." She rolled her eyes, but her jaw was tight.

"Reconsidering my offer to . . . helpfully intervene?"

"I am."

"Do you need to go back?"

Jane shook her head. "A few days won't matter. I'll talk to Chance tomorrow. He can't be on board with this bullshit. And Susan pretended not to know about the tail. They're hers, I'm sure of it. I know how she sounds when she's lying."

Lila began to reply, then seemed to think better of it. She nodded, squeezed Jane's hand. "Let's go," she said.

Outside, the rain had stopped and a rank wind blew across the plains and down the lonely street. They walked back to the motel. As Lila undressed, Jane admired her movements: deft, economical. The way she unhooked her bra and pulled on a tee shirt had the brisk efficiency of a military drill. She had a scar on her lower back that suggested someone had once stabbed her in the kidney. "I'm taking a shower," Jane said, as Lila climbed into bed. Jane stood under the spray, despising Susan, disgusted with herself, and almost fell asleep on her feet. She wrapped herself in a towel, collapsed onto the bed, and woke shivering at dawn.

They drove US 212 west through the Northern Cheyenne Indian Reservation, got gas and coffee in Lame Deer, and continued toward Bozeman as the mountains loomed closer. A black SUV approached them at breakneck speed, then blew past. "Not them," Lila said. "Cops." Just before Livingston they turned north on 89, which took them through rolling brown hills, past cattle and sheep ranches. For a few minutes, antelope ran alongside the car, and Jane was surprised by a herd of shaggy animals she realized were bison. "Are those . . . wild?"

Lila shook her head. "There's a preserve in the western part of the state, but those are some rancher's."

They turned west at the town of Wilsall and, over the next twenty miles of paved road, saw a total of three pickup trucks. The day was bright, the sky clear. The Bridger Mountains surrounded them in the distance, and sometimes a wandering stream was visible to the south. At long last, a few minutes past noon, Lila turned off onto a neatly maintained gravel road marked by a small painted wooden sign reading FLATHEAD CREEK EARLY CYCLES.

"That's it?"

"That's it."

The tires rumbled over a surprisingly modern steel-and-timber bridge that carried them over the creek. Up ahead, a stand of pines seemed to demark a hidden lot; the road led to a break in the trees that revealed a tall chain-link fence topped with razor wire and interrupted by a rolling security gate. Lila slowed and came to a stop alongside a freestanding steel intercom and keypad. She rolled down the window and pressed a button marked CALL.

A man's voice crackled out of the speaker. "Yep?"

"Gramps? We're here."

"Yep," the voice repeated, "I see you. Meet me at the office."

After a moment, Jane heard an electric motor thunking to life, and the gate rolled slowly aside.

The facility consisted of several warehouse-style buildings with gray corrugated metal roofs surrounding a wide gravel lot. A log cabin at the far end bore a sign marked OFFICE. Pickup trucks were parked there. One entire side of one warehouse consisted of garage doors, three of them, opening up to an apron of smooth concrete. The rightmost garage door was open, and a couple of motorcycles were parked outside. Two young men sat on roller stools, surrounded by tools and bike parts. On the left side of the lot, two vans were nestled side by side, one anonymous white, the other bearing the company logo, a silhouette of a seventies-style long-haired rider astride an elongated chopper.

Lila parked at the office, beside the pickups, and the women got out and stretched. The creak of a screen-door spring directed their gazes to the man who'd just appeared: tall, hale, around seventy-five, dressed in clean denim overalls, flannel shirt, and work boots. A grease-stained trucker hat partially covered a head of wild gray hair and shaded a round, world-weary face dominated by an enormous beard.

"Hiya, kid," the man said. Jane could sense Lila wanting to move closer, to shake his hand or embrace him. But she kept her distance.

"This is my sister, Jane," she said.

The man doffed his hat, revealing a pink bald scalp.

"You must be Gramps."

"That I am." He turned to Lila. "Why don't you two come up to the house," he said, gesturing to the south, where the gravel path continued up behind a grassy foothill. Lila said, "Should we drive up?"

"The day I start driving home from work," he said, "is the day I start dying."

The path snaked up, alongside a small stream, into a sparsely wooded gorge. After a few minutes, a log house came into view, nestled into a notch in the hills. It was wrapped in a covered porch equipped with several wooden rocking chairs, a bench, and a charcoal grill. Behind the house, a tiny waterfall, tumbling among the rocks, fed the stream they'd walked along. Smoke poured out of a chimney and a raven alighted on the roof's peak.

"Nice place," Jane said.

"Built it" was the reply.

They climbed the front steps. As they entered, Gramps called out, "Ellie!"

Gramps led them through a front room dominated by a rack of fishing gear, rifles, boots, and raincoats, and into a high-ceilinged kitchen built around a woodstove. Beyond it, through an open doorway, they could see a comfortable living room with sofa, love seat, and coffee table. A fire burned in a wide stone hearth. A woman was getting up from a recliner and setting an iPad down on the coffee table. She was in her sixties, and dressed in jeans, bedroom slippers, and a tucked-in western shirt. She was wearing more makeup than Jane might have expected from a casually dressed lady in the middle of nowhere. Was it for them?

"I've got some business with these ladies. Gonna take 'em into the study. Maybe you can bring in something to eat?"

Wordlessly, the woman headed past them to the kitchen.

Gramps led them down a hallway decorated with old maps and half-decent landscape paintings. "Ellie did those," he said. "You can see some more in Livingston. She's got a gallery."

The hallway terminated in an incongruous steel security door with a single tall, narrow, mesh-reinforced window. Gramps punched a code into a keypad, concealing it with his body, and they were admitted with a click into a large room—a wing of the house, really, about twenty-five by forty feet. High windows let in enough light to dispel the gloom, but Gramps flicked a wall switch and two giant warehouse pendant lights, dangling from the arched exposed-beam ceiling, flickered to life.

The room was dominated by two long wooden tables, one covered with binders, catalogs, ledgers, and other papers, as well as a laptop computer, and the other with motorcycle parts and various pistols and rifles, disassembled on squares of carpet. Metal bins contained screws and springs; a wooden caddy held bottles of oils and solvents, brushes, and cleaning rods. One wall was completely covered by file cabinets, another by locked cabinets that Jane suspected were filled with firearms. On top of the file cabinets, beside a row of curved painted metal objects Jane believed were motorcycle fuel tanks, conservative talk radio poured quietly out of an old boom box. Gramps went over to it and switched it off.

"Gramps is the foremost restorer and parts dealer for vintage American motorcycles in the United States," Lila said.

"Indian, anyway," Gramps elaborated. "Other guys have me beat on Harleys. Also into Vincent these days, and some Italian bikes, Ducati, Laverda."

"He helped me out with my BMWs," Lila said to Jane.

"You still have that R90S?"

"You bet." She turned to Jane. "He's brought me a fair amount of business, too," she said.

Gramps moved around the space, showing things to Lila—some repro gauges he was working on marketing, a brake assembly he was in the process of restoring. Before long, the door lock clicked and Ellie came into the room, bearing a dinner plate with food on it. Some of the food slid off as she clanked the plate down onto Gramps's work table: a handful of Ritz crackers and some hard sausage that had been sliced haphazardly into ragged discs. "Anything to drink?" she asked flatly. "Coffee? Beer?"

"We'll be fine," Gramps said, with some annoyance, as though she was acting on her own initiative and not in response to his request. His wife, if that's who she was, disappeared without another word. None of them touched the snacks.

"You girls want to take a seat?" He gestured toward the less cluttered end of the paperwork table. The three lowered themselves into patched vinyl office chairs. Gramps said, "I couldn't tell you all this before. I don't trust the phone."

Lila said, "Understood. Maybe you can tell my sister a little about your history out here, and the business."

Gramps hesitated. He leveled a serious look at Jane, then back at Lila. "Not to offend," he said, "but I don't know your sister."

"You can tell her anything you can tell me."

He seemed to think about it for a minute, then nodded. "All right, then," he said, and turned to Jane. "So, I've been out here for about forty years. I used to work at a little bike shop in Bozeman in the seventies, then when my boss retired I bought him out, and I bought another shop in town, both of which I still own. I got a reputation for fixing Indians, and when guys from the Northwest would roll into Sturgis every summer, they'd stop in my shop."

Lila touched Jane's arm and said, "There's a big bike rally in Sturgis every August."

"The biggest," Gramps went on. "It got so I never had the parts I needed. So I started going to auctions, visiting junkyards, driving out to visit old dudes who were supposed to have big collections rotting in barns, and I'd come home with Indian parts, but also all these other bikes. I rented a warehouse in town, and then around 1990 bought this place. It used to be a ranch where some hippies were trying to raise llamas, and that didn't work out. They were customers of mine."

"The llama hippies rode Indians?" Jane asked.

"No, they weren't bike customers." He explained that, back in Bozeman in the seventies, there was a guy at the bike shop where he worked who sold weed and quaaludes out of the garage. Eventually this guy aged out of the business — bike repair and drugs both — and Gramps took over. "That's how I got to be called Gramps," he said. "That guy was old, so that was what they called him. When I took over, they just kept using the name." For a while, the shop's owner was oblivious to what was going on; when he found out, he tried to fire Gramps. They agreed on a cut for the owner to take. "But eventually I had to force him out."

Gramps shrugged. There was a casual indifference to the gesture that sparked recognition in Jane. Forcing the shop owner out probably meant intimidation, violence. His story continued with an expansion into cocaine, weapons; he dabbled in vintage firearms for a short while but quickly realized that he could serve as a supplier of unregistered weapons for the wholesalers who supplied him. From there it was a short hop to forcing out the wholesalers. Jane was dimly aware of what this might entail. It was clear Gramps relished telling the story of his rise; his earlier reticence was an act.

"Anyway," Gramps said, "I eventually sold off the drugs operation, though I still maintain a stake. It was profitable but not interesting. Also, people wanted methamphetamine and I didn't feel like dealing with the assholes I'd need to deal with to get it. The guns and bikes I like, and I like getting my hands on them." As if to illustrate, he cracked his knuckles.

At this point a deep sigh issued from behind them. Jane turned to find that Ellie hadn't actually left; she was sitting on a folding chair by the door, sprawled like a teenager. She was rubbing something off one of her fingernails. Gramps glared, but she didn't look up.

In his line of work, Gramps went on, you get a lot of unusual people. Ex-cons, outcasts, conspiracy theorists. "Back in the seventies and eighties," he said, "a lot of these people were into UFOs." Montana had a long history of UFO conspiracy, he explained; one of the first films ever supposedly depicting alien spacecraft was taken in Great Falls in the fifties. The objects turned out to be fighter jets from nearby Malmstrom Air Force Base. A quarter century later, there was another incident at Malmstrom; some nuclear missile control systems malfunctioned just after unexplained lights appeared overhead. Investigations were inconclusive, but Malmstrom had become an object of intense curiosity for "UFO freaks," Gramps said.

"There were all these UFO movies, aliens and what have you, and when guys would come to me for bikes and guns they'd talk about this shit. Mind you, it is not my thing. I think it's all bullshit. There's bases all over the place out here, and stuff flying around all the time. It's not aliens."

"You don't know that," Ellie said.

"Ellie, I didn't ask your damn opinion."

"I'm just saying, you don't know what you don't know." Her voice was slow and slurred.

"Maybe you could go back to your iPad and leave us alone here," Gramps said. The woman shrugged but didn't move from the chair.

Gramps gathered himself and continued. "Anyway, around this time, a guy showed up at the shop on a Harley, asking for a tune-up. This was before I had this place — it was the shop in Bozeman. I thought he was a narc." The guy was in his late twenties. He wore a black tee shirt tucked into then-outdated dark flared jeans, cowboy boots, and a gray Bates leather jacket a little too long for his height. His hair was short and messy and he peered out at Gramps through dusty John Lennon glasses. He asked to buy weed and Gramps told him he couldn't do that here. The guy laughed, said, "You must be Gramps," and told him to call him Jonah. "Like the guy in the whale, he said, like I never heard the name before."

There was nothing wrong with Jonah's bike. In fact there was never anything wrong with Jonah's bike, and Gramps wondered if the guy only rode it when he wanted to come see him. What he mostly seemed to want to do was talk about the "characters" who passed through the shop, whether there were any weirdos with wild theories. Jonah shared a few tales of his own, about religious zealots and UFO cults in the woods, and Gramps got the idea he was making them up in an effort to get him talking. He started logging the odometer, and sure enough. The fourth time Jonah came in, "just to chat," Gramps called him on it, and the guy laughed. "You got me," he said. "I'm with the Agency."

"Just like that?" Jane asked him. "He just told you to your face?"

Gramps shrugged. "My guess, he never really was CIA. I think he was a contractor. There was a lot of latitude in those days about how and where money got spent — the whole Agency was a mess. Maybe it still is, I don't know."

Lila said, "So somebody was paying this guy."

"Right," Gramps said. "To infiltrate the UFO people." The intensity of paranoia and speculation about UFOs and aliens had caught the attention of the government, he explained. Throughout the eighties and nineties, certain elements in the CIA and NSA had become preoccupied with parapsychology and mind control, and they wondered if the UFO phenomenon was a Soviet psyop. Could a handful of well-placed Soviet spies, posing as conspiracy theorists, foment distrust of the American military and system of government? Whoever regarded this as a possibility — "and it couldn't have gone too far up the chain, because it was fucking stupid" — had enough latitude to pay Jonah to insinuate himself into the UFO "community" and gather intel. He was looking for evidence that the UFO craze had been created by, and was under the control of, the KGB.

Gramps said, "He ended up getting chummy with these freaks. He'd travel with them to all the supposed UFO hot spots in the west, Great Falls, Cheyenne, places up along the Hi-Line. He told me he was paid in cash for his reports, so he started looking for more excuses to write reports, including making shit up and getting the yahoos to go along with it. He literally created fake blurry UFO photos by throwing various objects up in the air. Once, he saw me working on the electronics on somebody's bike and asked me if I wanted to make a few bucks creating some UFO wreckage. He wanted to photograph it and then get rid of it, and tell the yahoos the government showed up and confiscated it."

"So, if I'm hearing you right," Jane said, "Jonah was literally generating the kind of anti-government propaganda the CIA was accusing the Russians of making."

"Yeah," Gramps said, laughing. "And getting the government to pay him for it! He liked to brag about it. A couple of times he actually gave the photos he made himself to his Agency contact and told him they were recovered Russian propaganda. He said he found some old Russian military stuff in an army surplus store in Missoula, including this leather document case with Russian lettering in it. And he messed up the photos, made them look all distressed as though he dragged them out of a burning building, and stuck them in this bag, and gave the whole thing to his guy."

Jane heard a whispered voice behind her and peered over her shoulder. Ellie was staring at her. Her lips were moving. It took a moment to understand what the woman was saying: "Blah, blah, blah."

"The last time I saw him was, I dunno, I guess 2002 or so. I think the money dried up for the UFO stuff after he failed to produce the spies he claimed to have evidence of, and all anybody cared about then was the war on terror. He was also an addict, and wasn't in great shape. Maybe he's dead now. I'm giving you the impression this guy was an idiot, but he really was good at getting information out of people, and he had an ear for a great story. So, even though I didn't trust him, exactly, we were friends. I admit I liked it when he showed up. Eventually his bike really did need work, I think talking to me got him into riding for real. I'd have a guy work on it for him and we'd drink and talk."

Lila said, "Is that where our mom comes in?"

"Right. Well," Gramps said, "don't get too excited. It's not the freshest intel." He reached out toward the plate Ellie had brought, then hesitated. He glanced past Jane's shoulder at where the woman sat, and the two exchanged glares. Finally, he selected three crackers, the ones that had slid onto the table, and a piece of sausage. He resettled himself in his chair and ate.

"Jonah told me a story," Gramps said, brushing the dust off his fingertips, "that had been told to him by the guy he said was his handler — an old-school operative who'd been with the Agency since the postwar glory days, when they were trying to keep Soviet influence out of Europe. Again, I don't think Jonah was a real agent, and I sometimes wonder if this guy, his contact, just paid him as a source of entertainment. Anyway.

"Evidently there was this legend about a lady who had been working for the Agency in Central America in the eighties, a Russian speaker who could manipulate Soviet spies into giving her information. For decades the US backed a bunch of anti-communist governments in the region, goosing various dictators, supporting coups. They helped Hugo Banzer kick out Torres in Bolivia, then they tracked Torres down and killed him. They were paying Noriega in Panama, supposedly to oppose the drug trade, but instead he was going around behind their backs to launder money for drug dealers. They backed the contras in Nicaragua, helped overthrow Arbenz in Guatemala.

"Anyway, they were always looking for Soviet influence down there, whenever anybody opposed them. So they would send agents to find out. And one of them was this lady, the Holy Ghost, who could get information out of Soviet intelligence officers."

"You mean," Lila said, "fuck dudes."

Ellie laughed.

"Yeah, well," Gramps said. "Around when Bush invaded Panama, the lady disappeared. The Agency figured she got caught and killed, but they never found any evidence of it. But then, a few years later — this was the early aughts, when Jonah was still coming to see me — a rumor was going around that she was living in the mountains somewhere, she had some kind of horticultural research lab and was getting paid by an up-and-coming cartel to develop a new kind of coca plant, way more potent than the known varieties, and denser, too, so you could get a much higher yield in a much smaller space. There were stories about her showing up in various towns and villages; the locals called her Espiritu Santo, the Holy Ghost, as a kind of joke. It's this orchid that grows in the hills. And the lady acted kind of self-important, and she was white, so. Holy Ghost."

Jane said, "And you're telling us . . ."

"This is our mom," Lila said, beaming. "Mom's the Holy Ghost."

"She was a CIA agent?" Jane said. "Turned . . . cocaine grower?"

"It fits," Lila said. "I suspected it even when we were kids. Child of diplomats, master of languages, mysterious absences."

"I still don't buy it."

"Think about it," Lila said, her excitement clearly growing. "If she was CIA, Central America's where they would have sent her in the eighties, right? And the coca — remember her plants? She didn't just *have plants,* she was practically running a lab. All the tweezing and snipping, jotting things down in her little notebook, daubing at pollen with a brush. She was doing research."

The two stared at each other. Lila said, "There's one other thing. Remember the postcards?"

"Postcards?"

Lila reached into her satchel and pulled out a wrinkled paper sack. From it she produced a small stack of cards.

"Are these . . . the ones we got from Aunt Ruth?"

Lila nodded. Jane remembered them now — handed over with a shrug years ago, almost as an afterthought, a consolation prize. At first they'd seemed exciting, but there was barely anything written on them. Jane was surprised her sister had kept them.

Lila shuffled one card to the top of the stack and handed them over to Jane. The card depicted a mountainous green landscape, photographed from the air. A bold legend read PARQUE NACIONAL SANTA FE, PANAMÁ. A white mist hung over distant hills; a waterfall emptied into a shimmering lake. Jane turned the card over. Printed Spanish text described this forest reserve in Veraguas Province, its many plant and animal species. The card was addressed to Aunt Ruth; Jane recognized the handwriting immediately. Two canceled stamps celebrated a Panamanian essayist and an international conference on nutrition. There was nothing written in the space allotted for a personal message. She idly flipped through the rest of the stack.

"The postmark says Santa Fe," Lila said.

"That's just where you'd go if you were going to the park," Gramps said, somewhat dismissively.

"You think she's there?" Jane asked.

"She *was* there," Lila said. "At some point." She snatched back the pile. "And this one's from David . . . Colón . . . Santa Catalina. She was buying these and mailing them from those places. Montería, Colombia. Puerto Jiménez, Costa Rica."

"Yeah, but also . . ." Jane gestured for the cards, and Lila handed them back. "Paris . . . Los Angeles . . . Prague?" The Prague card read, "You'd like the absinthe." She was starting to become annoyed — is this what she'd just unraveled her life for? "Lila. We are hearing, thirdhand, that somebody who *might* be Mom toured the world *two decades ago*. Drinking booze and probably getting laid. And *one* of the places she went was Central America. Which is big."

"Well," Gramps said.

"What?"

"I asked around. Whether it's her or not, the Holy Ghost is still alive, and still operating."

Lila said, "Asked around?"

"There's a guy I use for charter flights," Gramps explained. "Matías Gil. He's got a fleet of blocked planes he runs out of Seattle."

"Wait, what are blocked planes?"

"People think that all flights in and out of the US are publicly tracked. But if you meet the criteria, you can get a plane blocked from public view, legally, by the FAA. The bar's not very high; all you need is a legitimate-sounding business reason. For instance, let's say you're a tech CEO, and you have a deal with a Korean factory to make your products. If people can see that you're flying to, say, Zhengzhou, China, instead of Pangyo, your stock price could be affected."

Jane said, "So, if you're rich enough, the government lets you have secret flights?"

"Right," Gramps said. "My guy has a bunch of these planes, for ferrying around these bigwigs. You just go to the airport and get on the plane—no luggage scanning, no TSA. The Holy Ghost is a customer of his."

Lila said, "He just straight-up told you this? Isn't he supposed to be discreet?"

Gramps scowled. "We go way back. Anyway, the point is, she's here. There's some kind of disturbance in the supply chain out in Seattle, where the coke comes into North America. My guy thinks she's trying to straighten it out."

"Jane," Lila said, leaning close. "It's *her.* I know it."

"I don't—"

In the pocket of her jacket, Jane's phone rang. She pulled it out, stared at the small screen. Recognized Chance's number. "Chance?"

"It's me," said Chloe.

# 19

# Nestor, NY: *Then*

———————

Jane's instinct, seeing George Framingham step onto the auditorium stage, was to stand up and leave. And she did stand up. She turned to Lila, expecting a similar reaction. But her sister wasn't looking back at her; she was gazing, eyes narrowed, past Mr. Framingham, past the stage, her lips moving in a barely perceptible rhythm, like a secret prayer.

"What should we do?" Jane whispered.

Lila appeared startled. "Do?"

"Should we leave?"

Her eyebrows rose. "No. Why?"

Jane sat back down.

"All right, folks," Mr. Framingham said, clapping his hands together. "Welcome to the tryouts for the fall drama. I am your director. You may call me George."

"Hi, George!" some boy shouted.

"Hi to you as well. *Bombshells* is a play by Gage Hemming-Farro about brave women, aviation factory workers during the Second World War, wronged by their government and by capitalism, who fight back against the system. They win their battle, but the play makes clear that the larger battle—that of women against a society that doesn't respect them, and of the worker against the state—has not yet been won. It's a romance, a history play, and a courtroom drama. There are plenty of roles, big and small, so you'll all be cast. There are two leads: Betty Faith, aircraft manufacturer, injured on the job, who fights for the safety of all patriotic wage earners. And August Sterling, factory owner, who wants to keep the workers down."

"Subtle!" shouted the boy from earlier.

"It's not," George said, eliciting mild laughter. "Oh boy, I'm going to like working with you. What's your name?"

"Aaron!"

"Aaron, we're going to be good friends. All right, I'm going to pass around this clipboard. Print your name and student ID, clearly, please, and I'll give you some pages to study. In about half an hour, I'll start calling you up one by one. Cast list will go up in the morning."

"Are we seriously doing this?" Jane muttered as the clipboard reached them.

"It was your idea."

"But it's *him*."

Lila said, "Aren't you curious?"

"No."

But she was. And she was already savoring the moment when their mother found out. How angry she'd be. How powerful Jane would feel.

"We can't tell her," Lila said, reading her mind. She wrote her name and ID on the form and passed it to Jane.

"Why not?"

"She can keep us out of drama club."

"No, she can't."

Lila shot her a look. "Sure she can. We're fifteen. Even if we wanted to go to court to be emancipated, we'd have to wait until February. And even then, it would be hard."

Jane shouldn't have been surprised, but she was. Emancipated? "You . . . researched this?"

Lila nodded. "We'd have to get a lawyer to represent us, for free, I guess. We'd also need to be self-supporting, so, like, a job and an apartment. We'd have to basically run away from home."

"Jesus."

"Which we could do. We've effectively been heads of our household for years. Money is the problem. We'd live together, of course. Maybe get jobs at the health food store? Someplace we could walk, since we can't drive until February, either."

A kid said, "Hey, pass the clipboard."

Jane hurriedly filled it out and handed it over. "This is, like, a serious plan?" she said to Lila.

"I guess? Job, apartment, turn sixteen, get a lawyer, go to court. That would be the way to do it."

"What about Dad?" Jane said.

"What about him?"

"We do all the cooking and laundry."

"What," Lila said. "You think he'd die?"

"Well, no, but—"

"I know you have a soft spot for him," Lila said. "But he's a loser. He lets Mom abuse him and he's a drunk."

"Well, he drinks, but—"

"Jane," Lila said, growing angry, "he is literally an alcoholic. You've dragged the recycling to the curb, have you seen how many bottles are in there?"

"I guess I didn't notice."

"People probably think we're running a nightclub or something."

They studied the script they'd been given and watched as the other kids tried out. The loud kid, Aaron, was pretty good—he affected a cruel snarl that really seemed to fit the sinister boss character. Another boy seemed a shoo-in as Betty Faith's lawyer. Jane thought she did all right as Betty, but then two other girls, upperclassmen, absolutely killed it, and it was clear she wouldn't get the part. She had wondered if Mr. Framingham—George—would acknowledge her, or even remember her from the theater camp four summers ago. But aside from a lingering glance when she stood up, he betrayed nothing.

When Lila took the stage, she asked if she could read for the lawyer.

"I'd like to hear you for Betty," George said.

"Gage Hemming-Farro is supposed to be a feminist playwright, isn't he?" Lila said. "The lawyer could be a woman, couldn't she?"

A titter from the group. Wearily, George said, "Carry on."

The next morning, the cast list was posted on the stage door. Jane had gotten the part of Marge, one of Betty's three co-workers—a fairly meaty supporting role. Lila didn't get the lawyer part, but George had indeed cast a girl, an upperclassman named Sara.

"Touché," Lila said, squinting at the list. "I'm Juror Number Four."

"How did you know about Gage what's-his-name being a feminist? Did you look him up?"

Lila raised an eyebrow. "Seriously?"

"What."

"You didn't figure it out? It's obvious."

"Figure what out?"

"Hey, move it," somebody said behind them. They stepped out of the way and moved down the hall toward homeroom.

"The name," Lila said. "It's in the name."

"What is?"

"*George Framingham.* It's an anagram. He wrote the play."

"Oh my god."

Lila rolled her eyes. "He's just dying for somebody to say it. I'm not going to give him the satisfaction."

In retrospect, Jane would consider that fall to be the happiest of her life. For the first time, it felt like the twins were making real friends — they drank and smoked with the theater kids, went out late to the diner, gossiped, fooled around. Jane dated Aaron, and then another boy, James, and then Aaron again. Nell Timmons, a condescending and imperious thespian who couldn't wait to move to New York and forget about all of them, became everyone's nemesis and foil. On the weekends, George had Sunday morning pancake brunches for anyone who could drag themselves to his weird little house in the woods. You could only get there via a twisting gravel road that led behind the public pool and driving range. The place was long, low, a little saggy; he'd bought it for a song, he told them, with money he made licensing his plays to Samuel French. (Someone had finally mentioned the acronym to him and he'd copped to it, proudly.) A large, overgrown, sloping back yard led to the water, where a rowboat was tied to a crooked pier. There was a fire pit with benches around it, and he let them smoke weed there when the weather turned cold.

Gradually Jane's resentment of him faded away. Gradually her mother began to seem like the bad actor, George the innocent bystander. He paid attention to them, praised their skill on stage, their style, their personalities. When was the last time their mother had anything for Lila and her but criticism? She was absent nearly all that fall, anyway; it was easy concealing the play from her, because she wasn't there to notice it. When she was home, she was perpetually in a state of agitation and distraction. Even the solarium was being neglected; things were drying up and crumbling to dust, and the mice had returned.

Most of the kids assumed George was gay, and the twins did nothing to disabuse them of the idea. But halfway through the semester, they noticed Sara, the lead, directing doleful looks at George during breaks; Aaron saw her try to kiss him when he was getting into his car after school one day. He pushed her away, but in the end, she got in the passenger seat and they drove off together.

"It's pathetic," Nell said, at the diner the night after their first dress rehearsal. Sara had stopped coming out with them; she wouldn't talk to anyone about what was going on. "She's hopeless."

"She'll get over it," James said. "It's a crush." He shot an embarrassed look at Jane.

"Yeah, don't blame her, she's sensitive," another girl said to Nell.

"At least he's being a gentleman about it," somebody agreed.

Lila and Jane exchanged a look but didn't say anything. Was he, in fact, being a gentleman about it? The performance run began, and Sara didn't seem to let her feelings get in the way of her acting; the play went off without a hitch, and they packed the house all three nights. George threw a kids-only cast party at his place — a rager. Parents were told to pick the children up at the top of the drive; one or two of them made their way all the way down to the house and George met them there, gently pushing their child to the car door. No parents inside, please! "This is a sacred space. Theater nerds only!" George himself didn't drink or do drugs, something he proclaimed at every available opportunity when parents were around, and it went a long way toward reassuring them that their kids were safe. At the party's ragged end, a few parents had already turned in for the night, so George drove as many home as could fit into his Subaru station wagon. They packed into the back like clowns; Jane and Lila spilled out into a cloud of exhaust and staggered to bed.

Sara wasn't at the party. When school started again in the new year, she'd dropped out. Jane walked past her house one snowy morning, hoping to find out what was up, and discovered that new people had moved in. Her school email returned messages with an error. She was just gone.

# 20

# Bridger Range, MT to Coeur d'Alene, ID: *Now*

⸺

C hloe?" Jane said. "Is that you?"

"Yes."

"Hold on, sweetie, hold on." She turned to Lila and Gramps. "I'm going outside for a minute." She thought she caught a sour expression on her sister's face — irritation that the unveiling of her grand plan had been interrupted? — or perhaps she was reading too much into it. She got up, threw herself against the panic bar of the heavy steel door, ran down the hall and onto the porch.

"Chloe? Are you there?"

"I said I was."

"It's so good to hear your voice, baby. Are you all right?"

"I'm fine."

Jane knew her tone — she was angry. "What is it, kiddo?" She tried to say it brightly, but she sounded like a desperate lunatic.

"Mom, is this true? Grandma said you ran off with your *sister*?"

"Listen to me," Jane said. "I'm going to explain all of this to you someday, and I'm sorry I didn't tell you before. I promised your dad I wouldn't."

"Dad said she was *dead*."

"Yes, I know. I'm sorry. Your father —"

"And Grandma said you went to jail? I was literally born in *jail*?"

Jane thought her head was going to explode. Keeping this from her until she was older had been Susan's idea! Chance had agreed, and Jane had only gone along with it to keep the peace. She said, "Chloe, please listen! I am coming back next week. I will tell you everything."

"So it's true? You're a criminal?"

"It wasn't like that."

A silence from Chloe.

"Listen, Chloe, please wait until I come home and explain. Your father didn't want us to tell you about my past until you were older, and I agreed to it. I am very surprised your grandmother did this."

"Is it true you're not coming back?"

"Chloe, *no*. Aunt Lila thinks our mother is still alive, and that's why I went on this trip. I am coming back soon."

"Mom," Chloe said, crying now. "I am confused. For real. Why do you have a new number? You wouldn't change your number unless you were leaving us."

"It's temporary! It's not —"

"Are you and Dad getting a divorce? I heard him talking to Grandma."

"Baby," Jane said, "I promise you. I will explain everything when I get back next week."

"So you are getting divorced."

"Chloe. I don't know. I don't know what's going on. But I would never leave you. I will never leave you."

"Why should I believe you now!" Chloe said. Jane could hear Chance in the background now, telling her that was enough.

"I'm sorry I lied about prison. I'm sorry I lied about your aunt. I hadn't heard from her in a decade, we really did think she was dead." Another lie, and she hated herself for telling it.

"I have to go, Mom."

"I will never leave you, sweetie. I promise."

"She didn't hear that," Chance said. "She went to her room."

Hearing his voice made every muscle in her body tense up. The cheap phone creaked in her hand. "How could you do this," Jane said. "Frighten her. Break the promise you made me make. There are easier ways to end our marriage, Chance, if that's what you want. Not this."

"We both know I should have taken her away when she was born. I shouldn't have let you keep her."

There was a silence between them as they both absorbed this. Jesus Christ. "How could you," Jane said again. But he had hung up.

She threw the phone as hard as she could, for the second time in as many days. It skittered to a stop on the gravel lot. She collapsed onto the porch bench and lowered her head into her hands. After a moment, she heard footsteps and felt a hand on her shoulder.

Lila said, "I heard most of that."

"This is all your fucking fault," Jane said.

"Hm" was the reply. The hand massaged her shoulders and Jane let it. After a while, Lila said, "I can make up for it now. I've been following your life closely for a while. I've been . . . following Susan and Chance."

Jane sat up straight and pushed Lila's hand off her shoulder. "What the fuck is that supposed to mean?"

"I told you I knew things about them. Mostly Susan and your father-in-law. Chance doesn't have his hands in anything bad, though his boss, Jacob C. Kemp of Onteo Stone and Landscaping, is a tax cheat who violently abuses his wife."

"*Lila.*"

"Susan's money is mostly ill-gotten," she went on. "Your father-in-law, Charles, is a real estate investment criminal."

"He's just some kind of local landlord."

Lila shook her head. "He's a slumlord with very high-up connections in state and local governments. When you were in jail, one of his properties burned down, an apartment building on the inlet in Nestor. The satellite office of a medical center is there now?"

"I know where you mean."

"So, those apartments. Your father-in-law had wanted to tear the place down and cut a deal with the hospital. But the zoning board voted three to two to deny the permits, after meeting with the tenants. So then he tried to evict everybody, and the tenants' association got a lawyer and fought it. Eventually the lawyer was accused of possession of child pornography. There was an investigation, and he was cleared of criminal wrongdoing, but by then he'd been disbarred, and he hanged himself within a year. When the building burned, four people died, three adults and an infant. Pretty soon after that, three people on the zoning board, the ones who had opposed the project, resigned and never talked to anyone in the press about why. They were replaced by three people sympathetic to your father-in-law, who were appointed thanks to a sudden change of heart on the part of several previously recalcitrant members of the town board. The permits went through and the medical center went up."

Jane just blinked at her now.

"Everything here that sounds bad, was bad. The fire was arson, the cops could have proved it, but they didn't have a suspect. Your father-in-law's money led me to an expert in Buffalo I've come across before in my research — I'm pretty sure he set the fire. I've also gotten access to bank accounts and private correspondence of the disgraced lawyer, two of the zoning board members, and one of the town board members. Everyone was either threatened or bribed."

"Jesus Christ."

"Oh, I think the lawyer's suicide was real. But the kiddie pictures were planted."

"How — How long have you known all this?"

"A long time. It's been a hobby, I guess." She looked out over the hills. "I can bring any of these people down whenever I want, Jane. I can expose them. There's a reporter at the Nestor paper who's been working on all this stuff for years, and I can threaten to dump all of this information into her lap. We can use this information as leverage, to make sure you keep custody of your daughter. You can make it clear that you have the power to destroy them. Charles, anyway. It's up to you."

"I don't want any more illegal things in my life," Jane said, knowing how naive she sounded.

Lila said, "I know. But sometimes the law protects the wrong people. And somebody should protect the right ones. Especially when they're people I love."

"I missed you," Jane said, before she could stop herself.

"I missed you, too. I almost reached out a thousand times. You were always right there, close enough to touch. But I knew you wouldn't want it. I knew you thought things were stable, even though I could see some of the rot underneath. I've always had your best interests in mind, I swear."

They sat in silence for a few minutes. The air was cool and the sun was bright. A crow landed beside Jane's phone and began to work at it with its beak. Inside, Gramps and Ellie began to argue about something. Jane said, "Don't harm Chance. It's not his fault."

"All right."

"Was Susan aware of any of this?"

"I honestly don't know. She wasn't directly involved, anyway."

"I don't care what you do to Charles."

Lila nodded. "Will you come to Seattle with me?"

"Yes."

"Well then," she said, standing. "I'll let Gramps know we're going. Do you want to wait for me out here?"

Jane nodded. "I don't like him," she said.

"Yeah, no, I get it. He's an ally, not a friend." The two nodded at each other, then Lila went inside.

Five minutes south of Gramps's compound, on their way back to the interstate, they passed a black SUV with tinted windows, just sitting on a wide spot of shoulder, in plain view. Jane looked back and saw them pulling onto the road behind them.

"You've gotta be fucking kidding me," Lila said.

"Jesus Christ. Fucking Susan!"

Lila adjusted the rearview. "Jane, I don't think it's her."

Jane was casting her mind back to her departure from Nestor, the days before. She hadn't told any of them where she was going. She hadn't written Lila's address down anywhere, as she'd requested. So—

Oh no.

"No, Lila, I think Chloe told them. I said the name of your town out loud. On the phone. She must have heard me and told her father."

"Well," Lila said, "I wish you hadn't done that, but . . . again, I doubt it. I know all the guys they'd use and these guys aren't them. Also, that wouldn't explain how they found us here."

"They must be tracking us again, somehow."

"No. The car's clean."

"So, how . . . we haven't seen them since Sioux Falls, right? How do they . . . ?"

"The only way they know where we are," Lila said, "is if they know where we're going."

"Do *we* even know where we're going?" The car was keeping a decent distance behind them, not close enough to be threatening. They just wanted to remind Jane and Lila they were there.

"We're going to a private airport, run by Gramps's guy. These have to be his people."

"If they know that's where we're headed, why would they follow us there?"

Lila scowled. "I don't know."

"Well, what are we going to do?"

"I don't know. Nothing, I guess. Ignore them. Let them be bored."

They drove south to meet the interstate, then headed west, where the Virgin Mary stood like a robotic sentinel in the hills over Butte and over the poisoned pit that used to be the rest of Butte. They refueled in Missoula at sunset while their tail waited patiently at the edge of the parking lot, and checked into a motel outside Coeur d'Alene for the night. The SUV didn't pull over with them, just rolled slowly past and out of sight around the bend.

In their room, Jane tried to read a paperback while Lila tapped away at a laptop computer. "Do you want to know what I'm doing?" she asked, and Jane said, "I do not." In the morning they ate at a diner attached to a truck stop, where, halfway through their eggs, two men in suits walked through the door, passed their table without a glance, and settled into a booth in the corner.

"I think it's them," Jane said. "The guy facing us is the one who opened the curtain in Sioux Falls."

"No sidearms."

"Well, that's good news, I guess."

Lila craned her neck. "They must have parked around the corner." She got up, followed a sign to the rest rooms, then came back a few minutes later. "Their car's here. Washington plates. So, not your mother-in-law."

The men ordered, sipped their coffee, and ate in silence.

Jane said, "What are they *doing*?"

"Eating breakfast, looks like."

"You know what I mean."

"Let's fuck with them." Lila signaled to the waiter. "Bring us their bill," she said, gesturing at the men.

The waiter raised an eyebrow. He opened his notebook, ripped off a ticket, and handed it to Lila. Then he filled out one for them, too.

Lila slapped two twenties and a ten down on the checks without a glance at them. A few minutes later, they watched the waiter talk with the men, point over at their table. One of the men raised a hand in confused gratitude. When they passed the sisters on their way out, they didn't spare them a glance.

"Let's go," Lila said. Out the door, around the corner. The two men were standing outside the SUV, thirty feet away. One of them, on the passenger side, was short, stocky, with big ears. On the driver's side, the other, the guy who'd opened the curtain, was taller and had a prominent, blocky chin. Their suits were shiny, their hair cut military-close. They were cleaning some trash out of the car — receipts, drink cups — and tossing it into a trash can at the curb.

"Just keep walking, fast," Lila said. "Don't slow down or hesitate. Get the short one."

"Okay," Jane said, sweat breaking out under her arms, the nerve endings tingling in her fingertips.

"Go."

They came at the men briskly, jauntily even, as though they were their boyfriends. It didn't take long to get there. There was just enough time, only a moment, for Jane to register their expressions of puzzlement before Lila grabbed Chin's arm with both hands, twisted it, and slammed the hand into the car window. Ears allowed his gaze to be drawn to this unexpected event, giving Jane the opportunity to knee him in the balls and then, when he doubled over, brace herself and drive that same knee into his face. She felt his nose crack, and the man fell back on his ass. Lila stamped Chin in the knee, and he dropped to the ground with a grunt and rolled, keening, onto his side.

There was a guy they met in Flagstaff twenty years ago called Rayburn. He was one of the few rock-solid allies they'd had during their six years together on the run, a disabled Iraq War veteran who'd undergone an epiphanic conversion — both religious and philosophical — while recovering from PTSD. He had gotten them out of a jam once and they paid him back by helping him run his dojo for a few months and serving as helpmates in his ramshackle suburban house. It was the longest they'd stayed in one place. Rayburn had made a whole personal philosophy out of the idea of disarming the aggressor: first and ideally with words (in his case, usually about Jesus and salvation), secondarily by using the attacker's own momentum, and, as a last resort, by modest, carefully applied force. He taught them his self-defense method and they taught it to teenage girls, leaving out the Bible lessons.

Jane liked step one of Rayburn's "Trinity of Tactics," as he called it. Project confidence and calm. Don't betray fear. Speak loudly and clearly. If your attacker is trying to rob you, give them what they want—it isn't worth risking injury just to protect some credit cards. If you think they want to rape you, let them know you're not an easy target. Make it clear you've gotten a good look at their face. Tell them you're going to fight. You're not helpless, and you don't want to have to be attacked to prove it. Jane would end up talking herself out of a few fights her first few months in prison, usually by bringing up her pregnancy, which wasn't yet obvious. She hadn't gotten into this kind of situation since she was released, but that's what she would probably use even now—she would claim to be pregnant.

Lila tended to give step one short shrift, though, both in her self-defense classes and out in the world. She thought it was better to skip to step two. She *liked* to skip to step two. Here, in this Idaho truck-stop parking lot, she and Jane had sailed straight to step three.

There was a pause in the action. Jane took in their SUV, a very shiny, recent-model Chevy Suburban. It was enormous, high enough to make climbing inside a presumably embarrassing experience, at least for Ears. A decal on the driver's side, at the rear of the vehicle, bore the number 05. So, part of a fleet. It was parked two slots away from the Volvo. Theirs were the only two vehicles on this side of the building, save for two big rigs, parked fifty yards away in their long diagonal slots.

Lila was clearly a few mental steps ahead of her. She reached into Chin's jacket pocket and pulled out a ring of keys.

"Aw, come on!" he managed to stammer.

The truck stop was situated at the base of a high grassy hill dotted with scrub. Between the hill and the parking lot flowed a low, wide, rocky creek. Jane could see, off in the distance, a couple of men in waders, fly-casting into the shadows beneath a stand of quaking aspens. Rather than a guard rail, the lot was separated from the creek by a crooked row of crumbling curb stops, spray-painted yellow.

Lila strode to the driver's-side door of the SUV, climbed in, and started the engine. She pulled out of the spot as the men rolled themselves clear, then cut the wheel hard, leaving the car pointed at the highway entrance ramp. She revved the engine.

"Come *on*!" Chin repeated, scrambling to his feet, spitting blood. He staggered over in front of the car, waving his arms. "Lady! Give it back! Seriously!"

Lila's face was invisible in the windshield's glare, as the car idled. A few seconds passed. Then, as though in surrender, the driver's-side door opened. Jane heard the telltale clunk of the doors locking. Lila hopped down to the pavement and slammed the door shut in one smooth motion, and the car, which she had put into reverse, began to roll slowly backward toward the creek.

"Fuck fuck fuck!" Chin said, and began to give chase. He passed Lila, stumbling, and she ignored the opportunity to trip him; clearly she was content merely to draw him away from the scene. She made her way over to where Ears still sat on the ground, his cupped hands full of blood.

"You didn't have to do that," he blubbered.

"You didn't have to follow us," Lila said.

The man moaned. "Yes, we did!"

The two women calmly walked to the Volvo. The SUV had nearly reached the creek, with Chin madly scrabbling at the door handle. He now ran around to the front and grabbed the fender, in an effort to slow the truck. His shiny black oxfords scraped the gravel as the truck continued, perhaps more slowly but probably not.

The events in the lot had caught the attention of the fishermen in the distance. As they watched, the pickup's rear wheels bumped over the curb stops and began their descent of the bank.

The sisters climbed into the Volvo, rolled the windows down, and watched. For a moment, as Lila started the engine and began to pull away, it seemed as though the front wheels of the SUV would arrest its motion. It came to a stop and a little shudder ran through its frame. Chin released the fender and stood, panting, appearing to assess the situation.

Then the front wheels heaved up and rolled over the stops, and the SUV, like an infant pushed at last from the womb, slid swiftly down the bank to be baptized. Chin let out a wordless shout as the truck disappeared from view.

Ears gave them the finger. Lila honked, and they both waved. A minute later, the Volvo was back on the interstate, headed toward Seattle.

# 21

# Nestor, NY: *Then*

The drama club did three one-act student plays that winter, one of which Lila had written. George told her that this was a rare honor for a sophomore. It was a murder mystery about two sisters, serial killers of rich, abusive men whose alibis depended upon nobody realizing they were twins. Of course they played the twins. The play was a hit, particularly with audience members who didn't see the twist coming, and even though they were fraternal, not identical. "Close enough, if you're good enough," George had told them, "and you are." He embraced them in the wings on opening night, told them they were "sexy and dangerous." His hand lingered on Jane's bare arm — the play had ended with her wearing a black silk négligé that she altered by hand, to meet the principal's standards for modesty.

George was hot for her. The possibility had occurred to her early in the fall semester. At the time, it disgusted her, but as the semester wore on, she got used to the idea, began to savor it. She thought often of how enraged their mother would be if she ever saw the way George looked at her: intimate, knowing. Understanding had passed between them, and he had judged Jane to be her mother's superior. "You're so controlled, so mature," he'd told her during rehearsals for the one-act, during a smoke break in the parking lot. "You're not dominated by your emotions. It's powerful, it's attractive."

"Thanks, Georgie," Jane told him, blowing smoke in his face. "Better not let the other kids hear you say that."

"They already know you're the best, and they know I think so."

"You're supposed to treat us all like we're equal."

"I'm supposed to," he said. "But you're not."

Now, backstage at the one-acts, she realized she wanted to sleep with him. Lila knew immediately. "Oh my god, Jane, no," she said, as George slunk off and the girls headed for the bathroom to change.

"I'm not going to actually *do* it."

"He slept with Mom. And probably Crissy, and Amber. And Sara."

"Not Sara!"

"No?" Lila said.

"Maybe."

"Maybe he took what he wanted."

"Come on, Lila."

The bathroom was full of girls talking excitedly. Nell Timmons saw them and rolled her eyes. Jane stuck out her tongue at her. "She disappeared from school," Lila said, her voice low. "Then she moved away, never contacted a single one of us again. What the hell else could have happened?"

Jane shrugged off her costume, pulled on her jeans. "Her dad got a new job, I'm sure."

"Her mother was the one with the powerful job. I think her dad just worked at the guitar shop."

"Whatever. She didn't like us, that's why she never got in touch. Anyway, don't worry, I'm not going to bone him, I'm not an idiot."

Until this point, their parents hadn't seemed to notice that they were acting in plays. Neither had asked where they were every evening; it was assumed that they had their own lives, their own friends, and didn't want to be bothered. Their mother had been home since a few days before Christmas, which passed without acknowledgment.

But on the second night of the one-acts, Lila gripped Jane's arm backstage and said, "She's here."

"Who?"

"Mom. In the audience. She looks furious."

"Jesus," Jane said. "How do you think she found out?"

"No idea. Saw a poster, maybe."

Jane peeked out from between the curtains. There she was, wrapped in a fur coat, staring daggers at the stage. Every minute or so she scanned the room, as if planning to fight her way out. "Do you think she knows about George?"

"She's holding the program. She has to know."

Their performance was uneven, though the audience didn't seem to care. At the end, George joined them onstage for their curtain call. He stood between Lila and Jane, arms around them, and let his hand brush down Jane's back as the audience rose and applauded.

They expected she would be waiting for them after the show, but she wasn't. She wasn't waiting for them at home, either. They asked their father where she was and he didn't know — appeared, in fact, pained by the question. Her car was gone, but her suitcases were in her bedroom — formerly the spare room, which she'd taken over the year before — still half-packed from her last disappearance.

The plays finished strong, but the cast party at George's was muted, maybe because of the weather, which was as cold as Jane had ever felt — nearly ten below. George tried to start a fire in the fire pit, but it was too cold and nobody wanted to sit around it. It fizzled out. In the kitchen, briefly alone with him, Jane leaned drunkenly against George, and his fingers brushed her hip. "Hm," she said, and he withdrew. In the end, the sisters got a ride home with Aaron's father.

Their mother woke them the next morning by switching on the overhead light and kicking their beds.

"What the fuck?" Jane said, startling out of sleep.

"Don't get up," she said. "I've been driving, trying to decide what to do. And I've decided that there is nothing to do. You have already decided."

Lila, squinting, rubbing her face, said, "What?"

"I tried to protect you from that man. You clearly have no respect for my judgment."

"Oh god," Jane said. "He's just the theater director, we're not going to marry him."

"If you can't see what he is, you deserve what is coming to you."

"What is that supposed to mean?"

Lila said, "It means he's a predator."

She pointed at Lila. "One of you understands."

Jane could see, behind her in the hall, the bags she'd been living out of. "What time is it, even?"

"I wish I could say that I regret nothing. But I have many regrets. I hope you learn to make better decisions than I have." She shook her head. "You and your spy games. I thought you were smarter."

"Jesus Christ, Mom!" Jane screamed, pounding her pillow. "Turn out the light and fuck off already!"

"Good luck," Lila said, soberly.

Their mother stared at her, as though noticing something for the first time. Then she reached out, flicked off the light switch, and walked out.

Early in the new year, Jane met a senior named Chance. He wasn't her type—rugged, sandy-haired, outfielder on the school baseball team—but he was nice and had a charming air of innocence, as though he thought the world had been made just for him and would never steer him wrong. She expected never to talk to him again, but he called her the next day and arranged a date—an actual date, where he picked her up in a truck and brought her to a restaurant, like an adult. This led to more dates. After a while, she realized he thought he was her boyfriend.

"Why do you hang out with those people?" he asked her over dinner one night, referring to her theater friends. The twins weren't great singers, but they had tried out for the spring musical, *Into the Woods*. They were cast in minor roles, Jane Rapunzel and Lila Florinda. They spent their sixteenth birthday smoking weed and eating french fries in Aaron's cast-stuffed car, roaring through the dark. Chance had been hurt that Jane wouldn't go out with him instead and was waiting for her at home when she returned in the middle of the night. He was clutching a present, a little gold bracelet in a pink-wrapped box, which he'd been saving up for, for weeks.

"They're my friends, Chance," she told him, kissing his cheek. "I wanted to spend my birthday with my friends."

"You could have invited me," he said.

"You said you don't like them!"

"I didn't *say* that."

Once the show got underway, Jane ignored Chance's calls and began to savor her flirtation with George, smoking with him on breaks, talking about her future, imagining her mother seething with fury.

"You should consider coming to work for me in the summer," he suggested one night in March. "Rachel is leaving for college."

"I don't know who that is," Jane said. They were standing in the parking lot, apart from the group, watching the last snowflakes of winter die on the pavement.

"Oh, right—I guess it was a while ago that you came to camp."

"Ah, so you do remember."

"Of course I remember, Jane. You're a memorable person."

"Right," she said. "I think you're thinking of my mom?"

He turned his head to blow smoke and left it there, gazing up at the blank, low sky. "I didn't mean to embarrass you then."

"Please. She's the embarrassment."

"How's she doing these days?" he asked.

"Ask the wind. She's in it."

This made him laugh. "What a flair you have for drama."

"This is literally drama club, George."

"True," he said, "true," and put his hand on her shoulder. Slowly, he dragged it down her arm, then held her hand, briefly, by the fingertips alone. He released it, gazing meaningfully into her eyes.

Then he tossed his cigarette on the ground, turned, clapped his hands. "Time, people!"

"You two are disgusting," Nell Timmons said as they flowed in through the stage door.

"Oh, Nell, please go eat a bag of dicks."

"Someone should tell your boyfriend you're flirting with a teacher."

"I don't have a *boyfriend,* Nell," she said, flipping her the bird, but the remark had worked—she felt guilty. She ended up calling Chance and going out with him. He even talked her into meeting his mother, a small, intense woman with a blond bob. Their house was fancy, expensive-looking, and clean. Later, they parked at the dead end by the burned-out firefighters' practice station. Chance left the truck running, they had sex on the tilted-back passenger seat, and when he came, he said he loved her. She shocked herself by saying it back—involuntarily, embarrassingly, like a fart. What have I done, she thought, but she imagined herself in that big, clean house, in front of a warm fire.

The final show was to be a Sunday matinee, followed by the party at George's. Jane told Chance not to come — he would have a terrible time — and he made her feel guilty for wanting to go without him. She got mad at him, and he didn't come to the show, though he'd dutifully attended every other performance. She figured she'd see him in school Monday morning and apologize.

It rained all morning and all during the performance, and when the kids emerged from the stage door, a warm front had arrived, pushing the clouds away and garlanding the world with glittering, steaming light. Everything felt perfect. Everything *was* perfect.

The party was epic. No one stayed away, everyone stayed late. Jane started drinking the moment she arrived and didn't slow down the entire night. She smoked and ate some pills. At some point she found herself standing outside the bathroom with Nell, waiting to pee. Jane slumped against the wall, which was covered in some kind of textured wainscotting. It felt weird. She rubbed up against it.

"Oh Jesus," Nell said. "You're a mess. Go home."

"Not until I seduce George!"

"Vomit on him, is what you're going to do."

"Whatever, bitch!"

"He's ancient. Also, he's a creep." The bathroom door opened and a boy from the crew stumbled out, still buckling his pants. "Jesus, Frank," Nell said. He stuck out his tongue at her.

"You're just jealous!" Jane said.

Nell shook her head, stepped into the bathroom. "You fucking pretty girls are all the same. Go be an idiot, if that's what you want." When she slammed the door shut, Jane gave up, went outside, and pissed sloppily in the long grass, her dress bunched in her hands.

A few times that night, she stumbled against, or threw herself against, George; he pushed her gently aside, but not without first stroking her hip or the side of her breast. At some point she fell asleep on the sofa, woke up, and fell asleep again, or maybe passed out.

Most of what happened next came from Lila's recollection.

Lila was not drunk. She'd stopped early, once she saw how heavily Jane was drinking. Sometime between 1 and 2 a.m., only they and two other guests remained, a boy and a girl, freshman and sophomore siblings, who lived on the other side of the inlet. George was supposed to drive them home, but he felt sick—could Lila walk them over the bridge? He was going to bed. Jane would be fine on the couch.

Lila agreed but felt funny about it. On the way out, she swiped George's car keys from the dish by the door and drove the kids over the water instead. When she returned, the front door had been locked. Lila hadn't locked it when she left. After letting herself in with the key, she called out to Jane. There was no answer, and she wasn't on the sofa anymore.

Lila would tell Jane that she searched every room, including George's bedroom, before realizing there had to be a basement and discovering the door hidden in the back of the pantry. Stairs led down to a space finished in rust-colored carpet, floors, and walls; lava lamps bubbled on tables throughout. There was a bar there, decorated in tiki style, with a "roof" of palm fronds, and candleholders shaped like Easter Island heads. Beyond it, some bean bag chairs were arranged around a hookah.

When she turned to survey the space behind the stairs, she saw a futon lying on the floor in the corner, and this was where she found Jane, grunting insensibly, with her dress hiked up and her underwear pulled halfway off. George was there, too, naked from the waist down, trying to spread her legs.

Lila didn't hesitate. She picked up one of the Easter Island heads from the bar, strode to the corner, and, screaming in rage, smashed it into George's head just as he turned to see who was there. He fell unconscious back onto the pillow beside Jane, his body twisting. The candleholders were made of rough cement—she vaguely remembered that some kid had molded them for George in shop class, as a gift, and this creepy sex basement was where they'd ended up. The wound was bleeding now, and the blood pooled in the wells of his eyes. Beside him on the bed lay the half-burned votive candle that had fallen out of the holder.

When Jane came to, Lila was kneeling on the bed, holding the Easter Island head and staring at it in bewilderment. Jane remembered George trying to get her up off the couch—she had thought Lila had come back and that George would bring them home now. But then he started kissing her, licking her neck. She tried kissing back, briefly, but she felt sick. He cajoled, whispered things to her, touched her breasts and crotch. She just needed to vomit, pushed him away, stumbled toward the bathroom. Did she make it? She wasn't sure. She did remember George holding her up, dragging her really, to the kitchen and down the stairs. She remembered stumbling on the stairs, George catching her, calling her baby. She could recall a vague sense of unease and wrongness. She really, really wanted to sleep. She didn't remember reaching the futon.

But that's where she found herself, exposed, staring at her sister staring at the concrete head. Lila touched her cheek, asked if she was all right. Jane propped herself up on her elbows, took in George's unconscious form, one arm thrown out, the other pinned under his body. His pants and underwear lay tangled on the carpet at the foot of the futon. She took in his large flaccid dick, the small tattoo on his hairy belly — was it a snail? a whirlpool? — the bleeding wound on his head.

"What — what happened?"

"He was raping you."

"I think — I don't think — Oh god."

The two of them stared. George's chest rose and fell shallowly, unevenly. He hiccuped and they both jumped. There was a divot on his forehead: Lila had staved in his skull.

"The blood," Jane said. "He's going to bleed on the pillow." In fact, it was weird that he wasn't bleeding more.

Jane pulled her underwear back on, sat up, pushed her dress down. A wave of deep shame ran through her, and fear, and she began to shake. She could smell the boozy sweat pumping into her underarms. She was so tired. Lila said, "We have to do something."

A second pillow was wadded up against the wall behind Jane. Lila pointed, said, "Give me that." Jane did as she was asked.

Lila held the pillow in both hands, pressed it over George's face.

"What — What are you —"

"Shh."

Lila leaned in, putting more of her weight on the pillow. After a few seconds, she just flopped over completely, covering George's face with her body.

The tableau was so shocking, so preposterous, that Jane barked out a laugh. She suppressed a wave of dizziness and nausea. She was very much awake now, but with every second that passed, the scene seemed less real. She felt small, weak; her fists came together and she resisted the strong temptation to shove them into her mouth. "Lila. Stop!"

"Quiet," Lila said, into the futon.

"You're going to kill him!"

"He was already going to die," she said. "We just need to finish it."

It was true that George was not struggling. His body remained mostly inert. Jane watched his hand, the one thrown out, that lay beside her. It twitched a couple of times. Then it stopped.

"How long does it take?" Jane whispered.

"I don't know."

The three of them remained very still for a very long time. Jane drew her knees up and buried her face between them. She thought about how much she really had wanted to go to bed with George. If she hadn't been so drunk, maybe she would have. Why did he do this?

As if she'd followed Jane's train of thought, Lila said, "How much did you drink, really?"

"A lot."

"But did he refill it for you?"

Jane thought about it. "Maybe?"

"Maybe you got roofied."

"Maybe."

Lila craned her neck and peered at her through strands of hair. "Jane. Look for his pulse."

"I don't want to touch it."

Lila sighed. Gently, carefully, she lifted herself up off the pillow. She crawled around his body to kneel beside Jane and took his hand in hers. She pressed her index and middle fingers to his wrist and held them there for a minute at least.

"I think he's dead. I keep thinking I feel something but it's just my own pulse or something."

"I smell shit."

Lila dropped the arm, placed her palms on his naked hip, and gently rolled him. Rank odor wafted up.

"Jesus," Lila said, and Jane vomited on the bed between them, splattering her sister and George's body. Lila didn't jerk away. She reached out and stroked Jane's head. She said, "I already know what to do. I thought about it while I was lying on him. You just have to do what I say, all right? We're going to get through it together."

"Okay."

"It's not complicated. We just have to go one step at a time."

"Yes."

"Do you feel a little better?"

"Yes."

"All right," Lila said. "Your mascara's a mess. Clean yourself up and let's go."

# 22

# Near Seattle, WA: *Now*

The place they were looking for was called Pine Valley Aviation and it was located near an unnamed lake south of Tiger Mountain State Forest. At 2 p.m. they turned off Route 18 onto a two-lane local highway, which led them through thick woods occasionally interrupted by farms and private roads. A small wooden sign announced the airport entrance road, which was neatly paved and painted, and which topped a small rise and led them into a long, deforested valley populated by a terminal, several outbuildings, and planes of various sizes. As they arrived a small jet was landing. Jane experienced a moment of irrational fear: it was coming too fast and couldn't stop in time! But of course it landed smoothly and taxied to a stop in front of one of the gates.

They parked in a lot that seemed large for even the airport's maximum imaginable capacity. A clutch of businesspeople dragging roller bags with briefcases lashed on top passed them in the opposite direction, betraying not a hint of travel fatigue.

Signs directed them toward a hangar at the far west end of the complex marked by a logo of an arrow piercing a circle and the words INCOGNITO AIR LINES.

"Subtle," Jane said.

"I guess you don't have to be, when you're rich."

Beneath the logo, a steel door stood beside a single wire-reinforced window. To its right was a row of numbered spaces occupied by a fleet of black Suburbans. One space, marked by a bold yellow 05 painted on the pavement, was empty. Jane and Lila stood before it, arms crossed, considering.

"So, Gramps is asking around about somebody resembling our mother," Lila said. "He gets wind of this Holy Ghost, and mentions it to his friend, this Gil, who runs a private airline. Suddenly, this guy knows exactly where we are, before we've even left, and where we're headed." She gazed at Jane. "How? How does he know?"

"I don't know."

"And why does he have us followed? If he knows we're coming anyway."

"He sent those guys halfway across the country."

Lila nodded. "Just to watch and report."

They stared at each other. Jane said, "It has to be her."

"The Holy Ghost. She's pulling the strings. Keeping tabs." Lila's face began to curdle into dismay, then anger. "How long has she known? Did Gil tell her or did she know before that?"

"How long have you been asking around?"

"Years," Lila said. Her jaw was trembling. She spat on the ground. "Goddammit."

"You thought she was a spy," Jane said. "Even when we were kids."

Lila shook her head. "It was just a fantasy. Or, I thought it was."

"How much did Dad know? How much does he know now?"

Jane gave it a moment's thought. "On the one hand," she said, "he's out of it. But on the other, he's a Cold War historian. He must have known something."

"He knew. And didn't tell us, when she left."

A loudspeaker announced boarding for a flight, in English and Spanish. A crow cawed and alighted on the fence separating the parking lot from the airfield. Jane said, "So what now?"

"We go talk to Matías Gil."

They passed through the steel door of the hangar and into an enormous space, separated from where they stood by a grimy yellow formica counter backed by a freestanding wall that ended ten feet up. Beyond it, several planes were being worked on: two twin-engine propeller crafts and a small jet, similar to the one they'd seen land, all marked with the Incognito logo. Another, unbranded jet, visible through the open hangar door, stood out on the tarmac about a hundred yards away. Workers were pushing a wheeled staircase up to it, and a group of people — a tall, thin woman and two ripped goons in polo shirts — were standing out in the sun with their bags, talking to a third man in a suit.

A buzzer was sounding, conveyed through speakers throughout the hangar. It stopped when the door shut behind them. A man in a yellow vest and protective earmuffs walked over and entered the space via a narrow door. The whole wall shook when he closed it. He removed the earmuffs and approached them from behind the counter.

"Hello, folks, what can I do for you."

"We're here to see Matías Gil," Jane said. Lila was standing on her toes, peering out at the group of people. They separated now, the woman and big men moving toward the plane and the third man turning to head back toward the hangar.

"Jane," Lila said.

"Is he expecting you?" the man said.

"He sure is."

"*Jane.*"

The man turned, picked up a wall-mounted microphone, and pressed a button. His voice rang out over the intercom. "Mr. Gil to the desk, please."

"What?" Jane said.

"I think . . . I think that's her."

The man in the suit was jogging toward them. Before he could arrive, Lila lunged for the door and ran through it.

"Hey!" said the man in the vest.

Jane followed. Her sister was headed toward the open hangar door. The trio of travelers had reached the staircase and were climbing into the plane.

Matías Gil opened his arms wide, as if to block Lila from passing. "No, no, no!" he shouted. A couple of other workers took notice and began to run after her, onto the tarmac.

Jane allowed herself to be corralled by Gil. He smelled like sandalwood and cigar smoke and appeared ready to hit her if he had to. The men had reached Lila, out in the sun, and took her by the arms.

The woman stood alone at the top of the boarding stairs, shielding her eyes from the sun. She gazed down at Lila. Jane realized that she'd known it before she knew it, the moment she'd seen the woman walk-ing—the way her dress billowed around her legs, the way her suitcase trundled along beside her, like a pet. She hadn't believed her mother was alive, that she was the Holy Ghost, that she was real. But she was. The face was indistinct, but it was hers.

"Mother!" Lila screamed, and the men held her back.

The Holy Ghost turned and entered the jet, and the door shut behind her.

"No, no, no, no," Matías Gil continued to say, though Jane had no inten-tion of trying to pass him. He was a compact bulldozer of a man, and Jane didn't think she could take him, even if she weren't frozen here in a state of shock.

Because she was paralyzed—by indecision, by confusion, and by something unexpected, a kind of recognition from which she ordinarily felt distant. She felt palpably rejected and abandoned. The suitcase, the closing aircraft door. The crew were wheeling away the stairs and the plane's engines were roaring. Jane felt like a child again, watching her mother disappear. Their mother had known they were coming and wanted them to watch her turn her back on them one more time. Had gone out of her way to make sure that's what they saw.

Was that how Chloe had felt, just the other day?

On the tarmac, even Lila had stopped struggling. Instead, she watched the plane taxi into position. After a minute, she gave up. She shook off the workers, turned, and stalked toward Gil, fists clenched.

"Enough. Enough. This is my hangar, these are my planes, you do not belong here."

"You knew we were coming! Why didn't you keep her?"

"No, no, no. Do not make demands of me, please. You are not my cli-ent. That is my client." He pointed to where the plane had begun its jour-ney down the runway. "I do not control her actions. I make the hangar available to her, that is my job."

"And have us *followed*?" Lila lunged forward and pushed him with the heels of her palms. The yellow-vest workers shouted and reached for her, but Gil waved them off. He hadn't moved an inch.

"Yes. You damage my car. This is not necessary."

"Of course it was fucking necessary! Your men were harassing and menacing us. They're lucky they didn't end up in that river."

"As they say it, they keep a safe distance and merely observe."

Jane said, "That's literally what menacing is."

He looked from one to the other, scowling. "Your friend, Mr. Gramps, he tells me you are looking for my client, so I inform my client. She instructs me to follow and report, so I tell my men to follow and report. That is all. She does not ask to meet with you. She wants to leave, we prepare the aircraft."

"Where is that plane going," Lila demanded. It was nearly out of sight now, a speck against the clouds.

"This is confidential information."

"How often does she come here?"

"This is confidential information! I cannot share the information of my client. You are a professional, no? You do not give client information to any stranger who comes to your place of work and punches your chest, no?"

Jane said, "All right. We're not here to cause you trouble. Your men frightened us." She hazarded a significant glance at Lila, who was still scowling, her fingers twitching. If they were going to find anything out, they would need to butter Gil up. Right? At the very least, get into his office, see how the operation worked. Lila returned a barely perceptible nod. "Just . . . can you give us a little bit of your time? We've come all this way."

"You never know, Mr. Gil," Lila said, more calmly now. "We may one day be heirs to our mother's empire."

He glowered at Lila, then Jane, shook his head. "Very well. Come to my office, ladies, please." He dismissed the two workers with a wave and beckoned Lila and Jane back toward the counter area.

On the other end of the room, a flight of steel stairs led up to a cat-walk, which ran around three sides of the space and was interrupted by a windowed, boxlike room. They followed Gil inside. The space had an industrial feel, with Steelcase office furniture on linoleum floors, and a couple of fluorescent fixtures dangling overhead. A woman was working quietly at a computer and nodded at them as they entered; pink and yellow sticky notes were stuck to everything around her desk, and a clipboard hung on a hook on the wall above it. Her screen displayed a calendar, with colored blocks denoting various events. Jane watched Lila take in the room, the security cameras in the corners, the small high windows. Gil invited them to sit in wheeled office chairs and offered them cups of water from a cooler. Jane accepted.

Gil sat down. He said, "I regret answering Mr. Gramps's query about your mother. In retrospect, I should not be involved in your doings. He is an old friend, though, and I owe him my career."

Jane tucked her hair behind her ear, managed a sly smile. "I bet there's an interesting story there."

He shrugged. "Not so interesting," he said. He had been a gang member at one time, he told them, a Norteño in the Yakima Valley, an underling who was serving as a mule for their drug and weapons trade. He delivered guns and gun parts to Gramps's compound. "My car broke down, he let me repair in his garages. He likes me, sees that I am good with cars—I learn the trade in prison, you see. I tell him I want a better life, and he gives me one. Eventually, I meet a man with small planes, wanting to sell, and Gramps help me to buy and repair. So, he wants to know something, I tell him."

"How did you come to do business with our mother?" Lila asked.

"This is confidential."

Jane said, "Understandable. Is most of your business to and from Central America?"

"I see what you do there, miss."

"But you're from there, right?" Lila said. "You don't sound Mexican to me. Are you Guatemalan?"

Gil narrowed his eyes, said something in Spanish. Lila responded. They conversed for a moment, tensely. In English, Gil said, to both of them, "My mother was Honduran. My father American, Mexican American, a soldier. Your Reagan sends him to stop communism. Then he is sent elsewhere, goodbye to him, and I am born." Palms up, he sighed. "When my mother dies, I come to live with him, it doesn't go too well."

"We haven't seen our mother in twenty years," Jane said. "Until today."

"That is your business and your mother's."

For a moment Jane thought Lila would get up and try to strangle the man. The tension in the room rose. Gil gripped the arms of his chair. Finally, Lila extended a hand and said, "Well, thank you, Mr. Gil."

He appeared wary but loosened his grip on the chair. He shook the hand. The sisters stood. Gil stood.

"We appreciate your time," Jane said.

"I apologize for my men. I will instruct them to be more discreet."

"No hard feelings," Lila said.

He walked them down the stairs and past the front counter. He opened the door for them. "Farewell, ladies. Good luck to you."

"Same to you, Mr. Gil," Lila said. He appeared puzzled for a moment, then shut the door behind them.

On the way to the car, Lila was incensed, muttering under her breath, clenching and unclenching her fingers. She resembled a child — not the strangely composed one she'd actually been, but a normal one, barely warding off a tantrum.

"Well," Jane said. "We saw her, anyway. She's real."

"I guess that's enough for you?" Lila growled. "I guess you want to pack up and go home?"

"Oh no," Jane said. "No, I don't."

"No?"

"She gave us the chance to catch her here, just to watch us fail. She doesn't think we'll follow her."

They slowed to a stop, still thirty feet from the car. Lila said, "Or maybe it's a test? Maybe she wants us to follow."

"I think it is. She wants to know if we can do it."

"What happens if we do?"

Jane threw her hands in the air. "This whole thing was your idea, you tell me."

"Only one way to find out. We have to go there."

"Yeah, but how?"

Lila pointed at the hangar. "We'll fly."

"Right, but . . . we can't hijack a plane."

"I mean," Lila said, "we could. But no. I have an idea. Let's see what we find tonight."

"What are we doing tonight?"

Lila smiled. "Breaking and entering," she said.

# 23

# Nestor, NY: *Then*

I n George Framingham's basement, Lila helped her to her feet. They
dragged his body to the center of the futon, covered it with the bloody
pillows. Then they folded the fitted sheet around it and carried it, in this
makeshift sling, up the stairs and out the back door, taking breaks every
twenty feet or so.

"Where are we going?"

"The boat."

The rowboat was surprisingly robust—watertight and freshly painted.
What had George used it for? He didn't seem the type to fish. The body
was heavy and Jane tripped on a warped board, but they managed to
lower him in without dropping him or capsizing it.

"We need rocks," Lila said. She gestured for Jane to follow. They
walked south along the inlet, collecting small boulders. "Fill in the holes
in the dirt," Lila said. "So they can't figure it out." The stones unstuck
themselves from the mud with a viscous pop and rolled into the bedsheet
shroud with a gentle thunk. When they had what they thought would be
enough, they climbed in, twisted and tied the elastic corners of the sheet
together. It was hard to fold his legs up—the body had begun to
stiffen—so his socked feet stuck out, one crossed over the other, like a
baby's. The package filled the prow of the small boat, leaving barely

enough room aft for the sisters to fit. Lila untied the line and took up the oars. She handed one to Jane.

Wordlessly, they moved north toward the lake. The sky was clear, the stars bright, the moon near full. The boat rode low in the water and its motion nauseated Jane, who was still drunk. She threw up again into the dark water and Lila paused for a moment to rub her back.

They were rowing against the current, but the current was slow, and the inlet widened until it was lake. From behind a clump of trees the defunct lighthouse hove into view, beyond it the lights of the county highway, snaking its way up into the hills. They made better progress now that they'd escaped the inlet. There were no other boats. The clunking and splashing of the oars, the smacking of small waves against the gunwale, and the girls' shallow breaths were the only sounds. Jane cried, Lila did not. After a time — Jane could not have said how long — Lila told her to stop. They laid the oars on the bottom boards.

"We have to stand up and swing him," she said.

"I don't know if I can."

Grunting, Lila pulled the bundle closer, then climbed over it into the prow. The boat rocked. She stood, took handfuls of sheet in each of her hands, and with a nod indicated that Jane should do the same. After a moment, the two girls stood, bent over, gazing at each other through loose strands of sweaty hair.

"Lift," Lila said, and they hoisted the bundle up.

She continued: "We're going to swing three times, first to your left, then to your right. Release on three, okay?"

"Okay."

"Swing left . . . one. Swing . . . two." The boat wobbled; Jane stumbled. "Swing . . ." Lila said, and Jane knew already that the body was not going to clear the gunwale. But there was no way to stop now. "Three!" Lila grunted, and they released it.

George almost made it all the way off. But one of the rocks was weighing a corner down, and the bundle caught as it fell and nearly capsized the boat. Lila got her foot up under the rock and flipped it off, but the boat rocked again as the weight was released and Jane lost her footing. She fell, following the body into the dark water.

The water was so brutally, stultifyingly cold that Jane thought it had broken every bone in her body. She drew breath to scream and ended up inhaling a mouthful of it, rank and needle sharp, and coughing and vomiting it back into the lake. Beside her, the white dumpling of the burial shroud bobbed and gurgled as it filled. Jane could swim — one of their mother's only successful acts of parenting had been to pay for, and sternly watch over, intensive swimming lessons from a former bronze medalist who coached at the college — but her drunkenness, and the shock of the cold, made her believe for a moment that she was doomed to go down with George.

Instead, a pale hand appeared before her. She grabbed it. Soon she was clutching the gunwale with both hands, panting. Lila said, "I'm going to sit on the other side as a counterweight. When I do, you climb in, okay?"

"Okay," Jane sputtered.

Lila shifted, and Jane felt her side of the boat pull up. If she let go, it would capsize and flip over onto her sister. Instead she pulled down, hard, hoisted herself up. She threw a leg over the side and rolled the rest of the way in as Lila dove onto her, trying to center their weight. The boat pitched wildly, then steadied.

The girls sat up. The package was disappearing beneath the surface. They watched as it slowly sank. Soon only the feet were visible, and then they disappeared and the body was gone from sight.

Jane was shivering uncontrollably. Lila held her, whispered, "We need to row back. That will warm you up and stop you shaking." Jane nodded, wrapped her numb hands around her oar. She couldn't feel it but trusted her eyes that she held it. Together they fell into a rhythm, and the boat began to move back toward the inlet. Lila glanced over her shoulder from time to time, turned her oar in the water to adjust their trajectory. Before long they were able to stop, and they let the current carry them the rest of the way to the dock.

"Is there anything in the boat? Stains?" Lila said, tying the line.

"I can't see anything. But there's so much water."

"Come on." She climbed out and helped Jane to follow. "We're not done. We need to go back inside."

"No," Jane said.

"We have to."

"I can't."

But she could, and did. She blubbered like a child as she descended the stairs; her nose ran and she coughed and choked. Lila held her hand. Soon they stood facing the bare futon, which was stained by blood and vomit.

"Can we . . . clean it?" Jane said.

"No."

"What do we do?"

Lila said nothing for a moment. Then: "Just flip it over."

"They'll find it."

"They're going to figure it out no matter what we do."

"Then why?"

"Maybe it'll buy us some time," Lila said. "Enough time, anyway."

"For what?"

Lila turned and gazed at her in evident wonder. As if to say, Don't you already know? Haven't you figured it out?

"To disappear," she said.

They stole his laptop and car. The Subaru reeked of mold; at some point, he must have left the sunroof open in the rain. The glove compartment was full of original cast recording tapes and the ashtray was full of cigarettes. Lila dumped these out the window as she drove. The clock on the dash read 4:23.

"It'll be light soon. We have to be quick."

"I don't understand what we're doing," Jane said.

"We're going to pack the essentials and get on the road. I have his cash and his credit cards. Did you know his name is Leslie?"

"What?"

"Leslie George Framingham. It's a stroke of luck. A girl's name. We'll probably get away with using the cards for a little while. Until they figure out he's missing."

Jane wanted to press her for details, but she was having difficulty processing what had happened. She was soaking wet and had begun to shiver again. The heat was on full blast but it hadn't gotten hot yet.

"I think we'll have a few days, at least. Do you know if he has friends?"

"What?"

"George. Who will miss him? The show just ended. Maybe it'll be a while—he's basically done for the semester. Like, I guess we're supposed to clean up the cast room or something?"

"I can't remember."

"The laptop. We could send an email as him. Saying he has a family emergency. Ask the cast to do cleanup without him. Tell Principal Kovacs, too."

"I — I don't —"

Lila patted her leg. "You take a shower. You need to warm up. I'll pack your clothes. I'm going to take care of everything."

They sneaked in so as not to wake their father, though it hardly mattered; he barely noticed their comings and goings. Would they say goodbye? They would see him again someday, wouldn't they? Shouldn't they have just told the police after they knocked him out? Lila had been trying to protect her. Surely they would have been treated leniently. Or would they?

In the shower, she made the water as hot as she could stand and silently sobbed until the shivering stopped. She wrapped herself in a towel and went to the bedroom. Her suitcase was already open on the bed, full of clothes. She pulled on a pair of jeans, sweatshirt, high-tops. Gathered her hair into an elastic band. She added her phone and charger to the bag, then stared at it uncomprehendingly.

Lila came into the room. She hugged Jane, then said, "It's time to go. I took some money from Dad and left him a note."

"Okay."

"You can't bring the phone. They'll know where we are. Just leave it behind."

"What?"

"We'll get new phones." She gripped Jane by the shoulders. "Look at me. You're in shock. It's been a long night. Look at me, Jane."

Jane hiccuped. She gazed into her sister's eyes.

"We were always going to run," Lila said. "We were going to do it our own way, but now things have changed. This isn't the best, but it's what we're doing. We have each other. We're going to start a new life."

"What about Dad?"

"Jane. You have to stop worrying about Dad. He's not a child."

"I feel . . . bad. For him. And wait," she said. "What about Chance? I have to call Chance."

"What? No, Jane. I thought you said he wasn't your boyfriend."

"He's not." He is, she thought.

Lila hadn't looked angry when she was killing George Framingham, but she looked angry now. She said, "So, don't. Don't feel bad for any-body. We are wiping the slate clean, starting now."

"But..." Jane said. "But where are we going?"

Lila took the phone and charger out of Jane's bag and dropped them onto the bed. "Chicago."

"What's in Chicago?"

Lila said, "Aunt Ruth."

# 24

# Nestor, NY: *Now and Then*

---

Showered, dressed, the pounding in his head reduced by analgesics to a dull throb, Harry prepared and devoured some eggs and toast and set to putting things right. While the washing machine churned, he rolled up the threadbare, piss-stained oriental rug he'd lain upon the night before and dragged it out to the trash hutch. He opened the office window and mopped the hardwood floor with oil soap. While attempting to clean the bathroom he vomited up his breakfast, then had to go back to bed, but when he woke he finished cleaning the bathroom and was able to eat again — just the toast this time. He called Mrs. Vesey's number and left on her voicemail as sincere an apology as he could muster.

Pouring all the booze down the drain was harder, in part because he truly didn't want to see it go, in part because he knew the act was futile. He'd done it before, so often that it had become a familiar bit of theater, with its own silly tropes and applause lines: the way he raised and lowered the gin bottle with a kind of flourish, like a Moroccan tea server; the way he pirouetted and leapt toward the recycling bin. This time, though, felt different. Not effective, necessarily, but different. Like it meant something, he didn't know what, yet. When he was done, he dragged the bin of empty bottles to the curb, though god knew whether the truck was coming today or tomorrow or next week. Eventually it would come.

In the office, he sat by the open window. The breeze was cold so he buttoned up his cardigan to the neck. He opened the box of notebooks and spread them out on the desk.

Considering everything that had changed in the world over the past five decades, it was astounding that the spiral reporter's notebook had been left relatively untouched. He'd been buying the same brand, the very same product, at the college bookstore since 1973. He remembered the spring day, not unlike this one, the similar hangover (the first hangover of his life, he was fairly certain), entering the bookstore, feeling as though he were being watched, trying to remember the events of the night before. His bleary insensibility, the birth of his paranoia. He was sure someone had pounded on his Binghamton hotel room door the night before, demanding something from him: his money, he supposed. But then, rising at some ungodly hour, finding the bill slipped under the door, paying it at the front desk without incident, the Factor nowhere to be seen. He drove home in a fog, pulling over twice to be sick, then showered, dressed, went back to sleep, and walked unsteadily to campus to begin his new assignment.

He sorted through the notebooks, looking for the earliest. May 1973. He'd met with the Factor just after semester's end, this time at a joint closer to home, a steak house called the Deer Blind, decorated with the remains of animals: pelts on the walls, antler chandelier, infernal assemblages made of two hoofs that sprouted from a slab of wood and awkwardly clutched a thick pile of paper napkins. Most of the patrons of this place didn't look like they were from the college, though its owners were former fraternity brothers, economists who'd shunned academic life. Lots of jeans and sweatshirts. Lots of beards. Not the Factor, who wore brown herringbone pants, a mustard paisley shirt, and a wide necktie with a pattern of yellow roses. The Factor ordered them whiskies and invited Harry to report his findings. Harry tried to hand him the notebook, but the Factor, wide-eyed, threw his hands up in refusal.

"My god, Harry, put that away," he said in a stage whisper. "This is supposed to look like a conversation, not an exchange of intelligence. Just two gentlemen of a mindly bent, enjoying the charm of their rustic surrounds."

"Sorry," Harry said, pocketing the notebook. "How am I—— That is, how do you want——"

"Just give me a verbal summary of your findings, Harry. As though we're speaking of old friends."

"Should I — What should I do with the notebook? After we've . . . had our conversation?" He glanced over at the restaurant's dominating feature, an enormous central hearth, open on three sides, that filled the center of the room. Firewood was carefully arranged in anticipation of a day cold enough for a fire. Harry imagined a winter's evening, casually tossing the notebook into the roaring flames on his way out. But no, that wouldn't work, would it. Any counterspy lurking in the place could dash over and extract the half-burned intelligence, then dunk it, smoking, into a glass of water before secreting it away in his document case.

"Keep it somewhere safe, Harry," the Factor was telling him, draining his whiskey and raising the empty glass in the air to signal his enduring thirst. "Somewhere very safe. Also, do you have a gun?"

"A gun? No!"

"Buy a gun. Learn to use it. You never know when you'll need it."

"I — All right."

"So tell me," the Factor said, wiggling his behind into the leather of his log-framed chair, accepting with a nod his third or fourth drink. "What have you learned?"

The answer, Harry was afraid, was not much. But he repeated what he'd heard, mostly through eavesdropping, partly through gentle questioning. Students' summer travel plans abroad, their thoughts about the war. Some of them had lost a brother or high school acquaintance in Vietnam. One boy opposed the military dictatorship of Thailand and seemed keen on the idea that there might be an uprising against it. One girl expressed admiration for Bettina Aptheker. "Very good, Harry, very good," the Factor said, writing nothing down. At one point — maybe it was the booze — Harry thought he saw flames reflected in the Factor's eyes and glanced at the hearth to see if it had been lit when he wasn't looking. It hadn't been.

He would meet up with the Factor about twice a year for the next decade, always at some local watering hole, always while doing plenty of watering. When Harry completed his dissertation and prepared to go on the job market, a position suddenly opened up at Nestor. When his book neared its first full draft, a press came calling, having heard about it through "the grapevine." When tenure time rolled around, Harry passed muster with nary a hitch. And when it was time to buy a house, it was the Factor who alerted him to a charming property in a hidden, leafy area of downtown, with a big wild yard, situated on the creek, that was going cheap. In truth, Harry didn't know to what extent his success and luck were his own, and what was the Factor's doing. But the Factor always seemed to know about impending good news before Harry did. If he wasn't pulling the strings, he was certainly tight with the puppetmaster.

Even Anabel, the greatest surprise of Harry's life, was foretold, if vaguely, by the Factor during their meeting of January 1983. They were back at the Deer Blind, and the fire reflected in the Factor's eyes was real this time. Over gin on the rocks — the Factor had switched from whiskey and Harry had followed suit — after their official exchange of intelligence, he said, "Have you thought of settling down with a woman, Harry?"

In truth, Harry had dated from time to time, not very successfully. His most enduring affair had been with the history department accountant, Mary Beth, who had mysteriously disappeared from the office after their embarrassing breakup at the annual Christmas party. He was fairly certain he'd broken up with her rather than the other way around, but he'd been too drunk to know for sure. Nowadays he occasionally spied Mary Beth bustling into or out of the philosophy building and always averted his eyes. He was glad to be relieved of the responsibility of sex with her, which had never worked very well.

"I suppose? I don't — That is — I wouldn't say I'm actively looking."

"Well, don't miss what's right before your eyes, Harry," the Factor said, winking lasciviously.

"Wh — where?"

"Come now, surely you find some of your students to be comely? You notice their admiring gazes, their coquettishness as they swan into your office?"

"Oh. I suppose."

"I don't mean the undergraduates, of course; we want to find you a woman, not a child."

"Of course."

"I'm sure there are a few graduate students seeking a mate," the Factor went on. "You should want respect first, Harry, professional admiration. Lust will doubtless follow."

Harry would probably have forgotten this strange conversation if Anabel hadn't expressed her romantic interest in him just a few months later, over glasses of beer in the faculty lounge, beside an open window letting in the unseasonable warmth of late spring. "Professor Pool," she said. "Harry. Why don't you invite me to your home?" He did, and they strolled down the hill together toward the house where they would eventually be husband and wife, argue and weep, go months without sex, raise the twins. Leaving campus that first night, Harry feared he'd misinterpreted her intentions, that they'd arrive at his door and he would try to kiss her and she would slap him, call him perverted, report him to the dean. But no, she took his hand halfway down the hill, followed him happily inside, and ultimately beckoned him to his own bed.

Now Harry endured another wave of nausea, another bout of longing for a drink to push it back. The breeze coming in the window was turning warmer, as though in response to his memory of that breeze in 1984. He was thirty-three years old that year; Anabel was twenty-four. How could they ever have been so young? And how could he have been so lucky as to have her in his life? He still felt that way, even now, even after everything that had happened. He didn't blame her for leaving him, not anymore; he'd felt anguish, yes, betrayal, frustration. But never anger. It wasn't Harry she was running away from, or even the girls, but her own nature, with which she had never managed to make peace.

He met less and less with the Factor after he married Anabel—in part because he was busy with the children and with his complicated marriage, and in part, he supposed, because the Agency's appetite for evidence of campus agitation had waned. Also, Harry got tenure, he got his raise, he got his house. There was nothing left to pay him with but money, and it seemed there was none of that to give.

The strange thing? When he found evidence of these students' lives online, he never could connect their fates to his actions. Most of them seemed to have grown into ordinary adults. Most had moved on from scholarship, into jobs in finance, travel, international commerce. A few were teachers themselves. He reached out to some of them, and most recalled his classes and a few his writing—an unexpected pleasure. None, however, reported that they were followed by shadowy figures late at night, or that they were mysteriously turned down for a home loan, or that they'd been interrogated in illegal prisons.

Gazing out the window, dying for a drink, Harry realized that he might literally die tomorrow — or, more terrifying still, he might die in twenty years. What in the ever-loving fuck would those years be like? Was it ever too late to change? What if he actually got the answers to his questions? What if he found the Factor, demanded explanations?

Just last night, he thought random people on the street were planning to follow him home and kill him. Now all he wanted was to contact the source of his torment, the man he assumed wanted to silence him. Well — he supposed he was brave now. Hand trembling, he picked up his phone, let his face unlock it (and why wasn't he paranoid about that?), and called Julius's office.

"Arts and Sciences, dean's office," chirped a woman's voice. Harry knew this woman, Elena; during his abortive attempt at psychotherapy he encountered her as he was leaving the therapist's. She was standing near the door, waiting for her turn, which was evidently next. He'd said, "Why, hello, Elena," and she'd blanched and turned away.

Now he said, "Harry Pool for the dean, please," and she wordlessly put him on hold. The dean's office hold music sounded like the soundtrack to a seventies pornographic film, recorded from a television speaker into a portable cassette player and stored underwater for five decades. Nestor could pretend, occasionally, to be a legitimate institution of higher learning, but its true nature always parted the proscenium curtains and peered shyly out.

"Harry!" Julius said. "I've been waiting to hear from you."

"You have?"

"About my offer."

"Your offer."

His old friend sighed. Not just audibly, but ostentatiously. "About — Never mind, Harry, what can I do for you."

"Do you remember Franklin Hastings?"

This was, of course, the Factor's real name. It had been easy to figure out: after one of their on-campus encounters, Harry simply followed him back to his office at a cautious distance and read the nameplate beside the door. At the time, he was proud to have evaded the great spy's notice, but now he wondered if the Factor had known he was following, had expected it of him all along.

A long pause. "Franklin . . . Hastings, you say?"

185

Fucking liar. "You know who I mean, Julius. He was a director or associate dean in admissions and financial aid. He disappeared in the late nineties. Is he dead?"

Another pause. Harry heard him move the receiver away from his face. "Elena, would you be kind enough to bring me a coffee from downstairs?" An unintelligible reply. "Yes, I know it's not in your job description, but — Look, please just leave. You don't have to do anything. Take a break." He sighed. "All right, Harry. Franklin Hastings."

"Yes. Is he alive?"

"Oh, I suppose."

"What do you know about him?"

"I should ask you the same, Harry," Julius said. "What do *you* know about him?"

"He recruited me for a project," Harry said boldly. "An interdisciplinary project."

"Oh god."

"I want to talk with him. To settle old scores."

"Harry," the dean said, groaning mildly, as though he were stretching out, catlike, preparing to go to sleep, "I would like for you to think about the future, for once."

"Actually, that's what I'm doing. Put me in touch with him, Julius, and I will discuss your offer with you."

Julius hesitated. "Is that so?"

"I know you want to give my office to some dynamic young scholar, Julius. Somebody who will look good in the alumni magazine."

"Hm."

"I'm considering retirement. But I'd like this from you, if you please. Tell me how to contact Franklin Hastings."

"Hold on." Harry heard the old dean cross the room, jangle a key, haul open a file drawer. Eventually he returned. "I want you to know something," he said. "The pressure I've been putting on you? Let me tell you. Our new provost is fifty-three."

"She is."

"We are both long overdue for pasture, Harry. We are both living on borrowed time. Borrowed from the young. Do you have something to write with?"

"Always."

"What will I do in retirement? I've given my life to this miserable institution. Oh Jesus Christ, excuse me. Elena, please leave! Four minutes lurking in the hallway does not constitute a break!" A rustling, a clunk. Eventually Julius returned. "Look, Harry, Hastings might be dead. I honestly don't know. I'd tell you to call him and find out, but he doesn't have a phone."

"A cell phone?"

"*Any* phone. Howard Underwood went to see him and Hastings wouldn't let him in. He peered through the window and could see the old coot in there, solving crosswords. Eventually some thug appeared to escort him back to his car! Do you have your pencil?"

Harry hadn't the faintest idea who Howard Underwood was. "I do."

"All right. Here you go." He rattled off an address, which Harry dutifully transcribed. He recognized the municipality, a village two hundred miles to the northeast where he had once bought a stack of paperback thrillers for a quarter a pop at a church fundraiser, on the way to a conference in Middlebury, Vermont, that had turned out to be canceled. He'd read the cancellation email but forgotten.

"Thank you, Julius."

"I expect an audience with you after break, Harry. To discuss the terms of your surrender."

"I hope they'll serve as a model for the terms of yours."

"I hope so, too, Harry, I hope so, too."

In the summer of his sixty-eighth year, Harry had discovered the joys of leasing. Previously he had exclusively owned and maintained used Volvos, right up until Nestor's used Volvo mechanic had perished, almost too ironically to be believed, crossing the street on foot in front of a Ford pickup. Once he'd secured himself a brand-new Subaru, he was astounded to discover how smooth a new car could feel to drive — like a dream of driving, a motorized womb. He'd nearly fallen asleep at the wheel several times since. Two years ago he traded his car in for another one, and it was with deep satisfaction that he realized he would do this every three years until he was dead.

It didn't take long to prepare for the trip. A thermos of tap water, an apple, his phone, and the Colt—loaded for sure this time, thanks to a YouTube video that jogged his failing memory—all tossed into a worn floral Lands' End backpack that had once accompanied one of the girls to school. He'd learned how to tell his phone to give him directions and bought a caddy for it that mounted on the heating vent, and he used these things now to set him on his path. As he drove, he thought of Anabel, specifically his greatest regret in life: recruiting her at the behest of the Factor.

He shouldn't have agreed to any of it. He could have renounced his assignment, retreated to their little home on the flats, by the creek. Instead, he listened to reason. "Now, Harry, your fiancée," the Factor said, this time on an uncharacteristic walk in the woods, on a path through a poorly maintained and largely ignored state park. "You're aware of her heritage, her facility for language."

"Of course."

"She could be of use to us, don't you agree? Her talents are many, her charm, undeniable."

"Wait," Harry said. "How do you know about her? *What* do you know?"

"Harry!" the Factor said, slapping his shoulder. "Come now!" He was wearing a preposterous outfit: a two-piece Dior-style safari suit in cream, and a pith helmet. Somehow, though, he radiated confidence, while Harry felt out of place in jeans and boots. It was 1985, when espionage was actually in the news for a change: multiple high-profile arrests of persons living inside the United States, caught spying for communist nations. John Anthony Walker, Jonathan Pollard, Edward Lee Howard. Talented agents were needed, Harry supposed. He sensed desperation in the Factor's plea: surely quiet, independent Anabel could never pass herself off as something she wasn't, would never work for a government?

"All right," Harry said. "You know things. But this is my wife we're talking about."

"Fiancée, Harry, fiancée."

"Fine."

"I hereby give you permission"—he paused to nod a greeting at a pair of teenagers, probably young lovers, stumbling along the path with guilty looks on their faces—"permission to invite her into our employ. If she agrees, she'll meet up with me, and I'll introduce her to my betters."

"Your betters?" Harry wanted to know. "You've never offered to introduce me."

"My dear friend," the Factor said with a laugh, "we suspect your betrothed of talents you lack. Take this as a compliment — your cover is perfect. You're an absent-minded professor through and through."

"I'm not absent-minded."

"But your Anabel could sell mukluks to an Arab."

The conversation was increasingly disturbing to Harry, not only for the Factor's strangely confident assessment of Anabel's personality — one that Harry himself wouldn't have been able to deliver, if he'd been asked — but the ease with which the man was able to thicken any plot, even if the thickening agent were another man's wife. Fiancée.

Harry agreed, of course — at this point, he didn't have tenure. He decided the request was a blessing in disguise: he'd wanted to clear the air with Anabel anyway, rather than worry, over the course of their lives together, that she'd find him out, be appalled, pack her bags, and leave. That night he sat down with her and explained that, for many years now, he had been working in secret for the CIA, monitoring student political activity, and he wanted to give her a chance to withdraw from their engagement if this changed her opinion of him, if this made him a liar in her eyes.

Instead she gazed at him intently and said, "On the contrary, Harry. It makes you a patriot."

To the Factor's offer, she appeared pensive. She'd never thought of herself as potential spy material, she said. She'd planned to live an ordinary life as an academic, and perhaps as a mother. Wasn't that what he wanted? Of course they should have children, if that would make her happy, Harry said. But for now, she should give the offer serious consideration. There would be time for family later. Now she had the opportunity to serve her country.

If he was being honest with himself, he hoped and expected that she would decline. His bookish Anabel, brilliant scholar, beloved young teacher, European beauty. Instead, when she said, "This is a very interesting offer, Harry — I need time to think," he knew that she was going to say yes, and his heart sank.

Thus began their years of disharmony — her mysterious trips, from which she would return exhausted, diminished somehow. Not just drawn, but worn down. She would recover her old self, then be called back, disappear again. Late 1987 and early 1988 were the worst times: her fall semester was a pedagogical patchwork held together by TAs and pinch-hitting faculty. She promised to do better in the spring, then didn't return to the US in time to begin her classes. They were reassigned. When she finally returned in late February, she slept for twenty hours straight, withdrew from the PhD program. "I'm done," she said. "I'm going to stay home and be a wife and mother."

"I'm so, so happy," Harry lied.

Anabel wept. "I am, too," she lied.

The sun was low when Harry passed the Essex County line, and setting as he entered the Town of Ghorum, where the GPS informed him the Factor's cabin was located. This particular nowhere seemed strangely chosen, for a man whose eccentricities were quite different from the ones other denizens of this place were likely to display. It was near nothing and its natural assets consisted of low hills, scrub trees, and stony creeks. The road the phone commanded him to navigate turned from smooth pavement to cracked asphalt to gravel to dirt, and just as the Factor's destination dot appeared at the top of the app, the cell signal gave up the ghost and the map went blank.

Never mind. It was right this way, over the crest of this hill. The Subaru shuddered and rumbled. If he was still driving old Volvos, he'd likely be shedding parts right now. He nearly missed the turnoff, which was narrow and crowded by untrimmed brush, but once he navigated onto it, he could see the lights of the house ahead, and the glimmer of a creek beyond, reflecting the last of the day's light.

The track gave way to a flattened gravel lot, where an old Jeep and an even older Mercedes were parked. The Mercedes's tires looked slightly flat. Harry pulled in, cut the lights. He sat quietly, listening to the engine tick. After a moment, he reached into the Lands' End bag and took out the Colt. Then he put it back in. He sat for a little while longer. Then he said, "Oh, for fuck's sake," and removed it a second time.

He got out of the car with a groan, slammed the door shut, and was promptly struck from the side by a tremendous, hard, warm force. The Colt fell onto the gravel and Harry's body was thrown against the car. He felt fingers close around his wrists, and his hands smacked against the roof. The breath in his ear stank of coffee and cigarettes.

"The fuck are you," a voice demanded.

Ugh. His arm and hip would be throbbing for days, if not for the rest of his life. He said, gasping, "Tell him . . . Harry Pool is here . . . to see him."

# 25

# Chicago, IL: *Then*

---

Their first day on the run was rainy and cold, April weather lingering into the first week of May. Jane slept through the first leg of the trip, and when she woke they were approaching Erie, Pennsylvania. She gazed in confusion out the windshield, then around the unfamiliar car. Gradually it all came back to her: the party, the basement, the boat, the lake. Lila noticed her stirring and said, "How are you feeling?"

The question reminded Jane that it was possible to feel things, and that she was feeling something now. "I feel sick," she said. They pulled over, the highway rumble strips deepening her nausea. She barely made it to the grassy verge, where she knelt and emptied her stomach again.

"You should eat," Lila said when she'd buckled herself back in.

"Yeah."

They drove another fifteen miles until they came to a service plaza. Lila pumped gas while Jane dozed. Then they parked and bought McDonald's breakfast sandwiches and coffee with George's money. They found a table far away from the other travelers.

"You know where we're going?"

"Her return address was on the letters Dad had." She patted her backpack. "I took them."

"How do you know she still lives there?"

Lila shrugged. "I don't."

The Sausage McMuffin was like medicine. When Jane was through eating it, she went back and bought another. When she got back to the table, Lila had George's laptop out and was trying to find a wireless network. "No public one. There's an office network but I haven't been able to guess the password."

"We can find a motel with internet."

"Yeah. I sort of wanted to bomb it all the way. But maybe we should be well rested for tomorrow." Lila clicked and swiped. "I'm going through his folders. Jesus. All these pictures from years of shows. It looks like he used to teach at some other school . . . Riverton High? Where's that?"

"Could be anywhere."

"He's cropped a bunch so it's just girls he likes. Fucking gross!" She gasped. "Oh my god, Jane."

"What!"

"I don't want to show you." She half closed the laptop lid, glanced behind her. "Girls he brought home. He photographed them naked when they were asleep. Or maybe when they were roofied."

Jane put the second McMuffin down. She could smell the basement, musty and fecal. She thought she might be sick again, took a moment to get control.

"I want to see," she said, pushing the tray away.

"Are you sure?"

"Yeah."

Lila slid the laptop over. The pictures were in a folder marked, disgustingly, RESEARCH. Various girls, naked and unconscious, shot from different angles. She knew she ought to feel righteous anger, but she only felt shame. A family came over with their trays and sat down behind her. She closed the lid and gave the laptop back to Lila.

"Are you okay to drive?" Lila asked her. "I want to go through his email."

"Why?"

"I want a sense of his style for when I write to Principal Kovacs. He uses a lot of ellipses, it's very weird. He leaves out the word 'the' and calls us 'children' instead of, like, students or kids."

"That is creepy."

"Yeah."

They drove for several hours more, into Ohio and past Cleveland. Jane kept the radio on low, adjusting the stations every now and then, switching between pop and country and talk. "What a fucking asshole," Lila said every now and then. "You can tell from the emails which girls he wants to fuck and which ones he doesn't."

"Gross." Were there emails to her in there? Lila didn't say, but there had to be — Jane could remember reading and rereading them, trying to detect hidden meaning. So hungry for love she missed George's actual intentions. She felt like an idiot.

When they had to pee, Jane found a rest stop and pulled over. A vinyl banner, new-looking, hung over the entrance. It read, FREE PUBLIC WI-FI.

"Hell yes!" Lila said. Inside, they got burgers and Dr Peppers from Hardee's and Lila composed the fake email. After a little while she slid the laptop over to Jane.

Dear Dr. Kovacs...
Thank you for your kind support of theater program this year......spring musical was huge success and the children performed like true professionals......very sorry but I just received bad news, brother is dying, I must request emergency leave. Not much work to clean up stage and dressing rooms, I will write to drama club with instructions. Again my apologies......school is full of such talent......I will miss the children this summer......thank you
Sincerely George Framingham

"I guess it's convincing?" Jane said.

"It is. I'll write one to drama club, too."

Lila tapped away with one hand while she ate her burger with the other. At one point a young custodian, a slick, objectively hot dude with both arms fully tattooed, ambled by and said, "What are you girls, like, twins?"

"Us?" Lila said, barely looking up. "We don't know each other."

On the man's arms, women's naked bodies twisted and intertwined like vines. "We just met," Jane said.

"I get off at six," the guy said. "Maybe you wanna get off at six, too."

"Lame," Lila said.

"We're going to have to be prepared for guys like that," Lila went on, once the custodian had moved off with his mop. "We have to get better at defending ourselves."

"How?"

"I don't know. Books."

Jane imagined the custodian cornering them in the restroom hallway, groping them. Imagined his hot breath, his hand around her neck. She imagined driving her knee into his balls, clawing out his eyes. The custodian wailing in agony, begging for mercy.

But why? He was a harmless flirt. Wasn't he? Is this what it was going to be like now? Every Romeo a secret rapist? Jane turned away, fighting back tears. "You're right," she said. "We should."

They got back on the road. In Indiana they found a motel grubby enough to take cash. The lobby stank of cigarettes. An old woman watched a Spanish-language news show on a black-and-white television. Their room was relatively clean; it smelled like cigarettes, but also bleach. Jane took a long, very hot shower and the two of them watched sitcom reruns between advertisements for new cars. After a while Lila took out George's laptop and began to click through the photos again.

"Look." She angled the screen so Jane could see.

It was a picture of her. It had been taken outside the school, presumably during a rehearsal for the fall drama, where kids were standing around, smoking. Behind them, the stage door was propped open with a cinder block. She could tell from her posture that she was relating an anecdote, a funny story. Her hands were in the air, she was slightly bent at the waist, her eyes were wide in joyful mock surprise. Around her, the other kids were laughing.

Jane almost couldn't recognize herself. She looked so happy. She realized that she ought to feel nostalgia, sadness, but she had no memory of this moment. It seemed fake. Or like something that would appear in the newspaper after a tragedy.

"In happier times," she said, a joke. But of course there had been a tragedy. Photos like this really would appear in the newspaper.

In the morning they got gas and bought a map. Jane drove while Lila marked the address they were looking for, on Belle Plaine Avenue, near a park. They were there in under three hours. The address was a small, neat, brown-brick apartment building with a rock garden and a sculpted yew hedge. The girls hurried up the front walk and read the names — ten of them — on the list of occupants. But there was no R. Bortnik, no R. anything. The number corresponding to the address they had was occupied by a P. Cruz.

"She must have moved," Jane said.

Lila said, "Maybe P. Cruz is her husband." She rang the buzzer.

No one answered. It was eleven in the morning on a weekday and this neighborhood seemed to be occupied by professionals, young couples. People would be at work. Lila rang several other buzzers. The intercom crackled and a man's voice said, "Yes?"

"We're looking for Ruth Bortnik."

"Don't know her."

They sat on the steps and watched the rain. Jane said, "Do you know what her job is?"

"No."

"I don't remember Mom ever mentioning her. Did we meet her?"

"Maybe when we were babies?"

Jane said, "Do you think anybody wonders where he is? Like, when's his first appointment that he's going to miss."

"George? I don't know."

"Lila. Maybe this was the wrong thing to do. Maybe we should have just . . . called the cops. The stuff on this laptop . . . it's obvious he was a creep."

Lila stared at her, hard. "Do you want to go back?"

"No."

"I saved you from him. I'm the one who would go to jail."

"I know."

"And do you think they'd let me off? Wayward girls from a broken home. They'd probably manage to charge you with something, too. It's the kind of story people love. They'd make it look like we seduced him so we could rob and kill him."

But Jane really had wanted to seduce him, at first, before they killed and robbed him. Lila was right. They'd both be blamed. Maybe their aunt would take them in, or at least tell them what to do.

The rain picked up. They watched a woman hurrying up the front walk, carrying a bunch of plastic grocery sacks. She had no umbrella or raincoat and wore a business suit and low heels. The girls jumped up.

"Oh! Excuse me."

They stepped to the side to let her by. She was in her early forties, friendly-looking, Indian features but with an American accent. She dumped her bags onto the stoop and fussed with a ring of keys.

"Can we give you a hand?" Lila asked.

"Oh . . . no." She unlocked and opened the door. "Well, you can hold that. I figured I could get groceries over lunch and it started to rain."

Jane held the door and the woman gathered up the bags. "Thank you," the woman said. "Are you waiting for somebody?"

"We're looking for our aunt. But we think she moved. Ruth Bortnik?"

"I know Ruth," the woman said. "I took over her apartment." She frowned. "She never mentioned you."

"We don't really know her."

The woman hesitated, then passed a handful of bags to Lila. "I'm Padma. Come in."


Padma Cruz's apartment was sparsely furnished, and without much decor. There was a television, its screen grayed over with dust, and a nonfunctional fireplace with a potted plant in it. A photo on the wall showed young Padma in graduation cap and gown, posing with an older couple, presumably her parents. The mother wore a sari and bindi, the father a dhoti.

"Why is your name Cruz?" Lila asked, more bluntly than Jane would have.

"Ex-husband," she said, hoisting her bags onto the counter of her small kitchen. "I got off track for a while there, didn't finish my law degree. My parents were furious. Eventually I divorced him, went back to school, and met your aunt."

Jane said, "In school?"

"She was my teacher."

"In . . . law?"

Padma looked from one of them to the other. "You really don't know her at all, do you. Are you lying to me? Are you going to rob me?" She appeared determined—both irritated and accepting of this fate.

"No!" Jane said.

"She was practically a secret," Lila explained. "I don't think our mother even knew we knew about her. But we found letters."

"So your mother . . . has passed away?"

"Yes," Jane said. "Cancer."

Padma Cruz nodded once. "I'm sorry." She gestured to a small dining table, where the three sat down. "Your aunt is an intellectual rights attorney and professor of law at Northwestern. We bonded over our divorces and the fact that we're the same age. I don't have her address and wouldn't feel comfortable giving it to you if I did. But I can call her and ask."

"Yes, please."

She reached into her purse and flipped open a phone. After pushing a couple of buttons, she listened. Jane could hear her aunt's voicemail pick up. Then, before Padma could leave a message, the phone rang in her hand.

The girls listened as Padma explained the situation. She took a small notebook and pen out of her bag and wrote something down. "It's good hearing from you, too," she said. "Let's have dinner." She hung up, ripped a page out of the notebook, and handed it to Lila. "That's her home. She says to meet her there at seven."

"Thank you," Lila said.

Padma scowled at Lila, then at Jane. "How old are you two?"

"Nineteen," Lila said.

"Hm. I do not believe that. Whatever you're doing, please be careful."

Lila said, not without a degree of defiance, "We're just looking for our aunt."

In response, Padma stood up and showed them to the door.

Their aunt lived on Orrington Avenue in Evanston, nearly ten miles away. The rain had stopped and the sun was out, and they had some time to kill. They wandered through the neighborhoods around Wrigley Field, bought sandwiches, ate them in a park. Jane tried to enjoy the unseasonably warm breeze, the experience of a new city, but, suddenly without an immediate goal, she remembered what they had done. Lila's body, crushing the pillow into George's face. The ice-cold lake.

Lila grew thoughtful, and her expression increasingly grim. On a bench facing Lake Michigan, alongside a paved path where runners passed, she took Jane's hand.

"I think we should get rid of the car," she said.

"What! Why?"

Instead of answering, she squeezed harder. "Just, like, leave it in a rough neighborhood." She turned to Jane. "We can take a bus to Aunt Ruth's."

"But then what? Say she won't help us? Or tells us to turn ourselves in?"

Lila shook her head. "Then we get on a Greyhound. Make our way someplace. West, maybe."

"And do what?"

"Change our names. Become, I dunno . . . private eyes."

Jane laughed.

"I'm serious!" Lila said. "What else would we be, Broadway stars?"

They sat in silence. After a while, Jane said, "I actually never thought of being anything. Like, anything real. I figured I would have a job, it didn't matter what. Maybe I'd end up a drunk, like Dad, or, like, married to somebody I don't like. All the stuff we wanted to be as kids was just fantasy."

"It's not," Lila said, releasing her hand. "Real people live interesting lives. For themselves. We can be them."

Jane looked at Lila a long time, as Lila looked fiercely out at the water. Every time a jogger passed, she clocked them with her eyes, never budging her head an inch.

"Okay," Jane said. "Let's go ditch the car."

They drove around until they found a promising spot across Route 14 from a large cemetery, between a check-cashing place and an abandoned auto shop. Safe enough for walking during the day, marginal enough that somebody who found the car would be more likely to drive off than call the police. They gathered their possessions, rolled down the windows. Lila said they should wipe all the fingerprints off the surfaces, so they did. They also emptied the glove compartment into a plastic grocery sack and dropped it into a nearby trash can. Then they left the keys in the ignition and started walking north. Nobody noticed them. Nobody cared.

Aunt Ruth lived in a pretty, quiet neighborhood full of big trees and professional-looking people walking dogs. The sun was going down, the air was getting cold, and delivery trucks rumbled past, distributing their last packages of the day. The house was large, clean-lined, and set back from the street behind a high wrought iron fence. But the fence was decorative, not practical; there was no gate. The girls stood at the end of the walk, gazing up at the warm lights behind curtained windows, the flowering shrubs just now coming into bud. And as they looked, the door opened and they saw their aunt for the first time.

Her silhouette — curious, wary, reluctant, as though the girls might harm her in some way, might steal her time, her attention, her emotions — triggered a memory of childhood, of playing in the bramble of the back yard and failing to heed, or even to hear, the call to dinner, and facing their mother's disapproval, her frustration and exasperation, communicated by that rigid, focused, bent-over form. Jane's heart overflowed with anger and confusion and love, and she wanted to march up the walk and slap her aunt, demand to know where she'd been, why she hadn't cared enough to visit or write or call, to confirm her existence in any way. She turned to Lila, expecting to see the same feelings playing themselves out on her face. But instead Lila's eyes were narrowed, her jaw set in calculation.

"Ruth Bortnik?" Lila said, as though she were a military officer come to tell her that her husband had died in battle.

The silhouette's arm extended and the porch light came on with a snap. There she was: not their mother at all, but an impostor, the woman you run to and embrace by mistake in the department store.

"Hello, girls," she said. "Come in."

Aunt Ruth, it was clear, wasn't happy to see them, though she was curious. She looked the part of the attorney she was: alert, self-possessed, observant. She wore expensive-looking eyeglasses, gray-blond hair pulled back into a casual chignon, a white oxford blouse tucked into pressed blue jeans. Jane and Lila faced her across a long, dark hardwood dining table. They'd just finished eating the sandwiches they'd been offered, which had been made by Ruth's husband (their uncle, Jane supposed, though it seemed strange they could have such a thing), a tall, dignified-looking man who now sipped a cup of tea and read the *Chicago Tribune* in front of a blazing fireplace in the next room. An ornate crystal chandelier hung over Aunt Ruth and the sisters, bathing them in cold, fragmented light. It felt like an interrogation.

"Give me a reason why I shouldn't call your father immediately."

The girls looked at each other. Jane said, "He knows we're gone. We left a note."

"The less he knows," Lila blurted out, "the better."

Aunt Ruth narrowed her eyes. "Why is that."

"We just don't want him to worry," Jane said.

"About what?" Ruth said. "You said you're on a road trip. If I tell him you're here, he ought to be reassured, not alarmed."

"Please don't," Lila said.

"Why aren't you in school?" Ruth asked them. "I doubt you're on break."

"We are on break," Lila said.

"Is there something going on at home? With your father?"

Jane said, "No. Nothing is going on with our father."

"He hasn't been . . . abusive?"

"He doesn't pay any attention to us at all," Lila said.

"Neglectful, then."

"We don't need him," Lila said, her voice hardening. "We're on our own."

"Have you run away from home, girls?"

"No," Jane said.

"Yes," said Lila.

She stared at them for long moments, first Lila, then Jane, then back to Lila. "Why did you track me down?" she asked. "If you're looking for your mother, I can't help you. I haven't spoken to her in years. Your father wrote me asking about her, too. And later, phoned. I told him the same thing."

"We don't need her, either," Lila said.

"Did you do something wrong?"

"No," Lila said.

Aunt Ruth turned to Jane, as though anticipating her "yes." It was on Jane's lips, but she managed to keep them shut.

"All right," Aunt Ruth said. She stood up, left the room. They heard rummaging from the kitchen, the sound of an ice machine. Aunt Ruth returned with three tumblers of ice in one hand and a bottle of whiskey in the other. She set the bottle down on the table, pulled open a drawer on the breakfront cabinet that dominated one wall of the room, and removed three coasters, along with a small kraft paper bag. She distributed the glasses and coasters and poured two fingers into each glass from the bottle. Then she reclaimed her seat. She set the small bag on the table before her, folded her hands, and said, "I don't want to seem cruel or unfeeling. But I am not going to take you in. I've worked hard to achieve this life, and I have no interest in the responsibility of children."

"We're not—" Lila began. Aunt Ruth silenced her with a raised hand.

"In exchange for this refusal, I won't ask again why you're here, I won't contact your father, and I won't make any demands of you, other than that you do not remain here beyond one week. I will rearrange my schedule to the best of my ability to provide for you during this brief time. I will give you money, if you need it, and any other practical resources you might require in order to live your lives safely and independently after you leave. I'll also tell you anything you want to know about your mother. I'm bound to disappoint you on that count, but I'll do my best. Deal?"

Jane was the first to answer. "Deal," she said.

"All right," Lila agreed.

"I have only one other thing to give you. Every now and then, your mother would send me a postcard. I'm not sure why; she didn't write much on them. They were from various places—Europe, California, Central America."

"Screwing her way around the globe," Jane said. Aunt Ruth's eyes widened.

Lila, gesturing toward the bag, said, "That's them?"

Their aunt slid the bag across the table toward them. Lila picked it up. "Those are all I have of your mother."

Lila reached into the bag, examined the postcards. Jane could see that they were just photos of cathedrals, forests, brightly colored birds. On the back, Aunt Ruth's address and an occasional word or two of greeting.

"Why did you keep them?" Jane asked.

She shrugged. "I suppose I felt bad for throwing out the others. I expected we'd see one another again, eventually. But by the time these arrived, I had realized we never would."

"That's sad," Jane said.

Aunt Ruth cocked her head. "Perhaps? It was a relief, to be honest. I admit that the thought of our eventual reunion caused me some anxiety. I don't like a social situation in which I don't have control. I would have had to drink my way through it, no doubt."

She raised her glass and the girls did the same. "Anyway, cheers," she said, and they drank.

## 26

# Near Seattle, WA: *Now*

—————

The conference center was an imposing, wedge-shaped structure with windows overlooking the airfield. Arrows directed them to separate lots for hotel check-in, conference rooms, and offices. Towering glass doors parted as they approached. The café was a bright, antiseptic area with colorful metal tables and chairs where businesspeople sat, typing into laptop computers and talking on phones.

Jane was famished. She bought a grilled cheese sandwich, a banana, and a cappuccino. Lila ordered only a black coffee and watched Jane eat in disapproval. "Do you really need all that?" she said. "We just had breakfast."

"That was five hours ago. Also, shut up. Normal people eat lunch."

"Hm."

"So what's the plan."

When they emerged from Incognito's office, Lila had beelined for the back of the Volvo and pulled her laptop out of its briefcase. She'd spent about five minutes typing and clicking before putting the machine away and walking here with Jane. Now she opened up the laptop on their table and swiveled it to face her. A video feed of a patch of concrete was displayed on the screen; a man in a yellow vest walked across it.

"What am I looking at?"

"This is the security feed from Incognito Air. They use a network with a known vulnerability, but a lot of people haven't patched their devices yet. I grabbed the UIDs off the cameras from the parking lot and reregistered them through the network. So they're mine now. When we go in later, I can turn the whole security system off."

"Okay, wow."

"What we'll be looking for are the flight manifests. We find out where Mom went, then figure out a way to get on the next plane going somewhere close."

Jane said, "How do we do that?"

"We could pretend to be somebody else."

"Who?"

"Whoever's going where she's going. If we're right, and he mostly flies to Central America, it shouldn't be too hard. Oh!" Lila said. "I almost forgot. By now, your father-in-law has probably learned that he is fucked."

"What! How did—"

She grabbed back the laptop, clicked open an application. "There we go. I sent him a big encrypted package containing all my evidence via an ephemeral email. Like the one I sent you. He's already responded." She turned the computer around.

A message from Jane's father-in-law read, "What do you want."

"Jesus!" said Jane.

"How should I proceed?"

"I . . . I don't know."

Lila closed the laptop. "Well," she said. "What *do* you want? And I mean . . . in life. What kind of relationship do you want with Chloe? With Chance?"

"I want shared custody. I want to get along."

"And Susan? Do you want her to see Chloe?"

Jane gave it a moment's thought. "Chloe is her grandchild. And she's Chloe's only grandmother, effectively. She's not a monster. I want them in her life. But I want to be in control."

Lila nodded. "What about assets? Do you want the house?"

"Not really?" Jane said. "Susan owns it, it isn't what I would have picked. I could move in with Dad until I figure something out."

"You sure you want to live with Dad?"

"Chloe likes it there. She plays in the yard." Jane was surprised to find herself overcome by emotion. "I mean, she used to."

"Okay." Lila started typing. "I'm telling him our demands. When you get home, you can hire a lawyer — I'll find you a good one — and divorce amicably. I think they'll be very quick to agree to whatever you want."

"Thank you," Jane said.

"Thank *you*," Lila told her. "I'm glad I can help." After a moment, she drew breath, as though about to say something, then exhaled, as though she'd thought better of it.

"What?"

"I was going to say . . . I got married once."

"No!"

"He was a good guy, or so I thought. A helicopter pilot, ex-military. Our lines of work overlapped. We talked about combining our resources, going big together. It was a whirlwind romance, we got married in Vegas. Then he disappeared."

"Lila, I'm sorry."

"I thought he'd changed his mind or something. But he actually legit disappeared. Dropped off the face of the earth. Assets swept up and vanished, properties sold through an anonymous broker." She nodded at the laptop. "If you exist, I can usually find evidence of it. Everyone leaves traces. But not him. The last thing he said to me, when he left for the last time, was, 'Back in three days.' It's always bothered me. Such a specific amount of time, and he didn't tell me where he was going or why. I was accustomed to that, of course. Until we joined forces we'd agreed to keep our professional lives to ourselves.

"I'm sure we would have had problems, like every couple, you know? But when he left, everything was perfect. I was happy. We were in New Mexico then, but I couldn't stand to stay. I went looking for somewhere to settle, alone. That's when I found Timber Fell, and Loretta.

"His name was Dwight. Dwight Kilmer."

They went for a drive. The sun had warmed the day and was beginning to set; the trees were greening and they rolled the windows down. Jane called Chance and Susan, hoping to talk to Chloe, but no one answered.

When night fell, they parked out of sight of Incognito, near the conference center, and watched the office. A plane landed, and people disembarked: a couple of businessmen and some rich vacationers. The former climbed into a pair of SUVs, the latter into a Ferrari. Half an hour later, the pilot and crew left, and the lights went out in the office windows. The woman from upstairs walked out with Gil, their arms around each other's waists.

"Aw," Lila said.

Gil locked the office door, and then, after they passed through, padlocked the gate of the chain-link fence. The couple drove away in a black BMW.

"All right," Lila said. "Here we go."

Lila opened her laptop on the hood of the car. A minute later, she had turned off the airline's security system. As they walked calmly to the fence, Jane said, "You know how to open the lock?"

"Please," Lila said. She reached into her bag and pulled out a small folded nylon case that contained a collection of small tools. It took her about as long to pick the lock as it would have taken Jane to open it with a key.

"Neat," Jane said, as Lila pulled the gate closed behind them.

"I mean," Lila said, "we could have just gone into the trees over there and climbed over."

"I'm too dainty for that," Jane said.

"Right. Ladies enter with dignity."

The office door proved equally easy, and soon they'd closed it behind them. Lila produced a small flashlight and led them up the stairs to the office. Jane woke the woman's computer, which asked for a password.

"I could probably get in via remote desktop," Lila said.

"Hold on." Jane was thinking of Lydia, from the history office, whose computer looked just like this, covered with sticky notes. She couldn't remember her passwords and had difficulty using the password manager the IT department had installed. As Jane tried out the passwords she found, she heard Lila clomp down the metal stairs and move around below.

None of the passwords worked, so she got down on her hands and knees and peered into the hollow beneath the desk.

"Shine that over here," she said to Lila, who was climbing up the stairs holding a clipboard.

Lila obliged. There were no stickies here. But a piece of masking tape bearing a random series of numbers and letters adhered to the exterior of the file drawers. She peeled it off.

"Here we go."

The password worked, and the computer opened.

"Excellent," Lila said. "So, this clipboard is the same as the one there on the wall. It's the week's printed-out flight manifests. I'm sure there's another in the hangar. She flew into another private airport."

"So you were right."

"Look up Aeropuerto Área 17."

Jane clicked over to a web browser and opened a map. "It's in Costa Rica . . . seems to mostly be for palm-oil plantation bigwigs? It's not far from the Panamanian border."

Lila flipped through the clipped sheets, reading by flashlight. "Looks like she owns the plane. Most of these belong to Gil." She looked up at the screen. "They haven't printed out tomorrow's yet."

Jane clicked an icon marked TotalFlight. This proved to be the software that generated the manifests. One part of it displayed the calendar Jane had seen open on the screen earlier in the day. "Okay. Tomorrow there are . . . three flights. Bogotá . . ."

"Nope."

". . . uh, Guatemala City . . ."

"No."

". . . and . . . San José."

"Dammit. Wait, California?"

"Costa Rica."

Lila leaned over. "Open it up."

The flight had been chartered by a company called El Festejo. Six passengers. Return flight three days later. Jane opened a browser and searched. "They make . . . liquor. Guaro, do you know what that is?"

"Costa Rican rum, basically."

Lila, impatient, pulled out her laptop, clicked, and swiped. A minute later she said, "I think this flight is a PR junket. They had a contest in the Seattle area. Like, a cocktail recipe contest. The winners go on a trip to the distillery and some kind of beach party."

"What are you looking at?"

"Instagram. Is there anyone on the manifest named . . . uh . . . Madison Klon?"

The name was there. "Yes!"

"How about Nicole Lamb?"

"She's on there, too."

Lila turned the laptop around to show it to Jane. It displayed a photo of two women in their twenties, each holding a bottle of El Festejo guaro in one hand and a tall, fancily bedecked daiquiri glass in the other. They looked happy and drunk.

"What do you think?" Lila said. "You want to be them?"

Jane laughed. "How would that work?"

"We call them, tell them the flight's been canceled. Put ourselves on the manifest in their place. Hop the flight to San José."

"Won't we need passports, visas, that kind of thing?"

Lila dug into her laptop case and extracted a resealable plastic bag. It contained a stack of American passports bearing different versions of her own photo, and different names. She compared them to the women on the screen, then handed one to Jane. In the photo, Lila had straight dark brown hair and the name read Sarah Matthews. "You'll be Nicole Lamb."

"So, to customs, I'm Sarah Matthews, and to the El Festejo people, I'm Nicole."

"And never the twain shall meet," Lila said, choosing a passport for herself.

"We hope."

"We just have to fake it until we're in the air. Then we're home free."

Jane replaced Nicole Lamb's name with Sarah Matthews in the manifest software, then Madison Klon with Francine Stillman, the name on the passport Lila had chosen. Then she put the computer to sleep, replaced the piece of masking tape, and followed Lila out the door, stopping in the hangar to replace the manifest clipboard. Back in the parking lot, Lila used her computer to turn the security system back on.

They spent the night at an anonymous motel in Monroe. Jane took out her phone and called Chance. He answered with "What the fuck are you doing?"

"May I speak to Chloe, please?"

"My parents are losing their fucking minds," he shout-whispered. "They won't tell me what's going on."

"Chance," Jane said, "I think you should calm down and follow their lead here. I might be out of touch for a few days, but I wanted to talk to Chloe first."

"Whatever you're doing, Jane," he said, "it is not acceptable."

"Please put her on, Chance. There will be plenty of time to argue soon."

She listened to his breathing for a few seconds. Footsteps, muffled voices. Then: "Mom! They're freaking out. What did you do?"

"I didn't do anything."

"That's not what they're saying. They're saying you're a criminal and you're trying to destroy them."

Jane could hear skepticism in her voice: that was good. "Not a criminal," she said. "They aren't destroyed."

"I don't believe you."

Jane sighed. "Chloe," she said, "whatever I'm doing, it's all for the best. I will be home soon, and everything will be back to normal."

"It's not normal if you went to jail."

"All right, then everything will be weird. But I'll be home."

There was a long silence. "I looked you up. Under your old name. There was a whole trial. There's video and everything, from the news."

"Yeah, I know."

"Some people said you were a hero or something."

"I wasn't. I was stupid. But it was a long time ago. I was just a kid."

"What else did you lie to me about?"

"Honestly? I don't remember. Honey, parents tell lies. There's stuff we don't think you're ready to know because you're a kid. I wish I'd told you about this sooner. I'm angry at your grandmother for telling you. It's something your dad and I were going to do."

Another silence. Then: "I have to go."

"Okay," Jane said. "You might not hear from me for a couple of days. But after that, I'll be coming home."

"Whatever. Maybe I should just live here now," Chloe said. "With Dad."

A silence opened up between them, and widened. Jane fought back tears. Eventually, she said, "I hope you'll want to live with us both."

"Maybe," Chloe said, and she could tell the girl was also trying not to cry.

Jane hung up before Chance could get back on the line. "Well," she said to Lila, "looks like your plan is working."

If Lila could hear the anger in Jane's voice, she had no visible reaction.

"Of course it is," she said. She'd copied down the other names from the manifest and was doing research on the other four passengers. "The PR flack is a guy named Chet, if you can believe that. He'd be the one to call to tell them their flight's canceled." She picked up her phone and called Loretta, asked her to do this in the morning. "Just tell them it's delayed by a day, due to weather. So they won't text or email the real Chet. Spoof a number from their office."

Loretta said something Jane couldn't hear.

"Better still," Lila said. "And could you arrange a car for us? Tell them we might have to go over the border. We're landing at . . . Aeropuerto Internacional Román Macaya. Flight gets there at seven in the morning. Oh, and one other thing — could you find a way to get Matías Gil out of the way for a couple of hours? He probably wouldn't recognize us or even see us at all, but I don't want to take the chance."

When she hung up, Jane said, "Over what border?"

"Panama."

"What makes you think we're going to Panama?"

Lila wouldn't look her in the eye. "Just covering all the bases," she said.

Jane woke up in a better mood. The matter with Chloe would resolve itself. Wouldn't it? Every kid is mad when their parents divorce. She couldn't have really meant it. Could she?

Lila found a secondhand store in Issaquah called Thrifty Pick and they bought some clothes for their boozy alter egos to wear. At a drugstore they found makeup and hair dye. "Excellence creme," Jane read, selecting a box and holding it up to Nicole Lamb's Instagram. "I guess it must be good. Hashtag party!"

"Hashtag good times!" said Lila.

"Hashtag identity theft!"

"Hashtag felony impersonation!"

Lila paid the hotel owner, a tired-looking man with a mustache, to let her park the Volvo there for a few days. Outside, she opened one of the military equipment cases that dominated the cargo area of the car and removed two banded stacks of cash, then, as an apparent afterthought, a third.

"Jesus! How much do you leave in there?"

"Not too much. A few thousand. I don't use ATMs."

"No," Jane said, "I guess you wouldn't."

Lila called for a cab to take them to Pine Valley. While they waited they assessed each other's appearance: ripped jeans, baseball caps with sports logos, big sunglasses, tennis shoes. Lila wore a white blouse, tied at the waist, over a bikini top; Jane a hoodie over a tank. "Oh my *god*," Lila said.

"Madison, you look *hot*."

"You look *hot*, Nicole."

"No, but seriously, Madison. So hot."

"Thank you, Nicole. You are *hot*."

"My boyfriend Jake is dogsitting my Pomeranian, Nugget."

"I love roller skating and my job managing a Red Lion Inn in Redmond."

"My niece, Kayleigh, loves Princess Peach and playing the recorder."

"My nephew Sage just learned to walk."

In the car, Lila called Loretta and verified that everything was going according to plan. "Actually," she said hanging up, "Nicole was delighted about the delay, because she has a stomach bug and would have had a terrible flight. And Mr. Gil is on his way to his lake cabin, where 'the police' just told him there's been a break-in."

"Perfect."

They met up with the rest of the junket in the hangar. Chet was a handsome, reedlike gay man with a curly undercut and beard stubble. The other three execs were weathered outdoorsy women around the twins' age. They squealed in fake recognition, hugged them, said how excited they were. The counterfeit passports were accepted without complaint, and they all filed onto the plane, a twenty-seat Learjet. The pilot announced that the flight would take about eleven hours, including two refueling stops. Jane and Lila left their sunglasses on, claiming hangovers, and took seats in the back, to try to put a little distance between them and the strangers they were supposed to know.

"How did you get the idea for the Maroon Lagoon?" one of the women asked.

"Seriously," another one said. "Blood orange juice and black walnut bitters? Fucking genius."

"Oh my god," Lila said. "Somebody sent one of our guests a fruit basket and they never picked it up? And it had, like, these blood oranges? So when I got home I just started, like, trying things out? Nicole brought over the bitters."

Jane said, "I was, like, you know what else should go in here? Fucking *rhubarb.*"

"Incredible," Chet said, poking at his phone. "Hey, can I get a snap for our Insta?"

"Oh god," Lila said. "I'm a wreck. Wait until I get a little sleep."

"Same here," said Jane.

They woke during the first refueling stop. When the plane took to the air again, Jane said, "What are you going to tell Loretta's guy? The driver? Where do we go first?"

"I'm still thinking. I guess someplace on one of the postcards."

"Yeah, but," Jane said, "that's thousands of square miles, hundreds of little towns. And she sent them years ago. Who's to say she's actually at one of these places?"

"Uh-huh."

"Even if we assume she's close to where her plane landed—"

"We don't know that. It could be a refueling stop on the way to a private airstrip. It probably is."

"Right. So . . . where do we go?"

Through gritted teeth, Lila said, "I'm *thinking.*"

The two sat in silence for a minute, Lila staring out the window, Jane picking threads off the holes in her jeans. Finally she nudged her sister.

"Do you have them? The postcards. Lemme see them."

With a dismissive grunt, Lila dug into her bag, handed over the little brown paper sack, and closed her eyes.

The postcards were in better condition than Jane remembered from their brief appearance at Gramps's compound. The paper had yellowed, they were slightly furred at the edges, but what little wear there was seemed to have resulted from the trip through the mail to Chicago: smeared postmarks, indentations from machine rollers. According to Aunt Ruth, these were the only things their mother had sent. They'd arrived over the course of many years, to judge by the postmarks; Jane assumed the dates would correspond to her absences from home. Why on earth couldn't she have sent a few to her husband and daughters? Even a blank one would have meant something.

Jane nodded off and woke when the stack of cards tumbled to the floor of the plane. When she bent down to pick them up, she had a memory: a game she used to play with Chloe when the girl was seven or eight. Jane would hide a gift of some kind somewhere in the house, then invent a cryptic clue in verse describing where it was. If it was stashed in the freezer, for instance, she'd take up a note card and write something like, "Your special gift / is nearly found. / Check where it's winter / all year round." And then she'd hide the note card in, say, the garage, and prepare another note card about that. "A trip to the mall / because you're bored? / Proceed to where / your ride is stored." Then hide *that* note card, and so on. A trail of bread crumbs. She still had most of these strings of clues, packed away in a box in the closet. Stacks of cards of clues.

She looked more closely at the postcards. What if these *had* been intended for Lila and her? Did she predict they would track Ruth down someday, and sent her these as a message for them to decode? A bread crumb trail?

But the card she was holding—the one from David, a city on Panama's southern coast—offered her literally nothing. There wasn't even a message, just Aunt Ruth's address. She studied the handwriting, compared it to the writing on the other cards, but it was all the same. The generic text on the bottom of the card read, "San José de David, o David, es la capital de la provincia de Chiriquí, en el oeste de Panamá. En el frondoso Parque Miguel de Cervantes Saavedra hay vendedores . . ." The only anomaly, if you could call it that, was a small flaw where a postal machine had scraped away one of the letters, the *m* in "Panama."

Jane brought the card closer. Actually, a machine hadn't done this—it appeared to have been removed precisely, scored with a sharp knife, the top layer of paper lifted off. A little shallow white grave where the letter used to be.

Excited, she examined the other cards. Some of them hadn't been altered at all. Most of these had a brief scribbled message to Ruth on them—"Be well," "Thought of you," "You'd like it here." But from each of the blank cards, that single tiny letter had been meticulously removed. The *c* from "Parque Nacional." The *o* from "Colón."

And now, with a start, Jane realized something else—every one of these blank cards was sent *after* their mother disappeared for good. There was a gap of many years, in fact, between the last card with a message on it—sent from Washington, DC, it read "Belly of beast"—and the first

214

blank one. And all of the blank cards were sent from somewhere in Central America.

Jane reached into her pack for a notebook and pen and wrote down the missing letters.

CIMNENOAIT

"Wait," Lila said. "What are you doing?"

"It's a code. The postcards. All of these blank ones are from Central America, and each one is missing a letter."

Lila snatched the pile away from her, held them up to the light. "Jesus Christ," she said. The PR crew glanced back at them, then returned to whatever gossip they were busy exchanging. "You're right," Lila whispered.

"What does this mean?" Jane said, holding out the paper.

"It's a place name. Right? The letters spell out a town." Lila reached into her bag and brought out a map. She spread it out over their laps. "Look for ten-letter places."

"Llano Marín."

"Río de Jesús."

"Puerto Vidal."

"That's eleven."

"Whatever!"

"Nacimiento."

"Cerro Banco. Wait!" Lila said. "What was that one?"

"Nacimiento?"

"Nacimiento, Panama," Lila said. "That fits."

"Nacimiento."

"Nacimiento!"

"It was" — Jane glanced at the postmarks — "well, a long time ago, but she was there."

"Ohmigod, *Nicole,*" Lila shout-whispered. "You're, like, a fucking skanky-ass *genius*?"

"*Madison,*" Jane said back, "no *duh,* you legendary inebriated slut!"

As the plane taxied for the final leg of the trip, hushed conversation broke out among the El Festejo group. "Madison," Chet called back to them. "Did you text me last night? About the trip being delayed?"

They had both gone back to sleep, waking up only briefly during the second refueling. There was something in Chet's voice, though, that brought Jane fully awake. Her stomach rose into her chest as the plane descended.

Jane watched as Lila pretended to dispel her grogginess, giving herself a few seconds to figure out what to say. "What? No, I texted you two nights ago. There was a storm or something, I was worried we'd get canceled."

"No, the one last night. 'Feeling much better, see you tomorrow.'"

"Oh god, I remember now—my stomach bug. No, I sent that two nights ago."

"I just got it."

"Weird."

"I texted you question marks. And now . . . you just texted me back? Just now?"

The plane was in the air now. "Yeah, no!" Lila said. "I don't think so?"

Jane was gazing in horror at the PR crew, who were gazing back in puzzlement. Chet looked at his phone and back up at Lila and Jane. He said to the others, "No signal now, so . . ."

"Guys, I'm going back to sleep," Lila said.

"Same," said Jane. "See you in Costa Rica, woo-hoo!"

At one point during the two-hour flight, Chet stood up, moved quietly to where they sat feigning sleep behind their sunglasses, and stared at them, eyes narrowed. He looked at his phone, then at them, then at the phone again. When he returned to his seat, the four huddled together in hushed conversation.

"I think our cover is blown," Jane whispered.

"Whatever," Lila said. "What are they going to do, turn the plane around?"

She was right. The El Festejo group were helpless. When the plane touched down, the four pulled out their phones and began furiously typing and making hushed calls. Lila, meanwhile, called Loretta. She spoke for a moment, then put the phone away and said, "Our guy will be waiting for us just beyond the fence to the left of the terminal. She says not to go through customs." The day was bright, and when the single flight attendant, a stern man with a neatly trimmed beard, threw open the exit door, a sweet hot wind swirled through the cramped cabin.

The PR group gathered their possessions and hastily climbed out of the plane, casting glances at Lila and Jane over their shoulders. When the sisters emerged, they found the four standing on the tarmac, huddled together in obvious alarm. One of them was talking on the phone. Chet exchanged a few words with the others, drew himself up, and took a deep breath. He met them at the bottom of the stairs.

"I don't know what kind of bullshit this is," he said, his voice quavering. "But we are calling the Fuerza Pública right now."

"Relax, Chet," Lila said. "Mr. Gil will bring your booze girls down here tomorrow."

"You are fucking terrorists and you're going to jail" was his response. Behind him, the three women were gesturing toward a couple of cops standing by the door to the customs office. When they didn't react, one of the women ran over to them, pointing back at the plane.

They were in a region surrounded by green hills; the air was warm and moist. Jane scanned the chain-link fence enclosing the airfield, saw a gap and, beyond it, a path. "Hey," she said, nudging Lila. "We should go."

"Chet thinks we're going to jail," Lila said, not taking her eyes off the man. Chet's jaw was trembling. Beyond him, the PR woman had gotten the cops' attention and appeared to be having difficulty making herself understood.

"Oh, you *are*," Chet said.

"Not," Lila replied, then feinted at him. He flinched, stumbled back.

"You people are crazy," he said, backing away.

"Have a great weekend, Chet!" Lila said, moving toward the fence. "Give our best to Madison and Nicole!"

He turned and ran for the group, who now surrounded the customs cops. Jane said, "Let's go, let's go."

"That was fun," Lila said.

"Not fun."

"Fun."

They crossed the tarmac to the gap in the fence, actually a gate, disused and hanging open. It led to a narrow paved path, which brought them to the shoulder of an access road. A little red Hyundai was parked there. The driver climbed out and introduced himself as Saúl. Lila talked to him in Spanish for a minute, then shook his hand and counted out some bills.

"I'm not sure if I have the nuance right," she said to Jane, "but he seemed to be suggesting that we'd have an easier crossing in a small town. Like, less friction. I told him fine."

As they pulled away, Jane peered out the back window, expecting lights and a siren. But there was nothing, and eventually she calmed down. A little while later, Lila asked Saúl to pull over at a desolate spot of road. To Jane, she said, "Give me your passport and phone."

Jane handed them over. "Why?"

"The passports are burned. Phones, I throw out every time I cross a border. I'll get you a new one."

Lila climbed out, crouched down, and, with a pocketknife, dug a hole beside a drainage ditch. She tore the passports in half, crushed the phones under her heel, and buried the mess in the hole. When they were back on the road, she handed Jane a new passport.

"Maria Bolaño?"

"Yeah. You're an American, Mexican-born. Or, she was."

"And twenty-nine, huh."

"Time to dust off those acting chops," Lila said, flashing a smile.

"Hardy-fuckin'-har."

The driver took them south, past hills and farms, and up, via winding highway, into the mountains. He gestured to either side of the car and spoke to them.

"He says we're in between two national parks. Those are the Talamanca Mountains." In the distance, white mist enveloped the peaks, and below them, rivers wound through green valleys.

It was a long drive. Jane slept for a while. When she woke, the land was lower and the road narrower; every now and then they passed through a small town. The road began to rise again and turned to tan dirt and gravel. Eventually the car slowed in a tiny village. Behind a fence, a low building was marked by a hanging sign: OFICINA REG. SABA-LITO. A small line of people waited at the door, and cars occupied a parking lot. Saúl pulled in and turned off the engine. He spoke to the two of them and held out his hand.

"Okay," Lila said. "He's asking for the passports. I think he's got a friend in there." The sisters handed over the passports. Jane noted a small pile of American twenties poking out of Lila's.

"I see," she said.

They waited in the sun outside the car. It was humid here, but cooler than at the airport. A few people waiting in the line glanced over at them, vaguely curious.

After a moment, Saúl exited the building. He walked past them, beckoning for them to follow. He led them up a small hill to another tin-roofed building. A second sign read MINISTERIO DE SEGURIDAD PÚBLICA MIGRACIÓN. There were two small lines of people. One of the groups wore shorts, tee shirts, running shoes, and tank tops. The other, beneath a sign marked GRUPOS ORIGINARIOS, consisted mostly of women in colorful print dresses. One elderly lady was holding out a finger, and on the finger was perched a small bird, its leg leashed to her thumb by a piece of string. She fed it seeds from her other palm. Saúl again told them to stay outside and disappeared around the corner of the building. When the bird woman reached the door, she embraced a companion, perhaps her daughter, and said goodbye. She trudged down the hill toward town, nodding to the sisters as she passed.

Saúl emerged, handed them their passports, and led them back to the car. They got back on the road and rumbled slowly through the village toward the border. In English, he said, "You go to Nacimiento?"

"Yes," Lila told him.

"After the border, taxi," he said.

"Sure."

A few minutes later, they crossed into Panama.

# 27

# Chicago, IL: *Then*

The girls' grandfather, Aunt Ruth told them, was a Russian-born American named Alexander Bortnik who grew up in Washington, DC, a child of low-level diplomats who elected to remain in the United States rather than repatriate at the start of the Second World War. Their grandmother, Mariana Castillo, was the native-born product of a short-lived marriage between a Spanish American intelligence officer and a socialite from Madrid. The couple's parents knew one another from the Embassy Row cocktail circuit of the 1950s; Sasha and Mariana met at a mixer between their two private high schools. Anabel, the girls' mother, was born in 1960, and Ruth three years later.

"Like the two of you," Aunt Ruth told them, "I did not know my mother well. My sense is that she regarded her marriage to my father as an inconvenience. She was a heavy drinker and frequently traveled back to Spain, drawn by her very large, very rich family. Your mother and I visited their villa in Cádiz exactly once, when we were ten and seven, respectively. Our Spanish was execrable and it was clear that we and our father were embarrassments to our mother. Eventually she took a trip and never returned; our father confessed that she had had multiple affairs with young men and eventually left him for one. He, too, became an alcoholic and died before you girls were born." She raised her glass to punctuate the point.

Alexander would squander most of the money left to him by his well-off but fiscally imprudent parents, but he did have enough to send Anabel and Ruth to Ivy League colleges. Ruth continued on to law school, Anabel to a graduate program in American history. "Which, as you know, is where she met your father."

Ruth refilled her glass but did not offer to refill the sisters'. She said, "I admit I despised my father. It couldn't have been easy, raising two head-strong girls who took after the imperious, self-important mother who abandoned them. But the older we got, the more we seemed to remind him of her. As his disease worsened, his hostility increased. He struck us both, and when drunk would attempt to touch us sexually. Your mother once knocked him unconscious with an empty wine bottle."

This detail made Lila sit up straighter. Jane watched as, beneath the table, she struck her knee with her fist in a steady rhythm.

"Our father doesn't treat us that way," Jane blurted.

Aunt Ruth turned to her, eyes narrowed. "I'm glad."

"Like I said. He doesn't treat us any way at all," Lila said.

"I don't know your father," Aunt Ruth said. "I have, in fact, never met him. If your parents had a wedding, I was not invited to it."

"They got married in a park, by a judge," Lila said. "With some random guy as a witness."

"There's one picture," Jane added. "But I think Mom said they took it later. Dad talked her into getting dressed up again after he bought a camera."

Aunt Ruth nodded. "Lloyd and I were wed in a courthouse as well, though his parents insisted on a lavish reception afterward. I think our mother's self-importance gave your mother and me both something to rebel against. But of course shunning all pomp and circumstance can become its own kind of narcissism.

"It sounds as though, like my own mother, she traveled frequently?"

"Yeah," Lila said. "You could definitely say that."

"And was unfaithful to your father."

"Yes," Jane said.

Aunt Ruth gazed at her with what she read as sympathy. Though it was hard to tell. "When he contacted me," she said, "he wanted me to speculate about where she might be, how I could find her. I just didn't know. By the time I graduated from college, your mother and I were independent women with our own lives. We had little in common, other than a family that had neglected and traumatized us."

"Do you remember the last time you spoke with her?" Lila asked. "What did you talk about?"

Aunt Ruth sat in silence for a moment, running her finger around the rim of her glass. "You have to understand, our conversations were not memorable. They were infrequent enough to be noteworthy, but little of importance was said between us. Before you girls were born, we discussed our work. And for a short while after, we discussed you. First as a source of anxiety and exhaustion, and later with some degree of pleasure. At some point, though, she stopped mentioning the two of you, or anything else specific about her life. She became cryptic, philosophical. I suspected that she was suffering from some mental illness, or was under the effect of some drug."

Jane turned to look at Lila, but her sister ignored her. She leaned forward, rapt.

"Cryptic how?" Lila asked.

"She mused about morality, responsibility. In part, I think she felt guilty for her inadequacy as a parent. But her questions were larger than that—about the morality of nations, a government's obligation to its citizens. How responsible we are for our small roles in the suffering of others far away. She wondered about our grandparents' work as diplomats. I'm making it sound much more coherent than it was. She often called very late at night, or early in the morning. There were long silences, sudden pivots in mid-sentence. I'd often lose the thread—I was tired.

"The last time we spoke, I told her that we were moving to a new house—this one—and that we wouldn't be using a conventional landline. I gave her the number to my cell phone. But I got the sense that she wasn't writing it down, and she never called after that."

"When was that last call?" Lila asked.

"Three years ago? Four?"

The three sat in silence for a while. Aunt Ruth drained her glass, stood up, and took hold of the bottle. "Well. That's twice as much as I usually drink. I suspect by now Lloyd has prepared the guest rooms for the two of you. I'm going to bed. You may help yourself to whatever you like from the refrigerator. Please place your dishes in the sink when you're through; Rosie will attend to them tomorrow." She moved, slightly unsteadily, through the doorway and disappeared up the stairs.

The girls ate cold cuts and a block of cheddar cheese while leaning against the sink. Soon Lloyd appeared and led them to their rooms. Jane couldn't sleep. She sneaked into Lila's room and climbed into bed with her. "Are you awake?" she asked after a while.

"Yes."

"Do you think they noticed him gone yet?"

"Maybe. I don't know."

"Did you check the computer?"

"Tomorrow."

A little while later, Jane said, "What else is in there? Like, did he have a family and stuff? Did he email his mother?"

She felt her sister stiffen and turn over. Lila's hands found her face. She smelled cold cut breath. Lila said, "Stop trying to humanize a rapist."

"I can't help it," Jane whispered, beginning to cry.

"The world is better without him. We have done it a huge favor."

"I know."

"Say it to me. The world is better without him."

"The world . . . is better without him."

"We have saved dozens of girls from pain."

"We have . . . we have . . ."

The hands gripped Jane's head harder as the sobs tore through her. Eventually Lila took her into her arms and rocked her as she cried. She tried to be quiet, but it was impossible. Even in this big house with its thick walls, they could hear her. But nobody came to them in the night, and eventually they slept.


The days they spent at Aunt Ruth's felt uneasy, unreal—as though they were waiting in the lobby of a theater, about to see a horror movie. Aunt Ruth and Lloyd (Jane tried to call him "Uncle Lloyd" just once, and he smiled politely and said "Lloyd" in his nature-documentary-narrator baritone and that was that) treated them with polite detachment, gave them house keys, fed them meals, and otherwise left them alone. Aunt Ruth went to work at Northwestern each day; Lloyd, a decade her elder and already retired from some kind of rich-person job, withdrew to his study, emerging occasionally for a cup of tea, a sandwich, or a walk. They didn't tell Aunt Ruth anything about their situation and she radiated a disinclination to know more.

Lila became obsessed with learning whether George's death had been discovered. Their second night, she opened the laptop and logged into his email; Principal Kovacs had replied. "Look at this," Lila said, handing the laptop to Jane, who lay beside her, too exhausted to sleep, on the guest bed.

> Dear George —
>
> I'm very sorry to hear about your brother. I wish you and your family the best of luck. The students and custodial staff were able to clean up in half a day, so you don't need to worry your absence has been a burden.
>
> I do want to tell you that Janice Thiel has decided not to return to Nestor High, and will be retiring. So the permanent position of theater director will be open. I encourage you to apply.
>
> Lawrence Kovacs

"So he was just filling in," Lila said, her eyes gleaming. "Do you know what this means? Nobody's expecting him to be anywhere."

"We don't know that. I'm sure he has friends or family."

"I'm not. Does somebody with a life invite high school students over to party?"

Jane thought about it. "Maybe not."

"Did he own that house or rent it?"

"He owned it, remember? He said he bought it with money from the plays he wrote."

"Right, perfect."

"It could be a long time," Jane said.

"It's a weird location, too. It's not like a lot of people are going to be walking by, wondering what's up."

Something about Lila's excitement was making Jane feel a little sick. Or maybe it was the takeout she'd eaten too much of, or the exhaustion, or the memory of the basement, the smell of mildew and sweat and death, the cold of the lake water. All of that, incredibly, was just the other day. She felt despair watching all the alternate choices recede in the rearview mirror. Not flirting with George. Not getting drunk. Not trusting him. Stopping Lila when she brought the pillow down over his face. Calling the cops. Not stealing his car, not going on the run. Nothing the girls had done that night was wrong. Jane was being raped. Lila was protecting her. This laptop would have ended up in the hands of the detectives and they would have found the pictures and interviewed the girls, and the girls would have told them what George did. If he'd recovered from the tiki candle, he would have been prosecuted for his crimes. Lila and Jane would be heroes, not killers.

"I don't want this hanging over us forever," Jane said. "When they finally find him, they're going to think about what else happened then, and somebody will tell them that the Pool sisters disappeared."

"We won't be the Pool sisters anymore," Lila said.

Jane let a long moment pass. Then she said, "What are we going to be, then?"

Lila turned and gazed into her eyes. "Whatever we want. We can be whatever we want, Jane."

On the fourth night of their stay, Jane and Lila, reading by the fireplace, heard the kitchen landline ring. From Aunt Ruth's side of the conversation that followed, it was clear that the caller was their father. They listened, two rooms away, as Aunt Ruth told him that she hadn't seen or heard from the girls and didn't know a thing about them. No, she hadn't heard from Anabel, either. Yes, she was fine, thanks for asking. Yes, she'd call if the girls tried to contact her.

Jane expected Aunt Ruth would come into the library and ask to speak with them, but she didn't, not then. It was another two days before that conversation happened. The girls had been out for a walk and were sitting at the dining room table with a road atlas, plotting their next move. Aunt Ruth called them into the library, where, for the first time since they arrived, no fire burned. It had been an unseasonably hot day, and now, at sunset, a warm breeze billowed in through the open windows. Lloyd joined the three of them there but remained with his hands clasped in the corner of the room, placidly observing. Jane and Lila took the sofa and Aunt Ruth the armchair by the cold black fireplace. Aunt Ruth laid a white paper envelope on the ottoman before her.

"Tomorrow will be your last night," she began.

Lila interrupted immediately. "We'll be leaving tomorrow, actually," she said, though she and Jane hadn't discussed it.

Aunt Ruth nodded. "Very well. Before you go, I wanted to reiterate my position that I will not ask about your reasons for leaving home, and I will not tell your father I've seen you. You may be aware that he discovered our phone number and called me the other night. He seemed worried, and not in the way of someone who has done something wrong. I understand that he's not an active or enthusiastic parent, but, unless you have reason to despise him, you may want to find a way to let him know you're alive.

"I've talked this over with Lloyd, and we've agreed to extend you this offer: you may come to stay with us for seven nights each year. We'd like you to consider our home a haven, but not a shelter. As a defender of the law, I must regard you as runaway children, whose welfare I am endangering with this policy. But as your aunt, I regard you as emancipated adults."

"Thank you," Lila said.

"Yes, thank you," Jane echoed, and Aunt Ruth glared at her, clearly perceiving the lack of conviction in her tone.

"I don't want to regret this," Aunt Ruth said, her eyes still on Jane's. "If you turn up dead at seventeen, regardless of my legal culpability, I will be to blame. In my heart." The words *my heart* seemed to catch in her throat, and for an astonishing moment, Jane thought she might cry. But she righted herself and continued. "If you are like your mother and me, then you won't turn up dead. You will find your way somehow, and thrive. If you are like your father, however, I don't know what awaits you." She paused a moment, eyes on the ceiling now. "I don't mean to cast aspersions on the man. I don't know him."

"We're like you and Mom," Lila said confidently. But Aunt Ruth trained a withering look at her.

"At the risk of insulting you, Lila, you do not, in fact, know what or whom you are like."

Lila appeared angered but remained silent.

"Girls," Aunt Ruth said, "you really may stay tomorrow night. Lloyd and I had planned on taking you to dinner. Someplace nice."

"That won't be necessary," Lila said. "Thank you, Aunt Ruth."

Aunt Ruth turned to Jane, anticipating her response. She wanted Jane, it was clear, to stand up for herself, accept the offer of another night in the house. But Lila was the leader now. Jane would let her sister call the shots. "No, thank you," she said. "We've made plans to go."

Aunt Ruth's eyes narrowed, but she nodded. She leaned over and picked up the envelope, then handed it, somewhat pointedly, to Jane. "That's fifteen hundred dollars in cash. I'll also give that to you every year, if you show up. Please let us know at least one week in advance."

Lila glared at the envelope, her mouth tight. She wanted to reject it, Jane could tell. So she quickly said, "Thank you, Aunt Ruth, this means a lot to us."

"You're welcome. Well!" she said, pushing herself up out of the chair. "I'm going to bed to read. Stay up as late as you like. Don't drink all the scotch." In the corner, Lloyd, too, got to his feet.

When they were gone, Jane said, "We need the money and I am not going to leave it behind tomorrow."

"Actually, I think we should leave tonight."

"What?"

"We can walk to Northwestern and get a bus to the Greyhound station. And then we'll be on our way."

Jane stared at her. Lila stared back. Jane said, "This is not how I would have handled all this."

She feigned offense. "What are you even talking about? This *is* how you're handling it. We're in this together. Do you have a better plan?"

"Not anymore," Jane said. "You know what I'm talking about. I was in shock."

"If you want to go back," Lila said, "with your envelope of cash, and turn me in to the police, I can't stop you."

"That's not what I mean!"

"Then what?" Incredibly, Lila was crying. "What do you mean?"

Jane, too, was crying now. "I . . . I don't know! I guess . . . I just want things to be different from this."

"Well, so do I! But this is how things are now!"

"I know."

Jane leaned over, took Lila into her arms. She stiffened, then relented, stroked Jane's hair. They sat in silence for a while. "You need a shower," Lila said.

"Wow, thanks."

"Whereas I . . ."

". . . am a wild rose in June," Jane finished, laughing. A thing their mother would say, when they were little, in response to any accusation of uncleanliness. "Oh, Lila."

"Oh, Jane."

They climbed the stairs, quietly used the guest bathroom, packed their bags, made the beds. They crept downstairs and out to the porch. Lila locked the door. Then they dropped their keys through the mail slot and set off for the bus.

## 28

# Nacimiento, Panama: *Now*

The border was marked only by a sign—no soldiers, no building, no gate. They passed through Río Sereno, a small town with a sunbaked park, where children climbed in a playground and some folk musicians performed on a concrete stage for an audience of tired-looking mothers. Town gave way to countryside. Old men stood on a dock in front of a church, fishing. Dairy cattle grazed on hillsides, and the cab slowed down to pass tractors hauling hay, fence posts, barbed wire. The cabdriver greeted the farmers with frantic honking, and the farmers returned their waves with evident reluctance and alarm.

Everything about the cabdriver was frantic, and Jane feared that he was under the influence of alcohol or drugs. But no, it seemed he was just that way. His English was fluent and he described their switchback-heavy climb into the mountains in lavish detail, translating road signs aloud and inviting praise for the region's natural beauty. Lila asked him to drop them off somewhere they could stay in Nacimiento that took American cash, and he said, "That's everywhere. I'll take you to my cousin's hotel! He loves Americans, he'll pay half your fare."

"Why don't you just drop us off in the city center," Lila said, "and we'll find something on our own."

"Of course, of course!" He picked up a wide-brimmed straw hat from the passenger seat and put it on his head so that he could tip it to them. Then he took it off again.

Nacimiento lay in a wide, flat valley among low green mountains. They passed beneath an arch that read BIENVENIDOS A NACIMIENTO, the words bookended by a picture of a plow and a picture of a pickaxe. They soon arrived at a commercial district where people strolled along the side of the road carrying groceries, packages, and children. Some adolescent kids wobbled by on bicycles, playing music out of a phone. The sisters were briefly unnerved by a policía traffic stop, but it turned out to be a car registration check, with which their driver enthusiastically complied.

The cabdriver dropped them off in front of a bar and grill with an open-air dining room. It was unclear what it was called — the sign said RESTAURANT, in English — but it was popular, its lot full of cars and pickup trucks and the bar packed with patrons. Spanish pop music issued from hidden speakers. The driver said, "This place you will love, my friend owns it."

"Great," Lila said, paying him. They climbed out, shouldered their bags, and entered the place. Jane smelled steaks searing and realized she was intensely hungry. They managed to find two seats at the bar and ordered chicken sandwiches and Atlas beers. The beer came in cans and tasted like Budweiser. They ate in silence, watching and listening.

"First time here?" the bartender wanted to know.

They told her it was. She suggested a motel a few blocks away, and some places to visit in the morning. "If you're here for the birding, I can recommend some tour guides." The woman's face and accent suggested that she was local, but she told them she was American. "Born in New York, moved back here to be with my grandma. I own this place with my husband, who's from Santiago."

"We're actually looking for an American," Lila said.

"If it's a conservative Republican from the South, you're in luck."

"A white woman in her sixties," Jane said. "Who looks like us. And maybe lives nearby."

Lila shot her a look. The bartender seemed to take stock of them both for a moment. Then she said, "Well, this isn't the kind of place where everyone's going to immediately know the white lady you mean. Most of these people are farmers or work in the tourist trade, and the expats keep to themselves and each other. There's a few hundred of them. They live in a neighborhood at the northern edge of town called La Aldea." She shrugged. "More of a gated community, really. With a fence and armed guards and what have you. There was supposed to be a golf course but one of the farmers wouldn't sell."

"Aw, too bad," Jane said.

"Ha! Right. Anyway, there's a guy, this land developer, he's the one who built the neighborhood. Bennett something. Maybe he would know. He goes way back — like, since before the invasion. He doesn't hang out here, but I see him around. You might find him at the expat bar on the north end of the strip. Big, tall, pink-faced guy. Loud talker."

This got Lila's attention. "Wait, he was here in the eighties?"

"Yeah," the bartender said, arching an eyebrow. "My grandma used to say, any Americans in Panama back then had to be in the CIA."

Night was falling. The motel the bartender recommended was actually delightful and not a motel at all but a quaint arrangement of guest cottages situated along a winding creek. The lobby provided brochures in English and Spanish, filling in the history of the property; these had once been miners' quarters, before the nearby gold mine closed. Out front, a wheelbarrow held a pile of rusted conical pans. A laminated sign explained that prospectors had once used these to find gold in the creek.

They left their bags in the room and headed back out. The sun was setting and the smells of livestock and woodsmoke drifted past them on the breeze. The expat bar the bartender had referred to was called Southern Glory; the motel clerk gave them directions, though it was easily found without them. The place was long, low, ramshackle, with a corrugated metal roof and an open-air dining room and bar; it looked like a Mississippi juke joint that had made it halfway through a tiki renovation. The parking lot was filled with white SUVs and a couple of sleek-looking motorcycles.

"Are those any good?" Jane asked.

"Those are for retirees who want to feel like Batman."

"Got it."

Inside, white people in their sixties were drinking beer from pint glasses and eating steaks. A couple of drunk women at the bar were complaining about their husbands. A bit of eavesdropping revealed that the husbands were down at Piñas Bay on a big-game fishing trip.

"Marlin, right?" Lila said. "Oh boy, ladies, I've been a marlin widow, too."

"Oh yeah?" one of the women said. Her silver-gray hair was tied back and her eyes had a perpetual squint, perhaps cosmetic-surgery related.

"As soon as he said he wanted to hang that thing over the fireplace, I called my lawyer."

Laughter. Jane bought a round of drinks. The women had further complaints. Jane wouldn't have had to lie to participate, but found it hard to engage; she realized she didn't know how. She didn't have women friends, or any friends. She endured a brief, very intense, and unhappy craving for Chloe. She shouldn't be here with Lila, courting danger. She should have brought Chloe instead, and gone birdwatching, like all the other tourists. Racked with emotion she was determined not to express, she gasped, swallowed, tried to put it out of her mind. She promised herself she would take the girl on a trip, just the two of them.

The women asked what they were doing here, and Jane said, "My sister and I are thinking of buying a place. Our daughters are into birds. We took them to the national forest last year and they loved it. It could be, like, a home away from home."

Lila glanced at her with what seemed like approval. "Somebody at another bar told us to look for this guy Bennett."

"Souder?" the other woman said. Her hair was dyed black and she wore hoop earrings the size of tennis balls. "Honey, you don't want to talk to him."

"He literally owns this place," said the one with the squint. "And half of this side of town. He built the development where we live." She pointed. "Just up past the church."

"If you want to buy a vacation place," Earrings said, "I can recommend a real estate agent. But Souder's paranoid. He doesn't do land and houses anymore. His place has, like, an electrified fence."

"He's still into crypto."

"Like, apes, was it?"

"Yeah," Squint said. "Right, Johnny?" She glanced over her shoulder at the bartender, a tall young man with high cheekbones, a local by the look of him. Johnny said nothing. "Johnny can't crap on his boss, but he knows."

"Apes was some time ago," Johnny intoned.

"Right," said Earrings. "Now it's— What was he bragging about the other day? Unicorns?"

"Rainbows," said Johnny.

"Rainbows! It's pictures of rainbows with, like, little bears under them or something."

"It's something my kid would do," said Squint. "Used to do," she added, lips pursed in distaste. "Now he drives a taxi in Portland."

"It's worse," said Earrings. "He pays, like, six figures for something you put on the fridge."

"Except you can't even," said Squint. "It's not on paper."

"You can print it out," said Earrings. "Or maybe that's illegal?"

Johnny raised an eyebrow. The women were very drunk now. Lila and Jane managed to extricate themselves and left in a flurry of hugs.

It was dark now, and the air was heavy and warm. La Aldea was visible from the road outside the bar, a cluster of white buildings climbing up a hillside and clustered around a central spire, illuminated from below, that resembled a Mexican bell tower in a spaghetti western.

The sisters walked there. The entire development was surrounded by a security fence, but a compound within, just beyond the tower and overlooking the rest of the neighborhood from the hill, was enclosed by a second fence, patrolled by the promised guards: men in black pants, collarless white button-down shirts, and waistband holsters, who milled around, smoking. They had the air of people who didn't see much action.

"We could stake the place out," Lila said, "wait for the guards' shifts to change, maybe climb in from above him on the hill."

"I'm not wild about the idea," Jane admitted.

"Me neither, to be honest. Let's go back to the motel and I'll see if I can fuck with his rainbows."

They stopped at a convenience store on the strip and bought snacks. In their room, Lila sat cross-legged with the laptop on her bed, eating plantain chips and taking sips from a water bottle. "It's Souder with a *d*," she said. "I think this is him, on a couple of crypto forums. He goes by Panama underscore Hack."

"Of course he does."

"There are a bunch of Panama Hacks listed in the StillRockin24 breach, lemme see if any of these are him."

"What is that?"

"Big text file of stolen credentials from earlier this year. You can buy these on hacker forums." She clicked and typed. "Okay, here we go. He uses the same password for both of these forums. Let's see what's in his DMs." She looked up, nodded at the bag in Jane's hands. "Are those any good?"

"They're just regular cheese curls. Are you looking for anything in particular in there?"

"Somebody he trusts who I can spoof. Tell him there are some newly minted rainbows or something, email him a link that leads him to a fake website where he'll hand over the keys."

"You think he'll actually fall for it?"

"People are bad at computers," Lila said. "But the people who are worst at computers are the people who think they're good at computers." She laughed. "Okay, here's somebody. This is going to take a little while, feel free to go to sleep."

Souder hadn't yet taken the bait when they woke up, so they ventured out into the bright day. They found a bakery and had pastries and Nescafé. Beside them, a family of three—a man, a woman, and a teenage boy—talked in German about Volcán Barú, a nearby national park. They wore expensive-looking Zeiss binoculars around their necks and the mother kept looking at her watch. There was a bus to catch, it seemed.

"You know what we never did?" Jane said. "We never went on vacation. Just, you know, a family vacation."

"Would you have wanted to, with them?"

"Guess not. The irony is, whenever we take Chloe someplace, Disney World, the beach, whatever, I just want to escape. You'd think I would love it."

"Is Chloe the reason you don't love it?" Lila asked. Jane searched her face for malice but didn't find any. It was, she supposed, a reasonable question.

"No. Or, yes, kind of . . . She's difficult on trips. But I don't think it's because of the trip, I think it's . . ."

"Chance?"

"If it was just Chloe and me, it would be fun. But the balance of power gets skewed with him. He doesn't like making travel plans, so that falls to me. But then he doesn't like the plans I make, and doesn't tell me until we're doing the stuff. I get Chloe all psyched up for some activity, then he suggests something else and makes it sound great, and then if it's not, she's mad at me because we didn't do what I promised. Or he goes along with my plans resentfully and that rubs off on her. And then, if his mother comes along, it's a whole other dynamic."

"So, maybe you're not the problem."

"Maybe not."

"Maybe escaping from that is a normal thing to want."

The two of them looked at each other. "Maybe," Jane admitted.

Back at the motel, Lila opened her laptop and laughed. "Too bad, Benny," she said, "your 'bows are mine. Let's set up a meeting." She began typing.

"Seriously?"

"A fool and his money, as they say."

Lila stashed the laptop and they set out for La Aldea. They passed the church and a mechanic, the former closed and silent, the latter open and at work, servicing a couple of SUVs.

"Those have to be the expats' cars," Lila said. "All the farmers are driving Toyota pickups."

"Why are the expats here, exactly?"

"Taxes, I'd imagine. Americans don't have to pay any."

"Ah."

"And the tourism economy means the locals tend to be nice to white people, whatever their real feelings might be. I suspect we're about to enter a pure domain of embittered racist jackassery. People who think America started going down the shitter in 1863. Here, they can enjoy the feigned respect of a perceived underclass."

"So you don't think Souder is going to be a sweetheart, you're saying."

Lila shrugged. "He'll be the least stupid one, anyway. Though still, as we've demonstrated, fairly stupid."

La Aldea really did resemble a Las Vegas–casino version of a spaghetti western set. The central tower was about three stories high, four-sided, and whitewashed; an array of loudspeakers, now silent, occupied the space where a bell ought to go. It stood in an open white-gravel plaza, from which paved streets, bordered by low stone walls, snaked out in several directions, leading to white villas with terra-cotta roofs. Workers, locals by the look of them, were busy touching up mortar, painting gates, and replenishing the gravel in the square. As the two women approached the guard kiosk, a white SUV crunched slowly past. Its inhabitants, a red-faced couple in late middle age, peered down at them through the windshield as the gate rolled aside.

"We have a meeting with Bennett Souder," Lila told the guard.

"You're . . . Team Rainbow?" the guy said, glancing at a computer screen. Lila nodded and he waved them through.

Souder's house was the only multistory structure and occupied a central spot on the hillside, overlooking the entire neighborhood. It had been built to resemble an eighteenth-century Spanish Mission–style villa, with arched roofs, stucco walls, and ornate wooden window casings. Another guard let them through the second fence; beyond it a stone wall enclosed neat, symmetrical gardens punctuated by fountains.

"Classy," Lila drawled.

They followed a driveway to a suburban-style garage wide enough to accommodate three cars. A woman was standing in the garden, aiming a hose at the base of some banana trees. Lila spoke to her in Spanish, and the woman pointed toward a gravel walkway that led past the front door and around to the other side of the property.

They walked where she pointed and found a man sitting on an incongruously cheap aluminum-framed beach chair, smoking cigarettes next to a cement pond. Koi swam in its murky waters as a central fountain burbled. The man was in his seventies. He wore cutoff jeans shorts, a button-down shirt, and a sweat-stained pink baseball cap with the word "Detroit" embroidered on it. A pair of flip-flops, an ashtray, and a half-drunk bloody mary were arranged on the ground beside him. Upturned on his lap lay a thick discolored novel with a picture of a dragon on the cover. His scowl looked incongruous framed by a wide, round face, like a hand grenade served on a china plate. The pistol he was pointing at them trembled slightly — the product, Jane surmised, of age, rather than nerves. "I could just kill you, you know," he said. "I don't give a fuck about the rainbows. They're a hobby. And I don't like being backed into a corner."

"Give us an hour of your time and you'll get your shit back," Lila said. "And you won't need to clean up a couple of corpses."

"Who the fuck are you? What is this all about?"

"We're looking for somebody. An American."

"Jesus Christ." He hauled himself up out of the chair to his full height, which had to be close to six and a half feet, and, with one hand, carefully dog-eared the book and set it down on his chair. The gun remained pointed in their general direction, though the arm that held it had begun to droop. He resembled a bear, awakened from hibernation, who wanted nothing more than to return to its cave.

"I heard you've been here for forty years," Lila said. "So has she. Somewhere near here, anyway."

"Lady . . ." Souder said.

"People call her the Holy Ghost," Lila said.

He looked hard at Lila, then at Jane. He began to laugh. "You cannot be for real. Where are you people from?"

"Her name was Anabel."

"Yeah, I know what her fucking name was."

Jane gasped. Lila said, "You knew her."

"Again, who are you people? Did she send you for me?"

Souder looked from one of them to the other, squinting. He took a step closer. Then he began to laugh again. "Holy shit," he said. "Are you her kids? You're her kids, aren't you."

They said nothing.

"Absolutely incredible. You came all this way, for what reason exactly?"

"She abandoned us," Lila said.

"So, you're going to go up into the mountains to find out . . . what? Why Mommy left?"

"So you're saying she's near," Lila said. "In the mountains?"

He got up close, bent down to put his face in hers. "You're going to march up to her and tell her she hurt your feelings, what, twenty years ago?" he said. "And she's going to fall into your arms and beg you for forgiveness? Is that the plan?"

"Which mountains, Souder," Lila demanded.

Off in the distance, a birdcall echoed through the hills. "I mean, I could tell you where to go," Souder said, waving the gun, which he might have forgotten he was holding, "if you want to get shot. Maybe that is what you want? You'll show her the error of her fucking ways by making the ultimate sacrifice?"

They didn't respond. For the first time since Incognito Air, Jane doubted herself. What if the stunt at the airport wasn't a challenge, but a warning? Their mother had devised the postcard code a long time ago — an enticement for a couple of kids she thought she could make use of, kids who she knew read spy books, kept secrets, defied their betters. Maybe, for a time, she thought she could draw them into the business, form an old-school crime family with the women as the bosses. But now? Maybe now Souder was right. She'd just had them threatened, pursued. She turned her back the second they drew near. The Anabel of today really might shoot them on sight, for the folly of taking a childish game to heart.

Souder shook his head. "Jesus Christ. Why don't you both come inside and have a drink."

"It's ten in the morning," Jane said.

"Oh, who fucking cares," Souder sighed, then turned, crossed the patio, and flung aside the sliding door.

They followed him into a clean, open-plan kitchen with stone-tile floors, marble countertops, and a massive island upon which Jane suspected no meal had ever been cooked. They could easily have been standing in any American suburb; there was no decor here, save for what some interior designer must have bought for the place when it was built: some plastic flowers in a vase decorated with faux-primitive, generically "native" designs. Framed photographs of mountains and lakes, perhaps nearby ones, perhaps not. A plaque printed with platitudes about the kitchen as a family meeting place.

A black plastic trash bag gaped open in the corner of the room. Flies buzzed around it. Souder shambled toward it, draining the last of his bloody mary, then threw a depleted lime wedge and stalk of celery into the open bag. He then moved to the counter and set the pistol down on it with a clunk, beside a forest of liquor bottles and a tray of glasses.

"Help yourself to a drink from the fridge," he said. "There's soda and bottled water."

"How long have you been living here?" Lila asked him brightly. Jane went to the fridge for water and had to dodge Souder's massive arm as it gathered ice cubes from the freezer.

"This place? Five years. I was back in the States for a funeral, got talking to some people, and saw an opportunity. A lot of Americans watching their country going to shit and looking for a place where locals have some fucking manners." He dropped his ice cubes into the tumbler he'd just drained and filled it half with vodka and half with tonic water. "I got this plot for a song from the daughter of a drunk who used to farm here. The cost of labor and materials is excellent, and there are more flexible ways to pay for it so you don't end up giving half your money to the fucking government."

He came over to the table, where Jane and Lila had sat down. He groaned as he lowered himself into a chair. "So, your mother. The Holy Fucking Ghost. I'm happy to tell you where she is. I can get out a map and point to the spot. But you have no fucking idea what you're getting yourself into."

"We think she's involved in the drug trade," Jane said, then immediately regretted it. Souder cackled, and his laughter echoed around the cold and empty space.

"Oh, involved in the drug trade," he said. "Sure."

"We heard she developed a new strain of coca," Lila said. "And she was in Seattle, overseeing something about the operation. We tried to catch her there, but missed. We heard she's working for some new capo."

Souder drained half his glass, leaned over, folded his hands together. His features—oversized, spaced too far apart, like a war mask—registered something resembling glee. "Girls," he said, "your mother is the fucking capo. She started taking over the business in this part of the country in the late nineties and has pushed out, taken over, or decapitated every other operation from the Costa Rican border to the Anton Valley. She's completely revolutionized and decentralized the manufacture and distribution of cocaine—she's got a hundred mom-and-pop growers working for her in secret, and she's cut out the Colombian and Bolivian supply lines completely. Most of the cocaine that comes into the US comes in by boat to California. Your mom is running container ships out of Puerto fucking Armuelles directly to the Pacific Northwest. The gangs up there usually bring in the stuff by land through the Yakima Valley, but your sainted mother has managed to bypass them through a bunch of white fishermen, who are loading up from the big boats out in international waters. What with the fisheries going to shit, it's a lot more profitable than what they used to do. She's turned these knuckleheads into a new gang. They literally call themselves the Snowmen.

"Most of the time, gangs up there get along. It's not like LA in the eighties, it's business. The Blacks, the Cambodians, Vietnamese, Mexicans—if those guys get the chance to make a buck together, they'll do it. But everybody fucking hates these assholes. So every now and then your mom has to send her people up there to smooth things over. If I know her, she's probably looking for a way to tempt the other gangs away from Colombian coke, to put her stuff in the hands of more competent distributors.

"Your mother," he said, "is a stone-cold genius with the balls of a fucking Tyrannosaurus rex. One of these days, the Colombians will probably come up here and rip her head off. But until then, she's king shit of coke mountain."

There was a brief silence as they digested this information. Jane sipped her bottle of water. Lila said, "How do you know all this?"

Souder's glee appeared to deepen. "Back when I thought such a thing was possible, girls, your mother was the love of my fucking life. I would have cut off my own arm for her. I ran her in Panama City during Iran-contra."

"So it's true?" Lila said. "She was CIA?"

Love of his life? Jane thought.

A snort. "Yeah she was fuckin' CIA." He got up, staggered deeper into the house, shouting down the hall as he went. "After the Iranian embassy hostage situation, back in '79, Carter instituted an arms embargo against Iran, right? But after Reagan took over, we got worried the Russians would slip in and arm the moderates. We sold 'em antitank and antiaircraft missiles in secret, through the back door, then used that money to train these guys in Nicaragua to fight the socialists."

They heard the sound of a file drawer opening and closing, and Souder came back with a thick pile of manila folders.

"Anyway, we wanted anti-communist allies, and Noriega, who we'd been working with for years, was in charge in the eighties. We had spy planes and ships running out of here, reconnaissance radio towers, that kind of thing, and we were using them to protect the canal and undermine the Sandinistas." He dumped the folders on the table, then fell back into his chair. "The Russians were sending guys to try and figure out what we were doing, so we needed somebody who spoke Russian to find them, keep an eye on them, figure out what they thought they knew.

"That was your mom. She was fearless and a fucking fox. After Iran-contra blew up in '87, she tried to get out of Agency business — went back to the States, I assume got married or something, since you're here?"

"Our parents got married in 1985," Jane said.

That silenced them all for a minute. "Fuck. Wow. Okay," said Souder. "I assume that didn't go too great."

"No," Lila said.

He opened the top folder, pushed it toward the sisters. It was full of newspaper clippings, printouts of articles, decades of them, about the drug trade in Central America and the US. Their hidden common denominator, their mother, the Holy Ghost. The man was obsessed.

"All I know is, she kept coming back to Panama. She used to live here, in Nacimiento, I mean. That's how I ended up here, I followed her, when I thought there was still a chance with her. Back in the city, she'd lived in this apartment with a greenhouse on the roof — she was obsessed with tropical flowers. She had a thing for Barú Volcano, the national park near here, she'd go up there and look for rare plants. She let me tag along a couple of times, but pretty soon she made it clear she'd rather be alone. Not just in the park, fucking forever."

The shambling old asshole looked for a moment as though he might cry. He drained his glass, then got up to fix another. "I guess she grew up rich, with diplomats or something?"

"Yeah," Jane said.

"She hated those people, the way they mostly looked out for other people like them. She hated that world. So she decided to exploit it." He shook his head. "Not that we did any good down here. Your mother ended up more disillusioned with the Agency than with her family. Any institution, she fucking loathes it. I wouldn't be surprised if that's why she took up coca, just a middle finger to the Colombians."

The room fell silent as Souder drank his drink. He issued a moan into his empty glass.

"You never knew she was married," Lila said. "You never knew she had kids."

"I never knew anything about her. One day she just up and vanished. I eventually found out from a real estate guy I know, he sold her some land. A lot of it, up in the mountains, a carve-out from Palo Seco, in the jungle north of Lago Fortuna. Actually, I wanted that land. He was supposed to sell it to me, once I got my investments in order, then your mother showed up with cash. That's where she is. She built a place there, you can see it in satellite pictures on the internet. She developed her plants and went into business."

He set his glass down, reached for a bottle. Seemed, at last, to think better of it. Blew breath out through puckered lips, then slumped down onto a chair at the table. Glowered at the pile of clippings. "It's been a long time since she's come into Nacimiento, as far as I know. I met a guy here once who used to be her helicopter pilot, before she bought her own rig — that's how she gets in and out. There's roads, though, old logging roads, if you want to get there by car. Just . . . if you go, she better know you're coming. Because nobody's gonna get up there who she doesn't want to see."

"Oh, she knows," Lila said. She stood, walked over to the counter, and picked up the gun. Removed the clip, examined the chamber, cycled the action, and clicked the clip back in. She said, "Give us directions. Print them out."

Souder looked hard at her. Little waves of emotion rippled over his big face. "Sure, girls."

"We'll also take one of your cars."

He barked out one single laugh, like a seal.

"Not kidding, Souder."

"Fucking incredible," he said, his eyes welling up, spilling over. "You are the spitting fucking image."

"Something with four-wheel drive, if you please."

It would take them three hours — two and a half to where the named roads ran out, and another thirty minutes north into the mountains. "The road follows the creek for ten miles, then it bends left," he said, out in the driveway, as they climbed into his Jeep. "That's probably where somebody will notice you. I'd leave the gun behind," he added, as Lila started the engine.

"Thanks for the tip."

"Do me a favor, girls," Souder said. "Return my rainbows to me before you leave town. Because you aren't coming back."

They returned to the motel and Lila did as he asked. Then they drove in silence for an hour through farms and villages, the landscape increasingly mountainous, traffic light. The day had warmed, but not uncomfortably so. Wind whistled in through the open windows and the gaps in the Jeep's cloth top.

"Do you want to leave the gun in the glovebox, maybe?" Jane asked.

Lila said nothing for a moment, then reached down between her legs and grabbed her satchel. She handed it to Jane, who fished out the gun and gingerly held it as she opened the glovebox door. She lifted up some papers — owner's manual, registration, what looked like service records — and slid the gun underneath. The snick of the door latch as she closed it brought her a small amount of calm.

"What's the endgame here?" Jane asked her. "What are you going to say to her?"

"I don't know," Lila said. But her face was hard and Jane got the idea that she had a plan. She glanced over, then back at the road. "You?"

"I think I know why she left us," Jane said, after a moment to gather her thoughts. "She was no good at family life. She stopped loving Dad. And I guess we just got in the way of the things she was good at. If I turned out to have that kind of power, would I want to pursue it to the ends of the earth? Maybe." A logging truck trundled past them, followed by a couple of sedans, looking for the opportunity to pass. "Maybe it's no different from being a great artist or something. You choose it over your family, and maybe you feel guilty about it, but that's life. You don't have children, Lila, I don't expect you to understand, but . . . it does change you. You're not the same afterward. You can change back, I guess, be selfish again, but . . . I want to make her tell me how it happened. I want to hear her say it. I want that closure."

"I think it's pretty simple," Lila said. "She got a better offer and chose it. That's all. She doesn't have normal emotions. She doesn't feel guilt like you do."

"Maybe."

"You don't think there's something like that for you? Something you'd abandon your daughter for?"

"I don't think so," Jane said. "I want Chloe in my life. I don't know if I'm good for her, but I want her."

"You don't think Mom ever felt that way about us?"

"I do, actually. That's what scares me. She wanted us, and then she didn't anymore. And I can feel that in myself, too. The potential for it." She turned to Lila. "I don't want that, though. I want to avoid it. I want her to show me that I'm different."

Quietly, Lila said, "What if you come out of there realizing you're the same?"

"I'm not," Jane said. "I can't be."

She dozed for a little while. When she came to, the glovebox door had fallen open and she closed it reflexively, like brushing away a wasp. The lake was visible on the right, stretching into the east, cradled in green and rounded hills. The car slowed.

"Look at that," Jane said.

"Yeah."

They didn't have to say what they were thinking, which was that it reminded them of home. They might have been in Nestor, at the southern tip of Onteo Lake, in some distant time before humans arrived to sully the waters and encrust the hills with concrete. Jane felt a strange, disconnected nostalgia for this world that didn't yet know ruin.

With the lake a few miles behind them, they slowed, searching for the place on the map where they were to head north. There it was, an unmarked turnoff, alongside a creek. They took the turn, then followed the road until it turned to gravel, then to hard-packed dirt carving two ruts through the grass. At the promised bend in the road, the one that would take them uphill, away from the creek, a clean, well-maintained sign read NO ENTRAR ILEGALMENTE. They passed it. Half a mile up into the hills, the road turned back to gravel.

There was no gate, no fence. Only a gravel lay-by with a guard hut and two unmarked white pickup trucks. Uniformed men stood outside the hut, smoking. The barrels of assault rifles peeked up over their shoulders. They saw the Jeep approaching and reached over their shoulders to brandish their weapons. One of them raised a walkie-talkie and spoke into it.

"Should we stop?" Jane said.

"Let's wait until they make us."

"I don't think —"

Lila kept going, slowly enough to indicate that they didn't expect to actually get away, fast enough to show disrespect. Jane didn't like it.

"Lila, they'll kill us."

Only now did Jane realize how angry she was. Lila's face had hardened into a series of lines and planes, and she spoke through a clenched jaw. "They won't. She's been waiting for us. She invited us."

One of the pickups appeared behind them and settled into close pursuit. They were going fifteen miles an hour. Another two minutes passed before a second lay-by came into view, with another guard hut, and this time the road was blocked by another pickup and a white Land Rover, and four more guards, three men and a woman, gripping their rifles. Three of them pointed the guns at the Jeep, which came to a stop. The fourth spoke into her walkie-talkie, then approached Lila.

"Get out," she said in English. "Both of you."

They climbed out, shouldering their bags, and stood on the gravel. The guard with the walkie-talkie approached Jane and patted her down, then gestured for her to open her bag. Jane did so, and the woman rummaged through her things, tissues and tampons and notebook and pens. She paused at a creased strip of photos Jane had taken with Chloe a few years ago at the movie theater, a digital effect rendering them as superheroes.

The woman's skin was smooth and unblemished and shone with sweat. To Jane's surprise, she smelled faintly of hibiscus — perfume. Did this woman have children? Was this something you were allowed to do, as the Holy Ghost's muscle?

The woman glanced up at her, expression unreadable, and back at the photos.

Jane tried to think of something to say, but before she could, the woman put the photos back and withdrew. She turned to Lila. A squawk issued from her walkie-talkie and she raised a finger in Lila's face — a moment, please — then moved away. She held the walkie-talkie to her ear, spoke inaudibly, listened.

Lila put an arm around Jane, pulled her close. "Are you all right?" she said quietly.

"Fine."

"I know that some people with . . . trauma don't want to be touched. By strangers."

It was an odd thing for Lila to say, and unexpectedly kind. Compassion ran through her like a warm wind and carried her energy away. She wilted. Her bag felt heavier, her breath tasted stale. She said, "I'm fine."

"Okay, good."

"Thank you."

The guard holstered the walkie-talkie on her utility belt and turned back to Lila. She patted her down, went through her bag. Removed a flip-style utility knife and wordlessly pocketed it. "Come with me," she said. She pointed at two of the guards and gestured for them to follow.

The sisters were instructed to get into the back seat of the Land Rover. One of the guards climbed into the cargo bay, where he watched them from behind. The other sat in the passenger seat, holding his rifle, glaring at the two. No one spoke. The road was clear, the gravel fresh. It took them higher and higher, bending, switching back. It was late afternoon now, and the sun was orange and low and filled the car with honeyed light. The driver's walkie-talkie crackled, somebody said something in Spanish, and the driver replied. A moment later, they topped a rise, the road widened, and the compound came into view.

The house itself was fairly modest, a long, low stucco structure contoured to the hilltop and dominated by an open-air second floor that doubtless offered views of the valley below. To the far left, a cluster of smaller buildings suggested a barracks, a small village of residences for workers. And to the right, a dome-like greenhouse as large as the house itself. From here, it looked like a diorama, a self-contained world, trees and other greenery rising to its roof. Even through the windshield of the Land Rover, Jane could see butterflies rising and falling inside its walls. The house and greenhouse were encircled by a low, whitewashed stone wall. A gap in the wall revealed a flagstone path that led to a carved wooden door.

The car doors opened and the sisters were led out at gunpoint. They stood on the gravel, facing the house, about twenty yards from the entrance.

"Now what?" Jane said.

Before Lila could answer, the heavy door swung open, and their mother appeared. She wore a baggy linen shirt tucked into green work pants tied with a shoelace belt. Her boots were brown and she held a trowel in one hand. Her hair was tied back from a tan face, lined and weathered by the sun, whose expression was inscrutable at this distance, and perhaps, Jane thought, would appear inscrutable even close up.

Jane was waiting to feel something. When it came, it wasn't what she expected. Not love, or longing, certainly, but weariness. Disappointment in herself for coming here. Embarrassment that she'd been persuaded. Their mother didn't approach them. She remained under the eaves just outside her door, which she had not closed behind her. Through the gloom inside the house, Jane could make out broad rear windows, hills giving way to more hills, and sky.

It was clear that they were expected to present themselves to her, to pass through the gap in the wall and walk down the path. They'd passed the test. Now it was time to receive their reward. Or their punishment. Jane turned to her sister and waited.

She waited about five seconds. Then Lila spoke, without taking her eyes off Anabel Bortnik, mother and kingpin, gardener and killer, lover and spy.

"Fuck her," Lila said, and turned to walk back down the hill.

# 29

# Illinois to California: *Then*

T he bus took them west on 290, then 88, then Interstate 80, through Davenport and Iowa City, through Des Moines and Omaha. They slept, and eventually got off in Denver. This period wasn't clear in Jane's memory; they slept in a lot of hostels, met people, did drugs, crashed in apartments. It was spring, then summer, and occasionally it was possible to feel free and happy. Jane fell in love with a boy for several days, became disenchanted, left in the night with Lila for another city. The world felt gentle and full of possibility; the people they met were kind and generous, at least on the surface: stoners with family money, college dropouts, musicians, hikers. Lila carried George's laptop around in a giant backpack she stole from a used sporting goods store in Boulder, and whenever she was able to find an electrical outlet and a Wi-Fi signal she read his email and checked for news of his absence.

In the second week of September 2006, they were living in a dilapidated shared ranch house in Holladay, Utah with a bunch of Mormon runaways, one of whom was receiving a secret stipend from a rich, sympathetic mother. When they moved in, they told their housemates they were college students and would just spend the rest of the summer, but nobody had asked why they hadn't left yet. They spent their time smoking weed, drinking beer, and teaching themselves how to fight dirty from a series of YouTube videos uploaded by a long-haired guy with a mustache called Defender Dan. Lila started spending a lot of time in another housemate's room, the one with the sympathetic mother. Jane assumed they were sleeping together. For her own part, she occasionally slept with a boy called Paul, who lived alone in the basement, but only when nobody else was in the house, which was rarely. Neither of them mentioned it to anyone else. It should have been exciting, but it wasn't.

Maybe this was a signal that their luck was about to change. Lila had been siphoning off a neighbor's Wi-Fi during the six weeks they'd been here and had seemed extra intent on the computer lately, until the night she finally called Jane over to the kitchen table and said she had news.

"There's something I haven't been telling you," she said.

She turned the laptop toward Jane and scrolled through what seemed to be a long email exchange, denoted by little cliff edges of carets. "I emailed with his sister."

"What!"

"I decided it was best to string her along. She wrote to him a while back saying their mother was dying and she needed his help. It was the kind of thing that . . . if they had ever been close, he'd reply. So . . . he replied. This was like a month and a half ago."

"What did he say?"

She scrolled for a moment, far back in the exchange, and pointed. The email read:

Beth—
    I'm sorry, I'm not in a good place right now........and I don't think I can be of much help..........if there's anything left, it's all yours
    George

The reply was livid.

The fuck??? Anything LEFT are you JOKING?? Look man I am asking you to devote a tiny fraction of your precious summer to the woman who treated you best in the world, for what reason I have no idea but there you have it. She is asking for you, the least you could do is call. I tried the only number I had and it's dead.

And then a number.

"Of course I can't call. So . . . I just ignored it for a little while. She emailed one more time here, which I ignored . . . and then . . ."

Buried Mom. Fuck you and good riddance.

"Which I thought was good news, he'd pissed her off and she was washing her hands of him. But then . . . I guess there was a fire at the house because the cops tracked her down to ask if she knew where he was. And she literally went to Nestor. She went to the house."

"Oh god."

George,

What is happening with you? I am at your house. It's obvious you haven't been here for months. There's mail and newspapers everywhere, some kids have been squatting and they started a fire. I assumed you were just being an asshole but if you're in trouble, I want to help. You're my little brother, I'm sorry I told you to fuck off.

Beth

"And then I wrote this. Which . . . I guess was not convincing."

Beth........thank you but I'm far away and can't be bothered........I give up on the house and all my worldly possessions.......I am at peace.......dont worry George

"And this just came this morning," Lila said.

Who is this

"Don't respond to it!" Jane said.

"I'm not going to."

"Did you check the news? Did she call the police?"

"No," Lila said, biting her lip. "Nothing yet."

But then, the next day, there was something. The online edition of the Nestor paper ran an article headlined WHERE DID MR. FRAMINGHAM GO? BELOVED NESTOR HIGH THEATER COACH REPORTED MISSING.

A fire that partially consumed a home along route 89 in Nestor has raised questions about its owner, former Nestor High School theater director George Framingham.

Framingham, 37, has not been seen since April 25, closing night of the spring musical he directed. A cast party held at his home after the play lasted well into the night, students say. Since that time, Framingham is said to have exchanged email with his former employer, Nestor High principal Lawrence Kovacs. He also communicated via email with his sister, Elizabeth Huntsman of Buffalo, but Huntsman claims the emails are counterfeit.

Firefighters from Nestor Fire Department and Herodotus Volunteer Fire Department responded to a fire at Framingham's home, 1448 West Lake Road, on Tuesday. The home appeared abandoned and the fire is believed to be the result of a campfire left burning nearby. Dry conditions and tall grass likely contributed to the blaze, officials said. The State Office of Fire Prevention and Control will continue to investigate.

Huntsman had been listed as an emergency contact in Framingham's employment contract, which expired in May. She was contacted via phone and alerted police to the possibility that her brother was in danger.

"Someone is writing to me, pretending to be my brother," she told reporters via email. "I believe he may have been harmed."

Huntsman has turned over the emails in question to police. Police have not commented on Huntsman's accusations and say the matter is presently under investigation.

Any readers with knowledge of Framingham's whereabouts, or of the fire that consumed a portion of his home Tuesday, should contact police.

"We have to get rid of this computer," Jane said. "Is it tracking us? Can they track it?"

"No," Lila said. Then: "Maybe. I'm not sure."

"Can they or can't they?"

Lila scowled, blinking. She gazed at the screen, then back at Jane. Lila stared through her. "I think they can read the IP address," she said. "On the emails. They might be able to tell where they're coming from. Like, geographically."

It was around noon. Their housemates were asleep. Outside, a brilliant day, the final breath of summer. "We have to get rid of it!" Jane cried.

"Yeah," Lila said. "Yeah. Actually, more than that, we have to leave. We have to leave right now."

There wasn't much to pack. In ten minutes they were walking down their suburban street in the heat, their hair pulled back, sunglasses on. "I wish I'd taken a shower," Jane said. They waved to a couple of neighbors, who didn't wave back; the house was regarded as a squat and Jane knew there had been meetings held about it. It probably wouldn't be long before they'd all be kicked out, anyway.

They took a bus into Salt Lake City, picked up some schedules at the Greyhound station, and found a Starbucks with outdoor tables. While Jane pored over possible destinations, Lila busied herself wiping the contents of the computer. After fifteen minutes, she declared herself finished. She shut the laptop, carried it to the other side of the outdoor seating area, and deposited it on another table. Then she came back, sat down, and pulled another, newer-looking laptop out of her backpack.

"Where did you get that?" Jane asked.

"Cyndi."

"She gave it to you?"

Lila raised an eyebrow. "Sure," she said. "Hey, though. Guess what I did before I wiped George's machine. I forwarded a bunch of those pictures to Kovacs."

"Oh my god."

They sat in silence for a minute. A tall guy loping by was brought up short and flung one long leg, then the other, over the low wrought iron divider that separated the Starbucks from the sidewalk. He approached the laptop, looked down at it, up at the sisters.

"Yo," he said, "this yours?"

"Nah," said Lila. "We've been here almost an hour, it's just been sitting there."

The guy nodded once, pulled his bucket hat down over his eyes, scooped up George's laptop, and reinserted himself into the flow of pedestrians. The two of them watched the laptop walk away.

"Lila," Jane said. "They're going to know pretty soon. That it's us, I mean."

"They won't *know*. But they'll want to talk to us."

"Dad won't say we disappeared, but the theater kids will."

"I'm sure," Lila said, "they already have."

Jane was beginning to cry. She let it happen. "We can't go back now."

"Did you want to go back?"

"No," she said, thinking of their father, of the overgrown yard, still harboring the broken, grassed-over playthings of their childhood. "But there's a difference between don't want to and can't."

They chose the Oregon coast, figuring it would be a mild and isolated place to winter. But on the way there, outside the depot in Boise, they were robbed at knifepoint by an addict. Lila tried to fight him and ended up with a slash on her arm, which they decided to keep quiet about. They bought disinfectant and bandages at a drugstore and got back on the bus as though nothing had happened.

"That bag had most of the money in it," Jane said.

Lila, luckily, had left her bag on the bus. It contained Cyndi's laptop and some clothes, but not much cash—about $50 that she'd stolen along with the laptop.

"I've got another ten or so in my pocket," she said. "You?"

"After the drugstore, like . . . eighteen."

They landed in Port Orford, Oregon, where they got a job cleaning a church and broke into it at night to sleep. They washed using paper towels and pump soap from the tiny bathroom; they laundered their underwear in the sink and draped them over folding chairs to dry. Lila studied computer networking and encryption at the public library, found out there was a thing called a virtual private network. In the library discard bin she found a book called *Steal This Computer*. From it she learned the kind of things that people did to invade your privacy and steal your stuff. She turned to the internet to learn how to do those things herself.

They followed news of George's disappearance via local news sites. Blood had been found in the basement of the empty house and police were now treating the case as a possible homicide. "We now believe Mr. Framingham's disappearance to have occurred in April of this year," a detective announced at a press conference. "A lot of potential evidence could have been stolen or washed away by now. If you know anything, please contact us." One article mentioned that there was "additional digital evidence" that had come to light but didn't cite a source and didn't elaborate. There was no mention of the missing laptop.

And then, the kicker, the thing that sent a chill down Jane's spine: the announcement that two children, Jane Pool and Lila Pool, were sought for questioning. "These youths have not been officially reported missing, but they appear to have departed the area around the time of Mr. Framingham's disappearance. We think they may have important information regarding his whereabouts." An article in the *Nestor News* ran their sophomore yearbook photos, which Jane was both pleased and dismayed to see no longer resembled them much.

"Is there going to be a national search? Will we be on TV?"

"Not if there's no body," Lila said. "There's plenty of reasons there might be blood on a futon."

"Seriously?"

Lila leveled a look at her. "Maybe you cut yourself while you were drunk and went to bed without realizing it. Maybe you attempted suicide."

The church where they were staying was cold and smelled like mildew. They were pretty sure the pastor knew they were living there, and eventually this notion was confirmed by the addition to the small basement kitchen of a hot plate, a saucepan, canned goods, and a can opener. Some washcloths and bars of soap. A thin, gentle, prematurely gray man named Steven, he told them he was collecting donations for the church's homeless food drive. He asked them what kind of things they would want to eat if they happened to be homeless. Not long after, they found these things stored in the kitchen.

"I don't know if we should eat them," Jane said. "I don't want to steal anything from the homeless."

"Are you kidding me?" Lila asked her, opening a can of chickpeas. "That's us. We're the homeless. The food drive is for us. Also, there's no food drive."

"I'm sure there's — That it's not just —"

Lila drained the can over the sink and began popping the chickpeas into her mouth. "We're the homeless," she repeated, holding out the can.

One night a few weeks into their stay, as they were trying to figure out where to go next, they heard a car door outside, then a key in the lock, and a young man walked into the basement. Jane had seen him before, at Sunday service, which they always attended, because they thought it was the polite thing to do and because there was singing. He was Jared, the pastor's son. Jane had felt bad for him before, as he had no mother — her absence had not been explained to them, but Steven's mournful disposition suggested that she had died — and appeared lost and angry during services. Once, coming out of the library, Jane had seen him in the parking lot of the Ray's Food Place across the street, smashing bottles against the concrete base of a light pole.

Jared was wearing loose, low-slung jeans and a black hoodie with the hood up. He smelled of liquor. He said, "I'm gonna tell the cops you're breaking in here and stealing our stuff."

"We're not," Lila said, setting down the road atlas. "Your father knows we're here."

"I don't care what he knows."

"What do you want, Jared?" Lila said, folding her hands together on her knees.

"Are you lesbians?"

"We're s —" Jane began.

But Lila raised a hand to silence her. "Just tell us why you're here."

"If you want me to keep the cops out of it," he said with a smirk, "there's stuff you can do."

Jane turned to Lila, expecting a glance back. But Lila was intent on the boy, her eyes narrowed, her shoulders pitched forward. "All right," Lila said. She patted the open road atlas. "We were just planning on leaving. Go ahead. Go tell them now. We might even still be here to say hi."

"Fine, bitches," Jared said. He scowled and turned to go. Then he pivoted on his heel and turned again to face them. He shook his head, then his whole body, the arms flapping, the legs trembling, like a cat trying to shake off water. "Nah," he said. "Nah."

"Nah?" Lila said.

"I'm not leaving."

It was dawning on Jane that they could be in danger — that this boy could be stronger than he looked, that he might try to overpower them. But Lila stood and walked right up to him. "Jared," she said quietly. "Are you going to rape us? Is that your plan?" She reached out and pushed his hood off his head.

Jane had thought he was their age or younger — he had the demeanor of a defeated child — but now she saw that he was an adult, at least twenty. His face was long, the cheeks full, the eyes far apart. A constellation of acne extended along his hairline. His hair was curly and lank. For all that, he wasn't ugly. But he appeared sad, pathetic, which somehow intensified her fear. She couldn't see her sister's face.

Jared didn't answer. He appeared mesmerized by Lila's closeness. "That's not how you get a girl to sleep with you," she said.

His mouth trembled. "How?" he croaked.

Lila said, "Money."

Jared appeared as surprised as Jane was. He glanced over Lila's shoulder at her, and Jane looked down at her own hand lying inert on the table, its chewed and dirty fingernails. "How much?" he asked Lila.

Jane heard her say, "One hundred dollars."

"What about . . . what about with both of you?" he mumbled.

Lila turned to look at her. Her confidence astonished Jane; she wouldn't have taken her eyes off the man for a second. The other thing that surprised her was the expression on her sister's face: the jaw set, the mouth serious, the eyes glittering with challenge. *I dare you.* She had changed. She was different now. Assured. In charge.

"Jesus, no!" Jane said.

Lila turned back to him. "Just me, then," she said. "Let's see the money."

His trembling hand produced a wallet. Lila plucked it from his hand, removed the bills. Counted them. "Not quite enough, Jared," she said.

"I can get more."

"Tell you what. I'll take this." She handed back the empty wallet. "But I'm the boss. You do what I say."

He swallowed. He looked like he was going to cry. "Can we . . . can we do it . . ."

"What?"

He pointed above his head. "In the church? At the altar?"

"Sure, Jared," she said, patting his arm. She turned, approached the table, placed the bills down on the road atlas. Jane could see a couple of cards, credit or debit, and a driver's license peeking out from under them. She nudged the bills over a little to cover the cards. Lila went to her backpack in the corner, rummaged in it, and pulled out a strip of condoms. She tore one off. "Let's go," she said, leading him to the stairs.

Jared offered one last glance over his shoulder. His eyes were glazed. She couldn't tell what he was feeling, whether it was excitement or fear or both, but she would have described his expression as pleading.

Later, Jane heard Jared's car start up and drive away. Lila came running down the steps and over to the table. "Come with me," she said, scooping up the money and cards.

"Where?"

"Ray's."

She followed her sister out the door and across the street. The air was hot and close and a mist-like rain was falling. It felt like sweat. The supermarket closed at ten; it was a quarter 'til. "What happened?" Jane said, as they hurried through the empty parking lot.

"I fucked him."

"I mean . . . are you all right?"

Lila smirked at her. "Yes, dummy," she said. "I almost feel bad for him. Wanting to defile his father's church. He's a child." Jane hadn't realized Lila had ever had sex, let alone become so blasé about it. She'd never said a word.

The automatic doors parted for them and they entered the cool brightness of the store. Lila made a beeline for the ATM standing next to the customer service counter. "Actually," she said, glancing at the driver's license in her hand, "he's twenty-two."

Jane watched her sister insert the ATM card into the machine. The PIN request appeared. "Let's try his birthday." She keyed in 5-8-8-4. Denied.

"How about his street address?" Jane said, looking over her shoulder. "It's four numbers."

1-7-3-2. Denied.

"I'm not sure how many chances we get," Lila said. She hesitated, then keyed in 1-9-8-4. Denied. The two of them stood there, thinking. Then Lila tried 0-5-0-8 and it worked.

He had $382.14 in his account. They withdrew $300, the maximum the machine would give them. Then Lila put the credit card in. "Cash advance," she said. The PIN was the same. They took another $300.

"That's six hundred and sixty-eight dollars for ten minutes banging some doofus in a church," Lila said. "Not bad. And you didn't even have to besmirch your precious honor."

"You are not," Jane said, as they made their way to the freezer section, "going to make me feel guilty for not prostituting myself." Except she had. Jane felt angry and disgusted and, yes, guilty. Was this a way they were supposed to make a living now? Would she just fall deeper and deeper into Lila's debt?

They picked out a couple of pints of ice cream and helped themselves to paper napkins and plastic spoons from the deli counter. In the checkout lane, the last one still open, Lila grabbed copies of *Guns & Ammo* and *Simple*. The items moved down the conveyor belt toward an exhausted-looking girl with black eyeliner and bangs. Behind her, on a low shelf beneath the plastic bags and above a wastebasket, Jane spied a haphazardly stashed black canvas tote printed with white grinning skulls. The tote was gaping open and she could see a couple of tampons, a denim wallet, and a set of keys.

"Can I have a pack of Luckies?" Jane asked the girl.

She sighed. "Are you eighteen?"

"I'm twenty!"

"Hold on." She turned, left her station, and headed for the cigarettes, which were behind a counter, in plexiglass-fronted cases. Nobody manned the counter; the checkout girl would have to go back there, out of sight.

Jane felt an opportunity to prove herself. To restore the balance of power between them. She leaned over and snatched the keys out of the bag. Ignoring Lila's gawp, she slipped them into the pocket of her jeans.

The girl returned and rang them up. They walked out and made for the cluster of employee cars parked on the far side of the lot.

"Holy shit," Lila said.

"You wanted to leave, didn't you?"

"We won't have time to eat the ice cream."

"We'll eat and drive."

The girl's car was the first one they tried, a dented Saturn with a mismatched hood. After a brief stop at the church to pick up their things, they headed south along the coast highway. "She'll get off work any minute," Lila said.

"It's an hour to the state line. We can ditch it in Crescent City and catch a bus."

"You sound like a true dirtbag."

"You smell like you fucked a pastor's son for sixty-eight bucks."

"Bitch," Lila said, grinning.

"Whore."

They laughed. Jane drove. They rolled down the windows and smoked. Lila fed her ice cream and read to her from *Guns & Ammo,* and just after 11 p.m. they crossed over into California.

# 30

# Town of Ghorum, NY: *Now*

―――――――

The goon who had knocked the wind out of Harry spoke into a walkie-talkie. "Harry Pool," he said. It was hard to accept that fingers so thick could also be so long; they stretched all the way around Harry's skinny arm like a blood pressure cuff. The two of them stood and listened to the creek rushing by, its burble mingled with the static from the goon's other hand.

"Harry *Pool*," he repeated.

The tiny speaker issued a faint moan, followed by a phlegmy drawing of breath, and at last a deep snore.

The goon grunted, released Harry's arm. He bent down and picked up the Colt. It disappeared into the pocket of an enormous satin jacket.

"Lemme go wake him up," the man said.

Harry watched him disappear through the house's panel door. By leaning over the hood of the Subaru, he could see the goon move into a messy-looking living room, bend over a plump sofa with an afghan draped over the back. After a minute, a small gray head appeared.

From the front door the goon motioned to Harry. "Come on in," he said. Harry walked past him, flinching, and entered. The goon came in behind him, dodged around him, disappeared deeper into the house.

It was not what he would have expected from the Factor's final resting place. It was . . . homey. The hardwood floor was covered in rag rugs. Amateur paintings of moose, bear, and eagle adorned walls paneled in stained pine. A gas fireplace was dark underneath a mantel arrayed with family photos. Nothing appeared to have changed in sixty years.

"Harry," said the sofa. He looked down. The Factor was now wrapped in the afghan Harry had seen through the window. Of course he seemed diminished. All elderly people do, himself included. But the Factor looked like the victim of a shrink ray. His hair was thin and white, the skull beneath it a sad little knob, a pencil eraser. He was pressed into the corner of the sofa as if by some brutal unseen hand. He said, "Do me a favor, Harry, turn on the fire."

"Where's the switch?"

"Over the mantel, next to the merry wanderer."

He was referring to a Hummel figurine, a little boy with a carpetbag, whistling as he walked. Harry flipped the switch and the fire whumped to life. He stole a few glances at the photos, most from the distant past, the old flamboyant Factor with a jovial-looking woman in various foreign lands. There was also a black-and-white of a child, a little boy of around four, sitting in a red wagon. A hand snaked in from the side, holding him up. He appeared ill, as bent and withered as the Factor was now.

The Factor had caught him looking. "That's my son. Hubert. He died soon after that was taken."

"I'm sorry."

"Eh," the Factor said. He waved at a chair, a dirty recliner, which Harry obediently took, despite his distaste.

"This isn't the kind of place I expected to find you in," Harry said.

"Not the kind of place I expected to be. My in-laws' retreat. When I retired, my investments didn't work out as I'd planned. We decided to sell the place in town and move out here — Georgina wanted the quiet. She was a fearful woman, I'm afraid. She passed away about three weeks after it was all settled."

His voice had changed, but it was still mesmerizing — soothing where it once provoked. It sounded like the pages of a storybook being turned.

"Why," the Factor said, "have you come to see me, Harry? I must admit, there aren't many people from my past I would have wanted to see. You're among them."

"Thank you, I suppose?" Harry wiped his sweaty palms on his pants, liked the way it felt, kept doing it. "Yes, well. It's the past I wanted to talk to you about."

"That's all we have left, Harry."

"I . . . I admit I was angry, coming here. I am angry. I even brought a gun."

He seemed mildly surprised, but not alarmed. "I assume Vince has it now."

Harry nodded. "It's the one you told me to buy, a long time ago."

"I don't recall that, but I believe you."

"My wife, Anabel. She left me. Not recently, ages ago. Our girls were teenagers."

"Ah," the Factor said.

Harry was rising to his subject, gripping the chair arms. "You gave me everything in my life, in payment for the terrible thing you asked me to do. My job, my tenure. My book. Anabel was the one thing I found on my own, the one thing that came to me out of the blue, my life's great stroke of luck. She was the most important thing in my life, more important than all the things you gave me, and you asked me to recruit her.

"And I did it! Out of a sense of duty! I invited her to join the Agency. And you sent her away, you took her from me! Wherever she went, whatever you people made her do, it ruined her for the life we had together. She abandoned me. She abandoned our children. And I would have given back the job and the promotions and the book to have her back. But I didn't get to choose."

The Factor was gazing at him in apparent wonder and concern. He coughed, coughed again. Plucked a tissue from a box on the end table and hacked something into it.

"That's what I wanted to say to you," Harry said. "I wish I'd said no to all of it. I betrayed my students and chased my wife away. All for fucking nothing. So, I don't know. I fantasized about shooting you. But I guess I'll just tell you to go to hell."

"All right, Harry."

"Go to hell!" The words felt less satisfying than Harry had hoped, perhaps because the Factor had just placidly approved their deployment.

The Factor nodded. He drew breath, sat up straighter. Threw off the blanket. Under his robe, he was wearing herringbone pants and a blue

Oxford shirt. He said, "You may get your wish. Hell is where I ought to end up, perhaps."

"Oh?"

"The one thing you have right is that I was a sadistic son of a bitch. I did, in fact, waste my life."

"You wasted *my* life," Harry said.

"Well. Let's not be dramatic. You've got a few things backward, Harry. Are you finished blowing your top? May I explain, or would you like to find some pistol alternative to murder me with first?"

Amazing that Harry could still feel chastened at the age of seventy-three. He tried to sound dangerous as he said, "No. Go on."

"First of all— Oh, pardon me, Harry, you just came off a long drive. Do you want anything to eat or drink?"

"No."

"I do. Please pour me something from the cart." He gestured toward an old English-style tea trolley in the corner behind a dining table, forested with booze.

Harry obliged. He selected several of the dustiest bottles — Campari, Pimm's, Fernet — and combined their contents into a vile slurry, which he handed off to the Factor untempered by ice cubes.

But the Factor didn't seem to notice the implied punishment. He slurped the drink, smacked his lips. Said thanks. Set it on the end table, beside the tissue box, inside a nest of spent, balled-up tissues.

"So," the Factor said. "All the things you think I did, I didn't. All the things you think I didn't do, I did."

"What?"

"Your job, at Nestor. People retire, Harry. A job opened and you applied. And your book. I've read it, you know. It's a good book. That's all. Of course a good press published it. It was good."

"I got a phone call, telling me to submit it!" Harry said.

"Yes, you published papers, did you not? In respected journals? This is the kind of thing an editor should notice, Harry. If you're writing papers, maybe you're writing a book. And they didn't just publish the thing. It went through review. The process was entirely normal."

"And my tenure?"

The Factor slurped his drink. A bit of it rolled down his chin, and he daubed at it with the collar of his robe. "Yes, Harry, your tenure. Good teaching reviews, well-received book. You earned tenure. I had nothing to do with it. Nothing to do with any of it."

"Then . . . then what were you giving me? In exchange for the information about the students?"

"Nothing," the Factor replied.

"I don't understand."

"I wasn't with the Agency, Harry. Yes, I'd worked for them, in the sixties, when I was a student. I was a contractor. I spied on my own cohort! I'd wanted to become an agent, or at least an analyst . . . I fantasized about having an office in Langley, where I'd pore over data hour after hour, extracting evidence of clandestine activity. That was my major, you see, statistics. But I wasn't careful enough concealing my personal activities, you see, and I was discovered with a truck driver in a motel. It was fine that I was a drunk, of course—that was practically a prerequisite in those days—but a faggot was out of the question. I married in haste, hoping to prove myself to the powers that were, but alas, I was denied. For a time, I was given a small stipend to continue work on campus, as a recruiter, but those funds quickly dried up. Campus agitators were no longer an important subject of Agency scrutiny.

"So yes, I was technically working for the Agency when I recruited you. But after a while, I wasn't. And neither were you. You were just working for me."

Harry was flabbergasted. He felt paralyzed, dense, but also impossibly light. Like a parade balloon. He said, "But . . . but why?"

"I was angry at the world and everyone in it, Harry. You were so obviously talented, but so pathetically self-deprecating. I just wanted to fuck with you. *And* I wanted to fuck you. I thought you wanted to fuck me, too—that first night in Binghamton? I pounded on your door to let me in. You slept through it. I lost confidence. Was I wrong?"

"Yes! No! Or—Yes, no, I didn't want that."

Didn't he, though? Or did he?

"You weren't the only one I was deceiving, Harry. But you were the only one I actually ended up liking. I truly regret that I treated you that way."

"But," Harry said, shaking now. "But . . . what about Anabel? If you weren't really Agency anymore . . . how did I recruit Anabel?"

"Ah, well, that. I keep waiting for you to confess that you already know all about this, Harry, but I'm beginning to think you actually don't."

"Already know what?"

"You didn't recruit Anabel, Harry. She was deceiving you, at least at first. She was already the real thing—an actual agent. They sent her to me. She wanted me to soften you up, engineer an affair."

Harry's hands seized the chair's arms in a death grip. "What! Why?"

"You know her family history, Harry. Foreign diplomats. They were Agency, too. She was groomed for the work, excelled at it, but she kept trying to extract herself from it. It was the family business, and she hated the family. Her graduate work was in earnest, Harry, she wanted to become a professor, like you." He drained the last of his medicine, fumbled the empty glass's return to the table. It thunked onto the rug. "But I guess enough of my reports had made it up the chain, and they asked her to check you out. They thought you might be a double agent, working for the Soviets to undermine the CIA's campus work. Just a looky-loo, they told her, get him into bed, extract his secrets, and report back, and you can return to civilian life. They sent her to me, I told her what I knew, and she went to work."

"You're lying," Harry said.

"You know I'm not. And look, Harry, she actually fell for you. That much was real! She thought you were her ticket out of the game. A cozy academic job, a couple of adorable moppets, happily ever after and all that. I should know, I played that game and lost. Anabel did, too, I suppose." He waggled a finger at Harry. "Of all of us, Harry, you're the only one who actually won. You got the house, the job, and, for a little while, anyway, the loving wife. You got the moppets."

"You bastard."

The Factor sighed. "Yes, yes," he said. "I know."

"Maybe I will kill you. Maybe I should strangle you."

Somewhere, a door opened. Harry flinched. Vince stumped into the kitchen, having listened in. "You want me to get rid of him, Uncle Frank?"

"No, no," the Factor said, waving him away. The man disappeared, and Harry heard the gentle click of a door. "The poor boy. His own failed marriage has beached him here. Thank god for it, he is a kind and useful companion. I think he's just trying to get into my will."

"No, I'm not!" came a voice from down the hall.

"It's fine, Vincent, there's no one else! It will all be yours!" To Harry, he said, "Honestly, he ought to be hoping you strangle me."

"I should, goddammit. I should strangle you."

The Factor sighed. "Look, Harry, come over here and do it if you can. God knows I deserve it." He stretched out his neck. Chin in the air, he said, "Come on. You can kill me if you like."

Harry stood—jerked up, as though controlled by strings. His fingers twitched.

"Come on. Come over here."

Harry took a step, then another. The distant door opened again, and Vince emerged, stepped into the kitchen. "Uncle Frank?"

"No, no, Vincent, stand down," the Factor said, holding up a trembling hand. "Let us finish this business, please. Harry. I'm sure it's clear to you, I'm going to die soon. If you want to hasten the process, I won't stop you. I can't promise you'll escape unharmed, but I'm ready. Take your revenge."

Harry took two more steps, then sat down on the sofa beside his nemesis, who smelled sour and sweet. He gazed into the Factor's eyes.

"Oh, Harry. I really am sorry." He reached over and plucked a tissue from the box. "Here."

"For what?"

"You're crying, you old fool." He opened his arms. "Come, Harry. Let me hold you. I'm so sorry. I've never been sorrier."

It was true! Harry was sobbing. He let himself lean heavily against the Factor, closed his eyes, and let the sobs rack his body. He felt the papery arms embracing him. He couldn't kill the Factor. Aside from Anabel, no one had ever known him better. Not Jane, certainly not Lila. Not Julius the dean or Mary Beth from the department. His friend was dying, and he was so sad—his best friend, the Factor, was dying.

# 31

# California to Nestor: *Then*

---

The California border was a Rubicon; Jane felt a chill as their head-lights illuminated the Highway 101 welcome sign, with its clutch of golden poppies. She was reminded of the poppies in *The Wizard of Oz,* their beauty and danger. The euphoria from stealing the car had worn off, their throats were raw from the cigarettes, and Jane felt bad for the clerk at Ray's.

In Crescent City they crashed with some freaks who were raising pit bulls, thinking they could sell them as attack dogs. But they didn't know how to train them, just played with them all day, and the dogs were as dumb and friendly as the freaks, wagging their tails and pissing from excitement all over the busted-ass house. They got a ride to Sacramento with the regional manager of a snack distributor. He wanted to sleep with them and seemed sad but resigned when they said no. "I shoulda known I'd never stand a chance with hard girls like you." He left them with a business card and half a dozen packages of creme-filled chocolate cupcakes. They fell in with some rich kids who proved to be heroin addicts, traveled with them to Oakland, left them behind. As the months passed, they moved south, ending up in Los Angeles; Lila met a C-list starlet in a boutique and they lived with her in Los Feliz until her Starz drama got canceled, she ran out of money, and she kicked them out. Lila spent a month in 2008 in Mexico with a brother and sister she was having affairs with, and Jane became depressed and almost died of heatstroke after a trip to the desert.

After that, things got bad. Someone stole everything they owned; they took a casino bus to Vegas, where they were cornered in a parking garage by a group of men they were trying to rob. A sympathetic casino employee saved their bacon and let them stay with her for a week, then set them up with a friend in Flagstaff who owned a florist's shop. That's how they met Rayburn, the dojo owner who would go on to teach them self-defense; he was buying a bouquet to propose to his girlfriend with. (She said no.) Gradually Lila got her shit together. She bought another computer and began making money playing online poker. She also learned how to create fake identities, which they used to rent an apartment.

Every spring, Jane asked Lila if they were going to go to Chicago, to take Aunt Ruth up on her offer of temporary annual asylum. And every spring, Jane alone stuffed her backpack with food and clothes, bought a bus ticket, and made the cross-country trip. Every spring for three years, she felt worse in body, mind, and spirit. Year one, the visit felt like a delightful vacation—a fantasy of order and plenty—from a life that she'd tried and failed to convince herself was already a permanent vacation. Year two, she spent most of the visit asleep, curled in a fetal ball in the plush and magisterial guest bed she'd found so alienating not that long ago. The balance of her time was spent raiding the refrigerator, pantry, and liquor cabinet, and eating and drinking herself sick. She departed nauseated and miserable. Year three, she arrived nauseated and miserable and spent much of the visit in tears. She'd lost her appetite and wasn't eating anything at all. Aunt Ruth got her a session with a shrink she knew, who, instead of asking about her father or life goals, wordlessly prescribed an antidepressant. Aunt Ruth sent her off with two bottles of the stuff and enough money to keep her on it until fall, and for a little while, it got her through her days. But life demanded the remaining money for other things and Jane handed it over.

By now Lila had lost interest in the Nestor local news. But in May 2009, something broke through nationally and appeared deep in section A of the *Daily Sun*, where Jane noticed it, folded back and abandoned, in a booth at a diner. Somebody running on a treadmill in the gym on the Onteo Lake inlet—a new business that hadn't been there when they left—noticed, through a second-floor window, something tangled up in the reeds among the decorative landscaping stones at the water's edge, and climbed down for a closer look. DNA tests revealed that George Framingham, by then a skeleton in a bag, had at last been found, and trauma to the skull strongly suggested foul play. His sister began a very public campaign to locate and arrest Jane and Lila Pool, who she was certain were the culprits.

Lila appeared unfazed by this discovery. Their names were no longer Jane and Lila Pool. They were Justine Geary and Roseanna James, college dropouts who were into martial arts. Lila had cut and dyed her hair and Jane wore fake glasses. The photos the FBI distributed were of a couple of innocent-looking flaxen-haired drama-club teenagers; Jane and Lila were working-class young women who no longer even looked related. Lila insisted they had nothing to worry about.

But as Lila thrived, Jane continued to wither. She lost herself in booze and shitty men and her depression deepened. She and Lila fought, and eventually Jane moved out. Lila had quit the dojo, so they saw each other less and less often; meanwhile parents began to complain to Rayburn about the children's classes Jane taught. She showed up late, she was short with them. She stank and yelled at the kids. She stopped visiting Aunt Ruth and Lloyd, partly out of inertia, partly out of shame.

By the winter of 2010–11 Jane was in a downspiral. Rayburn put her on indefinite leave and called Lila, who brought her sister back to the old apartment and helped her quit drinking. That spring, lying in bed, smoking, staring at the cracks in the bedroom ceiling and listening to the neighbor repair his Saab while classical music played through a transistor radio, Jane realized what she had to do. She waited until Lila was away for the weekend, camping with friends, and packed a bag. She bought a bus ticket and left without a word.

Jane went home, to confess to the 2006 murder of George Framingham.

She stepped off the bus in Nestor on an overcast, unseasonably cold afternoon in July 2011. She understood that her arrival would go unnoticed, but it was still unnerving, knowing what she was about to do, to feel so anonymous in her own home town. The air felt clammy and stank of the train tracks and inlet, both of which ran behind the station. If she followed them for a few miles, she would arrive at the former site of George's house, now likely razed. Instead, she shouldered her backpack and crossed the street to enter the health food store. Hippie mothers pushed their child-bearing carts down the narrow aisles; an old guy with a white ponytail restocked shelves. Jane bought an oatmeal cookie and ate it as she walked home.

The house looked the same, except cleaner. The overgrown yard was mowed and trimmed, and the siding had been given a coat of paint. An extra key was still hidden inside the wooden housing of the disused well pump. She let herself in, calling out to her father. But no one was here. She went to the kitchen and drank a glass of water. The refrigerator was covered with the unsigned postcards she and Lila had sent over the past few years. She realized that they'd inadvertently done to him, with these postcards, exactly what their mother had done to her sister — vanished without explanation, taunted from afar. She began to cry, then refilled her water glass and carried it around the house. Dad was paying someone to clean; that was good. Her room had remained untouched, save for the piles of cardboard boxes and old mail that he was storing on the floor. The same was true of Lila's room, except that it had become a repository for books, which covered the carpet in teetering stacks.

She went to the living room and lay down on the sofa. The end that had always been sunken where her father habitually sat was now sunken further. Her feet dangled into it as though into a hole in the ground. She fell asleep immediately with her water glass balanced on her belly, and didn't wake up when it fell onto the rag rug.

"My god," her father said some hours later. His key in the door had woken her, and she stood up to greet him. He looked old and frail, though he was not yet sixty. It occurred to her that the image she held of him in memory wasn't that of five years before, but rather the distant past, when their mother was still here. She held him as he trembled and sobbed.

"I'm sorry, Daddy."

"I missed you so much, Janie."

"I know. I missed you, too."

"Where's your sister?"

She didn't want to lie to her father, but this was what she'd decided to do. The less he knew, the better for both of them. "I don't know," she said. "She went to Mexico a while back, and we got separated. I lost track of her."

"Are you all right?"

She nodded.

He held her by the shoulders. "You know they're looking for you?"

"Yes."

"Do you want to tell me what happened?"

She said the words she had rehearsed in her mind. "We were at the party. Lila was drunk, I think he roofied her. I found them downstairs and he was raping her. I hit him with a candleholder. When she came to, we panicked and dumped him in the lake. I didn't mean to kill him."

"My god," he said again. He gazed at her steadily, and she gazed back. Surely he knew she was lying.

"I'm here to confess."

"You're not going to march into the police station," he said to her, with more force than she'd ever heard him speak. "You need a lawyer."

"I know, Daddy."

"I'm going to make some calls. You'll stay here. Don't go out. Do you understand?"

"Yes."

An hour later, a man like a small bear arrived, wearing a round beard, a cardigan sweater, and a soft leather briefcase. He introduced himself as Lamar and talked to her as if she were a child. She found that she didn't mind. They sat with her father at the kitchen table. Lamar produced a legal pad, a ballpoint pen, and a second, identical pen, which he laid down on the table as a backup. He asked her to tell the story from beginning to end, and she did, including their flight from Nestor, stealing the computer and car, emailing Principal Kovacs and forwarding the photos George had taken. It wasn't hard to lie; she just substituted herself for Lila. He asked her to describe the Easter Island head candleholder in detail, including the name of the student she thought had made it in the art studio. He asked her to describe the boat. He had her make a list of every kid who was at the party, and the names of the ones she remembered from the pictures. The only thing that she hadn't experienced firsthand was the blow itself, the one that broke George's skull; she'd been unconscious for that. But she knew Lila was right-handed and that George had been kneeling over her, his back to Lila. She said she struck him on the right side of his head, above the ear. That's where she would have hit him. That's where she thought she remembered the blood coming from. She left out the suffocation, figuring it had been too long, and the body too decayed, for there to be any evidence of that.

After an hour, Lamar asked her if she wanted to rest. She said no, and they talked for another hour. By now it was dark. Jane was hungry but she didn't say so. Lamar said, "Jane, you were a minor, and you acted in defense of your sister. In addition, police have spoken to the young women in the photos you sent. Some of them will doubtless confirm your experience with George Framingham." He cleared his throat. "It would be useful to have your sister's testimony. If you have some idea of where she might be, we can hire someone to find her."

"No, thank you," Jane said.

"It's unlikely she would be punished."

"No." Jane said. Then: "Will I be punished?"

Lamar sighed and set down his pad. He carefully capped his pen and set that down, too. "In hindsight, stealing Framingham's computer and car and concealing the crime may be worse offenses than what you did defending Lila. If you hadn't run, all of this would be years in the past, now. You could be charged with second-degree murder, which I would want to get down to justifiable homicide. It's possible you'd end up being tried for involuntary manslaughter, but I think a sympathetic jury would find you innocent of that. If things don't go our way, you could serve time in prison, yes. I will do everything in my power to prevent that."

"All right," she said. She didn't say what she was feeling, which was calm. A heavy weight that had been teetering had finally fallen.

The following week, Lamar made arrangements for her to turn herself in to the police. "I should be able to get you a bail reduction from the judge, and you can come home," he said. "But be prepared to spend the night in jail. Wear your jeans, no belt, a clean shirt." They arrived at the courthouse on a Wednesday morning to a massive crowd of reporters, some national, and spectators. Clearly the news had been leaked. There was a party atmosphere; people shouted questions, some cheered, some shouted "Murderer!" Jane didn't recognize any faces.

The police interrogated her for three hours. After a brief conference with a judge and the district attorney, Lamar managed to negotiate the charge down to involuntary manslaughter — not what he was hoping for, but not murder. She would be tried as an adult—a requirement for a violent crime committed by a sixteen-year-old in New York in 2006. He persuaded the judge that she was not a flight risk, having returned home specifically to turn herself in, and would be living with her father, a college professor. Lamar argued for a bail reduction and the judge set it at $10,000. Her father paid; Jane was mildly surprised that he had that much money. The trial was set for November, several months away. She went home at the end of the day, pursued by reporters, went to bed, and slept until midafternoon the next day. The reporters were gone when she awoke.

As far as Jane knew, Lila didn't try to contact her during this time. This was what she expected and ostensibly wanted, but it hurt. Her depression returned and she started drinking and smoking again. By the beginning of September she'd begun to get control of herself and took walks around the neighborhood, and then—after people started recognizing her and trying to talk to her—in the state forest on the northern edge of town. She quit drinking but kept smoking.

One cool and misty morning she was sitting, smoking, on a bench in a shelter next to a trail map when a man sat down next to her. He pulled an American Spirit out of a pack in his shirt pocket, lit it, and said, "This is the only place I smoke now."

He was tall, broad shouldered, around her age. He wore leather boots with yellow laces and his flannel shirt was tucked into dark, clean blue jeans.

"The birders give you the stink eye, right?" she said, turning to him, and then: "Oh my god. Chance."

"Hey!" he said, grinning.

They embraced, laughed. Walked and smoked together. He showed her an unmarked trail that led up behind the power company and ended at a hidden waterfall. She made a joke about the stacks of rocks teetering at the water's edge, attributing them to fairies. He surprised her by plucking a mushroom from the base of a tree, brushing it off gently with his cigarette hand, and popping it into his mouth.

That night, she let him take her to a steak house on Route 96. They'd been here before, back in high school, when it was a different steak house. A few people did a double take when they saw her. She said, "So, you know why I'm back, right?"

"Yeah, of course. I really meant to call you, but I kept thinking . . . I dunno, maybe you wouldn't want to hear from me."

She patted his hand. "It's all right."

"I was . . . really hurt. When you disappeared. There were rumors that you'd, like, run off with him. The dead guy."

"I guess there would be."

"I never believed them."

She laughed. "Seriously? I would have believed them!"

"Come on, Jane," he said, scowling. "I knew you better than that. Also, your sister was gone, it's not like you'd both go off with him. I figured you and her just had some kind of home troubles and had to get out."

"If that was the case, I would have called you."

He looked sad now. "Yeah. I guess I didn't know what to think." A waiter brought their meals: New York strip for him, Caesar salad with shrimp for her. "So . . . where is she?" Chance wanted to know. "Your sister."

"Don't know."

"Does she know you turned yourself in?"

"No idea," Jane said.

"Do you mind my asking?"

"I don't," she said. "I don't mind. Though I don't think I'm supposed to talk much about what happened."

"It seems to me that's pretty unfair," Chance said. "You going to trial for trying to help her, and her just"—he waved his hand in the air—"out there in the wind. She ought to be here, at your side. Telling the jury what happened."

"Chance," she said.

"I just can't believe she would betray you like this."

"Chance," she said, "I really don't want to talk about her, to be honest. Or the stuff that happened. Especially not here."

"What do you want to talk about?"

"Nothing," she said. "You talk. Just tell me whatever."

He talked about his job, which was stonemasonry; he'd become the head mason for a landscaping company. He talked about hunting and fishing, and his first wife, a hairdresser who left him for a woman. Jane could tell he felt particular bitterness about what he regarded as a betrayal not only of him, but of his entire gender, and it made her uneasy. But he quickly moved on. He talked about his parents, said his mother remembered her fondly in a way that made it clear the opposite was true.

She remembered why she liked him. Loved him? Liked him. He wasn't a clinging wimp, or a bored stoner, or a leech, like most of the boys she'd fallen in with during her travels. His skin was tan from work outside and he'd let his hair grow a little shaggy. It had some premature gray in it, which she found attractive. He'd shaved for this date but it almost seemed like a joke — beard stubble was part of his true form, and it would be restored within hours.

"I'll take you home," he said after dinner, an invitation for her to decline. She declined. "Drive me around," she said. He drove carefully down back roads, the radio playing classic country, the windows down. She was out of cigarettes so they shared one of his. "I thought you only smoked in the woods," she teased. "Busted," he said. "I guess I like to smoke in the truck, too. Sometimes." After a while a resolve came over him; he seemed to have a destination in mind. They arrived at the university's observatory, a place they'd parked before. A gravel lot, empty of cars, overlooked a valley. The night was clear and the stars shone. She said, "Is there anything else you like to do in the truck, sometimes?" He laughed, very low in his chest, and turned to her.

Their courtship was not what Jane imagined a courtship should be, and she didn't feel what she thought she was supposed to feel. But she didn't know what that was, and she felt something, anyway — some righting of an old wrong, or continuation of a plot — so she went along with it. Once, she came to his work site to meet him for lunch, and she saw a man and a woman, his co-workers, unrolling sod over fresh dirt. Instant, lush green. The image returned to her often. That's what their romance was like, a thick layer of luxuriant promise. Chance was steadfast, loyal. He was not ashamed to be dating an accused killer. Getting to know his mother gave her new insight; she clearly had wanted another kind of woman for him, and he was proving himself, asserting his independence. His first wife was an ill-conceived rebellion, Jane a definitive doubling down. Susan didn't bother to conceal her distaste, and this made Chance want Jane more. She did not mind being this to him. She didn't mind feeling as though she were being rescued.

Chance proposed to her the night before her trial was to begin, and they married at the courthouse during recess on the first day. The press loved it. They asked to see her ring and she held her hand aloft on the courthouse steps. The gesture, and the many photographs taken of it, would soon come to seem like hubris.

The prosecutor's opening statement was straightforward enough; she argued, as Lamar promised she would, that Jane's actions during her sister's supposed assault were extreme, vengeful, and unnecessary, and her actions afterward irresponsible and incriminating. "My job," she told the jury, "might be much more difficult if Lila Pool were here to corroborate her sister's version of events. But she is not. The only testimony we have comes from the defendant herself. And even if you believe that the defendant saved her sister from a bloodthirsty rapist — even if you give her the benefit of the doubt — you must still find that she did wrong. She did not have to end a man's life — and, having done so, she certainly did not need to conceal evidence of her crime. Even if you sympathize with Jane Pool, you must still find her guilty."

The trial spent several days on the disposal of the body, its discovery, the expert testimony pertaining to the remains: how they were identified, details about the wound. Jane had wanted to testify on her own behalf; Lamar had dissuaded her. It soon became clear that he was right to do so. As it happened, she was mistaken, in her statement to the police, about where on George's skull the blow had landed; evidently Lila had somehow managed to stave in his forehead. The prosecutor made hay of her incapacity to remember this, the moment she was asking the jury to believe was the single most traumatic of her life. She accused Jane of anger, fury above and beyond what would disable George. If Jane had had to answer to this directly, she wouldn't have been able to keep her composure. The case would have gone down in flames.

Chance had taken off work to sit in the gallery and watch the trial; Susan joined him. At the end of each day, Jane returned with Chance to his rental house outside of town, where she cried herself to sleep in his arms. Despite the setback about the killing blow, Lamar assured Jane that he was still confident in their case. Evidence of Framingham's predation was strong, and the remaining forensic evidence supported Jane's version of events. The medical examiner hadn't found evidence of the pillow smothering. She was glad she'd kept that detail to herself. Lamar's growing excitement offered her a glimmer of optimism; it was clear he was eager to show his case to the jury.

Then the prosecution brought Nell Timmons to the stand.

Jane had seen her name on the witness list but had only vague memories of her—didn't recall speaking with her that night, didn't imagine she could be a problem. Now, Nell stood straight as she was sworn in and stared blankly into the air above the gallery, and, with a horrific jolt, Jane remembered. She'd talked to her at the party. She was the one Jane gushed to about her plan to seduce George Framingham. She wore a new-looking navy suit and a turquoise blouse, and Jane realized that Nell still hated her, had hated her in high school and hated her now.

"Tell us about your encounter with the defendant at the victim's house on May 4, 2006," the prosecuting attorney said. She was a tall woman with a large round head. She bent toward the witness box like a flower straining to be pollinated.

"She was very drunk. We were waiting in line outside the bathroom and she was bragging that she planned to have sexual relations with George Framingham."

"Do you remember her exact words?"

Nell shifted in her seat.

"She said, 'I'm going to seduce George.' "

"Was this in response to a question on your part?" the prosecutor asked.

"No. She just said it, like a brag."

"And how did you respond?"

"I told her she was drunk, which she was, and she should go home."

"And how could you tell that the defendant was drunk?"

"She was slurring her words and walking like she was. Also I saw her drinking all night."

"Did it appear to you," the prosecutor asked, "that she might pass out from drinking?"

"Objection," Lamar called out beside her. "Speculation." He sounded tired.

"Sustained." The judge turned to the jury box. "Disregard that exchange, please."

"Did the defendant respond to your suggestion?" the prosecutor asked.

"She called me a bitch."

"And so," the prosecutor said, "do you think that drunk Jane Pool might have been jealous had she later discovered her twin sister in bed with the victim?"

"Objection, Your Honor! Speculation!"

"Sustained."

The prosecuting attorney also got several of Jane's own character witnesses to admit that she was extremely drunk that night. Several of them didn't recall Lila as being incapacitated; a few had the impression she hadn't been drinking at all.

"How bad was that?" Jane asked Lamar that night.

Lamar said, "It was bad."

"I'm sorry. I honestly did not remember her."

They were gathered around Harry's kitchen table, gloomily perched behind untouched cups of tea: Jane, Lamar, Harry, Chance. Chance brooded. Jane kept trying to catch his eye and he wouldn't look at her. He did this when he was emotional, whether it was with embarrassment or frustration or love. But she had the impression he was angry.

"It's all going to be all right," Harry said.

"You don't know that, Dad."

"I'm still confident," Lamar said, patting Jane's hand, not sounding confident at all. "The facts are on our side."

Then Chance broke his silence. He turned to Lamar and said, "I thought you were supposed to be good at this."

"Hey!" Jane said.

"Why didn't you cross-examine her? You could have proved she was full of shit!" Chance's face was red and his jaw trembled. Jane could hear his teeth grinding in the silence that followed.

"Chance," Jane said. "She wasn't. I did say those things."

"You were drunk! You could have said anything!"

"That hardly," Lamar interjected, "strengthens our case."

He leveled a sober, calculating gaze at Chance. For a moment, it seemed he might respond. Then he appeared to think better of it. Not long after, Lamar shrugged on his jacket and headed for the door.

The next day, Lamar's opening statement was clear and emotional, and the jury seemed sympathetic to him. A number of character witnesses attested to George's reputation as a lech and a predator. Rohypnol had indeed been found in a jar under the tiki bar. And the photographs Lila had emailed to Principal Kovacs clearly carried some weight.

Only George's sister, though clearly shaken by these revelations, maintained certainty in his innocence. She told the press that her brother was the victim, that his reputation was being smeared, that he could never do these things. But these claims seemed weak in the face of the near-unanimous testimony of the students Lamar had tracked down. For all that, though, it was clear — Jane could see it on the faces of the jurors — that none of it had dislodged Nell's testimony from their minds. To them, Jane was a jealous lover. Even if what she did was justified, they would be considering her actions in that light.

Lamar's closing argument was fine: a recapitulation of his opening statement, with an emphasis on Jane's youth, and of the evidence that had been presented in her favor. But the prosecutor's was excellent. She started with a speech about the severity and prevalence of rape. "Some of you may be victims of it," she told the jury. "Some of your loved ones certainly are. I am." Gasps sounded in the gallery, and the prosecutor hung her head. Then, for a moment, she seemed to argue in favor of Jane's innocence: if someone was raping a loved one, most people would do whatever was necessary to put a stop to it. And if everything the defense claimed were provably true, the defendant's actions would be justified, in the eyes of the law.

"But the defense's case is not provably true. The defendant openly admits that she was drunk, and that she desired the victim sexually. And the one person who could confirm her version of events, the person the defendant was ostensibly protecting, is not here today.

"You are not here to decide whether rape is wrong. We know it is. You are not here to decide whether protecting a loved one from it is right. We know it is. You are here to decide whether or not the evidence supports the defendant's version of events, or the prosecution's. You've heard some disturbing testimony about the deceased's character, but his character isn't on trial. Jane Pool is, for taking his life, then attempting to cover up the crime, instead of admitting to it, as we'd expect an innocent person, a person protecting a loved one, would do. If you think the defendant believed she was doing the right thing, but, in her drunkenness, made mistakes — that she may not have meant to kill George Framing-ham when she struck him — well, that's exactly what she is accused of today. I urge you to find her guilty of involuntary manslaughter."

That night, they gathered at Harry's house for what they all suspected might be Jane's last night of freedom: Lamar, Harry, Chance. Susan refused to see or speak to Jane, and Chance wasn't speaking to Susan. She clearly wished that Jane and Chance had never met, and had probably encouraged him to divorce her. He didn't want to talk about it.

They ate take-out pizza and drank beer. At the door, his eyes gleaming, Lamar said, "I'll be second-guessing this one for the rest of my life."

"It's not your fault," Jane told him. "You did the best you could with what I gave you."

"I'm at your disposal no matter what happens," he said, weeping openly. "Be ready for the worst tomorrow, but remember I will appeal on your behalf. I will keep fighting for you, no matter what."

"Thank you, Lamar," she said.

When it was time to go, Chance went out to the truck while she said goodbye to her father. He sat at the kitchen table, slumped in his chair. He said, "I was a terrible father."

"No."

"I was. I wish I could do it all over again. I wish I could fix it."

She held him as he cried. "None of this is your fault, Dad. It's on Lila and me. We knew better. We shouldn't have run."

"Should I be angry at her?" he said into his hands. "Because I'm angry at her."

"I don't know. I'm not."

"She should have been here. She should have defended you."

"Dad," Jane said, pulling his hands off his face. "Please trust me. This is how I wanted it." But it wasn't, was it. She'd expected, foolishly, to be exonerated. She had wanted to be the brave one, to prove herself to Lila. But not to go to prison.

That night, in bed, Jane said, "Chance. I need to say something."

"Don't."

"This isn't what you bargained for. If you —"

"Jane, don't. I don't want to hear it. You're my wife. You'll still be my wife when you get out."

"Your mother —"

"My mother doesn't have a say in this." He frowned, held her tighter. Too tight. She squirmed and he relented, slightly.

"All right," she said. "Love you."

"I shouldn't have gotten angry at Lamar."

"We're all under a lot of strain."

Late in the morning, they were called back to court and the decision was read. That afternoon, she was delivered to Boynton Ridge Correctional Facility, fingerprinted, photographed, strip-searched, relieved of her possessions, and led to her cell.

Three weeks later, having defended herself against several violent attacks and begun to make the alliances she believed would get her safely through the next year and a half, she missed her period, and then the one after that. The doctor told her what she already knew: she was pregnant. Eventually she would be moved to the nursery inside the Boynton Ridge complex. This was an unusual program, designed to treat incarcerated mothers with compassion; she was told by everyone she'd met inside how lucky she was. "At Auburn, they chained my cousin to the bed and took her baby away screaming," one woman told her. "She bled to death in shackles."

But it wasn't luck that got her into the nursery. It was Lamar. Harry later told her, on a visit to the prison, that the attorney had worked day and night to make it happen. "He feels like he let you down at trial. It was a crusade for him." Lamar himself downplayed his role in her transfer but accepted her thanks. Their meetings were brief and professional; it was clear that he felt nearly as much shame as she did for everything that had transpired.

Jane would give birth and serve out the last ten months of her sentence in the nursery with Chloe. Chance visited often and was allowed to play with their daughter; he confirmed what Susan had told her in a sternly worded, borderline-threatening letter: her mother-in-law wanted her to give the baby up and allow Susan to adopt her. Jane had a brief panic that Susan might have legal recourse to force the matter, but as it happened, the threat was empty. The child was treated well at Boynton Ridge and in any event was unlikely to remember anything about it. The other mothers knew why Jane was incarcerated and seemed to respect what she had done. Chance took Jane's side. The child should be with her mother.

But then he and Susan hatched their plan to keep the truth from Chloe until she was older. Much older, they agreed: thirteen years. She would never understand, they argued; she'd feel ashamed.

"You're the ones that feel ashamed," Jane told Chance on one of their visits. "If we tell her from the start, she'll think it's normal."

"It's not normal, no matter what we tell her."

"Also, Chance, how on earth will we prevent her from finding out? All the parents will know."

"You'll take my name," he said, "and go by your middle name."

"Martina Kelleher? That's my name now?"

"You can do your hair differently, change your makeup. Nobody will know. And Chloe is going to private school, anyway."

"What! We haven't talked about this, Chance," she said. They were sitting at a low table on tiny chairs made for children, surrounded by toddlers, and the mothers in their green prison uniforms. "We have to decide these things together."

"You want her to go to public school? In Nestor? Where everybody knows her mom is an ex-con?"

A few women glanced over. The guard stirred, shifting from one foot to the other. "Keep your voice down," Jane said. "These are my friends. Most of them don't have the advantages I will when I get out."

"So our daughter's life should be shitty because other people's lives are shitty?"

"That's not what I'm arguing! And public school isn't shitty."

He gaped, shook his head. "You had to kill your theater coach!"

In the end, Chance and Susan won. Jane agreed to their terms. It was easier that way, and anyway, it all seemed unreal to her—the trial, prison, Chloe, all of it. Life outside as a free woman was as unimaginable to her as prison had been just months before.

For all its danger, incarceration suited Jane, after the chaos of the preceding years. Her life of dissipation and petty crime had taught her, if nothing else, to live without fear. The inmates here had rivalries and disputes like anyone, but most people respected the pregnancy, and her allies helped her defend herself against the few who didn't. There were few choices to be made in the course of a day, and once Chloe was born—surprisingly swiftly, after just a few hours' labor, with the assistance of some extremely nervous nursing students visiting from a local college—her options dwindled to zero. She cared for her child, that was all. She fed her, changed her, gazed at her small, mysterious face.

Jane's worst day in prison came in the form of an envelope postmarked Chicago. She'd written to Aunt Ruth, who hadn't reached out during the drama of her confession and trial. Jane wondered if she felt betrayed when the visits stopped—after all she'd done, helping Jane with her depression, her poverty—and, in the days before Chloe was born, she wrote a long letter, telling her aunt everything that had happened since she last visited, years before, everything except the truth about the murder.

Months passed before a reply arrived from Lloyd. Laser printed on linen letterhead from his law practice, it was polite and brief. It informed her that Ruth was dead. She'd taken her own life in 2011, around the time Jane was gathering the courage to return to Nestor and confess. Lloyd offered no explanation for the news, commented only perfunctorily on Jane's life circumstances, and did not invite her to visit again. It was clear he had found Ruth's troubled nieces to be burdensome. Of course.

Chloe stirred in her sleep as Jane silently sobbed. The snipping of this final strand was somehow worse than anything that had come before—the trauma, the addiction, the eating disorders, the loss of her freedom. Ruth had represented some aspirational notion of home, above and beyond the sad reality of her father's crumbling house, and Jane realized that she'd imagined, in a humiliating fantasy she'd hidden even from herself, that someday Lloyd would die, that Ruth would grow ill, and that Jane alone would be willing to care for her. She would be needed, would inherit everything, would live in peace in that cold, palatial enclave. Instead, there would be nothing. Lloyd made no mention of a will.

When Jane was released, she was able to get the staff job in the history department through her father's influence. She introduced herself as Martina Kelleher and, eventually, drove half an hour each way every day to pick up her daughter from her private school for the arts outside Rochester. Susan had bought them a house in between the school and Nestor, and Jane wasn't in a position to refuse it. That became her life: she was a middle-class mother with a secret and an hour-long commute.

Of course she was bad at it: bored, resentful, quick to anger. Expected to maintain the home she hadn't asked for, to the standards of a woman she didn't like, she found herself taking it out on Chloe, overreacting to minor infractions, yelling for no good reason, locking herself in her bedroom to cry. Eventually she allowed herself to accept that, even before she was convicted of involuntary manslaughter, she hadn't wanted Chance to keep his promises to her. Their union, based on sentimental assumptions, had been a mistake. He should have quietly divorced her the moment the sentence came down, as his mother wanted. The latter days of her prison term came to seem idyllic to her: gloriously bored with her infant child, her basic needs being met, no social obligations other than not getting into fights.

Everyone in the history department knew who she really was. No one at the Tarbox Beals School did. Often, at school events — plays, fundraisers, student art exhibits and concerts — Jane wanted to tell these moneyed, cultured women the truth. She wanted to tell them her marriage was a joke, her daughter born in jail. She wanted to interrupt their anecdotes about home renovation or hired help or international vacations and tell them what it felt like to follow George Framingham's corpse into the frigid water.

But she never did. She kept the peace. Ruefully, inadequately, she cared for her daughter and father and lived her two lives. And then she opened her email inbox and found Lila inside.

# 32

# Bocas del Toro Province, Panama: *Now*

———

Jane stood on the gravel watching her sister slip into the shade beneath the trees. The guards seemed confused — weren't they supposed to enter the house? The woman who'd searched them gestured toward two of the other guards, who nodded and followed Lila down the hill.

"Hey!" Jane shouted.

Her sister stopped and turned.

"We came all this way!"

Lila shook her head. She looked small and dim, a shadow among shadows. She called out, "I'm not giving her the satisfaction."

"Come on."

Lila dismissed her with a wave of her hand.

Jane turned back to the house. Their mother had moved inside. She called down to Lila, "What am I supposed to do, then?"

"Whatever you want" was the reply. Jane watched her sister open the back door of the guards' SUV and climb in, leaving her crossed legs jutting out onto the gravel path.

Jane hitched her bag higher on her shoulder and marched up the flagstone path. Her heart was racing. She felt used and manipulated, both by her mother and by Lila.

Passing into the house was like stepping through a portal into a parallel universe. The ambient temperature dropped fifteen degrees, her eyes adjusted, and the interior snapped into focus. The floor was tile, the floor plan wide open. A wrought iron dining table lay in the glow from a skylight, and beyond it a modest kitchen was visible. A glass pitcher of water and two glasses stood on the table, beside the trowel her mother had been holding. Jane smelled flowers and heard the sound of a fountain but could see neither.

Anabel Bortnik stood before her. Her arms were crossed over her chest and she stood with one leg extended, as though readying herself to dance. Her hair was tied back, revealing a face ageless save for the eyes. Jane didn't see herself in her mother's face. She saw Chloe.

"You," her mother said.

"Mother."

She hadn't called anyone that in twenty years. The word felt dry on her tongue. She worked her jaw, licked her lips. Realized she was thirsty.

"I expected your sister."

Jane said, "I suspect she didn't want to give you the satisfaction. So, here I am."

Her mother let out a snort. "I can have her dragged in here if I like."

"So do it."

"Why don't you and I catch up first."

The voice was unchanged from the voice of Jane's memory, that crackling, strangely deep, flatly authoritative bark. It gave her a jolt, and she thought this was how the fury would be kindled: with the memory of that voice, demanding order, deflecting need, dismissing love.

Instead, she remembered the smell of her mother's solarium, the richness and heat and the moist air. The little electric fountain resembling a stream tumbling down a miniature mountain, through a series of natural pools. The fountain made a gentle trickling sound, like rain, like the sound she was hearing now. Her occasional kindness: showing them her plants, reciting their Latin names, identifying the parts, explaining how they absorbed sunlight, grew, reproduced. Jane recalled none of those facts, only the marvelous, elusive feeling of their mother's loving attention, so difficult to elicit anywhere else. She and Lila sat on folding chairs and listened to their mother talk, and to the sound of the fountain. They felt the warmth of the baseboard radiators and of the winter sun streaming through the glass.

Had Anabel Bortnik made that place her entire world, expressly to exclude them from it? Had she drawn them here to show what she had achieved without them? Was this her idea of love, this demonstration of power? Why did she trick them into crossing the country, only to show them her back? Jane tried to imagine what it would be like to leave her life behind, stay here for twenty years, and see Chloe again as a grown woman, wounded and angry before her. Surely she would collapse, devastated by the guilt and loss. What she would not do was stand there, as her mother was doing now, hand on her hip, eyes narrowed, a quizzical smile.

"Can you tell me what we're doing here, Mom?" Jane said. "Did you lead us out here just to rub our faces in it? Or is there something else you want to say?"

"I thought you both could learn something from what I'd made. Or that you might want to work for me. I didn't think it would take you so long to get here."

"Sorry to disappoint yet again."

Her mother shook her head. "So sarcastic. Just like when you were a child."

"If you had expectations for us, maybe you should have raised us."

"No one raised me." A shrug. "And it isn't like I left you in the woods. You were adults. Or you thought you were. And you had your father."

This last, she said with a little snort, almost as if it were a joke, and Jane experienced a burst of love for her father like a first breath after nearly drowning. The desire to defend him was like a boat capsizing in reverse: she flew up out of the cold dark water into safety. Anger gripped her and she said, "How could you be so cruel to him? You could have just divorced him. Anything but disappearing the way you did."

Her fingers drummed her elbow, a familiar tell of impatience. "My marriage to your father was a mistake. He knows it as well as I do. But we were useful to each other. And he knew what he was getting into."

"Oh, so he knew you were a spy?"

It looked like her mother might laugh. Again, Jane was reminded of Chloe. She realized that now, she would think of her mother whenever she looked at her daughter, and a fresh wave of fury pulsed through her.

"Of course he knew," her mother said dismissively. "He was Agency, too, you know."

It took a moment for this information to penetrate the fog of surreality; Jane wasn't sure she understood. "Wait," she said. "What?"

A bitter laugh. "He spied on his students. For decades. He won their trust, extracted their secrets, spilled them to the CIA. They let him think he recruited me, in fact. If he had any courage, he would have told you that by now."

Stunned, Jane didn't reply.

"I tried to love him, Jane. I tried to be part of a family. But, like my mother, I didn't have the knack. And I had greater aims than she ever did. Or your father. There was more that I could do here, for more people. I had ambitions the Agency couldn't satisfy, let alone the academy." She let her arms fall, allowed herself the indulgence of an exasperated shake of the hands. "Why would I waste my time on people who didn't care whether I was there or not? Who didn't listen to a thing I said? I saw the writing on the wall. I went out and *made* something of myself."

"Well, great job," Jane said.

"You should have enough self-respect to do the same, Jane. Your sister, at least, has tried to. But you . . ."

"How dare you."

"Admit it, Jane. Has your world ground to a halt without you since you left home? Does your daughter miss you?"

Jane's muscles were tensed, her legs trembled. Her body remembered the sensations of feeling cornered, stalked by every passing man, in the months — the years — after George Framingham. "Oh, fuck you, Mother."

"Come now, Jane. The thought hasn't crossed your mind that you're not the ideal mother? That you're passionate, unpredictable? Quietly seething with dissatisfaction and longing and dark secrets? Would anyone be surprised if you never came back?"

Jane's bag was slipping off her shoulder, and she pushed it impatiently back up. It bumped against her hip. There was something unfamiliar about the weight of it, and Jane's hand quickly found the culprit. The steel was still warm from the air outside. She remembered falling asleep in the car, waking to the open glovebox. Lila's embrace, after the pat down. The grip found her palm, and her finger, the trigger. She drew the pistol from the bag and held it loosely at her side.

For the second time, Anabel Bortnik appeared surprised. "How in God's name did you get that in here?"

"Apparently Lila wanted me to have it."

"Jane," her mother said quietly, "if my guards come in here, they will shoot you on sight. It doesn't matter that you're my daughter."

"Getting ready to blame somebody else again, I see."

"I mean it. Put it down on the floor at your feet."

"I'm not like you," Jane said. "I'm not the ideal mother, but I'm not like you."

"All right. You're different." Her face changed register, suddenly, a mask of fake compassion sliding into place to hide the contempt. Jane felt a click of recognition; this is something she'd done, too, when they were on the run, when she was an addict. To get what she wanted out of people. It made her angrier. Her mother went on: "Please put the gun down. You can kill me, but you will die. Your sister will die."

"So what?" Jane said. "The world won't grind to a halt without me."

"Your bodies will never be found," her mother said, a quaver in her voice, and for a moment Jane wondered if this theatrical fear was real. But it couldn't be. Could it? "Your loved ones will spend years and fortunes demanding that the institutions of justice discover what happened to you, and punish the people who took your lives." She stopped, drew breath. "But none of that will ever happen, Jane. Police will follow your trail to the outskirts of my land and will forget you ever existed."

She paused.

"Is that what you want?"

Jane said nothing. Maybe it was what she wanted—not just to die, but to be erased. If she'd made nothing of herself, why not become nothing? The most she could hope for was making her mother suffer. Maybe, as the bullets plowed into Jane, the woman would cry actual tears. Maybe she would run to Jane's lifeless body, fall to her knees and sob. What have I done, she would scream.

Or Jane could just shoot her, and they would die together. She raised the gun and pointed it.

"Think of your child," Anabel Bortnik said. "Think of your daughter, Chloe."

This was supposed to dissuade her. But why not just wipe the slate clean? She was no different from Anabel: She'd started a family to push away the truth about herself. She playacted as a woman with feelings. She should let Chloe start fresh, with no one to follow into the wilderness. Let the chain of error end here.

She heard footsteps behind her, someone coming in from the kitchen. In her peripheral vision, a rifle being raised to fire. Anabel shouted a command, raised a hand, and everyone froze. The smell of smoke: something, somewhere, was burning. "Jane, I want you to kneel on the floor and put the gun down. Then I want you to let my people take you away from here."

"Señora," a voice somewhere said quietly.

*"Your people,"* Jane said.

"Yes," said her mother. More footsteps. Long shadows in the rectangle of light framed by the door. "My people. The people who will seize this region back from the capos, from the mining companies."

The gun trembled at the end of Jane's arm. "You're a criminal, just like them," she said.

Anabel nodded. "That's right," she said. "Just like Noriega was, just like the CIA. The Sandinistas, the United States military, the Panama Canal Corporation, the British. The Spanish. Criminal enterprise is the only thing that will protect the people from criminal enterprise. And someday, after their power has curdled, someone will have to protect someone from them. That's how the world works. And killing us both won't stop it."

A voice behind Jane said, "Señora, algo está pasando." A small metallic sound followed. The safety catch, Jane presumed, of an assault rifle being disengaged. "Espera," said her mother to the man. The smell of smoke was sharper now, and distant voices exclaimed in alarm.

"I went to prison," Jane said. The gun was heavy and she was finding it difficult to keep her arm level. "Did you know that?"

"Of course."

"My daughter was born there. I was in for involuntary manslaughter. I killed George because he tried to rape Lila. You remember George."

Her mother stared at her in silence.

"He roofied her at a party. But you know all this."

A woman in white — a cook or maid — had been looking on in terror, a dishcloth twisting in her hands. Now she peered over her shoulder at the sound of some commotion in the kitchen.

"That's who you should have been protecting," Jane said. "Your people."

But the words seemed to dissolve before they reached their target. Anabel's face was distracted, concerned. She sniffed the air. Jane flinched as someone moved past, heading for her mother; rough hands grabbed her arms from behind, shoved her out of the way. Somebody plucked the gun from her hand as easily as an apple from a tree. Now she expected to be carried off—beaten? Locked up? Or just thrown off the grounds? But nothing happened. More people ran past her and fell into quiet consultation with her mother.

Something was happening. The woman in white ran off. Men outside were shouting, and someone screamed. Anabel Bortnik turned on her heel and marched through a sliding door in the windowed wall. Out on the rear patio, she looked left, then right; something caught her eye and she ran. The group of guards followed her.

Jane turned around. A moment ago, she was preparing to die, and now she was alone. Outside, shouts. A gunshot. She walked to the door.

The air was hazy and smoke burned her eyes. To her left, a wooden shed was engulfed in flames. Beyond it lay a structure that Jane had somehow failed to notice before, a great gray faceted hump stretching three stories into the sky. Its surface swirled and trembled like a soap bubble's, and it appeared lit from within.

Jane stared in wonder for several long moments at this inexplicable new addition to the compound before her brain processed it for what it was: the greenhouse, filled up with roiling smoke, its contents on fire. Its glass panels warped and twisted as the lattice that held them began to melt; as Jane watched, a panel shattered, then another, and the smoke poured into the sky in one, then two, then a half dozen thick columns.

Footsteps pounded on the gravel, and she turned. Someone was running toward her: Lila, clutching a rifle, her face aglow with sweat and streaked with soot. Her clothes, hands, and neck were splashed and spattered by blood. Someone else's, Jane presumed. "Come on!" she was shouting.

"What th—"

Lila grabbed her by the arm and began to drag her down the hill, where the courtyard narrowed to the entrance road. Jane's feet caught up with her and she ran after her sister. An object blocked their path, and Lila swerved around it: a human body, supine, a mess of blood and bone where a head ought to be. Farther down the path, a man lying on his side. The ground black beneath his chest, which appeared to have been blasted open by gunshots.

Jane stumbled to the edge of the road and vomited into the weeds. She felt Lila grabbing handfuls of her shirt, pulling her away. "Come on, come on," she was saying. "Get in the car." She was referring to the SUV that had brought them here, which was parked at an angle thirty feet away. The doors were open and bodies were spilling out. A guard with his throat cut, Jane saw, as they approached, one leg still thrown up into the passenger footwell; another tumbling out of the back with its head blown half off. "Help me!" Lila shouted, dragging the first man free of the car.

"I can't."

"Just push him out from inside!"

Jane opened the left rear door and climbed onto the back seat. She grabbed the man's booted feet and pushed, as Lila dragged the body clear. The SUV's windows were splashed with blood, and so were the seats; it covered Jane's hands.

She clambered out, gagged again. Slammed the back door shut. Lila was there, waiting for her, pulling her, then pushing. "Passenger side! Get in!"

"What— What did you—"

"Later!"

They pulled the doors closed, rolled the windows down to escape the stench. Lila started the car, executed a sloppy K-turn, and headed down the hill.

"Did you do it?" Lila wanted to know. "Did you shoot her?"

"No," Jane said quietly.

"Well," Lila said, wiping blood from her face, and then her hand on her jeans, "that's all right. I didn't really think you would."

Jane resisted the urge to scream. If they actually got out of here alive, she would find a quiet place for it. "What in the fuck is wrong with you?" she said.

"I thought I'd give you the chance. In case you wanted to take it."

"If you wanted her dead, why didn't you just do it yourself!"

"I didn't really. I don't *think* I did. I mean, I was *supposed* to, but . . ."

An animal ran out into the road—some sort of little pig—and both women gasped. Lila swerved to avoid it and branches scraped the side of the car.

"What do you mean," Jane said, "you were *supposed* to?"

"I mean, that's what they wanted, I'm sure," Lila said. "It was implied. But this should be enough to get them off my back."

The road was rough, they were going too fast, and Jane thought she could literally feel her brain bouncing around in her skull. She had no idea what Lila was talking about.

"Who is *they*?"

Lila hazarded a glance. "Come on, Jane."

"Lila!"

"I figured you would have pieced it together by now. The Agency."

They had arrived at an intersection, where Jane dimly remembered they'd been ushered out of Souder's SUV and into this one. Jane was trying to digest what she'd just been told, to understand its implications for the past week of her life, when Lila took the blind turn without stopping and nearly crashed into a pickup truck parked at a diagonal in the middle of the road. Behind it, blurred by the sun's glare, Jane could see the white hump of Souder's car, pulled off in the weeds. In front of the truck stood a woman. Jane remembered her as the one who had searched her purse. She stood straight, aiming her rifle directly at the windshield.

Lila slammed on the brakes, threw the car into park, and sank down out of sight. Jane did the same. The rifle chattered and the windshield rained down on them.

"Throw your weapon out the door," the woman shouted. "Then show me your hands and come out."

"She doesn't know there's two of us," Lila whispered. "From the glare. Climb over me." She tilted her head back and shouted, "I am unarmed."

"I don't believe you," the woman said.

"I'm coming out! You can search me!" To Jane, she mouthed, *Go.*

For a moment, Jane considered telling her to go to hell. Why did she have to be the bait? But she knew Lila was right. Jane couldn't fire an automatic rifle if her life depended on it, and evidently it did. She climbed over her sister, reeking of sweat and blood and gasoline, and thrust her hands out the door.

"Slowly," the woman said.

Jane slid her feet onto the gravel and stood up behind the open door. The guard was about twenty feet away, her weapon aimed and steady.

"Move away from the door."

Jane kept her eyes on the woman, shuffling sideways until she was clear. Where did Lila want her? She'd be hoping for a clean shot. Jane resisted the urge to glance back into the car for guidance. She said, "Please don't shoot me," and backed up as if terrified. Which she was.

"Stop where you are," the woman said, and took a step forward. "Where's the other one?"

"They killed her," Jane said, and manufactured a gasp of grief.

The guard glanced at the car, then back at Jane.

"Please," Jane said. "I have a daughter. Let me go."

"Yes, I remember." The woman began to move slowly toward her, the rifle never wavering.

Jane thought of the strip of photos, the woman's face as she held it in her hand. "You have a child, too. Don't you."

"Please be quiet," the woman said.

But Jane had to keep the woman listening and distracted. "You understand, then," she said. "My daughter can't lose me. No one knows where I've gone. To her, I'll have just disappeared." She forced her eyes to well up, for tears to fall down her cheeks. She thought she'd found the woman's soft spot, and now she pushed it harder. "A child can get over the death of a parent. But not knowing . . . that can ruin her life." In her peripheral vision, Lila adjusted her posture, leveled her weapon.

"I do not care about your child," the woman said, drawing closer. "You have brought death to my home. If I wasn't told to capture you, I would kill you now."

The woman came closer. Jane took a step back, and another. "Please. Let me go."

"Do not move."

Just a little more would do it. The guard would be clear of the door, giving Lila a shot, and Jane would be clear of the carnage. She took one more step back.

The guard swore, raised the rifle to strike Jane with its butt. Marched forward.

"I'm sorry," Jane said, and a moment of understanding flattened the guard's face. The woman turned to where Lila lay across the front seats of the SUV, drew a sharp breath, and collapsed in an eruption of noise and blood.

"She was sending clients to me," Lila said. "To find out how I did business." They had emerged from the woods and turned back onto the main road; Jane assumed the plan was to go back to Nacimiento, give Souder his car back, call Loretta, and arrange for some kind of passage out of the country. Or maybe they would just keep going, drive north until they made it to Texas. Jane didn't care. Lila had a plan, no doubt. She had all kinds of plans. "I should have known she was pulling the strings," she went on, "but my ego got in the way. I wanted to think I found those clients on my own. Solved their cases easily because I was so good.

"I learned it was her from this agent, a guy I'd seen hanging around town, supposed to be some kind of fisherman on a summer vacation. Turns out he was CIA, they'd been watching Mom, and that led them to me."

"I don't care," Jane said.

"It became this whole thing. I was supposed to share details of these cases with them, and they'd let me stay in business. In the end, Mom must have smelled a rat, because she went back underground. The cases dried up. And the Agency left me alone, for a while. But I guess they couldn't find her, because they told me to do it for them. If I did, they'd stop bothering me. Extra points for taking down the organization."

Grudgingly, Jane said, "That was never going to happen."

"No. Anyway, they knew she was running this new coke somewhere out of Central America, but they didn't know how, and they didn't know if she was down here, or running the show from someplace else. They knew it was coming into Seattle, though, and figured she might be living there. Turns out Gramps knew more than they did."

"That's why you were so sure about Central America," Jane said. "The CIA told you."

"They gave me the inkling, anyway. I mean, of course she would be here. The plants! It would have been paradise to her." She shook her head. "Obviously, it was. Is." The car had climbed up into the hills and now a vista opened up below them, little towns and farms as far as the eye could see. "She must have hired Gil's guys to make sure she got out of

Washington before we arrived. She wanted us to see all this. I should have noticed the thing with the postcards, actually. I can't believe it was sitting in front of me all that time." She patted Jane's knee. "I knew I needed you."

"You didn't need me. You would have figured it out."

"Maybe, eventually?" Lila said. "But . . . I missed you, I admit it. I wanted to get the band back together."

"How many people did you kill today," Jane said after a while.

Lila was as animated and unguarded as Jane had ever seen her. Years had fallen away from her face and she resembled the Lila who'd plotted their escape in the wake of George's murder. She said, "Ahhh . . . four, at least? The three guards who were holding me, for sure, and the lady just now. And then there were a couple of guys around the compound, and a guy who was sitting in the jeep I stole the gas can from. I put those guys out of action, but they're probably fine."

They rode in silence for a couple of minutes.

"Well," Lila said, "not the jeep guy. He might not have made it."

"Thanks for clarifying."

"I guess you're mad?" Lila said a few minutes later.

"No."

"I did get us out of there alive."

Jane didn't take the bait. Instead she reclined her seat, closed her eyes, and let the mountain air fill her lungs. All she had to do was endure and wait. Shower and change, throw away these clothes. Forget all this ever happened and let her sister lead them home.

# 33

# Geneva, NY and Nestor, NY: *Now*

She suggested a diner in Geneva, figuring it would be polite to meet them halfway geographically, since she was not meeting them halfway in any other sense. The lawyer Lila had found for her, a small, intense, laconic man named Arthur Kohl, had recommended that he accompany her, but Jane had refused. She wanted to see them alone.

Chloe had seemed relieved to reunite with her, though she tried to hide it. She was ostensibly still mad. It had only been a week and a half that Jane had been gone, though it felt like an eternity, and she'd catastrophized on the plane home that Chloe would greet her with renewed resentment and apprehension, that something between them would permanently have changed. But after a few days of coolness she began to tell Jane anecdotes about her frustration with Susan and Grandpa Chip, who had mostly sat in his study reading the news and playing solitaire on his iPad. "Also, he farts *incessantly*"—a new word in Chloe's vocabulary that she would deploy with exasperating frequency in the days to come. About her father, Chloe said little, and that was fine with Jane. It suggested the girl would say little about her to him. Jane had figured she would have some kind of conversation with Chance during the transfer. Instead, the pickup truck pulled up and Chloe hopped out with her backpack and suitcase. The truck zoomed away in a spray of passive-aggressive mud. She declared herself grossed out by Grandpa Harry's house and annoyed to be taken away from Susan and Chance but before long had made herself at home. She seemed more independent now, less needy. She made her own breakfast and lunch and only gave affection when Jane asked it of her. But Jane told herself it was for the better. She was growing up. When Jane apologized to her for the marriage breaking up, she said, "At least I won't have to put on headphones during your stupid fights anymore."

She'd expected there would have to be hearings before a judge, but everything was being handled privately. Chance's lawyer and Arthur would be handling the divorce, Charles's lawyer and Arthur would be handling the money, and Jane would appear only when it was absolutely necessary. "This is the procedure your sister has requested," Arthur told her. "It's how I'm accustomed to working."

It suited Jane. All of this, it seemed, had been orchestrated entirely to suit Jane — the closest thing to an apology she would likely ever get from Lila.

The diner, which was ten minutes outside town just off Route 90, was a low, square building that had been affixed with a faux Art Deco facade. It looked like a convenience store dressed as a diner for Halloween. She pulled into the only open space on the entrance side and looked up to see Chance and Susan staring gloomily out the window at her approach. Idiotically, she raised a hand in greeting.

Inside, the air was warm and smelled of hash browns, and Jane was hit by a wave of lunatic optimism. She understood, suddenly, that this meeting was the end of something bad and the beginning of something good. That it would be deeply unpleasant suddenly felt immaterial.

There was an awkward moment when she approached. Their booth was outfitted with an interlocking-boomerang formica table and seats that appeared salvaged from a decades-old Ford F-150. She stood gazing down at Susan and Chance, and they sat gazing up at her, until they realized that she didn't intend to sit beside either one of them. Chance grunted, got up, and slid in next to his mother. Jane took his seat, then scootched over, avoiding the patch of warmth he'd left behind. The man sitting behind him rattled his newspaper, annoyed at all the movement.

"This is not the end" was Susan's opener. "You have not won." She wore a cream cashmere cardigan sagging under the weight of a giant diamond floral brooch. Jane didn't think she realized that she was holding her fork and knife tightly in her fists, as though savagely eager to eat.

"Mom," said Chance.

"She's the one behind it all!"

"Okay, Mom. Just let it go for now."

A waitress approached, eyebrows raised. "Looks like your third's here. *Now* are you ready to order?"

"Mom wanted to leave home a little early," Chance said to Jane apologetically, and to the waitress, "Yeah, we're ready." Jane hadn't seen him this sheepish in years—maybe not since high school, during those wild months before everything went to pieces.

"I'm not hungry," Susan said.

"Well, Mom, you don't have to eat. Do you want a coffee?"

"I don't want anything."

Chance's face flushed with anger. He looked old. He dug into a pocket and brought out a set of keys. "Well, go sit in the truck, then."

Susan looked as though she might scream. Instead, she pushed Chance's hand away, stormed off, and disappeared beyond the end of the counter. After they'd ordered, Jane saw her emerge and take the stool on the end, where she typed furiously into her phone.

"Sorry about that," Chance said.

"Why are we even here?"

"Uh, well . . . I think she thought we were going to give you a piece of our mind. But, honestly, I've been kind of regretting things and don't want to fight anymore. I think I finally convinced her I meant it right before we got here."

"I don't want to be married to you, Chance," she said.

"No, no, I get it," he said. He sipped his coffee and looked out the window at the highway in the distance. "It's the right thing to do. We should have dealt with it a long time ago. I'm sorry I made everything so hard."

"Yeah, you did."

"Yeah," he said. "I did."

"I'm not backing down on my demands," Jane told him. "So if you're trying to butter me up . . ."

"No, no, that's what pissed her off so much in the truck. I told her I was giving up."

"Really."

The waitress brought their food, a turkey club for him and fries for her. She refilled their coffees.

"The lawyer pointed out, uh, that you could have got a lot more out of me. And the whole abandonment thing was, yeah, not a thing."

"No, it sure fucking wasn't."

"Hey, hey," he said, scowling. "I'm trying to be nice, here."

"Fine."

He took a bite of the sandwich, chewed thoughtfully for a minute. Glanced over his shoulder as though to make sure his mother was still there.

"I just wanna say, shared custody, the money, it's all reasonable and good. I think it's best for Chloe if we're getting along. And, you know, if you need to go out of town . . . like, I'll take her anytime. I didn't really think you weren't coming back."

"You could have fooled me."

He blushed. "Yeah, uh . . . I got swept up, I guess. I was hurt."

"Well. I appreciate the offer, anyhow. Let's see how things go."

A quick flash of anger on his face, then it was gone. She was glad she wouldn't be seeing those anymore, or at least less often. "Yeah, no, of course. One day at a time," he said. He ate more of his sandwich. "I don't regret marrying you."

"That's kind of you to say," Jane said, then winced at the hurt it clearly caused. "No, I mean . . . I don't regret it, either. Thank you for being there for me when I got out of jail. I'm glad we tried."

"Sure. Me too."

Over his shoulder, Susan stole furious looks at the two of them.

Chance daubed at his mouth with a napkin—a charmingly genteel gesture for such a coarse man—and dropped a few bills onto the table. "So, yeah, I . . . I don't want to keep Mom away from Chloe. I just wanna make sure you know that."

"I don't want that. Chloe can hold her own."

"Okay, good. Well . . . at some point, I guess I'll get the papers to sign?"

"Yeah," she said.

"Yeah, all right," he said, standing up. "I'll sign 'em. You coming?"

Jane laughed. "I'll finish my fries."

She watched them exit, then disappear around the corner of the building. A minute later, his truck came into view, crossing the parking lot toward the road. In the passenger seat, Susan was shouting. The waitress came and reached for Chance's plate, which still bore three-quarters of a sandwich. Jane reached out and touched her arm.

"I'll take that," she said.

The waitress nodded, picking up the bills. "I'll bring your change."

"Oh god, no, keep it," Jane said. "It's not my money."

After a few minutes, she reached over the back of the seat and tapped the shoulder of the man behind her. She gestured to his newspaper, neatly folded on the table beside the remains of his lunch.

"You still reading that?"

He shook his head, passed the paper over. With a deep, luxuriant sigh, Jane turned to the sports, a subject of which she knew nothing whatsoever, and, eating her husband's sandwich, began to read.

A couple of nights later, a knock came at the door. The door in question was Harry Pool's, behind which things had changed considerably since Mrs. Vesey fell into the bathtub in terror. The place was clean again, thanks to Jane and Chloe, and a rented dumpster was parked in the yard, where it was slowly filling with broken furniture, dead plants, mouse-gnawed books and papers, and rugs so saturated with spilled booze that they peeled the finish off the wood floor when Jane rolled them up for the trash.

She hadn't meant to move in; she and Chloe were planning to find a place of their own. But she'd returned to find a different Harry—not the helpless, beaten-down father she knew, but someone recommitted to living. A weight seemed to have been lifted from his shoulders; he was less furtive, less fearful. He apologized to her for being a burden and said he'd accepted an offer to go on phased retirement, which meant that he'd teach every other semester for a few years, giving him time, at last, to pick up the threads of the book he'd stopped writing.

Jane supposed the presence of his daughter and granddaughter had improved his state of mind, but she couldn't have said what else was at play. She hadn't brought up what Anabel had told her in Panama. It made her angry every time it crossed her mind and she didn't want to get into it with him.

While she and Chloe worked on the house proper, Harry had puttered in his office, arranging things into piles. One afternoon Jane had peered in to find him standing just outside the window holding a bottle of ammonia and a balled-up paper towel. The curtains had been parted and light streamed in. A few minutes later, when he came back inside, he said, "I didn't realize how dirty the windows had gotten. I think there was still grime on them from when I smoked."

"However . . ."

"Yes," he said, hands on hips, glancing around in evident disgust, "now you can see how grim it's gotten in here."

"You want a hand?"

Harry shook his head. "No, no, you're already doing more than enough. Let me earn back a bit of dignity in here."

Now the office looked more like a place where work might be done. "I didn't realize how many of my students' final papers I'd been keeping," he told Jane as she stared in wonder at the space. "About thirty years' worth."

"What! Why?"

He shrugged. "Well. At first, it's . . . what if they complain about their final grade? And I have to go back and justify it to them. Here's why you got a B, not an A!"

"Has that ever happened?"

"Sure! Well—maybe. I think so."

"So you should throw them out when the semester's over," Jane said.

"Ah, but what if they need to graduate, and records have been misplaced, and they'll be denied their degree unless I help them?"

"Has *that* ever happened?"

"No. No, it hasn't. But! What *has* happened is they eventually ask for recommendation letters, and it's good to have their work on hand, to remind me. Although I don't know that I've ever actually consulted the papers."

"Why didn't you just keep this all at the office?"

"You've seen my office," Harry said. "I ran out of space."

Then the knock came. They both appeared surprised. Chloe angrily called out from her bedroom—formerly Lila's. "Someone's at the *door!*"

It was an early evening in the third week of May. Darkness had begun to fall, but some light remained in the western sky, which served as a backdrop to the woman Jane saw through the spyhole. She wore sunglasses and a red knitted beret over short black hair. Her hands were shoved into the pockets of a zipped-up windbreaker.

She appeared harmless enough. Jane opened the door. "Yes?"

"You shouldn't have done that," Lila said, taking the glasses off. "I could have been anyone."

"Jesus!" Jane resisted the urge to embrace her. "You look different," she said. "You didn't dress up like this just to come here, did you?"

"No, no. It's for a thing. Not far from here." The two women stared at each other. "Are you going to invite me in?"

Was she? This was a moment that, if it ever came at all, she'd expected to have time to prepare for. To talk with Harry and Chloe about. She was still angry at Lila, despite all the help she'd given from afar. In the end, they'd driven to Mexico and parted without any promise to see each other again. And Jane had been glad, since she got back, to begin to clean up the mess she'd made of her life in a state of relative calm. People needed her here. She wasn't disappointing anyone. And she wondered, after their near demise at Anabel Bortnik's compound, if she and her sister were better off separated, for good. Bad things tended to happen when they were together.

"I guess that's a no," Lila said.

But before Jane could reply: "Lila?"

It was their father.

"Oh my god," said Chloe.

They stood in the kitchen behind her, Chloe illuminated by the open refrigerator door, holding a bottle of fruit juice in one hand and a book in the other, her finger marking a page. It was, Jane could see, *The Railway Children*. Harry held a sheaf of papers, which he appeared poised to add to one of several piles on the table.

Lila stepped around Jane and entered the house. "It looks different here," she said.

"You haven't been here in decades," Jane said.

"Well. I may have been. When you weren't looking."

"Lila," their father said, "it's really you."

"Hi, Dad."

He came over to them, still clutching his papers. Lila surprised Jane by opening her arms to him. In a fugue of guilt and jealousy, she watched them embrace. He crushed the papers against her back.

Chloe had put the juice and book down and sidled over to Jane. "She doesn't look like you," she whispered.

"She cut and dyed her hair," Jane said.

"She seems cool, though."

"Yeah," Jane said with a sigh, pulling her close. "I guess she does."

They were still in the kitchen an hour later, sitting around the table. Full night surrounded them and the window over the sink admitted the blessing of a warm front: a breeze heavy with blossoms and green. Lila talked about her life, clearly leaving out as many identifying details as possible without rendering her experiences boring. Chloe was rapt, Jane doubtful, Harry increasingly sad. Every now and then he would reach out, rest his hand on Lila's arm, grow uncomfortable, and withdraw it.

"I failed you," he said at last.

They didn't argue. Chloe gazed in wonder at one, then the other.

"That's all in the past," Lila told him. "It doesn't matter now. And anyway, Mom failed us first. You included. We didn't understand that we didn't need her."

"I did," Harry said.

"She's a vampire," Lila said. "Let it go."

He seemed impatient with this response, having already heard it from Jane more than once. He said, "Let's just say I do. I'm not sure what I'm supposed to do next, at least after the house is clean. I'll write my book, but who will want it?"

Jane said, "People want your book, Dad."

"Maybe," Lila said. "Maybe not. I've got another idea, though." She turned to Jane. "Where I'm at with my business, I'm finding my conventional clients more burdensome. I need somebody to handle that stuff. With Dad retiring, he's not going to need you on campus anymore. You can work here. I'll train you, and beat your current salary. And, Dad," she said, facing Harry, "you've spent your life doing research. When Loretta and I are on the road for my premium clients, I'm going to need somebody digging around for me. You might discover some interesting stuff."

"I don't know if I'm cut out for it," Harry said.

"Of course you are. You worked for the CIA, right?"

His head snapped up. "What! No, I didn't!" He'd gone pale and his mouth was a tight line.

"Jesus, Lila," Jane said.

"Well, he did!"

Chloe said, "You did?"

"Dad," Lila said, "Mom told Jane. And the CIA told me. It's fine."

Harry covered his face with his hands. Everyone was quiet. Then he got up, the chair barking behind him, and left the room. A moment later, they heard his office door slam shut.

Jane walked down the hall and knocked quietly. When he didn't respond, she let herself in. He was sitting at the desk in a pool of yellow lamplight, gazing mournfully at a cardboard banker's box on the floor. He tapped it with a bedroom-slippered foot.

"Just today," he said, "I was mentally preparing myself to burn everything. I didn't want you girls to know."

"Dad, it doesn't matter. You thought you were doing the right thing."

"I knew I wasn't, deep down." He looked up at her. "I think I was always trying to measure up to your mother. Even when she was young, and I was supposedly some impressive older man, an up-and-coming historian, she had the authority in our marriage. I didn't understand it for the longest time. She made me feel small."

"It's all right."

"It's not," he said, "but thank you." He kicked the box again, harder this time, denting it. "Someday I'll tell you how all this happened," he said. "My contact, the man who recruited me . . . I don't think that story's over, actually."

"I'll look forward to that." She went to him, put a hand on his shoulder. "Dad. Let's do it now. Let's burn it. Whatever's in that box."

"Yeah?"

"It's a nice night for a bonfire. A small one. The gravel clearing out by the shed. I'll have Chloe find some dry twigs."

"I want to start tidying up the yard anyway," he said.

"There's the spirit."

Twenty minutes later, the four of them were standing out under the stars, surrounding a little burning pile of branches, scrap lumber, and broken furniture. Harry held the banker's box by its handles, which appeared ready to tear down the middle, as though the box were full of lead. Sparks rose and darted and disappeared into the night. A distant train whistle sounded. A dog barked.

"Dad?" Jane asked. "You want to say anything?"

He frowned, sighed. He looked as though he wished he had a free hand to scratch his chin with. He opened and closed his mouth a couple of times, then finally said, "No."

"Well, okay, then."

Harry set the box down on the weedy gravel and removed the lid. Then he plunged his hands in and withdrew two fistfuls of little spiral reporter's notebooks. He drew a deep breath—too deep, too close to the fire—and began to cough. Then he dropped the notebooks on the pile.

Everybody watched them burn. Then Harry said, "Help me out," and the four of them slowly transferred the notebooks from the box to the flames. Only Jane seemed to notice when Lila slipped one into her jacket pocket between box and fire; their eyes met. Lila arched a single eyebrow—did you seriously think I wouldn't?

When the notebooks were gone, Harry tossed the lid onto the fire, and then the box itself. Soon they were both gone.

They continued to stand, watching the flames die down. Chloe moved closer to Jane, and Jane put an arm around her. When the light and heat were nearly gone, Harry said, "I'm in." He looked up at Lila. "Working for you, that is."

"Yeah?" Lila said.

"Yeah."

"Jane?"

Jane knew what was expected of her—capitulation, acceptance. Gratitude for being saved again. She was supposed to help her sister rebalance the books, get back into the black in the ledger of their relationship. But she wasn't having it this time.

"I'll work with you," Jane said. "Not for you."

"Well, sure," Lila said. "You'll just—"

"You cut me in on everything. I'm not going to sit here answering the phone, analyzing somebody's email spam. I don't want your shit clients. I can handle whatever you can."

Lila's eyes narrowed. "You sure about that?"

"I'm a killer, remember?" Jane said. "I saved your life."

A silence. Chloe and Harry stared at them, bewildered.

"That you did," Lila said quietly.

"So I'm all the way in, or I'm not in at all."

A grin slowly spread across her sister's face. Only Jane knew it was fake. She'd watched Lila seduce a dozen men and women, seen her draw enemies into false confidence. She knew her sister hadn't been fooled. "Fantastic," Lila said. "First payday's tomorrow. Feel free to quit your job, I'll be in touch with instructions." She stared hard at Jane. "Or . . . not instructions. First steps."

Jane nodded. "Good."

"Okay!" Lila said, rubbing her hands together. "It's a deal." Then she turned, walked off toward the house, and disappeared into the night. They waited another ten minutes, assuming she'd just slipped inside for a beer, but she never came back.

# ACKNOWLEDGMENTS

For their careful readings of early versions of this book, I want to thank Brian Hall, Adam O'Fallon Price, Lauren Schenkman, and Ed Skoog. Elizabeth Watkins Price (ebethwatkinsprice.com) served as sensitivity reader and legal consultant, and Caroline Levine as academic advisor. Katrina Carpenter and Christine Kelley suggested the creation of Loretta; Isaac Butler and David Burr Gerrard shared memories of theater camp; and fashion tips came from Emily Adrian, Catherine Nichols, Miranda Popkey, and Adalena Kavanagh. At Mulholland Books, Josh Kendall and Helen O'Hare gave indispensable editorial advice, much of it before I was even under contract, a first in my career. I thank my agent, Jim Rutman, for his energy and enthusiasm in helping me pursue something new, and Ethan Nosowsky and Fiona McCrae for their blessing. My writers' chat is good today, and every day. I'm most grateful to my wife, Stephanie Meissner, for being the greatest close reader I've ever known, and, along with my kids, Katrina, Olivia, and Eliza, making life perpetually interesting and fun.

## ABOUT THE AUTHOR

J. Robert Lennon is the author of three story collections and nine previous novels, including *Castle, Familiar,* and *Broken River.* He lives in Ithaca, New York.